RETURN OF THE
VENGEFUL QUEEN

Also available from C. J. Redwine

Defiance

Deception

Deliverance

The Shadow Queen

The Wish Granter

The Traitor Prince

The Blood Spell

Rise of the Vicious Princess

RETURN OF THE VENGEFUL QUEEN

C. J. REDWINE

BALZER + BRAY

An Imprint of HarperCollins*Publishers*

Balzer + Bray is an imprint of HarperCollins Publishers.

Return of the Vengeful Queen
Copyright © 2024 by C. J. Redwine
Map illustration © 2022 by Sveta Dorosheva
For information address HarperCollins Children's Books, a division of
HarperCollins Publishers, 195 Broadway, New York, NY 10007.
www.epicreads.com

Library of Congress Control Number: 2023933925
ISBN 978-0-06-290899-5

Typography by Jessie Gang
24 25 26 27 28 LBC 5 4 3 2 1

First Edition

*For Mary Weber, my ride or die in every era. I had
the time of my life fighting dragons with you.*

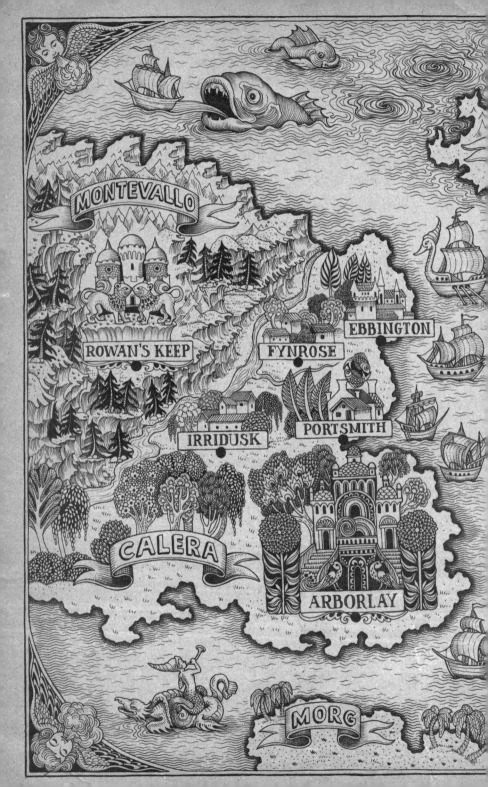

ONE

Dawn broke in shreds of crimson gold, spilling across the dark expanse of the Draiel Sea like liquid fire as Charis Willowthorn, exiled princess of Calera, readjusted her compass and drew an invisible line across the ship's map with her finger.

The upper corner of the map was anchored in place by the captain's log, the leather volume opened to a page of fresh notations in Orayn's looping scrawl. To Charis's left sat the tide chart, its edges smudged from use by the smugglers who'd once owned this vessel. She double-checked the chart, her throat tightening.

They'd make port in Solvang today.

Three weeks on the open seas, constantly scanning the waters for signs of pursuit by the monstrous Rakuuna who'd invaded Calera. Three weeks of sleepless nights and endless scheming to find a way to kill the enemy and rescue her people—and it all came down to this.

Somehow she had to convince the rulers of Solvang to stand with her against powerful creatures who moved faster than humans, could sink a ship with the brute strength of their hands, and whose reach was so long, swords were all but useless against them. Worry squirmed in her belly.

No ruler in their right mind would join her cause.

The blue lines of the map wavered before her, and she rubbed at the gritty exhaustion in her eyes. This was no time to lose focus.

"Good morning, Your Highness."

Charis jumped, sending the tide chart fluttering to the floor, and whirled to find Orayn in the doorway of the tiny room.

"I apologize for startling you." The big man ducked his shiny brown head beneath the doorjamb as he stepped inside and bent to retrieve the chart. He looked closely at her as he set it on the navigation table.

"Is something amiss?" Orayn's deep voice reminded Charis of King Edias's, and for an instant, she was back in Father's sun-warmed quarters, her head resting against him as he told her everything would be all right. A lance of pain pierced her heart, and she abruptly set the compass on the table and turned for the door.

"All is well," she said in a voice so hollow, she barely recognized it as her own.

"It's a fine day for a coronation. Everyone on board is looking forward to it." He bowed as she backed out of the little room, her heart knocking against her chest like a frantic bird in a cage.

Before the Rakuuna invasion, back when Charis was leading a secret group of loyalists to search the sea for the unseen enemy who was sinking Calera's ships, everyone aboard their boat had worn masks so that she could protect her identity from all but the few she trusted.

The memory of including her former bodyguard Tal on that list was a constant ache—a wound she didn't know how to close.

There was no point hiding her identity now. Still, revealing her true self and claiming her mother's title were very different things.

Charis hadn't wanted a coronation, but Holland, as next in line to the throne, had insisted. He'd argued that their people needed a queen, and that entering Solvang as Calera's sovereign ruler gave Charis far more leverage than entering as an exiled princess.

He'd been right, but Charis had fought him on it until the very last moment.

It was taking everything she had to move forward, to shove aside the grief when she thought of Mother, fierce and indomitable, falling to the ballroom floor beneath an onslaught of Rakuuna. And of Father, crumpled and lifeless in his bedroom. She was breathing by sheer force of will. Standing because she refused to let her knees give out.

How could she possibly do all that if she had to participate in a coronation?

Accepting the crown, the title, was real. It was final.

Charis couldn't bear for this ruin to be final.

Turning away from the navigation room, she climbed past the cannons resting in their metal rings along the edges of the ship. Past the hammocks hastily strung between the masts for the people who hadn't fit in the ship's eight cabins. A few children still slept, clinging to their mothers' arms, their dirty faces streaked with the remnants of tears.

Charis's own cheeks were dry. Everything soft within her had been burned to ash when she'd found her father's lifeless body and then learned that the boy she loved—the boy she'd *trusted*—was the son of her enemy, sent to spy on her.

A chilly breeze danced along the water and swept over the deck, prying at Charis's cloak. She tugged the garment close, stepped past the last of the hammocks, and then stopped.

Grim, the palace groom who'd been Tal's contact with Montevallo, and Dec, a sailor who'd turned out to be another Montevallian sent to look after their spy of a prince, were huddled in conversation at the bow.

Something cold and vicious unfurled in Charis's chest as she stalked toward them.

"You." She pointed at Grim. "You should be down in the brig taking care of the horses."

He held her gaze, and she ignored the worried grief in his eyes. Let him be terrified as he imagined Tal's fate at the hands of the Rakuuna who'd kidnapped him. Let it keep him up at night, eating at him until peace was nothing but a distant memory.

It still wouldn't be half of what he deserved.

The fact that worry over Tal's fate sometimes crept into her own thoughts as well was unfortunate, but it wasn't anything that a reminder of his betrayal couldn't fix.

Grim shot a look at Dec, his freckled brow collapsing into a frown. "Your Highness, if I might ask what you're planning once we reach port—"

In three steps, Charis closed the distance between them, her dagger in her hand. Before he could do more than blink in surprise, she had the point of the blade against his throat.

"Three weeks of silence from you isn't long enough. You will not speak to me unless I ask you to. You will not leave the brig unless I send for you. You will remember that this is a Caleran ship, and you are the enemy." She turned to lock eyes with Dec. The boy was taller than Tal, with black hair, brown skin, and brown eyes. As always, he was quiet and still, his body giving her no indication of what he was thinking.

She bared her teeth in a cruel smile, feeling every inch her mother. "As for you, traitor, the only reason I'm not sending you to the brig to care for the horses with your dishonorable friend is because Orayn needs competent sailors to help run this ship."

Dec inclined his head respectfully.

"I am keeping the two of you alive and fed solely for the purpose of providing me with useful information on the inner workings of the court at Montevallo." She drew her second dagger and aimed it at Dec. "If either of you refuses to cooperate, I will run you through with my sword, mount your head to the bow, and throw your body into the sea. Are we quite clear?"

"We're clear." Dec's voice was so quiet, she could barely hear him over the sound of the water slapping against the sides of the boat.

She sheathed her daggers as Grim moved toward the steps that led into the belly of the ship. Dec shifted as if to move away as well, then paused.

"You may cut out my tongue for saying this if you need to, Your Highness, but I'm truly sorry for what happened to your people and to you. It's horrifying, and if you want my help fighting back, I freely offer it."

Before she could respond, he bowed and then headed toward Orayn. She stepped to the edge of the ship, gripping the wooden railing so hard her palms ached.

There was no room inside her for being sorry. There was only rage and ruin and the desperate hope that, somehow, she could save her kingdom.

Mother had trained Charis to be smarter. Strike harder. To never falter, never waver, never break. Every interaction was a chess move, and only the most ruthless person on the board survived to win the game.

Maybe she could barely breathe past the grief. It was no excuse to stop thinking five steps ahead. No excuse to falter, even when the task in front of her would cut her to pieces.

"Charis?"

A soft voice spoke from behind her. Turning, she found her cousin Nalani Farragin—the closest thing she had to a best friend now that Tal no longer deserved the title.

"Are you ready?" Nalani's sleek black hair was braided and coiled around the top of her head, and the wind nipped a flush into her golden cheeks.

"Ready or not, it's time." Holland joined his twin sister, his black duster and battered sword sheath looking right at home aboard the ship. Hildy, the fluffy, multicolored kitten Tal had rescued and given to Father, perched on Holland's shoulder, blinking in the early morning sunlight. Holland swept Charis with a critical eye. "You look awful. Did you even try to sleep?"

"Holland!" Nalani smacked his stomach lightly with the back of her hand.

He raised his brows. "It's the truth."

"That doesn't mean you say it out loud."

"I'm fine." The lie rolled off her tongue with practiced ease. She'd spent the last three weeks repeating it until she no longer considered answering differently. "Let's get this done before we make port."

Holland stood to Charis's right as she turned to face the small crowd assembled on the deck. Nalani stood beside him. They both looked gravely serious, an expression shared by everyone on the ship. Every member of the royal staff that Charis had managed to take with her when the palace fell. Every sailor who'd scrambled to escape the chaos at the port. Every merchant, farmer, and peasant Holland, Nalani, and Delaire, a young noblewoman who'd escaped the ballroom with them, had whisked off the streets on their way to the dock—and quite a few who hadn't fit in the carriage but had followed on foot in a race for their lives. Sixty-two people who gathered in silence on the deck, staring up at Charis as she stood on the fore-castle above them.

Reuben, one of two remaining palace guards, was a few steps behind Charis's left shoulder, looking faintly ill, as sailing did not agree with his stomach. He kept his hand on his sword, his somewhat-bedraggled uniform buttoned up to his chin while his eyes scanned the crowd, hunting for threats, just as he would've done if she'd been standing on the dais in the palace throne room.

The thought of the throne room with its one golden chair where Charis had spent countless hours standing silently to Mother's right squeezed her chest until the next breath felt impossible to take.

Then Orayn stepped to her left side wearing the captain's jacket he'd had on the night of the invasion, pale blue braided tassels loop-ing over the shoulders as silver buttons gleamed against his chest. He held a crown in his large hands—a delicate concoction of twisted sil-ver wire that one of the merchant women had fashioned from spare supplies found in the cargo hold.

The thin metal shaped at the whim of the woman's hands reminded Charis of the dagger hairpiece Tal had made for her by twisting a simple updo cage into a weapon. Was that how he'd seen her? As a weapon he needed to keep close so he could predict where she would strike?

The memory of Tal drew blood.

She *was* a weapon. She had to be. Her kingdom's survival depended on it.

Orayn cleared his throat and then spoke in a voice that boomed across the length of the ship. "We, the remnant of Calera, gather on this, the twenty-third day after the enemy invasion, to formally acknowl-edge and accept as our sovereign ruler Charis Aliya Willowthorn, heir of Letha Roelle Willowthorn and Edias Stephren Lorrinton. Let our allies rejoice and our enemies tremble. Long live the queen!"

"Long live the queen!" the crowd yelled, their eyes lit with fervor.

Charis kept her expression regal and cold as Orayn settled the crown onto her head.

"Your Majesty." Orayn bowed. Instantly, the twins and Reuben followed suit.

Charis blinked rapidly as the crowd at her feet bowed, their murmured "Your Majesty" rolling through the air and slamming into Charis as if she'd been struck by the hilt of a sword.

Her chest heaved, a silent sob she trapped inside by sheer force of will. The featherlight weight of the crown on her head suddenly felt impossible to bear.

She shouldn't be queen.

Her family shouldn't be dead.

Her kingdom shouldn't be in ruins.

The salty air seemed to scour her throat raw as she drew in a breath.

"Would you like to say a few words, Your Majesty?" Holland asked beside her.

Another impossible thing. Even if she could force herself to speak past the ache in her throat, what could she say? She had nothing but grief and rage and the promise that she'd made to herself to see her vengeance through to the bitter end.

"Charis," Nalani breathed, a quiet plea that wouldn't reach the ears of those waiting below.

Tearing her gaze from the distant place where the sea met the sky, Charis looked at the faces below her.

They were full of grief and rage, too. But they had something else. Something more. A flicker of desperate hope as they gazed up at their new queen.

She forced herself to swallow against the ache. Licked her lips with a tongue gone bone-dry. And let her fury blaze within.

"People of Calera." Her voice shook with anger. She let it spill out of her and fill the air, a vicious, shimmering thing born of bloodshed and loss. "We have been through something unspeakable. We have been deeply wronged by the monstrous Rakuuna from Te'ash. We have been betrayed by our former ally Rullenvor, who aligned themselves with the monsters and set us up for destruction."

The words tore through her throat, raw and painful. "We lost countless loved ones on our most sacred night of the year. And an invader now resides in the palace. It would be easy to look at all of that and feel despair. But all is *not* lost."

She let the statement linger, let them see the unyielding determination on her face. Let the faint light of hope in their eyes burn a little brighter. And then she stepped forward until her stomach pressed against the carved wooden railing.

"We are not running away from Calera. This"—she flung out an arm to encompass the ship—"is not escape. This is strategy."

Slowly, she swept the crowd, meeting a sailor's gaze, a merchant's, a mother's. "We will go to Solvang for supplies and information about the Rakuuna. From there, we will send out a call to the rest of our allies, and especially to Montevallo. My betrothal treaty with them will ensure that they commit their army to our cause."

And if it didn't, then the threat of losing Tal, the king's youngest son, to Charis's blade should do the trick.

"I will personally see to your safety. And then I will bring all who are able to sail with me on a journey of vengeance. We will not rest until we march into our royal city of Arborlay with an army at our backs and cleanse our soil of every last invader who dared set foot on Calera's shores."

She paused, her words ringing across the water, and Holland

pulled his sword free of its sheath with a metallic scrape. Stepping to her side, he raised the blade above his head and yelled, "For the queen and for Calera!"

Reuben's sword flashed as he lifted it. "For the queen and for Calera!"

The crowd stirred, drawing weapons if they had them, raising fists when they didn't. "For the queen and for Calera!"

They chanted the words, louder and louder, until the deck seemed to tremble beneath Charis's feet. The thrum of their voices reverberated in her chest, a heartbeat that would not be denied.

She drew her own sword and raised it high, her skin prickling with goose bumps, the crown on her head the heaviest thing she'd ever worn.

"Death to our enemies and to all who fight against us!" Her voice cut through the air, and the crowd below her roared. Shaking their fists, screaming their approval, the wild light of hope alive on their faces.

She held her sword aloft and let them scream. Let their rage and their hope blister the air while she stood, crown firmly in place. It didn't matter that her knees wanted to buckle. That she was faint from both lack of sleep and lack of food. That everything in her longed to hear Mother's cold voice slice through the chaos as the queen took control.

It was real. It was final.

Charis was queen now. There was no looking back, no matter what her heart wanted. There was only the path in front of her and the fortitude she would need to see it through.

TWO

UNLIKE THE GENTLE, rolling hills and large fields that graced eastern Calera, Solvang's shoreline was a long strip of golden sand bordered by thick dunes that backed up to forested cliffs of rugged rock. Roads of pale crushed stone wound their way through the trees and into the capital city of Ooverstaad, where the streets were lined with tall, narrow buildings in dark cranberry, navy, or gray. Every few blocks, a well-tended park with benches, fountains, and swings for the children stood safely ensconced behind an iron fence. Ribbons of fog threaded their way through the city.

Ooverstaad was the picture of elegance, peace, and prosperity. Was it prosperous enough that the rulers wouldn't balk at helping Charis, though she had no way to pay her debts? Charis could promise to repay them in Montevallian jewels once she'd married Prince Vahn, but there were a lot of uncertainties lying between Charis and safely reaching the court at Montevallo. She would be asking the Solvanish rulers to extend their assistance purely on the hope that she could overcome every hurdle in front of her.

Which meant Charis had to exude unwavering confidence and

strength for the entirety of her time in the Solvanish palace.

"Remember that bakery?" Nalani leaned across Holland to point out the window of the carriage the royal family had sent for Charis once they'd learned of her arrival at port. "Best duvacca in the city."

"What's duvacca?" Delaire asked, her wide brown eyes taking in the sights. She'd been a member of the nobility in Calera, forever mooning over an irritable Holland, but three weeks of sailing had given her calluses on her fingers, a sunburned nose, and an ability to help with most tasks onboard the boat without losing her consider-able patience. The fact that the crew's morale had remained steady was almost entirely due to Delaire's sunny disposition and consistent kindness.

"It's a puffy square of layered pastry with chocolate and berries inside." Nalani bounced on the seat as they turned a corner. "There's the Royal Library! Those stained-glass windows depict scenes from Solvanish fairy tales. The library has the *best* selection of children's books. Remember, Holland? Great-aunt Estr used to take us there when we'd visit Father's side of the family. Most of them live farther inland, but she lives here in the capital."

"I liked the library's section on combat." Holland crossed his ankles and glanced at the passing buildings as the carriage sped toward the eastern ridge where the palace overlooked the city streets. His shoulder-length black hair looked windswept, and his already battered duster was definitely the worse for wear after weeks at sea.

"Why is the Royal Library not in the palace itself?" Delaire asked as she smoothed her curly black hair away from her face with a scarf she'd folded down to ribbon width.

"Because the Solvanish people value the pursuit of learning above all else. Placing the Royal Library in the center of the city where everyone has equal access to it shows that the royals share that value with their people." Nalani sounded as though she was reciting a line from one of Tutor Brannigan's textbooks. Actually, Charis was pretty sure that's exactly what her cousin was doing.

Charis barely acknowledged the view outside the carriage windows. She was too busy running scenarios in her head. What she would say to gain asylum for the people on the ship. What leverage she might use to get assistance on her trip to the Rakuuna kingdom of Te'ash if, indeed, rescuing Tal was necessary to force King Alaric's cooperation. If there were any promises she could make that would convince the royals to commit troops to the cause of retaking Calera.

And most of all, what she would do if King Gareth and Queen Vyllanthra refused to help at all.

As the carriage turned up the long, tree-lined drive that led to the palace, Nalani leaned over Holland and patted Charis's knee.

"Don't worry. The king is known to be generous. He'll help us."

"Generous enough to send his army to help free Calera?" Charis rolled her shoulders, trying to relieve the tension in her neck.

Holland snorted. "Not sure any ruler is going to be generous enough to send their soldiers to certain death."

"Honestly, just once, would you think before you speak?" Nalani glared at her twin while Delaire wrung her hands in distress.

"Holland's right." Charis sat up straight as the carriage slowed.

"No need to sound surprised." Holland uncrossed his feet.

Nalani sighed.

"But . . ." Delaire looked between Charis and Holland. "If he's right, then how are we ever going to go home?"

Charis met Delaire's eyes and forced every ounce of confidence she could muster into her voice. "Just because we can't see a path toward victory, doesn't mean one isn't there. We'll get help for our people."

"How are we going to do that when no one is going to want to go against the Rakuuna? I mean, besides Alaric, who will no doubt rejoice when we return his traitor of a son with all his limbs still attached." Holland sounded eager to hear her plan so he could do his part.

"One step at a time." Her stomach clenched as they neared the palace. She had no idea how to make the dangerous mission to retake her kingdom sound like a smart, strategic decision to any ruler but King Alaric of Montevallo, who'd already spent years sacrificing his soldiers in a bloody war with Calera so that he could have port access and a son on the throne. He wouldn't flinch at the chance to keep those hard-won prizes as long as Charis knew how to defeat the Rakuuna. Plus, she could use Tal's safety as leverage to sweeten the deal.

But why would any other ruler commit troops to her cause?

The carriage rolled to a stop, and a footman opened the door with a small bow. Charis exited first, moving as though she wore one of her gowns instead of the clean, but wrinkled, sparring clothes she'd worn during their escape from Calera. A dress didn't make one a queen. It was all in the attitude, in knowing down to one's very bones that the weight of the crown on your head was yours and yours alone.

Gazing up at the palace, Charis lifted her chin and smoothed her expression into one of icy calm, just like Mother had taught her. The palace was built of navy-and-white marble, threaded through with bands of silver that glittered in the sun. A pair of silver statues flanked the wide stairs that led to the entrance.

Reuben, Orayn, and Finn climbed down from the bench at the back of the carriage. Orayn and Finn took up their posts on either side of Holland and Nalani, while Reuben stepped to Charis's side, his gaze sweeping the area for threats.

Charis moved up the stairs, feeling grateful that she'd skipped breakfast as her empty stomach churned. Every expression, every word from this moment on had to be perfect. The fate of her people depended on it.

King Gareth and Queen Vyllanthra were waiting in an elegant parlor just inside the palace entrance. A page wearing a dark red uniform with silver accents opened the parlor door and announced, "Her Majesty, Queen Charis Willowthorn of Calera."

Charis entered, Reuben on her heels, and paused in front of the king and queen, who were standing shoulder to shoulder in the center of an ivory rug that appeared to have tiny replicas of their royal coat of arms embroidered across its surface. A queen did not curtsy to another ruler, so Charis allowed her lips to curve into a genuine smile.

"Your Majesty." King Gareth stepped forward first, his arms outstretched. His wide girth was encased in a shiny navy tunic with long braids of silver rope looped across his chest and then wrapped around his waist, their knotted ends dangling near his knees. Like Vyllanthra, he had golden skin and black hair. He gripped her forearms gently, his dark eyes sympathetic. "We welcome you to Solvang and hope to provide some comfort and aid during this distressing time."

Of course, they already knew about the invasion. There were plenty of Caleran families who could trace some of their ancestry back to Solvang, and vice versa. Pallorens carrying the news must have been sent to Solvang within hours of the Rakuuna overtaking the palace.

"Welcome, Your Majesty." Vyllanthra, a tall, broad-shouldered woman with a strikingly handsome face and strands of pure white threading her black hair, squeezed Charis's hands. "I was hoping the news out of Calera wasn't as dire as we've been hearing, but your new title tells me otherwise."

"Your Majesties." Charis returned Vyllanthra's squeeze and then let go. She might not be arriving from a position of strength, but she could avoid the weakness of appearing to need their sympathy.

Sympathy wouldn't bring back anyone Charis had lost. It might, however, grease the wheels of Gareth's famed generosity.

Reconsidering her strategy, Charis allowed herself to draw in a visibly shaky breath before saying, "I'm not sure what you've heard, but here is the truth. Rakuuna from the kingdom of Te'ash allied themselves with Rullenvor, attacked our ships and sealed off our harbor, and then invaded during our Sister Moons Festival."

The next breath wasn't meant to be shaky, but it trembled just the same. "In the invasion, both the queen and the king consort were lost."

Lost. As though her parents were something she'd misplaced. Something she could find again if she just looked hard enough.

"My dear, come. Sit. Let's see what we can do to help those who were able to escape." Gareth swept his arm toward the pair of red velvet couches that sat opposite each other in front of a window overlooking the palace's tidy courtyard. "Our staff will see to the comfort of your companions while we talk."

Charis kept her expression calm even as her thoughts raced. He'd offered help to those who were able to escape. That wasn't a slip of the tongue. It was a clear message that Solvang did not intend to interfere with Calera's fate.

Somehow she had to change their minds.

Charis sat on the sofa to the right. Gareth and Vyllanthra sat opposite her. A parlor maid entered with a tea cart, and Charis's stomach pitched uneasily as the smell of fillevun tea, buttery pastries, and pickled onion sandwiches filled the air. Once the maid had poured three cups and set the food on the low wooden table between the sofas, she backed out of the room.

Vyllanthra reached for her tea while Gareth took a hearty bite out of a savory biscuit. They were giving Charis permission to help herself to the food, but she knew better than to try swallowing anything of consequence. Not with her stomach in knots. And not when grief felt like a stone permanently lodged in the back of her throat. Instead, she took a delicate sip of the floral tea.

"How many were able to escape?" Vyllanthra asked as she set down her cup and folded her hands in her lap.

"Sixty-three." Charis set her own cup down.

"So few?" Gareth pressed a hand to his chest, the large ruby ring on his middle finger glittering in the rays of sun streaming in through the window.

"Most of them are merchants or tradespeople." Charis kept her voice even, though the horror of leaving thousands behind, trapped under the vicious rule of the Rakuuna, was an ever-present pain she couldn't get used to, no matter how much time passed. "We have a few families. Some of the palace staff and a handful of sailors. And then myself and the three members of the nobility who came with me today."

"You've all suffered a great tragedy." Vyllanthra leaned forward, and behind the sympathy in her gaze, Charis caught a hint of worry. "We've struggled to understand why Rullenvor and Te'ash, whom our master scholars assure us haven't been seen in the southern seas for over one hundred years, would ally themselves against an agricultural kingdom like Calera."

Charis heard the question embedded in the queen's statement. What had Calera done to bring this calamity upon themselves, and how could Solvang be sure they weren't next?

The answer was complicated, and Charis had to be careful how she framed it. She couldn't afford to be turned away from Solvang in a tiny smuggler's ship with few provisions and even fewer options.

Holding herself still to keep from giving too much away, Charis said, "It all seems to come down to Montevallo."

Gareth's eyes widened as he brushed crumbs from his tunic. "Montevallo is behind this? I thought you'd signed a treaty."

Charis nodded. "We have a treaty in place. King Alaric and I are allies." She hoped.

"Then what has Montevallo to do with the invasion?" Vyllanthra watched Charis closely.

People were more likely to trust someone whose body language matched theirs, so Charis folded her hands in her lap and leaned forward, like Vyllanthra. "Rullenvor made an alliance with the Rakuuna, ostensibly to have more protection for their ships in the northern seas.

"At some point, the Rakuuna began sinking any naval or merchant ship that tried to enter or leave our harbor. We didn't realize it was them at the time, of course." Charis flinched inwardly at the memory of standing on the deck of the smuggler's boat at night, practicing the seven rathmas with Tal's warm hand pressed to the center of her back as he adjusted her position while they quietly hunted the waters for the enemy who was attacking Calera's ships. Tal didn't deserve the flurry of desire that the memory of his hand caused, nor did he deserve the ache of misery that followed.

Shoving that thought away, Charis focused on the royals opposite her. "When they thought they had us at a true disadvantage, Rullenvor sent their ambassador with an offer. They'd colluded with Lady

Channing, a member of our royal council, to make the proposed alliance seem more trustworthy than it was. In exchange for protection at sea and help defeating Montevallo's army, they wanted us to allow both the Rakuuna and Rullenvor a place to set up an encampment and to grant them safe passage to Montevallo so they could mine for jewels."

Vyllanthra frowned. "An encampment for how long? How many troops?"

"I appreciate your immediate grasp of our misgivings. It is one thing to offer amnesty to people in need"—something Charis dearly hoped Solvang would extend to her people—"but it is quite another to welcome a military encampment. Especially one that would be difficult to defend against should that prove necessary."

"And all this because they wanted jewels from Montevallo?" Gareth dabbed at his mouth with a napkin. "What need could Rullenvor or the Rakuuna possibly have for so many jewels that it was worth sinking ships and offering to fight Montevallo with you?"

"I don't know. All I know is that we achieved peace with Montevallo through a treaty of our own design, turned down Rullenvor's offer, and within days of that refusal, the Rakuuna invaded."

"So they're using your kingdom as a staging ground to go after Montevallo?" Vyllanthra tapped a finger on her lips. "Does that mean when they've gained the jewels they want, they'll leave?"

"It's possible, though I hesitate to put much faith in that assumption." Charis met the queen's gaze as the answer she'd been hunting for fell into her lap—the one thing that might scare her allies enough to make them promise to help her reclaim Calera. It was time to show Gareth and Vyllanthra the picture Charis needed them to see.

"Prince Vahn of Montevallo sent a palloren to the Rakuuna's

armada with a promise to pay them any number of jewels they required in exchange for leaving Calera's harbor for good. Days later, the Rakuuna attacked us. They went straight for Mother—for the queen." Charis swallowed hard, but the stone in her throat refused to budge.

"They intended to kill the royal family and put themselves in charge immediately. Despite being offered what they said they wanted." Gareth shot a look at Vyllanthra.

"I believe they'd already done the same in Rullenvor. No one has heard from the High Emperor in some time, and Rullenvor's ambassador was arguing for the Rakuuna's interest, not for those of his own kingdom. I believe that the Rakuuna rule Rullenvor now, just like they rule Calera." Charis let the words sink in, fraught with dangerous implications for the safety of Solvang and the rest of the sea kingdoms.

"They're colonizing." Vyllanthra and Gareth seemed to share an unspoken conversation.

The memory of being so connected to Tal that she could read his mind from across a crowded room cut deep, but Charis ignored it. Locking eyes with Gareth and Vyllanthra, she spoke with vicious confidence.

"If the Rakuuna had only wanted jewels, they could have had their fill. They could have reached out to us for safe passage to negotiate directly with King Alaric instead of involving Rullenvor. As you know, we've long had a policy of providing protection to the ambassadors of our allies as they travel to the Montevallian border so they can assume their posts in Alaric's court." Charis's voice was cold as she went for the kill. "They could have left the High Emperor of Rullenvor alive. They could have left my parents alive. They didn't. They've now taken two of the seven sea kingdoms by force, and it's clear they mean to go after Montevallo as well. How long before they go after yet another kingdom on the map?"

Silence filled the room, broken only by the *tick-tick-tick* of a clock on the mantel behind Charis. Finally, Gareth and Vyllanthra seemed to reach an unspoken agreement. Turning to face Charis, Gareth said solemnly, "Tell us what you need."

THREE

"THIS IS A waste of time. I'd rather just sail straight to the Rakuuna kingdom and force them to tell us how to kill them than spend another day searching through old books for the solution." Holland paused to let Charis leave the Royal Library ahead of him.

In the fourteen days since their arrival in Solvang, a band of pressure had wrapped itself around Charis's chest and refused to leave. At Holland's words, the band squeezed a little tighter.

Most of the Calerans were staying in an older building that had been hastily converted into refugee apartments. As nobility, Charis, Holland, Nalani, and Delaire were housed in the palace with access to the city's palloren hub and a carriage at their disposal.

While Nalani and Delaire helped the refugees settle in, Charis and Holland had spent nearly every day studying the library's vast resources—scrolls, books, even the official diaries of ancient Solvanish royals—looking for the key to the Rakuuna's demise. They'd found almost nothing. There were few mentions of the reclusive species, and even fewer details beyond what Charis already knew: they were faster, stronger, and far more powerful than humans, and only a fool would go up against them in a fight.

The rulers of Solvang, Thallis, and Verace agreed.

Gareth and Vyllanthra had made it clear they would only commit troops to Charis's cause if she knew how to kill the Rakuuna. The messages she'd sent to Thallis and Verace had received similar answers. She'd sent a palloren to King Alaric of Montevallo as well but had yet to receive a reply, which made sense given how far Montevallo was from Solvang.

Still, the tension of not knowing if Alaric would honor the treaty ate at her composure until it thinned and frayed.

A pair of Solvanish guards left the library first, followed immediately by Reuben and then Charis. A second pair exited on Holland's heels, and the entire group moved quickly toward the carriage waiting at the curb.

Tendrils of fog snaked through the streets, clinging to rooftops and drifting through the gray afternoon sky like shreds of spun sugar. Charis was getting used to the frequent bouts of fog that blanketed the Solvanish coastline this time of year, but the inability to see more than a few carriage lengths in any direction never failed to unsettle her.

She stalked toward her carriage, the skin on the back of her neck prickling.

There were no assassins here waiting to kill her. No traitors standing by her side wearing the face of a friend. And still, every time she left a building, it took all her willpower not to flinch.

"This is getting us nowhere." Holland moved to her side. "Now that King Gareth has given us a map of the entire northern sea, we could just sail to Te'ash and—"

"Demand they tell us how to kill them?" Charis snapped as a footman opened the carriage door and bowed.

"You sound angry." Holland settled beside Charis on the slick black leather seat, while Reuben sat opposite them, his narrowed eyes examining the street beyond the carriage window, hunting for threats through the curtain of fog.

"Where to next, Your Majesty?" The coachmistress, a woman with silvery hair and deep creases in the corners of her eyes, stood at the doorway, her navy cap in her hands.

"Lady Estr's home, please." Charis made herself give the woman a tiny smile, her lips moving stiffly into the unfamiliar position.

There'd been precious little to smile about since the night of the invasion, and forcing a kind expression onto her face right now felt as natural as breathing water, but she couldn't aim her fury and despair at the Solvanish people.

As the carriage lurched into motion, Holland said, "If you keep tensing your jaw like that, you'll break your teeth."

She glared, and he shrugged. "Fine. Break your teeth. Good thing you like soup."

Shaking her head, she turned to look out the window as a patch of fog thinned enough to reveal elegant shops with neatly manicured flower boxes and tall, narrow doors. Her lungs ached with every breath.

How was she supposed to save her people and avenge her kingdom if she couldn't kill the invaders who'd taken her throne? She was trapped here, living off the generosity of the Solvanish royals, making promises she'd never be able to keep. A queen who didn't deserve her crown.

Her heart thudded frantically against her chest, and her head spun as the air in her lungs seemed to disappear.

She couldn't do this. Couldn't hold her people together, negotiate with allies, rescue Tal so she could leverage him against Alaric and take back her kingdom by force all while pretending she wasn't collapsing from the inside out.

A line of pine trees outside the window wavered as Charis's vision blurred. Clenching her fists in her skirt, she forced herself to breathe.

If Tal had been there, he'd have knelt at her feet, gathered her fists in his callused fingers, and ordered her to do something like count to ten or answer some silly question that distracted her long enough to let her body settle a bit.

Of course, if Tal had been there, she'd have been honor bound to run him through with a sword for being a traitor. The grief in her heart swelled, spilling heaviness into her veins until it felt as though she was made of stone.

Curse Tal for a thousand generations. The thought of giving him the death he deserved shouldn't hurt.

Her vision cleared as the carriage climbed a steep hill, the view outside her window swallowed whole by a thick blanket of white. Apparently, even just the memory of Tal interrupting her panic was enough to give her the brief distraction she needed to begin mastering her fear.

She cursed him again for good measure, even as her thoughts slowed and the deadly chess match she waged with her enemies once again came into focus.

There was a solution. There was *always* a solution. If she couldn't find it, that simply meant she wasn't looking in the right direction. She needed to step back and see the entire game board before she made her next move.

She could do this. Somehow. She had to.

"I meant what I said about relaxing your jaw," Holland said as the carriage turned a corner and slowed. "And maybe fix your face. You look like you want to kill the next person you see."

She blinked, reining in her thoughts as she turned to her cousin. Their eyes met, and a frown furrowed his brow.

"You're scared, aren't you?" Holland cocked his head to study her. Charis lifted her chin.

"I'm right." He shifted in his seat as the vehicle came to a stop. Reuben grabbed the hilt of his sword and faced the door, his expression unreadable, though Charis knew he was listening carefully to every word.

If ever there was a time for Holland to not speak every thought he had, this was it. Not that Charis didn't trust Reuben. She could grudgingly admit that while she often loathed his methods and would never forgive him for killing her handmaiden Milla on Mother's orders, he'd proven himself absolutely loyal to Charis since the moment she became Calera's ruler.

Still, a queen must not show weakness. The moment she behaved like prey instead of the predator she'd been raised to be, someone would be waiting to bring her down. Everyone either wanted to take her power or use it for themselves. Mother had repeatedly told her that, but it was Tal's betrayal that had truly carved the lesson into her heart.

"I am many things, but scared isn't one of them." Charis's voice was steely.

"If you say so."

"I do."

"Well, since you're the queen, I'm not supposed to argue. However—"

"Be careful how you finish that sentence." Charis met his eyes, sighing inwardly at the lazy way he arched one eyebrow as though not at all deterred by her threats. "What I really need from you right now is help navigating Solvanish polite society."

"And you think *I'm* the right person for that?"

"Nalani is busy, which makes you the only person in this carriage whose family are Solvanish nobility, so yes, I'm counting on you to help me through this."

"The last thing I want to do is eat tiny morsels of fancy food and pretend to listen to people I don't care about. I'm not even getting out of the carriage," he said with absolute conviction.

"Oh, yes you are. Your queen orders it." She took some pleasure in the expression of murderous defeat on his face. "Besides, it's your great-aunt Estr's tea party. If anything, you should be more comfortable here than most other places in Solvang."

"You're only saying that because you haven't met Great-Aunt Estr."

The footman opened the door, and Reuben exited, blocking the doorway with his body while he searched the courtyard for any danger to the queen and her heir. Not that it would be easy to see a threat through the fog that obscured all but the hazy glow of the lamplights burning on Lady Estr's porch.

Charis crossed the distance between the carriage and the porch in rapid strides, the copper tea gown her Solvanish seamstress had finished for her that morning whipping around her ankles.

"Your Majesty." A tiny woman who barely reached Charis's shoulders inclined her head respectfully and then studied Charis's face with sparkling eyes so dark brown, they looked nearly black. "Welcome. I see you've brought my rogue of a great-nephew with you."

"Thank you." Charis stepped across the threshold, grateful for the warmth of the fire burning in the gracious front parlor. "I promise your great-nephew will be on his best behavior."

"Oh, I hope not." Lady Estr winked at Holland. "What a boring afternoon we'd all have if that was the case."

The butler reached to remove Holland's duster, and Holland batted at his hand. "I'll keep my coat. I'm not staying long. Besides"—he turned to his great-aunt—"I doubt your friends would approve of me wandering your parlor with a sword in plain view."

"Given the threat your queen's presence has brought to us all, I think a sword would be quite welcome." Lady Estr tapped his arm none too gently. "Now, give Welsin your coat and go be sociable for at least ten minutes."

Charis schooled her face to conceal her racing thoughts.

If Lady Estr had no problem possibly offending Charis with her words, how many other members of the Solvanish nobility were whispering behind Charis's back? If too many of them felt unsafe, the warm welcome Gareth and Vyllanthra had extended could just as quickly turn cold.

Where would she take her people if Solvang turned them away?

The pressure in her chest sent a spike of pain into her jaw.

"Hmm, I'd wondered how much of your mother you had in you. Turns out, you have quite a bit." Lady Estr peered up at Charis, her expression open and direct.

Charis drew in a slow breath and then said quietly, "I'm not sure what you mean."

Lady Estr snorted none-too-delicately. "You heard me say that you've brought danger to our people. I know you've already calculated how much influence I have with my sovereigns, or you wouldn't have taken time out of your busy schedule to accept my invitation when you've turned down so many others."

The door opened behind Charis, and a gust of damp, chilly air swept the parlor as new guests arrived.

Lady Estr waved impatiently at the newcomers. "Yes, yes, you'll be introduced to the queen in a minute. Go have some tea and try not to look gobsmacked while you're at it."

As the new arrivals brushed past Charis and into the tearoom,

Lady Estr said, "I'm sure you started thinking about options the instant you heard me speak. But your face!" She gestured once more at Charis. "Just like your mother. Ice wouldn't melt on that one, no matter what was happening around her. It's good you have her self-control. Let's hope you have her brains as well."

Charis took a moment to assess Lady Estr once more. Sharp intelligence gleamed in her eyes, but there was no malice. No anger. Nothing sly or sinister.

A real smile lifted Charis's lips. "I see where Holland gets his . . . forthrightness."

"Thank you. Now, I'll do you the courtesy of being straightforward."

Lady Estr's voice lowered as a man in a deep-purple tea jacket and a pale violet scarf leaned against the tearoom door, glancing their way even as he spoke to someone still within the room. Flapping her hand at the man in the doorway, she said, "She'll be along when she's ready."

The man disappeared back into the tearoom. Lady Estr turned back to Charis. "The king and queen met with their advisors this morning. We have reason to believe pallorens sent to Calera are being intercepted by the Rakuuna."

A shiver crept up Charis's spine, but she held herself still and waited for Lady Estr to finish.

"As you know, all pallorens sent from Solvang must go through the royal hub, where officers of the crown make sure no message compromises our kingdom's security. However, your people use your own pallorens, and therein lies the threat." Lady Estr's eyes narrowed as she studied Charis. "The king and queen planned to inform you of this new development immediately, of course, but as you were scheduled to be here today, I volunteered to be the messenger. Be careful what your people are saying. It's one thing for the Rakuuna to ignore a small group of Calerans living in Solvang. It's quite another for them to discover you plan to wage war against them."

Charis nodded, her mind racing. "Thank you for that warning. Beyond checking in with family members to let them know we're safe, my people haven't said a word about my intentions."

Or had they? She'd certainly ordered them to keep quiet about her plans. Furthermore, she'd made sure several messages had contained the news that she'd sailed on from Solvang, though the refugees weren't sure where she was headed. It was the best she could do to assure the safety of both her people and those in Solvang, in case the Rakuuna decided their agreement with Tal to leave Charis unharmed was no longer valid.

"Better make sure it stays that way. The royal hub received word this morning that the Rakuuna queen has offered a generous reward to anyone who tells her where to find *you*." Lady Estr's short finger stabbed the air as she pointed to Charis. "Best hope every single member of the group you brought with you is absolutely loyal, or you'll have just invited the monsters to come fetch you back home."

FOUR

THE TEA PARTY seemed to take forever. Charis's head ached as she exchanged pleasantries, sipped spiced tea, and navigated her way through a slew of discreetly barbed questions.

Had she settled in Solvang, or would she be moving on soon?

Was she finding it difficult to plan for the future without the wisdom of her mother or her council at hand?

What had Calera done to attract the wrath of the Rakuuna in the first place?

By the time she'd worked her way through the thirty-some people in attendance, her smile felt sharp as a blade, and her tone was dipping dangerously close to the one Mother had used when she sentenced someone to the dungeons.

These people, in their velvets and silks, their plush carriages, and their comfortable homes free of monsters and bloodshed, couldn't possibly understand how their words affected her. They looked at Charis and saw someone who brought danger in her wake. Every bit of information they tried to pry out of her was simply to protect themselves and their families. She'd have done the same if the roles were reversed.

That knowledge didn't ease the pressure in her chest one bit.

She'd accepted Lady Estr's invitation because the woman was related to Holland and Nalani, which meant she was distant family to Charis as well. And because her connections to the palace and Solvang's nobility ran deep, which meant Charis could assess the Solvanish nobility's sentiment toward her people. If this afternoon was any indication, they were unsettled enough that even a hint of the Rakuuna's attention turning their way would send them running to Gareth and Vyllanthra to demand that the Calerans be forced out of their kingdom.

Charis was going to need to act quickly to assure the royals that her people posed no threat.

"I beg your pardon." The man in the purple tea jacket nodded respectfully to Charis as he accidentally bumped into her on his way to the refreshment table, which was being restocked by a pair of servers in crisp black-and-gold uniforms.

"Of course." Charis stretched her mouth into yet another smile and took a step back.

He paused and then turned to face her, his dark eyes intent on her face. "You won't remember me, of course, but I visited Calera often in my younger years."

She kept her smile in place and nodded. He was hardly the first in the room to tell her of a personal connection to Calera and its people.

"I study the stars, you see."

"How lovely." Her voice was polished marble, but at least her smile stayed intact.

"Yes, well." He reached up to smooth his graying goatee. "I made it a habit to establish correspondence with like-minded individuals in other kingdoms, comparing their understanding of the night skies with my own."

"An excellent habit."

He cleared his throat. "Yes, quite. I don't know if you're aware, but your father and I spent many years writing each other, until his health declined. And while we usually spoke of astronomy, we also mentioned our respective families. He was so proud of you and loved you deeply."

Charis's smile disappeared.

Tears shone in the man's eyes, and his voice caught, thick with grief. "I've mourned his loss since I heard the news and wanted to simply say that I'm so sorry. He was the kindest, most sincere man I ever had the pleasure of knowing, and he is missed."

The air in the room thinned until it was nothing but a wisp.

Charis opened her mouth to reply, but the words wouldn't come. All she could see was Father, crumpled on his bedroom floor. Gone. Ripped away from her without even the chance to say goodbye.

"I apologize if my words distress you." The man reached out as if to touch her arm, and Charis stumbled back.

The chasm of grief within bled darkness into her veins, heavy as stone, and she shook her head, though it was too late. He'd already torn away the thin wall she'd built to contain a loss she couldn't truly face.

Not if she wanted to be strong enough to save her people.

"Your Majesty." Lady Estr spoke from behind Charis.

Turning away from the man, Charis reached desperately for a shield of icy calm to cover the wreckage left in the wake of her memories. The room swayed slightly, and the pain in her head doubled as she faced Lady Estr and summoned every bit of willpower she possessed.

"Yes, Lady Estr?" Her voice was a husk of itself, but at least it didn't tremble.

Lady Estr frowned. "You look unwell. Perhaps you should visit the bath chamber. Nothing ruins a queen's formidable reputation like vomiting on a hostess's expensive rug."

"I'm fine." The lie left her lips, bold as a sword and just as sharp.

"If you say so." Lady Estr held a parchment letter in her hand, its purple seal already broken. Charis recognized the crest of Lord Jamison Thorsby, the head of Mother's royal council. "This was just delivered for you from the royal palloren hub."

Clearly those who ran the hub had either opened and read the message themselves or had brought it to Gareth and Vyllanthra before sending it on to Charis. She could only hope Lord Thorsby hadn't written anything that could jeopardize Charis's standing here.

"Thank you."

Charis couldn't bear to spend another moment pretending in this room full of strangers, and the message from Thorsby was the excuse she needed. "Lady Estr, I thank you for your gracious hospitality. Holland and I must take our leave now. I look forward to seeing you again soon."

"Last time I saw my great-nephew, he was hiding in the kitchen." Lady Estr snapped her fingers at a parlor maid. "Fetch Lord Holland. Have him meet his queen at her carriage."

The man in the purple coat opened his mouth as if to say something, but Charis was already moving toward the door, trusting Reuben to keep up.

She had no diplomacy left within her. No soft replies or smiles. No dexterity to answer questions without giving away anything of value.

All that was left was grief and rage and the terrible certainty that the Rakuuna queen setting a bounty on Charis's head meant something important had changed.

As Charis made her way back into the fog-drenched afternoon, her mind raced through scenarios, each one grimmer than the last.

Perhaps the Rakuuna had learned of the treaty between Calera and Montevallo and thought to use Charis as a bargaining chip, along with Tal.

Perhaps the Rakuuna regretted the deal they'd made with Tal allowing Charis to go free.

Or perhaps they needed Charis because Tal was dead.

Her knees weakened, and she sagged against the porch railing as a sickening wave of dread slammed into her. A hand wrapped around her upper arm and steadied her. She turned to find Reuben looking at her with the same implacable expectation she'd always seen in Mother's face.

Be stronger.

Strike harder.

Never falter, never waver, never break.

Not even if the boy who'd broken her heart was dead.

"What happened?" Holland rushed onto the porch, wiping crumbs from his chin.

"The porch is a bit slippery from the fog," Reuben said, his eyes darting toward the members of Lady Estr's staff who stood nearby, manning the entrance.

"Seems fine to me," Holland mumbled as he took the stairs quickly. "Let's go before Great-Aunt Estr finds someone else who simply must have a conversation with me."

Charis pulled her arm free of Reuben's grip and walked to the carriage with the same purposeful stride she'd once used to enter the throne room. When she was settled inside with Holland and Reuben, she instructed the coachmistress to take them to the refugee apartments where they would pick up Nalani and Delaire, and where Charis would face the unenviable task of informing her people that they could no longer send messages to family in Calera.

Not until Charis was long gone from Solvang.

She'd have to alter her plans. Rush any remaining repairs and upgrades to the ship. Secure letters of protection from Gareth and Vyllanthra to prove they were allies in case Charis needed help from another kingdom along the way. And head to Te'ash before the Rakuuna came looking for her here.

But how could she do that if she still didn't know how to kill them?

And what would she do if she arrived in Te'ash only to learn that the monsters had killed Tal?

Panic closed a fist around her throat, and she swallowed hard as the thudding of her heart matched the pounding in her head. She told herself it was simply because Tal's death would leave her without leverage against Alaric. It had nothing to do with never seeing Tal's warm brown eyes or crooked smile again.

"What's that?" Holland's voice broke through her spiraling thoughts. She followed his gaze to the parchment she still clutched in her hand.

As the carriage turned left and began winding down a steep hill, she smoothed the parchment open, her heart giving a twinge at the sight of Lord Thorsby's elegant scrawl. Focusing on his words was better than spinning useless scenarios in her head. The panic eased a bit, and she drew a steadying breath.

"It's a note from Lord Thorsby." She peered closer and realized that Gareth and Vyllanthra had opened the message because it was addressed to them. Thorsby, along with the rest of Calera, didn't know Charis was in Solvang.

Which meant the Rakuuna didn't know, either.

Charis had to keep it that way until she had time to learn how to kill them and then leave Solvang's shores far behind.

"What does he say?" Holland leaned closer.

"Let me read it, and then we'll see." Charis peered closely at the parchment in the dim light of the carriage interior.

A match flared, and then the lantern that hung on the wall opposite the door began to glow. Reuben shook the match's flame into smoke and nodded to Charis as soft, golden light filled the carriage, illuminating the parchment.

"Thank you." She scanned the parchment once and then went back to reread it with care, her heart swelling. "They're resisting." She handed the parchment to Holland as the carriage slowed to a stop in front of the building Nalani and Delaire had converted into makeshift apartments for the refugees. "Nobility, merchants, and peasants alike are organizing in the shadows and sabotaging the Rakuuna every chance they get."

Holland swore and pounded his fist against his thigh as he read Lord Thorsby's words, but his elation evaporated as he reached the last paragraph of the parchment. "Charis—"

"I know."

Holland turned to Reuben. "The Rakuuna placed a bounty on Charis's head. A generous reward for returning her to Calera, alive."

Reuben glared. "Best not to mention that to the traitors on board the ship, then."

"I hardly think Grim and Dec will return me to Calera just for some coin." Charis composed her expression as the door opened. "They're depending on me to rescue their prince."

"May he choke on every bite he ever swallows," Holland said.

"Indeed." Charis exited the carriage after Reuben and instructed a Caleran girl playing in the courtyard to spread the word that the queen needed to speak to everyone immediately.

Fifteen minutes later, everyone who'd sailed with Charis—with the exception of Orayn, Finn, Dec, and Grim, who all slept on the ship—was gathered in the community parlor on the first level of the building. Charis had stationed every Solvanish guard outside. Only Calerans needed to hear what she had to say.

"I've received word from Calera." She held up the parchment. A murmur spread throughout the room. Charis waited for silence, then continued. "There are three things you need to know. First, the Rakuuna queen has placed a bounty on my head."

Cries of shock and anger rippled through the crowd, and Charis held up her hand for quiet. "Second, the Rakuuna are intercepting pallorens sent to Calera and are reading the messages. I can only assume they are doing so to hunt for news of my whereabouts and to make sure no kingdom is sending an armada to Calera's rescue."

This time, she didn't have to ask for quiet. Silence settled over the room, thick as wool.

"Unfortunately, this means we must temporarily cease sending pallorens to your families as we cannot risk any accidental exposure of information that puts either Solvang or our people at risk. Once I've left for my next destination, you may resume communication."

People shifted uneasily, exchanging swift glances.

"I realize that's disappointing, and I'm sorry for that." She lifted the parchment, calling their attention back to its content. "Finally, we've received the welcome news that a contingent of Calerans from all backgrounds have loosely organized themselves in the shadows and are mounting a resistance in our fair capital city of Arborlay."

Conversation erupted, and Holland shouted them into silence again.

Charis's head ached so badly, she felt sick. She wanted nothing more than to take a tonic, crawl into bed, and beg the sister moons for sleep without nightmares. Instead she said with quiet vengeance, "I intend to finish my tasks here in Solvang within the next two weeks. At that point, I will set sail for the enemy's kingdom and turn the war to our favor. All Calerans who are in good health and do not have children to care for here will be sailing with me."

Charis dismissed the crowd and climbed into the carriage with the twins, Delaire, and Reuben, trying desperately to think past the pain in her head and the pressure in her chest.

She needed a new plan to find the Rakuuna's weakness, and she needed it fast.

FIVE

Ten days had passed since the unwelcome news that the Raku-una were intercepting pallorens and had posted a reward for Charis's capture, yet Charis was no closer to finding the key to her enemy's destruction. She'd talked to professors, visited shops in hopes that a merchant might know something, and stared at the sister moons long into the night, hoping inspiration would strike.

Today she was going to the docks to speak with sailors from returning vessels.

"I'll just be a minute, Your Majesty, and then we'll have you all sorted for the day."

Charis sat at the vanity in her suite of rooms and tried to control her impatience as Nita, the handmaid assigned to her, gathered her supplies.

She should've already been dressed and downstairs, but she'd spent most of the night staring at the ceiling, her thoughts racing in fruitless circles while jittery spikes of fear startled her awake every time her eyes closed. She'd finally drifted off as the sky outside her window lightened to a rosy blush, only waking when Nita came in with her breakfast.

"Your Majesty, would you like your hair parted in the middle or to the side?" Nita was a middle-aged woman with firm, competent hands and the devout belief that, despite Charis's natural curls, proper royals always wore their hair straight.

"A simple updo will be fine," Charis said, smoothing the skirt of her new navy-blue velvet day dress. A thin silver rope laced up the bodice, and tiny silver ferns were embroidered across the skirt. It was pretty, but Charis was uninterested in wasting time on a complicated hairstyle, no matter how fashionable it might be. The days of needing to send a clear message to her political opponents with her appearance were long gone. Now the only message her opponents needed to receive from her could be delivered with a sword.

Not that a sword was much use against the Rakuuna, but hopefully today's errand would give Charis another option.

Closing her eyes against the pain of Nita's firm brush, she focused on what she'd already gained since her arrival in Solvang.

She had an ancient map, painstakingly copied onto a new scroll of parchment over the span of several hours in the library, that showed Te'ash's location in the dangerous waters above Embre. She had weapons of every description donated by King Gareth, and Holland was happily studying technique and then training her crew how to use each item in the ship's new armory. She had amnesty for those who'd escaped Calera and a safe place for them to live.

Shifting in her seat, she clasped her hands tightly in her lap to resist the urge to fidget.

"I think perhaps a minucca today, Your Majesty," Nita said as she yanked another curl through her brush. "With your bone structure, it will look quite fetching."

Charis couldn't care less about looking fetching, but she nodded anyway. The faster she agreed to Nita's suggestions, the faster she would look presentable enough to leave the room.

It all came down to learning the Rakuuna's weakness so she could leave Solvang before they destroyed her kingdom. It had to be possible to kill them somehow—nothing was immortal.

"Just a moment more, please." Nita wielded a damp brush and a collection of hairpins like a sculptor determined to turn reluctant clay into whatever she wished. Charis tapped her foot and gripped the sides of the chair to keep herself from squirming.

Her suite was on the east side of the palace. The sun's rays streamed over the windowsills and puddled on the plush ivory rug in pools of golden light. Hildy slept in a patch of sunlight, her orange-and-black fur looking sleek and warm.

The kitten was her last connection to Father, but she was also a connection to Tal. Every stroke of her back reminded Charis of visiting Father, and every rumbly purr brought her back to her own sitting room, curled up in front of her fire while Tal tucked Hildy into her lap, handed her a mug, and told her to drink the cocoa, pet the kitten, and breathe for a while.

How had he done it? How had he slipped so far past her defenses that he knew what Charis needed before she did?

A knock sounded at her door, and Nalani entered.

"There, Your Majesty. You look a picture." Nita patted Charis's hair one last time and stepped back.

Pushing thoughts of the traitor into the darkest corner of her heart, Charis turned to examine the looking glass mounted above the vanity. Her brown curls had been tamed into a swirling coil of braids threaded through with red velvet ribbon and then twisted into an updo. The festive look was a stark contrast to the pallor of her cheeks and the smudges of exhaustion beneath her blue eyes, but there was little anyone could do about that.

"Thank you, Nita." Charis rose, ignoring the way the room swayed for a moment before righting itself.

The maid frowned. "I'll ring for breakfast, Your Majesty."

"That won't be necessary. I'm running late as it is. You are dismissed."

The instant Nita closed the door behind her, Nalani said firmly, "I'd like your permission to represent Calera in discussions with various members of Solvanish society."

Charis reached for her new white fur cloak, but then reconsidered. If recent rumors were true, public sentiment in Solvang had turned against her as news about the bounty spread. She would be much less conspicuous on the docks wearing her plain gray cloak.

"You're not even listening to me." Nalani stepped in front of Charis and fisted her hands on her hips.

Charis blinked, her focus momentarily shifting to her cousin. "Did you need something?"

Nalani's dark eyes narrowed. "Yes."

"What is it?" Charis's mind raced through the potential problems Nalani might be bringing to her attention. Trouble at the refugee apartments? Invitations to events Charis couldn't afford to decline when she needed to shore up support among the nobility? Holland offending yet another member of the palace staff?

"I need your permission to speak with your authority to members of Solvanish society."

Charis paused. "Speak about what?"

"Battle plans, medicinal supplies, schooling for our refugee children, and that's just for starters."

"Battle plans?" Charis moved toward her closet to retrieve her gray cloak.

"Father's brother knows a retired admiral. I'm certain I can get him to agree to discuss strategy with me. If you figure out how to kill the Rakuuna and our allies commit ships to our cause, we're going to need help developing a battle plan."

"I know what we need. What I don't understand is why you're asking to take care of that on my behalf." The words rushed out, sounding harsher than Charis intended. "A queen should work directly with her military advisors."

"Maybe so, but—oh, don't give me that look." Nalani's chin rose in a way that suddenly reminded Charis very much of herself. "You're wearing yourself out trying to find a way to stop the Rakuuna. You can't do everything, be everywhere, and speak to everyone at once. And the last Caleran ambassador to Solvang had returned home for the Sister Moons Festival. Who knows if he even survived the invasion? Either way, he isn't here, and we need a representative from the crown. Give me the job, and let me take care of this for you."

"You want to be my ambassador to Solvang?" Charis studied her cousin as if just now seeing her. The determined glint in her eye that signaled a battle for any who argued with her. The firm set of her jaw that belied the softness of her features and lulled people into believing she'd be easier to manipulate than her obstinate brother.

She could trust Nalani's loyalty and discernment. Even better, she could trust that Nalani understood exactly which situations Charis would prefer to handle herself. It was a good solution to a problem Charis had been too busy to even notice.

"I'm perfect for the job." Nalani raised her hand to tick items off on her fingers. "I'm related to nobility here, which establishes trust. I understand both Caleran and Solvanish culture. I know you, which means I know when I can confidently speak for you and when I need to bring something to your attention first. I'm diplomatic when I have to be and firm when it's needed. I realize you don't have many options at the moment, but even if you did, I'd still be the best person for the ambassadorship."

"I agree."

"And furthermore, I have connections to—oh. You agree?" Nalani leaned closer as though examining Charis's expression.

"I do. And I'm glad you brought this to my attention. I'll draw up a certificate—"

Nalani whipped a small roll of parchment from her dress pocket. "I already did. It just needs your signature."

"I pity the person who tries to derail you when you've made up your mind." Charis looked over the certificate and then grabbed a quill from the desk and scrawled her signature across the bottom.

"I'm heading to the docks with Reuben today to see if I can find any information on the Rakuuna." She tied the gray cloak at her throat and reached for a pair of buttery soft black leather gloves. "As you are now my ambassador, I'll expect daily reports on your conversations and actions. I don't want any surprises."

"Yes, Your Majesty." Nalani took the parchment, curtsied, flashed a smile at Charis, and left.

Charis quickly joined Reuben in the hallway and headed toward the carriage house, where a small buggy was waiting as requested.

"I don't like being the only guard, Your Majesty. You need more protection," Reuben grumbled as they settled into the buggy.

"I won't need that level of protection if I take care not to look like a queen. I need answers, not pomp and circumstance."

Tendrils of fog once again threaded the landscape like fraying ribbons. The bay was so shrouded in mist, it was impossible to see past its mouth and out into open waters. A lighthouse glowed at the edge of the bay, but even still, Charis wondered if ships ever collided simply because they couldn't see each other in time.

The buggy dropped them off half a block from the dock. Even though there was no royal shield on the vehicle's side, Charis didn't want the spectacle of arriving in what was clearly an expensive carriage.

The dock was busy. Two large vessels were being unloaded, with a stream of sailors carrying crates down ramps and over to merchant wagons. Other ships were being loaded, cleaned, or repaired. The hum of voices was punctuated by the slap of boots against the dock.

She'd sent a message to Orayn, and he was standing on the dock, a little way down from their ship, haggling with a merchant over what looked like a selection of spare tarps.

When she reached him, Orayn sent the merchant on his way, but not before the man gave Charis a long, bold stare. She ignored the instinct to burrow further into her hood.

"The ship at the far end just arrived from Verace. That's nearly as far north as you can get without going into the northern seas where Te'ash is located." Orayn gestured toward a sleek green ship with sailors hauling crates down its ramp.

"Let's go." Charis began weaving her way around sailors, merchants, and dockhands alike, with Orayn on her left and Reuben on her right. As they passed her ship, she caught a glimpse of Dec and Grim disembarking and ignored them.

The green ship had the name *Ell-roth-mi* painted on the side in delicate gold script. She could speak Veracian, though not as well as Solvanish. Still, she was grateful for Tutor Brannigan's endless hours of drilling her in the languages of the other sea kingdoms.

"Greetings," she said to a woman with sun-kissed brown skin and a constellation of scars along her cheekbones. The woman wore a green jacket with several patches embroidered on the sleeves, which

Charis assumed meant she was either the captain or the first mate.

The woman barely glanced at her. "We're selling fish at the market. Not here. Ahn-li, if you drop that crate, it's coming out of your pay!" She glared at one of the sailors, whose feet slid on the damp wood of the ramp before finding purchase again.

"I'll get straight to the point so that I don't waste your time," Charis said crisply. "We aren't here to buy fish. I'm looking for information about the kingdom of Te'ash and the Rakuuna who live there."

The woman's pale gray eyes found Charis's for an instant, and then she made a strange gesture with her hand, as though wiping something across her collarbone and then flinging it to the ground. "Cursed species. We have nothing to do with them."

Charis spoke quickly before the woman could turn away. "They're invading other sea kingdoms. Colonizing. I'm trying to find a way to stop them, but there's no information here in Solvang about how to kill them. Verace is much farther north. I'd hoped—"

"As I said, we have nothing to do with them. You'd do better finding someone from Embre. Much closer to Te'ash." She looked back at her ship and swore. "Mer-la, help him, please! I swear he couldn't find his own face in a mirror."

Charis pivoted and stared at the plethora of ships tied to the dock. "Any ships here from Embre?"

Orayn shook his head. "Not likely. They keep to themselves. Maybe those sailors who just returned from a merchant run to Thallis might—"

"You're not welcome here, queen of nothing." An older man in fish-stained overalls and a wide-brimmed hat spat at Charis as she moved away from the Veracian ship.

Reuben reached for his sword, but Charis breathed, "No."

She couldn't risk a scene. Not if she wanted others to feel comfortable talking to her. Ignoring the man, she kept walking, scanning the dock as she went.

In a port as busy as this one, surely someone had to have experience with Embre.

"Aye, that's right. I recognize you. Spitting image of your mother when she last visited." The man followed at her heels. "Look at you, trying to hide in that fancy cloak when you're bringing danger to our shores!"

"Your Majesty—"

"We will not react, Reuben. No, Orayn, ignore him." She touched Orayn's shoulder as his large hands curled into fists. "If you're caught fighting on the docks, you'll have trouble finding anyone willing to do business with you, and we still need more supplies and a repair or two for the ship before we sail."

She quickened her pace, but the man followed suit. How was she supposed to hold conversations when she had someone yelling at her wherever she went?

"Shoulda kept to your own," he shouted. "Or at least had the decency to sail into Dursley, where the likes of you belong."

Something struck Charis, sending her stumbling forward. Reuben snarled and reached for his sword as Charis turned to find a fish as long as her arm lying at her feet. The man was already reaching into a nearby bucket to pull out another one.

"That'll be enough out of you," Reuben said, violence shimmering in his rough voice. But before he could finish drawing his sword, Dec and Grim were there.

Dec stepped in front of the man, blocking his view of Charis, and put a firm hand on the man's shoulder, while Grim gave a dramatic gasp and yelled, "Thief! He's stealing your fish, Hilmer!"

A man nearly as large as Orayn, with a long brown beard and deeply creased skin, stalked away from a merchant's wagon, an angry flush rising in his cheeks. "Shab, you good-for-nothing dog, get your hands off my fish!"

Shab dropped the fish and backed away, his attention diverted to Hilmer, who looked ready to fillet the man with the knife in his hand.

"Come, Your Majesty," Reuben said with quiet urgency. "It's best we leave before we run into any more trouble."

Frustration hummed through Charis as she stalked toward the main road. She was going to have to delegate the search for information to someone else if she was that easily recognized. Who could she trust with the task?

Orayn wouldn't read people well enough to know when he should push for more information. Reuben was likely to run them through with a sword if they made threats against Charis. Holland could be ruled out for the same reason.

She paused when they reached the road. Turning, she was startled to see Dec and Grim had followed her as well. The fact that they'd demonstrated quick thinking and had acted to protect her was a bitter pill to swallow, but a queen who refused to be fair was a queen who didn't deserve her power.

"Thank you," she said stiffly, nodding to them. "Your intervention was well timed—and appreciated."

Dec nodded back, staying silent as usual. Grim, however, gave her a shy smile.

The day couldn't be a complete loss. She'd had too many of those in a row. Obviously, the two Montevallians were well acquainted with the dock and the people who worked there.

Gesturing toward an alley tucked between the dockmaster's office and a fishmonger's stall, she gathered the four men around her and said quietly, "The captain of the Veracian ship thought our best source for information on the Rakuuna would be someone from Embre. Do any of you know of a ship from Embre currently in port? Or maybe a sailor or merchant who's been there?"

Dec cocked his head as if thinking carefully and then said, "I don't know of anyone on the docks with ties to Embre, but Shab mentioned Dursley, and visiting there might actually be a good idea."

Charis frowned. "Where is Dursley?"

"It's a village on the north end of the island where foreigners who don't fit in so well with proper Solvanish society live," Orayn said.

A whisper of something that felt dangerously like hope flickered to life within Charis. "Are any of those foreigners from Embre?"

A slow smile creased Orayn's face. "It's been years since I visited there, but I think so."

Charis dug her fingers into the folds of her cloak to keep them from trembling. "Then let's go to Dursley and figure it out."

SIX

THE VILLAGE OF Dursley was a three-hour ride away, so Charis cleared her schedule for the second day in a row and requested a large, comfortable carriage. A note from Vyllanthra arrived as Charis finished securing her curls with a cocoa-brown ribbon. Nita hovered anxiously, brush in hand, but Charis didn't have time to waste if she was going to make the trip to Dursley, hunt for someone from Embre, extract information, and then return to the palace in time to keep her dinner appointment with Queen Vyllanthra.

Charis toyed with the idea of skipping the dinner entirely, but one glance at the note changed her mind.

As Nalani entered the room, dressed in a brushed wool gown of cream and gold, Charis slid the note into the drawer of her bedside table and said, "Nita, I'll need a bath prepared upon my return, and my evening dress should be pressed and ready. You are dismissed until then."

"Yes, Your Majesty." Nita bowed and left the room.

The instant the door shut, Nalani said, "Are you sure you can manage this trip and attend a dinner with the queen? Perhaps we should do the trip tomorrow instead."

"We need information immediately. I'm not willing to wait." Charis shook out her skirts and reached for her cloak.

"Then send your regrets and skip the dinner." Nalani hurried forward to pull a stray thread from the cloak's hem. "It's too much to fit into one day. Especially when you aren't sleeping, and"—she glanced at Charis's half-eaten breakfast—"well, at least you ate something. I'll give you that."

"I'm glad it meets with your approval." Charis gave her a small smile and then headed toward the door. "I have to be at the dinner. Vyllanthra made it clear she expects my attendance. Public sentiment has turned against me now that knowledge of the Rakuuna bounty on my head has spread."

"Great-Aunt Estr thinks you're being invited to dinner so the queen can question you and make up her mind about whether to continue supporting Solvang's alliance with what's left of Calera."

"Lady Estr is right." Charis paused at the door. "If Vyllanthra decides we're more risk than potential reward, I will have no choice but to leave Solvang."

"All the more reason to get answers from Dursley if there are any answers to be had." Nalani's voice firmed.

"Exactly." Charis opened the door and swept into the hall. Reuben took up his position at her right, Nalani on her left. Four Solvanish guards joined her, and the group moved quickly through the east wing and out into the misty morning air, where a large carriage pulled by four black horses awaited. Holland, along with Dec and Grim, was standing beside it.

She'd decided to include Dec and Grim in the day's outing because their actions yesterday spoke of loyalty to her. Not because she meant anything to them personally, but because they knew she was the best chance Tal had of being rescued. Alaric could hardly give in to the Rakuuna's demands if it meant jeopardizing his own kingdom's safety, even for the life of his youngest son. Charis had made it quite clear in the palloren she'd sent that she intended to take that burden off his shoulders.

She'd also included Dec and Grim because if the people of Dursley were outcasts in Solvanish society, they were far more likely to feel comfortable around those who didn't appear to be nobility.

Now she just had to endure hours in the company of the spies who'd helped Tal betray her. She'd endured far worse.

Holland, Dec, and Grim bowed and murmured, "Your Majesty" as she passed them and climbed inside the carriage, Reuben on her heels. Holland and Nalani sat on either side of her. Dec and Grim joined Reuben on the opposite bench.

As the vehicle began moving through the city streets, Holland scrutinized her face. "Are you feeling sick?"

"No."

"Well, you look like that time you had a stomach virus. You're all pale and thin, and your eyes look like you haven't slept in a week."

"I'm fine." The lie fell from her lips with practiced ease.

"You keep using that word." Holland raised a brow in her direction. "I don't think it means what you think it means."

Charis ignored him and turned to look out the window at the pristine buildings with their elegant window boxes full of the lush chordellia flowers that bloomed here in winter. Her breath puffed from her lips in a swirl of white condensation as she burrowed deeper into her wrap. The kingdoms north of Solvang were already experiencing snow and ice, and it wouldn't be long before the seas became difficult to navigate.

She intended to be long gone from Solvang before it was unsafe to sail past the northern kingdom of Embre. The worry that Tal was already dead—thus prompting the Rakuuna to place a bounty on Charis's head for leverage against Alaric—was one she steadfastly refused to consider. He was alive. He had to be. If the idea of his death caused panic within her, it was only because she'd decided he was the tool she would use to gain his father's cooperation.

The fog thinned beneath the midday sun as the carriage rumbled through fields with scattered stone cottages and rocky outcroppings full of goat herds that leaped nimbly from one craggy peak to another. The rattle of the carriage wheels and the rhythmic sway of its chassis beckoned Charis to close her eyes, but she pinched herself every time she felt her eyelids growing heavy.

That last time she'd accidentally fallen asleep in a carriage, she'd awakened with her head on Tal's shoulder, his arm braced across her waist to anchor her safely to the seat.

The memory stung, and she drew her spine straight as she glared across at Dec and Grim. She had no plans to ever speak to Tal again, even after she rescued him, which made getting answers to the questions that kept her up at night difficult, to say the least. But here were Tal's co-conspirators, worried she might change her mind and leave their prince to his fate. She had at least an hour left in the journey to Dursley. Might as well make the most of it.

Before she could think better of it, she said casually, "Your prince must have been quite pleased to be assigned as my bodyguard."

Beside her, Nalani stiffened, and Charis could practically feel her worry. Holland, on the other hand, stretched his legs out like a cat and let his hand come to rest on the hilt of his sword.

Grim shot an anxious look at Dec, who held himself as still and watchful as always, his dark eyes finding Charis's. When it became clear she was waiting for a response, Dec said quietly, "Nothing about being sent to Calera as a spy pleased Prince Tal."

Holland snorted.

"Well, he certainly had an aptitude for it." Charis settled back against her seat and smiled at Grim in a way that had beads of sweat suddenly dotting his forehead. She raised a hand to tick items off on her fingers. "Perfect Caleran accent—quite impressive, really. Friendliness that disarmed others. A familiarity with northern Calera that gained the trust of my father."

Fury crept into her voice. "That must have been a moment of pride for Tal. Father rarely let new staff get close to him, and he was so taken in by Tal that he trusted your traitor of a prince with that which was most precious to him. *Me.*"

Grim rubbed his palms against his thighs as if scrubbing them clean. Dec folded his arms across his chest, his eyes never leaving hers.

"I'm sure Tal was thrilled to report to King Alaric that he'd managed to deceive not only the king of Calera, but its princess as well. I can only imagine the celebration—"

"He was terrified of you at first," Grim blurted out, his voice shaking. Charis was surprised to note that the emotion in his words was anger nearly strong enough to match her own.

"Grim," Dec breathed, but the other boy paid no attention.

Charis leaned forward. "Not nearly terrified enough."

"You have no idea what it was like for him." Grim threw the words at her. "He wasn't happy to be assigned to you, but what choice did he have?"

He'd had plenty of choices. Becoming her friend had been a choice. Kissing her had been a choice. Not telling her the truth had been a choice. He'd been rich with choices, and at every turn, he'd done the wrong thing.

"Your Majesty." Dec unfolded his arms and clasped his hands in his lap. "Tal should be the one to explain himself to you. We can't pretend to know everything that happened between the two of you. We know how bad it was for him at home in Montevallo, and we know—"

"How bad could it have been?" Holland sounded genuinely curious. "He was a *prince*."

Dec considered Holland in silence for a long moment, and then said evenly, "He was unwanted, unloved by his father—"

"Abused by his father, more like," Grim muttered.

"Constantly told he was worthless and would never be of value to Montevallo like his older brother and sister were." Dec continued as if Grim hadn't spoken. "His older brother adopted the same attitude toward Tal and delighted in making his life miserable. When he was ordered to be a spy, he knew it was his one chance to redeem himself in his father's eyes."

"He had nothing to redeem!" Grim's voice rose. "He was sickly as a child, and that alone made the king decide he wasn't worthy of being a Penbyrn."

"Because he was sick?" Nalani asked.

"Growing up, he wasn't strong enough to be trained for the military, which is all a thirdborn royal is really expected to do in a kingdom constantly at war. Of course, he outgrew that and worked hard to turn himself into a capable warrior, but by then, his father had other plans for him." Dec met Charis's gaze again. "That's what we can tell you about his past. Any explanations about his actions toward you will have to come from him."

Charis looked away. How could a small part of her battered heart ache at the thought of young Tal, rejected by his father, bullied by his brother, adrift in a society that only valued him if he could contribute to their war with Calera?

He'd done more than contribute. He'd done more than spy. He'd broken through her defenses and left her in ruins.

The carriage slowed as it entered the fringes of Dursley. The stone buildings were shorter than those in the capital and spread loosely along the street, as though the inhabitants who lived and worked here preferred space between themselves and others.

Dec unclasped his hands. "Your Majesty, Grim and I volunteer to ask around for someone from Embre. Even in a cloak, you are unmistakably nobility, as is Lady Farragin"—he nodded respectfully toward Nalani—"and people like these might not want to speak with you."

"What about me?" Holland demanded.

Dec glanced at him. "No one would take you for nobility—"

"Thank you."

"Until you open your mouth and display your rather impressive education," Dec finished.

Holland glared at him. Charis studied Dec and Grim for a moment, but she already knew Dec was right. Sentiment had turned against her in Solvang, and people who felt like outcasts already would hardly be interested in speaking with the refugee queen who'd brought trouble to their shores.

"You have one hour," Charis said. "Knock on every door. If the information we need is here, we can't afford to miss it."

"I can knock on doors," Holland muttered as the two Montevallians exited the carriage and hurried down the closest street.

Charis, Reuben, and the twins sat in silence for a few moments, watching the Montevallians move from one building to the next, their shoulders hunched against the sharp winter wind that sent watery gray clouds scudding across the sky, momentarily obscuring the midday sun.

Finally, Nalani said softly, "I know you don't want to hear this, but it helps me a little to understand Tal's childhood."

"Being picked on as a kid, even by your own family, is no reason to act with dishonor." Holland gripped his sword hilt until his knuckles turned white.

"But he treated his father—his kingdom—with honor." Nalani leaned forward to look across Charis's lap and meet her brother's gaze. "We're angry because we thought he was one of us."

"Because he's a *liar*." Holland's lip curled around the word as if he could barely stomach it.

Charis's heartbeat shuddered, a jagged rhythm pulsing through her as if she was a hollow vessel capable of holding nothing more than the echo of who she used to be.

"He lied to us. Not to his family. His own people." Nalani clasped and unclasped her hands, her telltale sign of distress. "If you'd been assigned to spy in Alaric's palace, and you'd succeeded in getting close to the royal family, they'd be furious with you, but would you think of yourself as dishonorable?"

"He did more than just spy on Charis!" Holland's voice rose.

"I know that, but—"

"Enough." Charis meant to sound firm, but the word came out ragged and worn. Instantly, the twins turned to her.

"I'm sorry." Nalani grasped Charis's cold fingers in her own. "I didn't mean to upset you."

Holland bumped her shoulder with his. "Don't worry, Charis. I'll make sure the traitor regrets ever setting eyes on you."

"And if he doesn't, Your Majesty, I certainly will." Reuben's voice shimmered with violence—a part of him that used to make her deeply uncomfortable. Now it barely scratched the surface of the darkness in her heart.

The three of them were watching her closely. Slowly, she lifted her chin and blinked away any hint of emotion in her eyes.

She couldn't look weak. Even in front of her closest allies. Tal had taught her that.

The carriage door opened, and the Montevallians entered on a gust of frigid wind. "Found someone," Dec said as they settled into their seats. "A herbologist. The coachmistress is taking us to the shop now."

The vehicle took three turns and then rolled to a stop in front of a little hut made of gray stone. Ivy clung to the walls, and a gate to the left of the entrance led to an overgrown garden.

"You two, stay here," Charis said to Dec and Grim.

Charis left the carriage, followed by Holland, Nalani, and Reuben, and the four of them entered the shop.

An old woman was bent over a large pot stirring something that bubbled and steamed, filling the room with the scent of damp wood and bright citrus. A thick purple scarf was wrapped around her head, and her wrinkled skin resembled a crumpled piece of parchment.

She glanced up as Charis entered, one blue eye sizing up her visitor. The other eye was covered in white film. "The name's Lunay. Help you?" she asked in thickly accented Solvanish.

"I understand you're originally from Embre," Charis said.

"Oh, aye." Lunay reached for a dusty glass bottle full of something that looked like red seeds and poured a small amount into the bubbling mixture.

"Do you know who I am?"

Lunay stirred her pot. "Should I?"

"Probably not." Charis stepped closer. "I'm from Calera. We've recently been invaded by the Rakuuna. A small number of us escaped, but most of the kingdom is now trapped."

Lunay muttered something in the lilting language of Embre and spat on the floor.

"I have the difficult task of learning how to defeat the invaders so I can save my people. I've searched every resource in the Royal Library, but nothing there tells me how to kill the Rakuuna."

"Needs moriarthy." Lunay returned the red seeds to their shelf.

"I don't understand." Charis frowned. Did she mean her concoction needed something else, or was she speaking of the Rakuuna?

Lunay gave her pot another vigorous stir and then faced Charis. "Moriarthy. Dry beans from the moriar bush, crushed into powder, kills Rakuuna."

The pressure in Charis's chest burst, sending a rush of vicious hope through her veins that nearly brought her to her knees. Holland rapped his fist against his sword sheath and swore, while Nalani clasped her hands to her chest. Reuben's perpetual sneer widened into something that almost resembled a smile.

"How? Do we coat our weapons with it? Or do they have to ingest it?"

Lunay frowned and then shrugged. "Maybe both. Maybe not. Been many years since I was in Embre."

Charis was too triumphant to care about this small setback. She'd figure out the delivery system for the poison herself. She'd coat every weapon, fill tiny satchels for every warrior in her army, even pour it into Arborlay's water supply if she had to.

Finally, she had a way to secure the support of her allies. A way to rescue Tal and get King Alaric to honor the betrothal agreement she'd signed with their treaty.

A way to ruin those who'd ruined her.

She lifted her chin, fire burning through her as she said, "I'll buy all the moriarthy dust you have in stock."

"Don't have much." Lunay reached for another jar and shook the gritty red-brown contents at Charis. "Only grows on Embre."

Embre. How convenient. Charis had been planning to sail in that direction anyway.

The fact that Embre hadn't pursued trade with Calera in many decades was of no account. They would help Charis, or they would learn firsthand why Montevallo had called her the warmongering princess. She'd approach with honey but finish with a sword if that's what it took.

Nalani hurried forward to pay Lunay for the moriarthy dust. The herbologist poured the dust into a small leather satchel. Charis accepted the satchel from Nalani and attached it to the braided silver belt that wrapped around her stomach.

The group remained silent until they were safely back inside the carriage and the coachmistress had ordered the horses forward. The instant they were in motion, Grim leaned forward.

"Did she have what we need?" The frayed hope in his voice scraped against Charis, and she wrapped her hand around the satchel at her waist as she levied a cold stare in his direction. He was worried about his precious prince, but she had the fate of an entire kingdom on her shoulders.

"She had a small amount of poison that she says will kill Rakuuna. Not nearly enough, but at least now we know where to get more."

"Where?" Even Dec sounded eager.

"Embre." Charis turned toward Holland. "I have dinner with Vyllanthra tonight, and Nalani is meeting with your uncle's friend the retired admiral to discuss possible battle strategies, so I want you to prepare our crew to set sail at first light."

"Sailing through dense, early-morning fog." Holland raised a brow. "Sounds difficult."

Charis gritted her teeth. "You're right."

"A frequent occurrence," Holland said. Nalani huffed.

"We'll have to leave the harbor at midday, Your Majesty," Dec said. "But Grim and I can gather the rest of the crew and their belongings and make sure all final preparations are made while you're at dinner. Perhaps Reuben could give some of the palace staff the job of bringing your trunks on board?"

He glanced at Holland and Nalani, and Charis gathered herself for the argument that was about to erupt.

"Nalani is staying behind as my ambassador to Solvang. And Holland will be staying as well. Only my belongings will need to be transferred to the ship, Reuben."

There was a beat of silence, and then protests erupted from the twins.

Holland swore with such creative flourish, Charis felt sure he'd learned some new words during his time at the docks.

"You aren't going out there alone." Nalani leaned toward Charis. "Who will watch out for you?"

"I have an entire crew—"

"With me on it." Holland glared at her.

"Orayn, Finn, and Reuben are perfectly capable of keeping me safe."

"It's not just about your safety." Nalani's hand wrapped around Charis's and squeezed gently. "You need a friend, too."

Her words pierced Charis, and salt stung her eyes. Blinking, she drew herself up straight. "The northern waters are treacherous."

"Which means you should stay here and send me instead."

Holland's hands curled into fists.

"Embre needs to be handled by an expert negotiator," Charis said.

"I can negotiate with my sword." Holland turned to her, and she whipped a hand in the air to stop his next words.

"We must get that poison from Embre. Everything else fails if we don't achieve that. And we all know the dangerous waters are the least of what awaits us out there. Rakuuna must be searching for me if there's a bounty on my head, and they are hardly the only monster in the seas. And then there's the fact that I have to marry Vahn Penbyrn when we reach Montevallo, or we can't convince Alaric to lend us his army, even if we manage to rescue Tal to use him as leverage. I'm the one going."

Nalani's grip on her hand tightened. "But—"

"Our people have lost so much already. I'm going, and I'm leaving my heirs safely in Solvang in case I don't make it out of this alive." She kept her voice from trembling but had to swallow hard against the lump forming in her throat. A queen didn't get to flinch from shouldering the hardest burdens, but still, Charis wished she could keep her cousins close instead of facing the unknown all alone.

Tears shone in Nalani's eyes, and Holland muttered several things under his breath, but when she looked expectantly at them, they both bowed their heads and murmured, "Yes, Your Majesty."

Ignoring the twinge of loneliness that settled into her at the thought of continuing the journey without her closest friends, Charis smoothed her expression into one of serene confidence as the carriage slowed before the palace's entrance.

It was time to tell Gareth and Vyllanthra her plans and then make sure preparations were in place to set sail for Embre.

SEVEN

CHARIS MADE IT back to her quarters with an hour to spare before Vyllanthra expected her for a late dinner. Nita rushed to draw a bath while Charis instructed several other maids to pack her new wardrobe into a trunk. Once she'd reclaimed Calera and driven the monsters back into the sea where they belonged, she would have to send a generous gift to Solvang's rulers to begin repaying them for their kindness.

For tonight, a simple thank-you and the assurance that she was leaving the next day would have to suffice.

"The bath is ready, Your Majesty," Nita announced as a brusque knock sounded on the door. Before Nita could hurry to open it, Nalani burst in, a paper clutched in her hand. Delaire followed on her heels, her lips pressed tight as her wide eyes met Charis's.

"Your Majesty, we have a problem." Nalani hastily performed a sorry excuse for a curtsy and then waved the paper at Charis.

"Nita, please have this trunk taken down to my ship and be sure no one disturbs us." Charis waited until the trunk and the handmaiden were gone before reaching for the paper, her stomach clenching painfully as her thoughts skipped frantically through the options.

More disastrous news from Calera.

Allies who'd committed to her cause provided she could kill the Rakuuna were having second thoughts.

Tal was dead.

Each thought drew blood, and her hands shook as she opened the paper, silently cursing Tal for somehow still causing her pain when she should feel nothing for him at all. She scanned the message quickly, eyes skimming the words without really understanding any of them. She was simply searching for his name.

When she came to the end and found no mention of Tal, she drew in an unsteady breath and forced herself to slow down and reread carefully, hunting for the problem.

It was the long-awaited response from King Alaric, promising to abide by their treaty and help her retake Calera, provided she upheld her part of the bargain and married his oldest son, Vahn.

There wasn't a single mention of her offer to rescue his youngest son.

"I don't understand." Charis raised her gaze to Nalani and Delaire. "This is exactly what we've been hoping for. What's the problem?"

Besides the fact that there was no longer any reason to sail to the northern kingdom of Te'ash to rescue Tal—a fact that should have brought relief but instead left an unsettling sense of dread in her stomach.

"You can't sail tomorrow," Delaire said, her voice pitched higher than normal.

"Why not?" Charis turned to Nalani. "What's happening?"

"Finn sent a message from the docks. A trio of green lights has been spotted just outside the harbor." Nalani wrung her hands. "They can't see the ship because of the thick fog, but it's probably Rakuuna."

The air left Charis's lungs.

For a moment, she was back in the Farragins' ballroom, the silvery blue décor of the Sister Moons Festival glittering as Rakuuna swarmed the crowd, tearing people apart just to get to Charis and her mother. Her heart pounded in sickening jolts, and the edges of her vision went gray.

"Charis!" Nalani's warm hands gripped Charis's shoulders firmly, dragging her thoughts away from the horror of her memories and back into the present.

"Is he sure?" Her voice was a faint imitation of itself, but her muscles felt weak, and her skin tingled as though warning her to grab a weapon and brace for attack.

"Sure of the lights, yes." Nalani kept her grip firm. "We can't know for certain that it's Rakuuna until the fog lifts."

"By then, it will be too late." Charis forced herself to breathe deeply. Once. Twice. She couldn't afford to panic. Not when a single misstep would cost her and her people everything.

"We'll hide you." Delaire hurried forward. "I'm sure Queen Vyllanthra must know of a place—"

"I'm not hiding." Charis straightened her spine and stepped back, breaking Nalani's hold on her. "We finally know where to get a weapon we can use against them. I'm sailing to Embre."

"Or you could send someone else!" Nalani's voice rose. "Someone the Rakuuna aren't hunting."

"So that they can find me here and punish these people for helping us? I'm not going to be responsible for Gareth's and Vyllanthra's deaths." Charis squared her shoulders, her mind racing. She needed to attend her dinner with Vyllanthra, finalize preparations for the journey to Embre, and send a reply to King Alaric, but that all paled in comparison to the need to know for sure if the Rakuuna were anchored outside the harbor.

"Change of plans." Charis grabbed a pair of warm gray pants, a soft black shirt, and a shawl of shimmering cranberry cashmere that she'd intended as her sailing outfit for the next day. "Nalani, you'll attend the dinner with Vyllanthra as my ambassador and inform her of my plans to sail tomorrow. Make sure she understands I'm going to get the weapon we need to kill the Rakuuna. I want to hold them to their promise to help us fight for Calera."

"Where are you going?" Nalani folded her arms across her chest as Charis wiggled free of her evening dress and reached for the pants.

"I'm going to take a few sailors and our rowboat to see if the Rakuuna are there."

"That's a terrible idea," Nalani snapped.

"The fog will hide our activities, and if those monsters *are* lying in wait out there, I need to be at the docks anyway, because we're going to have to set sail immediately." Her voice didn't shake—a small mercy given the way everything inside of her tumbled and churned at the thought of seeing the Rakuuna again.

"But what if something happens?" Worry sharpened Nalani's voice.

"Exactly." Charis tugged on a pair of soft black boots and moved to the vanity.

"No, not *exactly*. This is serious, Charis." Nalani stalked toward the vanity while Charis rummaged for pins to subdue her tumble of brown curls into a bun.

"I agree." Charis shoved the pins into her hair and met her cousin's gaze in the mirror. "A queen doesn't flinch from facing danger to protect her people."

"Charis." Nalani's voice sounded wounded, and something in her eyes reminded Charis of Father. Charis looked away, feeling suddenly exposed.

"Why not trust Holland with it instead?" Delaire asked as she grabbed two extra pins and rescued Charis's bun from sliding to the left.

Because she'd lost too many people she loved to those monsters. And because a queen who failed to save her family and her kingdom didn't deserve to have anyone take risks for her.

"I've made up my mind." Charis's voice wavered, and she cleared her throat. "If all is well, I'll see you when I return to the palace tonight. If not, I'll send you a palloren once we reach Embre and secure the poison so that you can coordinate attack plans with the rest of our allies."

Nalani slid her hand around Charis's and squeezed gently. "You do realize you're worth protecting too, don't you?"

The chasm that had opened within Charis on the night of the invasion shivered, and she withdrew her hand. "So are you. If there are Rakuuna at port, they're after me, not you. You'll stay safe here; that way if something happens, there can be a seamless transfer of power. The Calerans need a ruler."

"No, the Calerans need *you*." Nalani pulled the shawl out of Charis's hands and wrapped it around the queen's shoulders before drawing her close for a hug. Charis stiffened at the contact, and Nalani just patted her back the way Father used to when he knew something was wrong and was just waiting for his daughter to finally drop her guard.

Charis couldn't drop her guard. There was a tidal wave of ruin within her, and if she let a single drop escape, the weight of it all would press against that crack until it shattered her.

Tears stung Charis's eyes, and she blinked rapidly as she stepped away. "Don't wait up," she said as she left Nalani and Delaire standing in the middle of her chambers.

☙

Twenty minutes later, Charis, Reuben, and Vellis met Finn and Orayn at the docks. The sky was a swath of black velvet punctured by the diamond-shine of stars. Ribbons of cloud drifted across its surface, limned with the sapphire light of the sister moons that hung in the sky like ghostly blue crescents. The wooden dock they stood on stretched out into the fog-drenched harbor, creaking and shifting as the ships tied to it rocked gently in the waves. The frantic activity of the day had subsided, leaving the docks nearly deserted.

"Your Majesty." Orayn and Finn bowed in unison.

Movement behind them caught Charis's eye, and she reached for her dagger. "Who's there?"

"It's just us, Your Majesty." Grim and Dec emerged from the shadows and bowed.

Charis gritted her teeth. "What are you doing here?" She kept her voice down, though it was unlikely their conversation would carry over the frothy splash of the waves against the shore.

"I asked them to join us," Orayn said. "We need extra rowers if we're going to move quickly. Thank the sister moons we've got this fog for protection."

Suppressing a shiver of dread, Charis said, "Let's get this done."

They followed Orayn down the creaking dock until they came to a boat the size of three carriages put together. It had a small, sheltered cabin overlooking the bow, and a collection of nets, barrels, and spears lining the outside of the cabin's wall.

Moments later, they were rowing the little vessel toward the mouth of the harbor, and Charis found herself willing the thick fog to blanket them. They hadn't lit a lantern, but she had no idea how well the Rakuuna could see in the dark. Since she'd personally witnessed them sink a merchant vessel in the dead of night, she assumed they could see much better than she.

"Your Majesty," Reuben spoke from beside her. "If you could take a step back from the bow, that would be safer. Let one of the Montevallian spies take your place."

Reuben hadn't seen what the Rakuuna could do at sea. If the monsters saw the vessel and decided to destroy it, they would come from beneath the waves, tear a hole right through the hull, and drag every person on board into the depths in less time than it would take to walk from one end of the boat to the other.

Her heart raced, and her nerves vibrated like the plucked strings of a violin. Forcing herself to draw a steadying breath of damp, salty air, she braced her feet against the swells and tried to smother the spark of panic that wanted to spread through her.

"I'll stay where I am," she whispered, pushing the words past a tongue gone bone-dry.

The boat nosed its way out of the harbor, hugging the shoreline, though being within swimming distance of land wouldn't help them if the Rakuuna were truly here.

Clouds scudded across the sister moons, and a sharp wind kicked up, rocking the vessel until Reuben had to grip the railing, swallowing audibly against the sickness that rose up his throat. Finn, Grim, and Dec left the oars on Orayn's quiet orders and came to stand near the bow with the rest of their small company. Vellis, accurately assessing Reuben's situation, positioned herself close to her queen, putting her body between Charis and the Montevallians.

For several long moments, they stood there, braced against the rocking motion of the sea, eyes streaming as the wind tore at them with icy fingers. Billows of fog crept over the surface of the water, smothering all sound, and Charis strained to see anything past the short span of visibility around their boat.

"Maybe we need to row farther out," Finn muttered as another cloud obscured the moonlight. "We can't see any—"

A haunting wail cut through the night, as though a woman was singing, screaming, and laughing all at once. The cry rose in pitch until she could barely stand the pain in her ears.

Her breath caught in her chest as the cry was met with several others.

It was impossible to tell how far away the creatures were. Charis reached for her dagger, though she knew it wouldn't save her.

The cries dropped into a series of rapid clicks, like dry bones rattling across cobblestones, and in the distance the mist gleamed a faint green as a single ship became visible for an instant before being swallowed whole by the fog.

Vellis swore softly. Orayn ordered the boys to row them back to the docks as quietly as possible. Reuben left the railing to stand between Charis and the distant ship, as though somehow his wiry body could save his queen from the monsters.

Charis gripped her dagger until her palm ached as the boat nosed its way back into the harbor.

The Rakuuna were here.

Maybe they'd somehow learned where she was and had come to take her home. Or maybe they were here to assess what it would take to do to Solvang what they'd done to Rullenvor and Calera.

No matter their reasons, there was only one play left for Charis. She had to warn Gareth and Vyllanthra and then leave Solvang before the monsters realized she was gone.

EIGHT

CHARIS STOOD ON the dock and struggled to breathe past the fist of panic closing around her throat. Every creak of a boat nudging against its mooring became the telltale sound of the Rakuuna ship closing in. Every slap of the waves against the pilings was a monster clawing its way out of the sea.

She hadn't been quick enough in her search for answers, and now she'd brought danger to the people of Solvang.

Charis's body trembled, and the ground shifted beneath her. From what felt like a great distance, the sound of voices pierced the faint ringing in her ears.

"—can't take that risk, can we?"

"Perhaps the king of Solvang would—"

"He can't do anything. No one can. We're—"

A warm hand wrapped around her arm, steadying her as her knees buckled. "Your Majesty."

She blinked, and Orayn's face swam into focus. His dark eyes held hers, calm and unflinching. His hand lent her strength while she slowly became aware of the icy wind scraping across her cheeks and the creaking dock resting solidly beneath her feet.

"There you go," Orayn said, as if he'd simply helped her over a slick patch of wood. "It's all right now."

She clenched her teeth to keep them from chattering. Nothing was all right. The enemy was here, and the only weapon Charis had was one tiny satchel of poison tied to her waist. Movement caught her eye, and she turned to find the others standing on the dock, watching her. Waiting.

She was supposed to have the answers. She was supposed to know what came next.

The faint light of the sister moons gleamed against Dec's dark eyes, and Charis flinched inwardly at the compassion she saw there.

Her chin rose, though her jaw was still tight. She took a step back, breaking Orayn's hold on her arm, and forced herself to quickly sort through her options and find a path forward.

One that didn't end in bloodshed.

"What should we do, Your Majesty?" Finn asked, sounding as if he was working hard to remain calm.

She drew in a ragged breath and reached for the voice Mother had used when her people needed to believe she was a shield of iron standing between them and what they feared. "We have only one real choice. We set sail immediately, using the fog as cover."

"How will we get out of the harbor when we can't see more than half a ship's length ahead?" Grim asked.

She glanced at Orayn, who said quickly, "We'll use our maps and a depth finder to keep ourselves away from the shoreline. If we take it slow, we can manage."

"We'll sail in absolute silence and will not light a single lamp until

we're far from Solvang." Charis looked to Dec. "You have forty minutes to gather any crew who aren't yet on board. Otherwise, we leave
without you."

He bowed and left the docks at a run.

Turning to the others, Charis spat out orders. "Grim, go make
sure everything is on board and secured. I don't want the sound of
a trunk sliding across the deck to give us away. Orayn, you and Finn
chart your course and get the depth finder ready."

She turned to her guards. "Vellis, you'll bring word to Lord Holland and Lady Nalani that we've had to sail early to avoid detection."

Heaviness filled her at the realization that there would be no good-
byes. No last chance to properly return Nalani's hug or tell Holland
what his stalwart support meant to her. Pushing her feelings aside,
she met Vellis's gaze. "Have them report the presence of the Rakuuna
to King Gareth and Queen Vyllanthra. Orayn, how long should it
take us to reach Embre?"

The big man counted on his fingers, his lips moving silently as he
calculated the distance, and then he said, "With winds like this, two
and a half weeks. Maybe three."

She turned back to Vellis. "Let Lady Nalani know that I will send
a palloren once we reach Embre. If she hasn't heard from me at the
end of five weeks, she should assume that we were lost at sea and work
with King Gareth to send a Solvanish ship to purchase the poison."

Vellis bowed, but Charis wasn't finished. "One more thing, and it
is the most important. You are to stay behind and guard Lady Nalani.
Create a security team around her the way you did for me."

Vellis's mouth dropped open, and she looked ready to protest. Charis
hurried on. "Reuben, you are to stay behind and guard Lord Holland.
I feel sure he'll make it difficult, but he is my heir, with Lady Nalani
second in line. You must let nothing happen to them. Am I clear?"

"Yes, Your Majesty," Vellis whispered, bowing again.

Reuben, on the other hand, glared. "I decline that assignment."

Charis set her teeth. "You don't get to decline anything. I'm your queen, and I gave you an order."

He folded his arms. "You are in imminent danger, Your Majesty."

"All the more reason to make sure my heirs are alive and well."

"I would rather make sure *you* are alive and well." His tone was mutinous.

She held his gaze for a long moment. "We both know the chances of me surviving both the Rakuuna who hunt me and the battle for Calera are small. I'm fighting to save our kingdom, but I don't necessarily expect to be alive to rule it. If Holland or Nalani can't take the throne, that leaves the leadership of Calera in the hands of my fourth cousin, Ferris Everly, and I believe we agree that's not an option that bears considering."

"Your Majesty—"

"I need to know my heirs are safe, Reuben. And while you and I often have our differences, I trust your ruthless dedication to your responsibility." She straightened her spine as another gust of wind whipped through her cloak. "You all have your orders. We leave in forty minutes. Get it done."

Precisely forty minutes later, Charis's ship quietly slipped its berth and began slowly moving toward the mouth of the harbor. Or at least Charis hoped that was the direction they were headed. It was impossible to see from one end of the ship to the other in the thick fog, much less track their surroundings.

Except for the creaking of the timbers and the snap of the mainmast in the wind, the deck was silent. Most of the crew were belowdecks, waiting as one agonizing minute bled into another. Orayn had advised

Charis to wait belowdecks as well, but she'd refused.

If the Rakuuna came for her, they wouldn't find her hiding. They'd find a fierce, vengeful queen facing them head-on from the bow of her ship.

Her hands shook as she gripped the railing, made slick by the fog.

She hadn't been able to say goodbye to those she loved, just like she hadn't been able to say goodbye to her parents. She was so far from her kingdom and the person she'd once been that the invisible threads binding her to her home felt stretched thin enough to snap. And Alaric had agreed to help her without mention of his youngest son, which meant she no longer had any strategic reason to rescue Tal—a fact that shouldn't have mattered to her and yet somehow did.

The darkness within shivered as one grief became tangled in the next, until all that remained was empty, all-consuming loss. Thick tendrils of mist drifted across the deck, brushing against Charis and moving on without breaking form, as though she had no substance. As though she was nothing but a memory.

Her eyes burned, and she blinked rapidly to keep tears from falling.

The mainmast flapped, timbers grinding as someone adjusted the sails, and then the ship began gently curving to the right.

They were leaving the harbor. At any moment, the Rakuuna might spot them and come swarming on board. Or maybe they would simply tear the ship to pieces, fish Charis out of the water, and take her back to Calera.

At least she had a plan in place to ensure the poison in Embre would be purchased and an armada would descend upon the Rakuuna in Calera's port. And Alaric could still be convinced to help since the treaty between their kingdoms stated that an heir of Calera would marry an heir of Montevallo. Charis needn't be alive for that to happen.

Holland would be furious to suddenly become both king and betrothed to Tal's older sister.

From a distance, muffled by the shroud of fog, the sound of bones rattling against cobblestones drifted through the air.

The breath froze in Charis's lungs.

She knew that sound. The first time she'd heard it, she'd been aboard this same ship, hunting for the enemy who was sinking Caleran vessels, blissfully ignorant of the calamity that was coming for her people. It was the strange language of the Rakuuna. The noise they made after the piercing wail that seemed to start their conversations.

Charis gripped the railing until her palms ached.

Where were they?

In their ship, anchored outside the harbor? Or in the water, hunting for Charis and her people?

Another rattle, like a gust of wind disturbing dry twigs.

The fog made it hard to tell what direction the sound was coming from, much less how far away it was.

Charis drew in an unsteady breath. If the fog was distorting the sound of the Rakuuna, then it should be doing the same for the tiny bit of noise her ship made as it sliced through the swells. As long as the wind held, they would be far away from Solvang by the time the midday sun burned through the mist.

The Rakuuna had no way of knowing which ship was Charis's, or even if she'd still been in Solvang, so it was unlikely they'd be immediately concerned about the ship that had set sail in the middle of the night. Who knew how long it would take them to realize they needed to keep searching the sea for her?

The faint echo of a high-pitched wail slithered through the fog, and someone behind Charis swore softly. She stiffened, her heart suddenly pounding as the person said, "Maybe we ought to load the cannons, just in case."

Equal parts fury and hope flooded her as she turned on her heel to find Holland standing there, clearly exhilarated by the prospect of risking his life. Reuben stood beside him, defiant.

Keeping her voice barely above a whisper, she said, "I explicitly ordered you to keep Holland in Solvang." She glared at Reuben, but the shadow of loneliness within her shrank a little as Holland grinned.

"No, you explicitly ordered him to guard me. And here he is"—Holland flung out a hand toward the older man— "guarding me."

"I told you to stay behind." She pinned Holland with her glare, for all the good that ever did.

"And I decided not to."

The ship swayed as it plowed through a patch of rough swells, and Charis braced herself while Reuben looked ill. Holland, however, looked even more excited than he had when he'd heard the Rakuuna.

"I was trying to keep you safe." The words drew blood from the most tender area of her heart. How was she supposed to shoulder the responsibility for the life of another person she loved? Especially when she was their enemy's primary target?

"I don't care much for being safe." Holland shrugged and then looked at her properly. His smile faded. "I'm staying at your side for as long as it takes to see this through. Nalani and I both agreed I was the best person to help you on the journey while she helps from Solvang. You might as well just accept my presence because you can't get rid of me."

"But you could *die*."

His eyes lit up as he whispered, "Yes, but life isn't worth much if you aren't risking everything for what you believe in. Just think of this as the best adventure I've ever had."

"Holland." Her whisper carried the words she couldn't bring herself to say. That she was furious he'd put himself in danger for her. That she was grateful to have a friend close by as she sailed into the unknown. That she'd never forgive herself if anything happened to him because of her.

He brushed a hand against her shoulder in a rare show of affection and said, "You're welcome. Now, are we staying out here all night listening for monsters, or are we trying to get some sleep so we can help relieve Orayn and Finn when the fog burns off?"

"You and Reuben go get some rest. I'll be along shortly." She raised a brow and waited for arguments, but the two men seemed to realize they'd pushed their luck enough for one night.

Turning back to the bow, she peered into the fog and listened for any sign that the monsters who hunted her were closing in.

NINE

THE CRAGGY SHORELINE of Embre came into view on their fifteenth day of travel. Squinting against the light of the winter sun as it reflected off the icy gray water, Charis nodded to Holland to release the palloren with her message to Embre's chancellor tied to its leg.

She expected a prompt response, though she'd hardly given the chancellor any warning about her impending arrival. It didn't serve her to allow him time to think through her reasons for showing up when Calera had no trade relations with Embre. She needed him off balance and scrambling to keep up with her.

As the palloren swooped through the pale sky, she scanned the waters, searching, as always, for a sign of the Rakuuna.

She'd barely slept for their first three days at sea. Instead, she'd stalked the deck, hunting for a glimpse of long, pale bodies that swam impossibly fast and examining the horizon for a glimmer of the green lanterns used by Rakuuna ships.

Twice, she'd heard ear-piercing wails that sounded like Rakuuna, but they were distant—drifting across foggy water like echoes of something half-forgotten.

It was a vast sea, and finding her ship would take time and a bit of luck, but Charis didn't fool herself. She couldn't risk staying in Embre, even overnight. The farther they were from land, the harder they'd be to find.

At least that's what she was counting on.

She'd filled her days by drilling the crew on using the weapons in the ship's arsenal, including teaching Holland, Reuben, and crew members Ayve and Lohan the basics of the seven rathmas sword-fighting style. If the lessons reminded her of long hours spent with Tal, his callused hands adjusting her stance while his breath warmed her neck, it was nothing the knife of his betrayal couldn't chase to the back of her mind.

"Palloren returning!" Finn called. Reuben hurried to untie the message and, when Charis nodded, scanned it quickly.

"Well?" she asked when he was done.

His lip curled. "Apparently they have procedures to follow, and that means we're to stay outside the harbor until his committee of advisors notifies us that we've been approved for a visit." He handed the paper to her.

"I volunteer to tell them exactly where they can put their procedures." Holland paced the length of the bow, his duster billowing in his wake.

Keeping a royal dignitary from a non-enemy kingdom anchored outside one's harbor was an unforgivable breach of courtesy. The chancellor was trying to make the point that he was the highest ranking official here, regardless of her title.

Charis could care less about outranking anyone. She just needed a weapon to destroy the Rakuuna. And she wasn't going to sit out here on the open sea, hoping a man on a power trip got around to selling it to her.

"If he wants the queen of Calera as his enemy, he's going to get his wish." Charis spun toward Ayve, who'd volunteered to help Charis when it came time to presenting herself like a queen. "I need a fancier dress than this, a crown—"

"A sword," Holland suggested.

"That too. And once I'm ready, we're sailing into that harbor and docking at his port. While his committee scrambles to figure out what to do with us, we will disembark and enter his kingdom. And we aren't leaving until we get what we came for."

Twenty minutes later, Charis was wearing a dark green gown embroidered with bronze falcons and the delicate golden crown Vyllanthra had gifted her. A sword strapped to her side, she stood at the bow of her ship as it sailed into the harbor as if she was heading into battle.

Her fingers trembled as she gripped the railing, struggling to keep the fear at bay. This had to work. If the chancellor refused to see her, much less sell moriarthy dust to her, everything was lost.

She'd sent a palloren moments ago expressing her intention as queen to seek refuge in Embre for a single day. There had been no reply, but in fairness, the ship had already been en route when the palloren took flight, so she'd hardly given the chancellor's committee time to follow their precious procedures.

She glared at the shoreline, and the fury in her heart spilled into her blood until she felt forged in fire. The leader of Embre would *not* be the reason Charis failed to save her people.

It took nearly fifteen minutes to cross the harbor and maneuver into an open slip at the dock, giving the chancellor and his committee plenty of time to hear the news that the Calerans were no longer content to play games. Therefore, it was no surprise to see a small delegation of people in green-and-gold uniforms waiting on the dock as the ship made port. Every member of the welcome party had their weapon out.

"I'm sensing some hostility," Holland said.

"They don't have to welcome us for long, but I'm not leaving without getting what we came for." Charis glared down at the delegation as two crew members lowered the gangplank.

A woman from the delegation stepped forward, her curved sword pointed at the ship. "Greetings, Charis Willowthorn, Queen of Calera." She spoke a rough form of Caleran, her consonants brusque and her vowels lengthened in the style of Embrian speech. "Chancellor Jhi sends you good wishes for your journey and respectfully requests that you sail from our harbor immediately."

Charis murmured softly to Holland, who in turn spoke flawless Embrian in a loud, commanding voice, "Her Royal Majesty, Queen Charis Willowthorn of Calera, offers her greetings to Chancellor Jhi, along with her sincere regret that she must refuse his directive without first speaking to him in person."

The woman blinked and shot a glance at the others in the delegation. They shifted uneasily, and a quick, whispered conversation ensued. Then the woman said, "Chancellor Jhi expects you to leave the harbor, Your Majesty. He will not be coming to the docks."

Charis let her lips curve into the smile that never failed to inspire instant obedience in those who'd earned her anger. A queen would not address a delegate, especially before being formally received by the chancellor. That Jhi had sent a spokesperson rather than greet the queen himself was very telling.

Maybe it was a foolish power play.

Or maybe even Embre had heard of Calera's fate, and he wanted no involvement in a potential conflict with Te'ash.

She spoke rapidly to Holland without breaking eye contact with the woman on the dock.

Holland's voice filled the space between the two parties. "Chancellor Jhi is either a friend to the alliance of Calera, Montevallo, Solvang, Thallis, and Verace, or he is our enemy. We will give him an hour to make his choice before sending pallorens to the rest of our armada with news that they must change course from their intended target and visit Embre first."

The delegation erupted into furious whispers. Charis remained still, pride and fury glittering in her eyes.

The key to selling a lie was to speak it once, with conviction, and then behave as though no other explanation was needed. Those who rushed to pad their words with justifications and excuses were easy to see through. Those who spoke as though they'd just had the final word on the matter sowed a seed of doubt, and the line between doubt and fear was thin and fragile.

"I think they believe you," Ayve breathed quietly from Charis's left. Beneath her heavy cloak, she also wore a dress with a sword strapped to her waist. Her skills as a seamstress had certainly served her well. The quality of her dress was easily equal to what the nobility wore, and it helped sell the idea that Charis was here on official business.

Two members of the delegation peeled off from the rest and hurried toward the town whose rooftops were just visible past the craggy rocks that comprised Embre's shoreline. Charis stood with Holland, Ayve, Reuben, Orayn, and Finn beside the lowered gangplank, waiting silently for the chancellor's response.

Charis kept her expression cold and distant as her thoughts raced. What would she do if the chancellor called her bluff? Her crew couldn't fight their way through the town until they found Jhi's home. And they certainly couldn't force the Embrians to sell them their supply of moriarthy dust. If Jhi didn't respond to Charis's threat, she had precious little room to maneuver.

Her hope was that the palloren Jhi had already received from her, which included one of the letters from King Gareth, would lend credibility to the idea that she'd managed to form an armada with the help of her allies.

Time passed slowly as they stood waiting, cloaks pulled close to shelter them from the frigid gusts of wind that stung their cheeks and numbed their noses. Dread crept into Charis's thoughts as the hour she'd given played out with no sign of Jhi.

She was going to have to somehow appear to make good on her threat.

"Captain," she called with bold confidence, "send pallorens to every admiral in our armada and instruct them to send a contingent of warships to Embre. Let them know we will wait in this harbor until they arrive."

"Yes, Your Majesty." Orayn didn't hesitate. Turning, he shouted, "Ready the pallorens!"

"Wait!" The spokeswoman for the Embrian delegate stepped forward again. "Chancellor Jhi will not allow you to disembark, but he will grant you a brief audience aboard your ship."

Relief rushed through Charis as she nodded to Holland. He said, "We will welcome Chancellor Jhi and assure his safety while in our presence. Captain, stay those pallorens until we speak with the chancellor."

Orayn yelled his counterorder as just beyond the craggy shoreline, a retinue approached the dock.

Chancellor Jhi was a short, middle-aged man with a graying black beard, brown skin, and a wickedly curved axe strapped across his back. His dark umber robe was embroidered with intricate swirls of peacock blue and brilliant yellow. Five guards in peacock-blue uniforms edged in scarlet accompanied him as he made his up the gangplank with measured, stately steps.

Charis appreciated a show of power when she saw one, though the effect was somewhat diminished by the fact that *he'd* come to *her* because his warriors had been unable to force her to comply. And because he was afraid of her nonexistent armada.

"Chancellor Jhi." She extended her hand.

"Queen Charis." He took her hand and raised it to his lips. His mustache scraped across her skin, and she suppressed a shiver of revulsion.

"Please, join me in our mess hall. I'm afraid it isn't as elegant a meeting place as I'd hoped to enjoy for our first conversation, but it will have to do." Her words were barbed beneath their polite veneer.

"Elegant surroundings are reserved for our invited guests." Jhi's polite veneer wore as thin as her own.

That was fine. Charis was well versed in navigating tricky political waters with an opponent who thought they were the predator and she the prey. They never realized their mistake until it was too late.

Jhi sat on one side of a long wooden table, his guards standing at attention beside him. Charis sat opposite him, Holland and Ayve standing to her right and on her left, Orayn, Finn, and Reuben forming a protective semicircle around the group, with Reuben close to Holland in case he needed to leap across the table to meet an oncoming threat.

If you needed information from an opponent, you waited to see how they would steer the conversation and played a careful game of cat and mouse, hunting for the crumbs they unwittingly dropped.

But if you wanted to establish dominance and quickly maneuver an opponent into a corner, you went for the jugular and held your grip until they surrendered.

Charis needed Jhi to feel backed into a corner, and she needed it fast. Before the Rakuuna who hunted her closed in, making a safe transfer of the poison impossible.

"I trust you received the palloren with messages from both me and King Gareth of Solvang. Because you understand the severity of the situation Calera faces, I will do you the courtesy of coming right to the point." She leaned forward, her words sharp as a blade.

"Every allied kingdom in the east and the north has made a commitment to drive the Rakuuna from Caleran lands except you and Rullenvor. Rullenvor has been overtaken by the Rakuuna, and we believe their High Emperor is dead, so I expected no help from that quarter. However, I certainly expected the kingdom closest to Te'ash to be concerned about the Rakuuna's colonization efforts and to join forces with the rest of us to defeat them. But you didn't, did you?"

Jhi opened his mouth, but Charis wasn't done.

"No, you remained silent. And then you tried to turn us away. I can only think of two reasons for that. First, you're scared of the Rakuuna coming to your shores. Or second, you're already aligned with them and hope to benefit from the destruction of my kingdom."

The chancellor drew back as if deeply offended. "We have nothing to gain from Calera's troubles."

"But you do have everything to lose." She met his gaze, the fire of her rage burning through her veins as the answer to making him give her what she needed came to her. "I don't believe you're scared of the Rakuuna. Why would you be when you alone have a supply of the poison that kills them?"

He shifted in his chair, his gaze darting momentarily away. She'd struck on the truth, and he didn't like it.

"They must know that you can defend yourselves against them."

"Our affairs are no business of yours." Jhi made as though to stand. "You are not granted entry into our kingdom, and therefore you must leave."

"If I leave without getting what I came for, you and your kingdom are as good as dead." Her words sliced the air like a weapon, and she let him see the fire that burned in her blood. He'd assumed he was dealing with a child playing at ruling a lost kingdom. It was time he understood that the girl before him was a queen, forged in war and ruin, willing to obliterate all who stood in her way.

"You can't defend yourself against the Rakuuna if they decide to attack in overwhelming numbers, and they will, Chancellor Jhi. They will."

He paused, halfway out of his chair. "That's absurd."

She ignored his response. "The Rakuuna invader who currently holds the throne in my kingdom is intercepting every palloren sent to Calera. When I send a message to my contact in the palace that you willingly gave us your entire supply of moriarthy dust in the hopes that we would destroy Te'ash so you could have its resources, what do you think will happen?"

Jhi slowly settled back into his chair, his short fingers gripping the edges of the table as though holding on for dear life. "You won't reach out to Calera. There's a bounty on your head."

"I'll do better than that. I'll send every palloren in my possession except one, just to make *sure* the Rakuuna intercept the message." She lifted her chin and stared him down. "Their queen will believe that Embre is now defenseless and that you also handed their enemy a weapon that can destroy them. How long do you think you'll have before they come for you?"

He waved a hand in the air as though her words were of no consequence, but a muscle along his jaw was tight as he said, "We can defend ourselves."

"Can you?" She infused her tone with sympathy. "They won't politely sail a ship into the harbor and use the dock to enter your city. They will anchor their warships all around your island and swim ashore. They'll come at you from every direction, and they'll tear everyone they meet into pieces. I've seen it firsthand."

She gave him a cold smile. "You'll kill some of them, certainly. But you won't kill them all. Not by a long shot. And do you know what is coming for you once the Rakuuna leave here?"

He frowned, glancing at his guards as though one of them might have the answer.

"Me." Charis stood, her hand on the hilt of her sword, though she kept it sheathed. Fear and fury warred within her until she couldn't tell the difference between the two. "I will send my armada to Embre, and we will take every last bit of moriarthy dust for our battle on Caleran soil. You couldn't defend yourself against us even without the Rakuuna wiping out half your people. What chance do you have of turning us away once those monsters get through with you?"

Jhi lunged to his feet, sending his chair flying. "How dare you threaten us!"

Her voice filled the mess hall with icy rage. "How dare you refuse to help when it is in your power to do so! You could easily sell us enough moriarthy dust to serve our purposes while keeping some back for your own defense. Te'ash would never know you'd done so, because they wouldn't believe you'd share your weapon and potentially weaken yourselves against them. And because they wouldn't believe it, they wouldn't come for you. Not when they are so singularly focused on destroying my kingdom instead."

She held herself utterly still, a fierce, immovable opponent he had no hope of beating. "You could have helped us willingly without cost to yourselves and gained staunch allies in Calera, Solvang, Verace, Montevallo, and Thallis. Instead, you chose the destruction of your kingdom, and I will still get what I came for. I just have to wait out the bloodshed."

Turning on her heel, she snapped to her retinue, "Tell the captain to ready the sails. I want us out on the open water within the hour. Lord Farragin, send ten identical messages to our contacts in Calera that Embre has been most generous in selling us all their moriarthy dust, believing Te'ash will never attack. Captain, send a palloren to the admiral—"

"Stop!" Jhi slammed his fist on the table.

Charis paused, one eyebrow raised as though mildly curious. Vicious triumph blazed in her chest, sending her heart pounding. She'd backed him into a corner so fast, he'd had no time to think. No time to sort through her words, hunting for cracks in the show of strength she'd presented. He was going to acquiesce. He had to. In his eyes, she was already setting in motion the chain of events that would ruin Embre.

When he glared at her and said nothing for a long moment, she shrugged and turned away. "You all have your orders. Get this ship moving and get those palloren into the air."

"You can buy some moriarthy dust." Jhi sounded furious.

Charis pivoted back toward the table. "I will buy enough to fill the barrels we brought for that purpose. I suggest you deliver it disguised with a shipment of food and water so that in case we are being watched, it appears as though all you did was reprovision us and send us on our way."

He looked as though he wanted to spit in her face, but instead, he said, "And if I do this, you will protect us from rumors reaching Te'ash, and you will call off your armada?"

"I will."

Slowly he nodded, his expression carved with bitterness, his chest puffed out in a last display of pride. "This will be our one and only dealing with Calera. Do not attempt to contact us again."

"As you wish," she said, because allowing him to collect the shreds of his dignity in front of his people was the best way to ensure his quick compliance. Now he could tell people he'd bargained fiercely with her and managed to drive away both her armada and the threat of Te'ash with the clever sale of a few barrels of moriarthy dust. He'd be hailed as a great and heroic leader, and Charis would leave him in peace unless she had no other recourse.

Less than two hours later, her ship loaded with barrels of poison, her casks full of fresh water, and her larder replenished with Embrian grain, root vegetables, and jars of pickled fruit, Charis sent a palloren to Nalani asking her to notify Calera's allies that Charis now had a powerful weapon they could use against the Rakuuna. Solvang's top admiral would coordinate with the leadership of the other kingdoms and plan an attack from the sea. She then sent a second palloren to King Alaric, asking him to meet her at the northern border between Calera and Montevallo with his army in tow.

"Where to, Your Majesty?" Orayn asked as they left Embre's harbor behind.

For a moment, Tal's face filled her mind. His crooked smile and the challenge in his eyes when he argued with her. The way his cheeks burned when she caught him staring at her, and the unspoken conversations they could have across a crowded room. She looked north, at the unforgiving gray seas where ice caps floated in the distance.

He was out there. Imprisoned on Te'ash by creatures who appeared to have no mercy. And Charis was going to have to leave him there if she wanted to rescue her people. She couldn't risk the dangerous journey—sailing around icebergs and sea monsters, in danger of being discovered by the Rakuuna—not when she had a huge supply of moriarthy dust in her hold. And not when Alaric had already agreed to help her.

It was a choice between saving her people or saving the boy who'd broken her heart, and it shouldn't hurt so much to leave him behind. The ache in her heart sent tendrils of pain down to her fingertips, and she balled up her fists.

She needed to reach northern Calera, where she could travel by horseback to the Montevallian border and meet up with King Alaric. But first she needed a way to deliver half of the moriarthy dust to Nalani so her allies could arm their ships as they came to Calera's defense along her shoreline. The fastest way would be to sail for Verace, give the poison to their navy for safe transport to Solvang, and then turn toward northern Calera.

She looked to Orayn. "Set a course for Verace. Get there as fast as you can. I want this poison divided up in case anything happens to us."

Moving to the bow of the ship as Orayn shouted orders, Charis set her gaze on the distant southern horizon, resolutely refusing to glance over her shoulder again for one last glimpse of the path that would have taken her to Tal.

TEN

THEY'D MADE GOOD time since leaving Embre's craggy coast behind five days ago, though a storm had pushed them much farther west than Charis was comfortable with. The faster she could hand over half the supply of moriarthy dust to Verace's king, the better. However, now there was a swath of shallow water with huge rocky outcroppings jutting from its surface between her ship and Verace, so the safest path was to travel southwest and then cut east once they were far enough past the outcroppings.

She had no idea where the Rakuuna were, but if they were still hunting for her, surely the last place they'd expect her to be was sailing out of the icy northern seas and into the gray-green waters of the west. There was nothing out there but caves, islands, pirates, and sea monsters. No one in their right mind would choose this course when they could instead use the merchant lanes farther east, closer to the sea kingdoms and the illusion of safety they provided.

The storm had cost her time she didn't have, but there was nothing she could do about it now. They would sail southwest for one more day and then turn east and pray for clear skies and favorable winds.

Making her way to the forecastle, she joined Orayn. "How long before we can go east?"

"I don't like it," Orayn muttered as he wrestled with the helm and barked an order for Finn to relay to the crew. Joren, a whip-thin boy with a shock of red hair, sprang into action, climbing the main mast with dexterity and speed.

"What don't you like?" Charis asked.

Orayn grunted, his large hands gripping the helm as a gust of wind rocked the boat. When he had it under control, he gestured to the right. "See that?"

She squinted against the shards of sunlight dancing across the water. A massive island was slowly coming into view off the starboard side. It looked like a tree-covered mountain bordered by a strip of sand, but there were large, gaping holes along the base, as though it was pockmarked with caves.

"Another island?" she asked.

"Not just an any island, Your Majesty." Orayn's voice was grim. "That's the basilisk cave. There's a whole system of caves and tunnels inside, all partially filled with water. Many a sailor has lost his life to one of those basilisks when his ship took shelter in there."

"Well, we have no plans to shelter there, so rather than worry over it, let's figure out how far southwest we should travel before it's safe to turn east for Verace."

"That's my point." Orayn met Charis's gaze, his dark brown eyes troubled. "The basilisk cave marks the line in the western sea where nothing is safe any longer. At least, not for the likes of us. Past that island, there are pirate hideaways, and they'd board us, kill us, and take everything we own before we could turn tail and run against this wind. Even if we do manage to avoid any pirate ships, there are sea monsters in those waters, and our ship isn't built with spikes along the bottom to deter them."

Charis pulled her cloak tight as the hairs on the back of her neck rose. It was bad enough they had to worry about the Rakuuna finding them. She didn't want to face pirates and sea monsters as well.

"If we run into a big enough creature, they'll get curious that we might be a food source, bump us hard enough to tilt the ship, and then take us down with their tentacles," Orayn said.

Her stomach twisted, making her thankful she'd eaten barely three bites for breakfast earlier.

"What if we trim the masts and turn east now?" An errant curl drifted across her face, and she tucked it behind her ear. "Maybe we could steer along the edge of the rocky outcroppings and avoid the western sea altogether."

"Not with this wind or this current. We need to either weigh anchor and wait for the wind to settle or keep heading southwest. Otherwise, we'd likely smash our ship into a rock."

Charis strove to keep her voice calm, even as the familiar vise around her chest squeezed mercilessly. "If we're anchored, I fear we'd be easier for the Rakuuna to find, but I also don't want to go up against a kraken."

"Are we going to see a kraken?" Holland bounded up the stairs to the helm, his face alight with eagerness.

"I'd strongly advise you to rethink that enthusiasm, Lord Farragin," Orayn said sternly. "Even a baby kraken could punch a hole through the bottom of our boat. A full-grown kraken could wrap itself around this entire ship, snap the masts in half, and drag us into the depths."

"Ship, ahoy!" Joren's voice echoed down from the crow's nest.

Charis whipped around, scanning the waters off their port side, her stomach knotting.

A small frigate with a trio of masts was on the horizon.

"Is it a pirate ship?" Her heart seemed to slam into her chest as she took a shaky step forward to peer into the distance.

"No one else would have reason to be out here." Orayn sounded grim.

Charis forced herself to speak, though her lips felt numb. "No one but the Rakuuna."

"I'll arm the crew," Holland said, already starting for the stairs.

"I'll get more speed out of the masts," Orayn said.

"Wait." Charis's voice was thin, the air in her lungs disappearing as the ship began speeding toward them.

The vessel moved unnaturally, as though the swells and currents of the northern sea had no effect on it. It was traveling in a straight line toward her ship, like an arrow released from a bow, and closing the distance between the two boats with impossible speed.

"How are they moving that fast?" Holland demanded. "And why aren't the swells slowing it down? Is it pirates?"

"No pirate ship I know moves like that," Orayn said.

The outline of the ship became clearer as it drew closer. A small frigate. Three tidy sails. And a trio of green lanterns hanging from the forecastle.

For an instant Charis couldn't breathe. Couldn't think. Couldn't do anything beyond fumble for the railing with trembling hands as panic slammed into her.

"It's the Rakuuna." She pushed the words through numb lips. "They've found us."

"Weapons!" Holland cried as he took the stairs two at a time. "All hands, arm yourselves!"

Orayn gripped the helm so hard his knuckles turned pale. "We can't outrun them, Your Majesty. Best to hide and hope they believe us when we tell them they've got the wrong ship."

But unless they could somehow manage to make themselves look like pirates within the next few minutes, they'd never be able to convince the Rakuuna they had any business this far away from civilized kingdoms. Besides, all the Rakuuna had to do was send a single scout into the water to check for spikes embedded on the ship's hull and the ruse would be discovered. Any ship that regularly sailed the western seas had spikes to defend against sea monsters.

"They won't believe we're pirates." Her voice shook as badly as her hands. "They'll either search the entire craft, finding our entire supply of poison, or they'll just tear the ship to pieces and sink us without asking a single question."

"But they're after you." He looked back at the ship, which was gaining on them rapidly. "They don't want to drown you."

"They'll just fish me out of the water, and we'll have lost our only weapon against them." She squinted at the horizon. Better to face the possibility of pirates and sea monsters than to be caught by the Rakuuna. "Get more speed out of the masts, Orayn. We need to run into the western sea."

Orayn shouted orders. Chaos broke out across the deck. Sailors trimmed the masts and grabbed weapons. Finn shouted orders to load the cannons. Holland ran from one end of the deck to the other, handing out weapons to those who didn't have one yet.

The ship picked up speed, but still, the Rakuuna vessel in pursuit was faster. Charis frantically looked around for options.

She had the poison stored in the belly of the ship but no idea how to use it.

They had cannons and swords, but so had every other ship the Rakuuna had sunk outside Arborlay's harbor.

Maybe if she loaded the poison into the cannons, she would have a chance at defending the ship, but doing that took time she wasn't going to have.

Mentally kicking herself for not having created some kind of weapon already, even though she didn't yet know whether the poison worked on contact or if it needed to be ingested, she started down the stairs toward the deck. Better to put up a fight than go quietly.

Her stomach pitched as she reached the bottom of the staircase, and she struggled to swallow past the terror clogging her throat.

She was going to be taken, and her crew was going to die.

Either the monsters would punch holes in her ship and drag them all to the depths, submerging the poison along with her crew, or they would board the ship, murder her crew who would surely try to protect her, and then take her back to Calera, where she would either be traded to Alaric for jewels or killed to put down the rebellion that was growing across Calera in her name.

Whichever choice the Rakuuna made, it all added up to the same thing: the poison would be lost, and Charis would have failed her people.

Bright anger lanced through the terror and flooded her veins like liquid fire.

She hadn't come this far to fail. She hadn't lost everything, only to be ruined by the very monsters she'd set out to destroy.

A gust of wind rocked the boat, and a flash of green caught the corner of her eye. Turning, she saw they'd been pushed closer to the basilisk cave.

"Get inside!" Reuben appeared next to her, grabbed her arm, and tried to pull her toward the cabin.

Charis dug her heels in as an idea, equal parts terrifying and exhilarating, took hold.

Maybe she didn't know how the poison worked. Maybe there was no outrunning the Rakuuna. But she could hide somewhere even the Rakuuna were scared to go, and maybe it would buy her and her crew enough time to come up with a plan to defend themselves using the moriarthy dust.

"Your Majesty!" Reuben barked as he tugged her arm.

She glanced once more at the pursuing ship, her pulse thundering in her ears. The monsters were closing in fast. There was no time for a better plan.

"Captain!" Charis yelled as she spun on her heel for the stairs. "Head toward the basilisk cave. Full speed ahead."

ELEVEN

SILENCE DESCENDED ACROSS the deck as the ship sped toward the basilisk cave. Behind them, the Rakuuna vessel was rapidly approaching. Every crew member was either on deck, weapons strapped to their waists as they helped sail the ship into the cave, or down below, ready to row the moment the sails lost the wind. They'd lowered fishing nets over the sides, covering as much of the ship as possible to make it easier to trap any basilisks that might try shimmying up the side of the boat.

Charis had ordered everyone who was on deck, except for Orayn, Finn, and herself, to keep their eyes shut. She couldn't risk a crew member meeting the gaze of a serpent and dropping dead.

Charis readied herself as the sea cave loomed closer.

It resembled a massive, hollowed-out mountain, with a copse of dark green trees growing up the sides and along the top, and thick, rubbery vines hanging across the closest entrance. The opening was just large enough to accommodate two small frigates side by side.

Charis's body shook like a plucked string.

She didn't close her eyes. She was responsible for supporting Orayn and Finn if they needed it and for keeping an eye on the crew to be sure none of them were in danger.

"Swimmers in the water!" Finn's voice, tense with worry, echoed over the quiet deck. Several sailors opened their eyes to look at the Rakuuna who were diving off their vessel and heading toward Charis's ship.

"They're trying to reach us before we get inside where they don't dare follow." Charis spun toward the first mate. "We need more speed, and we need it now. Sailors"—her voice rose— "close your eyes and keep them closed, or the basilisks and Rakuuna will be the least of your worries. That's an order."

Finn cursed. "If we trim the main mast, we might get a bit more out of it."

"Do it." Orayn gripped the helm and stared at the approaching cave entrance.

The main mast flapped for a moment and then it caught a gust of wind and held. The boat picked up speed, racing toward the cave.

"There'd better not be any sharp turns inside that thing, or we're going to smash this ship against the wall," Holland said.

Charis shook her head and said nothing. She'd wanted Holland to stay down with the rowers, but he'd refused, and she hadn't had time to argue.

The Rakuuna vessel was closing the distance between them. Four furlongs away.

Three.

She couldn't see the swimmers. Even now, they might be under the ship, preparing to tear it to pieces.

Charis held her breath as Orayn adjusted the helm, and the bow pierced the curtain of vines at the cave's entrance. A massive thud shook the bottom of the vessel.

"Rakuuna!" Finn called.

"Keep those eyes closed, sailors!" Orayn barked as the boat slid farther into the cave.

Sprinting for the helm stairs, Charis launched herself down their length, ignoring Reuben's curses as he scrambled to keep up.

"Holland!" She hurried to the stern as the ship plunged into the murky twilight of the cave.

Lantern light revealed glistening, damp walls covered with clumps of algae and bits of moss. The rough texture of the rock had uneven cracks running in horizontal lines. In several places, jagged ledges jutted out from its surface. Charis glanced at the wall closest to the starboard side as the ship nearly brushed against it, and a movement caught her eye. Something uncoiled from the closest ledge, hissing as it rose.

Instantly, she jerked her gaze to Holland and called out, "There are basilisks on the walls! Finn, mind the depth reader and nothing else. Orayn, steer the ship but keep your gaze on the bow as much as possible."

Holland reached toward the sound of her voice, his hand brushing her shoulder as he found her. "What is it?" His other hand was already on his sword. "Why did you call for me?"

Quietly, she said, "Go down into the hull. Make sure the Rakuuna who hit our ship didn't damage it, or worse, tear a hole and climb inside."

He reached for his sword, and she snatched the satchel of poison from her belt and pressed it into his hand. "If one of those creatures is on this boat, kill it."

Holland took the satchel and raced for the stairs that led below-decks.

A splash echoed in the muted silence of the cave as the ship slid farther in. They were moving much slower now without the wind to push them along. Orayn had already given the order for the dozen crew members who were manning the galley to start rowing.

"Snakes in the water, too," she whispered, drawing closer to Reuben and keeping her eyes trained on his boots in case more serpents were rising from the ledges, trying to catch her eye.

The ship turned slowly, nudging along a narrow curve that took them northeast. Finn was calling depth readings up to Orayn from the one spot on the port side where they'd left an opening between fishing nets. It was impossible to see beyond the pale glow of the ship's lanterns, but all around them came the sound of hissing and large bodies sliding across stone.

There were no more thuds against the ship's hull. No creature was immune to the basilisk's gaze, not even the Rakuuna. Had they given up pursuit before entering the cave?

Charis strained her ears to hear as the ship bumped against a wall, scraping its length along the rough surface before Orayn managed to turn them back toward the center of the channel. From behind them, far too close for comfort, came the sound of dry bones rattling.

"The Rakuuna," she breathed to Reuben. "They're talking to each other. They must be close. But that sounded like it came from outside the cave. Maybe they—"

A loud, wet thud sounded from the deck on the starboard side, and an anguished cry split the air. Charis whirled, her sword ready, her heart in her throat.

A basilisk had dropped from a ledge and landed on Joren. The young man's red hair was covered in blood, and the snake was just withdrawing its fangs from his head.

Charis lunged forward, her weapon raised. "Snake on the deck. Blades up! Hold your positions and keep your eyes closed. I will tell you if one is close to you. Uriah, snake to your left."

The man beside Joren opened his eyes, drove his dagger into the snake's back, and tried to drag his friend to safety. The basilisk whipped its head around, and Charis looked at the deck as Uriah dropped, his eyes covered in white film, his bloodless lips parted. Beside him, Joren was convulsing as the venom spread to his heart.

"Get back, Your Majesty," Reuben barked as he raced between her and the basilisk, his blade flashing. His weapon drove into the back of the snake's head. Charis pivoted around him, whipped her sword through the air, and severed the head from the rest of the snake.

"Don't look at the eyes." She turned to assess Joren's condition and found the young man lying dead, foam flecked around his mouth. "Just throw the head overboard, Reuben."

A high-pitched scream pierced the air behind the ship, rising to a fever pitch that drove Charis to her knees in pain. The noise undulated, sending shivers over Charis's skin. Something thrashed in the water close to the back of the ship, and more snakes slithered from the walls and plummeted into the water.

"I'm guessing a Rakuuna tried following us," Reuben said as he returned to her side.

Her enemies wanted her badly enough to send soldiers into basilisk-infested waters to get to her. How was she going to get herself and her crew out of this alive? Her entire plan hinged on being able to deliver the poison to Verace so they could take it to Solvang and the armada Nalani was gathering. She couldn't hide in the cave for long, and the Rakuuna would surely be waiting when they exited.

They were going to have to devise makeshift weapons with the moriarthy, and fast.

Holland entered the deck and came toward her, his eyes widening when he saw the beheaded basilisk nearby. "You fought one?" His face rose as if to scan their surroundings for the exciting possibility of finding another monster to kill.

"Close your eyes before you end up dead." Charis's voice was a whiplash, barely containing the furious panic that churned within at the thought of him dying at her feet. "Is the hull breached?"

"There's a small hole." Holland nudged the snake with his boot and then obediently closed his eyes as he reached Charis. "I patched it as best I could, but we've got a slow leak."

She drew in a slow breath as the ship bumped its way around another curve and added "fix the leak" to the short list of life-or-death tasks that had to be completed before they sailed out of the cave.

The ship nosed its way through a damp curtain of vines and turned down another tunnel. Orayn muttered as he consulted his map by the light of a lantern. "There should be a wide opening soon, and then we take another series of tunnels west until we finally meet one that heads due south. That's our exit."

"How long will that take?" Charis asked.

Tracing a large finger over the map, he grunted and then said, "Most of the night would be my guess."

"Then we'll use that time to fix the hull and load cannons with moriarthy dust," she said.

"If we put dust into the cannons, won't it just spray into the air?" Holland asked. "We'd have to wait until the Rakuuna were right next to the cannons for that to be effective, and I assume they'll just rip apart the bottom of the boat long before their ship is close enough for dust spray to hurt them."

"Then figure out a better delivery system," she snapped, though she knew it was unfair. It wasn't Holland's fault they were in such a precarious position. It wasn't her fault, either. It was the Rakuuna's—and somehow she had to fight off a ship full of the monsters without leaving any survivors.

A chill crept down her spine as the truth hit hard. If even one Rakuuna from the ship outside the cave survived, they would bring the news to their queen that Charis had moriarthy dust. She'd lose the element of surprise and give the Rakuuna ample time to come up with countermeasures to save themselves and destroy her people.

The tunnel expanded slowly, and then all at once it was gone, and they were floating in a lagoon half the size of Arborlay's harbor. The crack in the mountain above became a wide fissure, allowing the faint glow of moonlight to fill the space, turning their entire surroundings a shadowy, ghostly blue. She hadn't realized they'd been inside the cave long enough for night to fall.

"If we sail to the center of this, how far away are the basilisks, provided we don't look into the water?" Charis asked.

Reuben immediately squinted toward the craggy walls that enclosed the lagoon before once more looking down. "A pretty sizable distance, Your Majesty. And it's so dim that it would be hard to meet a direct gaze until we're back in the tunnels."

Charis considered their options for a moment, though really there was nothing to consider. The hull had to be fixed, and weapons capable of leaving no survivors had to be fashioned. However long that took was how long they would have to remain here.

Finally she said in a tone that projected absolute certainty, "Get us to the center of the lagoon and weigh anchor. We've got work to do."

TWELVE

THE SHIP ROCKED gently in the center of the lagoon, and Charis shivered at the occasional thud of a basilisk brushing against the bottom.

The lagoon was approximately the same size as the small bay at Portsmith where she'd seen the Rakuuna queen's armada several months ago. Craggy walls rose high on every side, and the ceiling was a lopsided dome with a long, jagged opening at the top, revealing the distant, star-flecked velvet of the night sky. Her chest squeezed painfully as she scanned her surroundings, but Reuben's assessment was correct. The walls where the snakes might be coiled on ledges were too far from the ship and the light was too dim for the basilisks to threaten her people. There was a large shadow in the water off to her right—maybe a rocky outcropping or a small island?—but it was also far enough away that her crew wouldn't risk meeting a basilisk's gaze by looking at it.

Another thud echoed from the bottom of the ship, and she turned to Finn. "Order the crew to stay away from the sides of the ship. I don't want anyone accidentally glancing at the water. Post guards at the bow and stern and on the port and starboard side, five paces in to protect them from looking into the water. I want them listening for anything trying to climb up the ship."

Could a snake shimmy its way up the side of a ship even with fishing nets in place? She thought it likely they'd get tangled in the netting, but her understanding of the creatures was limited at best.

Her people were safe, for now, but they couldn't hide in this lagoon indefinitely. They needed to fix the hull and make weapons capable of killing an entire ship full of Rakuuna, including any who jumped into the sea. The task seemed impossible, but a month ago finding a weapon capable of killing the Rakuuna had seemed impossible, too.

First, however, she had to deal with what was in front of her. They'd lost Joren and Uriah, and she could hardly bear to look at their bodies.

Entering the cave had been the right move, but she was so weary of feeling like every decision she made was paid for with someone's blood. Forcing herself to crouch beside their bodies, she gently closed their eyes and whispered her thanks for their service. There was an ache deep inside, like the dull pain of a bone bruise. Was this how Mother had felt every time she'd read the casualty lists from the war?

They couldn't keep the bodies aboard the ship. She was going to have to send two of her own into the cold, unforgiving arms of the sea, and nothing about that felt right. They should be buried in their family plots, nestled by loved ones in the soft, fertile ground of Calera. Seers should be reading blessings over them, and chimes should ring in their honor. Their loved ones should be able to bring flowers and fruit to their graves every birthday.

Instead, they'd be lost to the deep, and no one would have a way to visit them and remember. Her throat burned as the ache spread from her chest to her neck.

Her people deserved better.

Orayn crouched beside her, his large brown hands resting briefly on the shoulders of the fallen. "They were good lads, and they'll be missed. I know Joren's mother. When we've retaken Calera, I'll be sure to tell her how bravely her son served his queen."

It was difficult to breathe. Difficult to blink away the tears that stung her eyes.

"You made the right decision," Orayn said quietly. "We lost two, aye. And it's a hard loss. But we would have lost everyone aboard the ship *and* the poison we carry if you hadn't sent us into this cave."

"But how do I get us out of this cave alive?" she whispered, careful to keep her words from carrying to the nearby crew.

Orayn met her gaze. "I don't know, but I have faith that between you, me, and the rest of our people, we'll figure it out."

She nodded, because what else could she do? They had to come up with a plan. The alternative was unthinkable.

Orayn stood as she did and said softly, "Your father would be proud of you. He always said you'd be the best queen Calera has ever known, and I haven't seen anything yet that proves him wrong."

His words slipped into the hollow of her chest, sharp as knives, precious as gems. She drew in a shaky breath and found she had the strength to lift her chin and wipe her face clear of the doubt that crouched in the corners of her thoughts.

"Have Ayve and Finn prepare these two honorable men for burial at sea." Her voice caught on the last word, but she pushed through. "And then send several crew members down to patch the hull and bail out the water. Once those things are complete, we'll rest for tonight and tackle the problem of making weapons in the morning."

As Orayn moved to obey, Grim and Dec rushed to her side, Holland in their wake.

"Your Majesty." Grim sketched a hasty bow. "You know that big shadow off to the side in the lagoon? We thought maybe it was a large rock or even an island?"

"Yes."

"We looked at it through the telescope. It isn't either one of those."
She turned to face him "What is it?"

"A ship."

Hours later, with Joren and Uriah respectfully sent to their final resting place and the hull firmly patched, Charis stood on the deck as some of the crew manned the galley oars while Orayn and Finn carefully navigated their way to the ship that rested in the southwestern quarter of the lagoon. It was much easier to see it now that faint scraps of daylight filtered in from above, but still, it wasn't until they were close that Charis could truly make out the spiky mast timbers, the spacious deck, and the limp flag that hung above the crow's nest.

"Ahoy!" Orayn called, his voice booming across the space between the two vessels. "We come in peace."

That was a relative term. If the ship was a pirate vessel—and Orayn had assured Charis there was no other type of ship that might take refuge here—and if its crew thought they were going to rob Charis's people, then she had no intention of being anything close to peaceful.

"Ahoy!" Orayn called again.

No one replied.

Finn yelled instructions to the rowers, and Orayn brought the ship alongside the other. Still, there was no reply. No activity on the deck as far as Charis could tell. Were they asleep?

"Cease rowing and weigh anchor!" Finn called.

Her crew stood silently waiting while she watched the other ship. Nothing. No sounds, no movement. She turned to find that Orayn,

Reuben, and Holland had all joined her at the bow.

"Is it abandoned?" Reuben asked.

"No one abandons a ship," Orayn said. "Too valuable. If you don't want it anymore, you sell it."

"Maybe they anchored overnight like we did, and the basilisks climbed the sides of their boat and killed them." Holland leaned over the railing as if by peering closer he could determine whether there were any bodies on the ship.

"Snakes can't climb ships like this one." Orayn gestured toward the sides of the vessel, where silvery spikes gleamed in the faint daylight. "Those spikes will be all along the bottom as well. Pirate ship, for sure."

Orayn cursed and spat three times over his left shoulder, while the others shifted uneasily. All but Holland, who looked as if he'd been given an early birthday present.

"Do you think they left any of their loot inside?" Holland rubbed his hands together. "I've heard pirates collect the best weapons the sea kingdoms have to offer."

"We should not steal weapons from pirates," Orayn said firmly. "That's a good way to get ourselves killed."

"What's a bad way to get ourselves killed?" Holland sounded genuinely curious.

"Lord Farragin, pirates hunt down those who steal from them and make examples of them. The stories are enough to chase the sleep from your eyes for a month. We should leave this ship alone, don't you think, Your Majesty?" Orayn looked at Charis.

Orayn was correct. Pirates were rarely seen in the southern waters—the vigilance of the Caleran and Solvanish navies had seen to that—but they were a danger in the northern seas, especially to the west, where they had hideouts far from civilization.

However, pirates weren't the most ferocious predator on Charis's trail. And they'd first have to return to the cave to realize they'd been robbed. At that point, it was unlikely they could ever track down who did it.

Maybe she didn't have to figure out how to make weapons powerful enough to obliterate an entire Rakuuna crew. Maybe all that was needed was a simple bait and switch.

The idea took hold, and as her mind raced through the strategy, hunting for weaknesses, she arrived at one simple, stark truth.

There was only one person in this lagoon who could act as bait.

It would be worth it if it meant her crew and the poison were safe. They could sail for Verace without issue, which meant the invaders could still be driven from Calera, and her people could still be saved.

Pushing aside the sickening dread that filled her, she latched onto that hopeful thought and turned to the group surrounding her.

"Your Majesty." Orayn sounded strained. "Please tell Lord Farragin that we are not stealing weapons from pirates."

"We aren't stealing weapons from pirates." Before Orayn could sigh in relief, Charis continued. "We're stealing their entire ship."

There was a beat of silence, and then chaos erupted. Orayn spat until his mouth ran dry. Reuben shouted objections that were drowned out by Holland's enthusiastic celebration.

Charis interrupted them. "We have to work fast. Orayn, stop trying to ward off a pirate's curse. *We're* their curse now. Put together a system that will allow us to haul our supplies safely on board and do it fast. I want every speck of food, weaponry, clothing, first aid supplies, tools, ropes, and poison on that ship by noon. Faster, if you can manage it.

"Holland, make sure our weapons are transported securely. Put Rithni in charge of the food and first aid supplies. Ayve can put together a small team to get everyone's clothing and hygiene supplies. I want Finn in charge of moving the poison."

"What should I do?" Reuben asked as the others left to do their jobs.

Calling on the fury in her heart, Charis turned to face him. A queen did what was necessary to protect her people. Even if it meant sacrificing a few lives to save the many.

Even if it meant sacrificing herself.

With enough steel in her voice to meet Mother's exacting standards, Charis said, "You are going to help me figure out how to sail our original ship out of the cave with as few crew members as it is possible to have."

There was a moment of silence. She met Reuben's hard brown eyes and waited.

Finally, he said, "This ship is a decoy to lure the Rakuuna into attacking, isn't it?"

"Yes."

He stared her down for a long moment, his jaw flexing, his eyes burning with the violence that lurked just beneath his surface. Then he said, "As you wish."

She nodded as though she'd never expected an argument, though it was rare for Reuben to simply accept her bold ideas. "Good. The crew who stays behind to row must be given the choice if at all possible. I don't want to condemn anyone else to be either kidnapped or killed by the Rakuuna."

She ought to feel bad forcing Reuben to join her, but despite the fierce loyalty he'd shown once she became queen, he was still the same man who'd ruthlessly murdered her handmaiden Milla and her nighttime guards on orders from Charis's mother. She'd never forgive him for that.

He could pay the life debt he owed by helping her save Calera.

"How many crew do you think it will take to get the ship out of the cave?" Charis asked, turning away to run some calculations. "I can manage the helm. Orayn's been teaching me. You can have Finn explain the depth finder—"

"No, Your Majesty." His voice was as cold as hers.

She pivoted to face him, anger flickering. "I don't think I heard you, Reuben, because surely you know better than to tell your queen no."

"I will sail the ship, Your Majesty." He sounded resolute. "I'll assign crew to the oars and the depth finder. We'll leave the cave first and lure the Rakuuna into sinking the ship. But *you* are getting onto the pirate ship and sailing safely out of here."

"No, I'm not."

He matched her glare with one of his own. "The queen of Calera is not going to send herself out of this cave as bait."

She gritted her teeth. It was hard enough to take this step without having to argue with Reuben, of all people, that she was making the right choice—the only choice—for Calera.

"I'm the one with a bounty on my head. I'm the one the Rakuuna are hunting. If they drag me back to Calera, they'll stop hunting. They won't be looking for more Caleran threats, and that gives our people time to gather an armada and use the poison to destroy the Rakuuna. This plan doesn't work if I'm not the bait."

A small sound behind her had her turning on her heel. Holland stood there, looking for all the world as though she'd just run him through with her sword. For a long moment, they stared at each other, and then he squared his shoulders and said, "When do we leave?"

"Give us half a day's head start to make sure the Rakuuna take the bait, and then sail for Verace. Once you've delivered half the poison to them, set sail for Calera's northernmost port and arrange to meet King Alaric and his army." Her words were full of calm certainty, at odds with the way her heart ached.

Holland raised one brow. "No, I meant when do we"—he waved a hand to encompass Charis, Reuben, and himself—"set sail as bait?"

She sucked in an unsteady breath and locked eyes with him. "You're not coming with me."

He smiled. "Indeed I am."

"Holland, I forbid you to go. That's a direct command from your queen."

His smile disappeared. "Then kill me."

She recoiled. "What kind of nonsense are you—"

"I'm about to commit treason by disobeying my queen." He crossed his arms over his chest. "So either give me a traitor's reward or stop trying to convince me not to follow you every step of this journey, no matter the cost."

She shook her head, momentarily speechless. He was using the same tone of voice that always sent Nalani into fits of despair because it meant nothing would change his mind. Still, she had to try.

"I appreciate your loyalty, and you know I love you. But everyone on board this ship is going to an almost certain death—"

"And how dare you try to leave me out of such a grand adventure." He leaned closer, a rare move for him, and said softly, "I'm going. Now, let's figure out how to do this right."

She could force him to leave with the other ship. Have him tied up in a cabin until she was too far away for him to fight the fate she'd chosen for him. And maybe she should. Maybe that was the right choice for Calera.

But it would crush Holland. He would forever feel responsible for not fighting for her to his last breath.

And if she was honest, the despair that lurked within her lost some of its bite when she considered facing capture with her cousin by her side.

"Fine. You can come. Now, let's start planning. I want us sailing out of here by the end of the day."

THIRTEEN

By MIDDAY, EVERYTHING of value had been transferred to the abandoned pirate ship. Charis stood on the deck of the Caleran boat facing her entire crew one last time, feeling as hollow and delicate as spun glass. The small leather pouch of moriarthy dust she'd retrieved from Holland was tied to her belt.

There was no point putting off the inevitable. There was only her duty and the force of willpower it took to see it through.

"I'm proud of you," she said, grateful her voice didn't shake. "You carry the hope of Calera with you."

Rithni made a strangled noise and began sobbing into her hands. Several other crew members looked near tears themselves.

"I know some of you believed I was the salvation of our kingdom, but the truth is that, as long as there are loyal Calerans willing to fight for our people, we have hope. You have a very important task ahead of you. I hope to be alive to see you all in Calera again, but if Lord Farragin and I perish, you will have a new queen in Lady Nalani Farragin, and she is kind, fair, and committed to justice for every Caleran."

Her throat closed, and she paused while she worked to take one deep breath and then another. Beside her, Orayn sniffled, and the bruise in Charis's heart seemed to spread to her veins until she ached from head to toe.

Reaching out, she placed a hand on the big man's shoulder and squeezed gently. "Your captain was a close friend of my father's. Orayn is capable, wise, and loyal, and he will guide you all to Verace and then on to northern Calera, where King Alaric and his army will be waiting. I hereby transfer my authority to Orayn for as long as you are at sea. Obey him, respect him, and work hard for him, and you will be hailed as the heroes you are."

Turning to her right, she looked at Holland, Reuben, Dec, Grim, and the four other crew members who had elected to sail with their queen to bait their enemies into an attack. She'd been surprised when the Montevallian spies had volunteered, but they seemed to believe serving her best interests would make their traitor of a prince happy, and as it meant that two more Calerans got to stay on the newly acquired pirate ship, she didn't argue.

The Montevallians looked determined, as did the rest of the skeletal crew. Even Holland appeared somber.

To them, she said, "Each of you are heroes as well. Without your brave sacrifice, we couldn't fool our enemy into leaving the rest of our crew alone. Without you, the weapon that will destroy them would sink to the bottom of the sea." Her mouth was dry, her hands shaking. The weight of their faith in her—their willingness to follow her, even to an early grave—sat on her chest like a boulder.

When she was sure she could speak with the confidence their faith in her deserved, she said, "I thank you for your service to me and to Calera. Because of you, Calera will one day be free again."

Her gaze met Holland's, and he drew his sword from its sheath and raised it high. "For the queen and for Calera!"

His shout echoed across the lagoon. The rest of the crew raised their weapons and shouted, "For the queen and for Calera!"

For a moment, their fury, grief, and stalwart faith seemed to shimmer in the air like a living thing.

It should never have come to this. She shouldn't be choosing which of her people would be tasked with carrying a weapon to Verace and which would help her sail their boat into the arms of their enemy. She shouldn't be so far from home with a crew of Calerans who'd all lost loved ones to the invaders.

None of them should be facing death.

With everything in her, she wished she could undo it all. Wind back time to the moments before the Rakuuna set their sights on Calera as the bargaining chip that would give them access to the jewels in Montevallo.

But wishes were distractions, and she couldn't afford to lose sight of what was at stake. She had one move left in the deadly chess match she was waging against her enemy. It was time to let them take the queen and assume they'd won the war.

"Go in strength and fortitude," she said, holding herself as rigid as stone, an immovable pillar worthy of her people's faith. When the last of the crew had crossed the ramp from her boat to theirs, she turned to Orayn. "Thank you for everything, my friend. I'm trusting them to you."

Tears glittered in his eyes, and he bowed low. "It's an honor to be your subject, Your Majesty."

When Orayn was across the ramp, her crew disengaged from the pirate vessel and then turned to her. "All of you except Lord Farragin and Reuben, to the oars. Full speed ahead."

☙

It took four hours to navigate their way through the warren of tunnels and back onto the open sea. Snakes rose, coiling and hissing along the tunnel ledges. Charis spent the entire time hunched over the map Orayn left for her, carefully choosing her course while Reuben worked the depth finder to keep them from running aground, and Holland remained on guard in case a snake fell onto the deck.

With only half their usual rowing crew they moved slowly, and the strain of knowing what waited for them once they cleared the cave stretched Charis's nerves to the breaking point. She focused on the map, whispering calculations to herself as she made small adjustments based on Reuben's depth finder. It was better to focus on one curve, one tunnel, one small turn of the helm than to think about the Rakuuna.

When at last the dim haze of the tunnels began to lighten, and the map before her showed the exit, Charis's knees gave out. She sank to the deck in front of the helm, her body shaking as though a hurricane was trapped within.

It was impossible to think, to stand, to breathe.

There was a ringing in her ears. A pressure in her chest.

She wanted Calera. She wanted Father.

She wanted Tal.

The thought of Tal in the midst of her panic lit a fuse in the corner of her heart where she kept her rage. He'd betrayed her trust and broken her heart. He didn't deserve to be the last person she thought about before she faced her enemy.

"Take my hand, Your Majesty." Reuben stood beside her, hard eyes pinned to hers, his hand extended.

She pressed her lips together in a thin line. She was queen of Calera. She did not go to meet her fate huddled on the ground like a baby rabbit frightened of a hawk. *She* was the hawk, and the Rakuuna were her prey. They might be about to swallow her whole, but she was the poison that would kill them from the inside out.

"Your Majesty, the exit is approaching." Reuben's voice held the same implacable expectation of perfection that Mother's had.

Charis was not going to face the Rakuuna looking anything less than the queen she'd been raised to be. Ignoring Reuben's hand, she climbed to her feet, grabbed the helm with fingers as cold as the sea itself, and raised her chin.

As the bow pierced the curtain of vines that hung over the exit, Holland braced his feet, prepared for an immediate attack. Charis and Reuben did the same.

Wintery sunlight gilded the deck in a wash of pale gold as the boat nosed its way out of the cave and onto the open sea. A stiff wind snatched at the mast, filling it almost immediately. Charis squinted against the light and searched the seas around them. They were empty.

"We've come out the other side, Your Majesty," Reuben said. "It's possible the Rakuuna ship is still by the entrance."

"It's possible," she said, though that made little sense. It was more likely that her enemy hadn't been sure which gap they'd sail from as there were multiple options on every side of the mountain. "We act like all is normal. Call up the rowers. I want the masts filled while I plot a course south."

Holland stalked the starboard side, searching the water beneath them for trouble while Reuben called the rowers to the deck.

"Anything?" Charis called to Holland.

"Not even a baby kraken." He sounded disappointed, and for once she understood.

It was agony to wait for what they knew was coming. It was even worse to wonder if the Rakuuna would miss the bait and go for the other ship instead.

As the rowers rushed onto the deck, Holland issued orders to trim the sails and secure the rigging. They hurried to obey, though their faces were grim and their voices muted.

Charis adjusted the helm, turning the ship to catch enough wind to push them south. Maybe this was better. They could put distance between themselves and the other ship so that there was even less chance of the Rakuuna remaining near the basilisk cave once they came for Charis.

She was just making a final adjustment, fighting hard to keep the ship from drifting into the rapid current of the western sea, when Holland shouted, "Ship, ahoy!"

An instant later, something thudded against their vessel, sending Charis tumbling to her knees as the boat rocked precariously. Her crew grabbed their weapons and shouted to each other, rallying beside Holland, whose dark eyes were wild with the thrill of facing death.

Charis scrambled to her feet as a high-pitched wail pierced the air, sending an ache through her teeth and scraping against her eardrums. As the wail tapered off into a sound like dry bones tumbling across cobblestones, a long, nearly translucent hand grabbed the railing on the port side of the ship.

"Port side!" Charis yelled, abandoning the helm and drawing her sword.

Holland and her crew pivoted as a Rakuuna with long, ragged, gray-white hair, a beard that reached his waist, and gleaming black eyes leaped onto the deck. Three more immediately followed, their too-long limbs making the task of scaling the boat and flinging themselves over the railing look easy.

"How dare you trespass upon the vessel of her Royal Majesty,

Queen Charis Willowthorn!" Holland bellowed, his sword aimed at the first Rakuuna who'd come aboard.

One of the crew members, a middle-aged man named Losh, dove for the creature closest to him. The Rakuuna batted away Losh's sword, grasped his wrist, and twisted until the bones cracked. Losh screamed, and his sword clattered to the deck.

"We take the queen," the bearded Rakuuna spoke in halting Caleran, his voice as brittle and dry as autumn leaves.

"Over my dead body," Holland snarled.

"We accept your terms." The Rakuuna lunged for Holland.

"Wait!" Charis held herself still, though she longed to rush down the stairs and put herself between Holland and the attacker. The Rakuuna paused, his head swiveling around like an owl's until his black eyes met hers. "He does not bargain for me. If your queen has an offer, I will hear it."

A strange sound came out of the four Rakuuna, like pebbles scraping over tin in a windstorm. It took a moment for Charis to realize they were laughing. Her eyes narrowed.

"No offer. We take the queen," the leader said.

"And if we refuse to give her up?" Reuben asked, looking two seconds away from throwing his body between Charis and the monsters.

"Then we kill everyone except the queen, and we still take the queen. She stays alive until Calera."

Until Calera.

Charis froze, a statue on the outside as everything inside of her tumbled and fell.

She wasn't being brought back to Calera as a bargaining chip for Alaric, then. She was being brought home to be publicly executed, to drain the fire out of the rebellion. They'd killed the Rullenvor High Emperor when they'd taken over his kingdom. The only reason

Charis had been spared was Tal's fierce bargain for her life.

If that bargain no longer held, then the Rakuuna either had what they wanted from Alaric, or they'd realized the Caleran people would be difficult to subdue as long as she was still alive.

The Rakuuna turned toward Charis, and her crew instantly moved to place themselves between the monsters and their queen.

"Kill them," the lead Rakuuna said as casually as if he was stating what he wanted for breakfast.

A Rakuuna with thick white braids wrapped in a circle around her head and a bluish tint to her scaled skin leaped past her leader, snatched a crew member named Wenshel off his feet, and tore out his throat. Another ran straight for Holland.

"I surrender!" The words tore their way out of her, born of desperation and fury. "Let them live. I surrender."

She laid her sword down and then descended the stairs, every inch the regal queen she'd been trained to be. Surrender was strategy, not defeat. It kept her alive to learn her enemy's weaknesses and exploit them. And it saved her brave crew members, especially her fearless cousin, from death.

The bearded Rakuuna smiled, revealing both rows of fangs, and unease sank into her stomach.

Why so amused? He'd known he could tear through her people and take her. Her surrender did nothing more than speed the process along.

She paused at the bottom of the stairs, her mind racing.

He hadn't promised to spare her people's lives. He'd said there was no offer. They were going to take her, surrender or not. He'd said nothing about the fate of everyone else.

Already the other Rakuuna were spreading out, surrounding her crew, black eyes glowing as they flexed their long fingers and bared their fangs.

Frantically, she grasped at her spinning thoughts, hunting for a way to save her people. The Rakuuna didn't value human life. They'd demonstrated that over and over. So what did they value?

Power. Jewels from Montevallo. Having unimpeded access to the throne of any kingdom they invaded.

"I surrender my heirs, the heirs of Montevallo, and my uncle as well," she said crisply, giving Holland a look that ordered him, for once in his life, to keep his thoughts to himself.

Holland simply raised one brow and looked around him as if wondering which of the other crew members was posing as Charis's uncle.

The bearded Rakuuna studied her, tilting his head so far that his chin nearly pointed toward the sky. She *really* wished he'd stop.

"Heirs?"

"Surely your queen understood that the entire royal family fled from Calera, with the help of several heirs from Montevallo." She gestured at the crew and went for the jugular. "Of course, I suppose you could kill them now. They've already gained quite a reputation among the rebels in Calera. Killing them would turn them into martyrs for a cause that needs very little spark to turn into a firestorm you have no hope of extinguishing."

The Rakuuna blinked, and Charis gritted her teeth. How much of that had he understood?

"She means if you kill us, the rebellion gets bad." Reuben stepped forward, his wiry body somehow managing to look threatening even in the face of the monster before him.

"Rebellion bad?" The Rakuuna looked at the group and then chittered to the others in their language.

"King Alaric won't give you what you want if you kill his family," Grim said, the boldness of his words somewhat marred by the shakiness in his voice.

The Rakuuna spoke rapidly among themselves for a moment, and then the leader said, "We take all and sink the ship. Go."

Before any of them could react, each Rakuuna grabbed the humans closest to them and flung them over the railing and into the sea. The bearded Rakuuna wrapped his chilly webbed fingers around Charis's arms, lifted her as though she was a feather, and dove into the water with her in his grasp.

The shock of the icy water stole the breath in her lungs, and then she was plunging forward beneath the waves, dragged at incredible speed by the lead Rakuuna. In his other hand, he held Holland's wrist.

She needed air. Desperately. Fighting the Rakuuna's grip on her, she kicked and flailed, straining for the surface. The male turned his head, translucent skin glowing beneath the waves, dark eyes evaluating her struggles. Finally he soared upward, breaking the surface with a splash and pulling Charis and Holland up with him. They were beside a gray-green, barnacle-encrusted hull.

She choked on sea water, coughing and retching until she was hoarse. Before she could properly catch her breath or look to see if the rest of her crew had avoided drowning, she was hauled unceremoniously up the side of the ship and dumped onto the deck.

In seconds, Holland was dumped beside her. All around, she heard thuds as other crew members were tossed onto the ship. She drew in a ragged breath, coughed again, and then turned to make sure Holland was in one piece. His black hair was plastered to his face, and he was coughing violently, but he was alive.

A tremendous crack split the air, and she clambered to her feet, her clothes sticking to her, rivulets of water pouring out of her hair. In the distance, her little smuggler's ship rocked violently. The main mast was slowly falling toward the sea, still tangled in the rigging. As she watched, a swarm of pale bodies climbed out of the sea and up the sides, tearing chunks out of the boards and tossing them into the water.

Her eyes stung and a lump formed in her throat as the boat listed hard to port and began to sink.

"We go to Calera now," the bearded Rakuuna spoke from behind her. "You and other royals stay in rooms. Go this hallway, the deck, and the dining hall, but nowhere else. Try nothing against us, or die."

She watched her boat sink until all that remained was a constellation of debris floating on the swells, and then slowly turned to face her captor. He smiled again, and she returned his smile as viciously as she knew how.

His smile disappeared. "To the rooms."

Latching on to her arm, he reached for Holland as well and dragged them both down the stairs and into a long corridor with a mess hall at one end and twelve cabin doors staggered at regular intervals. "You and your heir live here." He flung open the first door, as other Rakuuna dumped her crew members into adjacent cabins.

"I stay with my queen—with my niece," Reuben said firmly.

The Rakuuna who held his arm ignored him, shoving him into the cabin beside Charis's. She and Holland tumbled into the room, and the door slammed shut behind them.

Shut but not locked. As the Rakuuna had said—they were free to wander about the ship. What did it matter? The Rakuuna believed they had no reason to fear the humans. They'd even left them with their weapons.

She pressed her arm against her belt, where her small satchel of moriarthy dust hung limply.

The Rakuuna didn't know it yet, but they had plenty of reason to fear her.

A whisper of sound behind her had her spinning to face the inside of the cabin. The world tilted, and her breath seemed to scorch her lungs as Tal walked into view.

FOURTEEN

Time stood still for seconds, minutes, years.

He looked thinner, and his blond hair was long enough to brush past his shoulders now, but he was alive, and the punch of relief she felt was a bitter pill to swallow.

Tal made a sound as though someone had knocked the air out of his lungs.

A tremor shook Charis, sending an ache through her veins that throbbed in her fingertips. She wanted to cry. To throw herself into his arms. To strike him hard enough that he would know some fraction of the pain she was feeling. To scream her rage until her throat was raw. How could grief, anger, and love become such a tangled knot, impossible to separate?

He'd read it on her face. He always had. And she'd rather be dragged beneath the water by a Rakuuna than appear vulnerable to him.

Desperately, she reached for some semblance of control. Pressing her lips together in a thin, firm line, she met his brown eyes as though the sight of him meant nothing.

Less than nothing.

Certainly not worthy of revealing even a hint of the wound he'd given her.

"Charis." He breathed her name like a prayer.

"She's not alone," Holland said.

"Holland." Tal met his gaze.

"Impostor." Holland stalked toward him. "I once promised to disembowel you if you ever hurt Charis."

"I remember." Tal held his ground.

Holland drew his sword. "This brings me no pleasure. No, that's a lie. It's going to bring me a little bit of pleasure."

Tal held up his hands in surrender. "I deserve whatever you want to do to me, but you might need me to help Charis deal with my father so she can retake Calera. I promise, once she's safely on her throne again, you can do as you please to me. I won't fight back."

Holland's eyes narrowed, and he stood in silence for a long moment. Finally, voice heavy with suspicion, he said, "You won't?"

"I swear it." Tal looked at Charis, his expression full of resignation and regret.

"Why would you do that?" Holland demanded.

Tal continued looking at Charis. "Because I deserve it. Besides, nothing you could do to me is worse than living with how much I've hurt her."

Holland glared. "You really know how to drain all the enjoyment out of this for me."

"I'm sorry," Tal said, but his eyes were only for Charis. "You have no idea how sorry—"

"Holland, let's take a look at the quarters and figure out how to get dry." She turned away from Tal, grateful that her voice, though thin, remained steady.

"Well, this is going to be awkward," Holland said to no one in particular.

Charis willed Tal to move aside as she came into the cabin, but he stayed where he was. Fine. She was a queen. She could handle anything.

The cabin was a cramped L-shaped room with two sets of bunk beds bolted to the walls, a vanity with a basin for water fixed to the top, a dresser, a tiny desk and chair, and a small bath closet.

One of the beds had obviously been slept in. The others appeared untouched.

"You're bleeding," Tal said softly as she swept past him.

She frowned and turned to the mirror above the vanity. The glass was warped, changing her face into a parody of itself, but there along her neck was a thin line of blood dripping onto the collar of her shirt. She must have been scraped by the Rakuuna's claws as she fought for air.

"Here." Tal brushed past her, reaching for the vanity, and she jumped back as if stung.

He froze and then said, "I apologize for startling you."

The bitter laugh that escaped her took them both by surprise. Quickly, he said, "I know I have far more important things to apologize for, but first can I help you stop the bleeding?"

Moving slowly, he reached into the top drawer and withdrew some gauze but made no move to come closer to her.

Wise decision. She might have left her sword on board her ship, but she could do a lot of damage with her dagger. Maybe she hadn't wanted him dead, but wounded was still on the table.

"I'll be careful. I promise," he said.

Like he'd been careful with her heart? No thank you.

She was exquisitely aware of Tal's presence. The way his chest rose and fell with every breath. The look of pain in his eyes when she refused to hold eye contact. The weight of everything left unsaid between them filled the cabin, an invisible wall Charis had no intention of breaching.

The ache in Charis's veins seemed to grow, scraping at her composure until she wanted to scream or cry or both. Turning to Holland, she said crisply, "You can help bandage my neck."

And after that, she would crawl under the covers of the bed furthest from Tal's. Under no circumstances was she going to be able to maintain her expression of cold indifference if she had to be around him much longer.

"Um . . . I'm not very good at helping people feel better," Holland said as he came toward them. "Maybe you should just let the impostor—"

"Not him." Charis spat the words without looking at Tal. "I'd rather lose every drop of blood in my body than have him help me."

"Understandable, but unnecessary." Holland snatched the gauze from Tal and shoved it against Charis's neck. "It's not bleeding fast enough for you to lose all your blood before the wound cauterizes on its own."

"Be gentle with her," Tal's voice sharpened.

"Oh, look who's giving lessons on how to treat Charis. Give me a moment. I'd like to take notes." Holland brushed roughly at the cut, and Charis hissed.

"Give me that." She took the gauze, folded it until she had a clean square, and pressed it gently to her neck. "Holland, please find me some dry clothes. I'm going to bed." She cut her eyes toward Tal. "And I expect to be left alone."

He held up his hands. "I won't disturb you while you sleep."

Her lips twisted. He'd been disturbing her sleep ever since she'd learned his true identity. At least now, if he woke her in the dead of night, she could actually cause him some of the pain he deserved.

Holland searched the dresser and came back with a linen tunic that, judging by the length, was made to fit a Rakuuna. She'd wear it as a nightgown while her own clothes dried and hope that there would be no emergency requiring her to leave the cabin while wearing such a flimsy garment.

"I'll change in the bath closet," she said.

"It's too small." Tal shrugged when she glared at him.

Since when was a bath closet too small for a quick outfit change? She took the tunic, opened the narrow door, and sighed.

Tal was right, curse him. There was barely enough room to turn around, much less strip off damp clothing.

"We'll turn our backs," Tal said.

"Trust us, nobody wants to see you undress." Holland shuddered as he turned away, blocking the mirror with his body and looking studiously at the ceiling.

Tal's ears were red as he stared out the small porthole window, and warmth flushed Charis's skin as well. There was a time when Tal had certainly been interested in watching her undress, though he'd been far too honorable to act upon it. Was he blushing because he still wanted her? Or was he remembering that he'd been honorable about her body while recklessly using her heart?

Hours later, Charis was sick of tossing and turning in the lumpy, uncomfortable bunk bed. Holland had insisted she take the lower bunk, even though that put her only two arm spans away from Tal's bed, because if the ship encountered turbulence at night, he wanted the risk of being flung to the floor instead of her.

She'd been sleeping fitfully ever since the invasion. Trying to rest now, while she was at the mercy of her enemies and Tal was close by, was impossible.

Moving as quietly as possible, she climbed from her bunk and went to stand at the porthole. The sister moons hung full and bright in the velvet sky, their sapphire light glistening against the dark water like a spill of blue silk. The ship was cutting through the swells with incredible speed. Charis gripped the edges of the porthole as a dizzy spell hit.

"They push the boat from underneath," Tal said softly from behind her.

She gritted her teeth and kept her attention on the sea.

"That's why the ship moves so fast. Part of the crew grabs handholds beneath the hull and swims." He stepped closer to the porthole.

She stiffened, and he stopped moving.

"I'm so sorry, Charis." Pain was a living, breathing thing within his voice. "I—"

"No." She gripped the wall as her knees trembled.

When was the last time she'd eaten? Or slept?

Maybe it wasn't her body giving out on her. Maybe it was that the idea of having a conversation with Tal was simply impossible.

He didn't deserve to know how much he'd hurt her.

"All right, we won't talk about that yet." Tal sounded as if he was feeling his way for a candle in the dark. "Since I've been a captive here, I've gathered information on the Rakuuna that I think you'll find useful. We can talk about that as we take care of your wound. We don't want it to get infected. I can go get clean water and real bandages. They don't have medicine our bodies would recognize, so we'll have to—"

"*We* will not be doing anything." Charis drew in a breath of freezing air and turned, her mask of indifference firmly in place. "I will take care of myself. You can do whatever you want. I really couldn't care less."

She stalked to her bed and climbed beneath the rough blanket once more, leaving him standing in the cold alone.

FIFTEEN

Two days after being taken captive by the Rakuuna, Charis had yet to sleep or eat. Her stomach clenched at the thought of food, her body thrumming with a strange, jittery energy that refused to let her relax. She jumped at every sound. Startled awake just as she began to doze off, convinced a monster was in her room. And withdrew into a shell of silence that no one could penetrate.

She felt one loose thread away from unraveling completely.

Halfway through yet another miserable day of being stuck belowdecks watching the vast, empty sea fly past her window as the Rakuuna vessel made the journey to Calera in half the time a regular boat would need, she decided she'd had enough of hiding. She might not have a crown on her head, but being queen of Calera was all she had left, and a queen didn't cower when her kingdom needed strength.

Nothing would save her from what her captors had planned for her, but that didn't mean she couldn't still help Nalani save their people. Information was the most priceless currency in any war, and she had her enemies so close she could reach out and touch them. It was time to do some spying of her own.

She had the fleeting thought that she should ask Tal for pointers, but the words stuck in her throat. Instead she left him in the cabin as he prepared to teach Holland the seven rathmas sword-fighting technique. Holland still called Tal by the name "impostor" and was rude to him, even by Holland's standards, but he was also fascinated by all the things Tal knew, and nothing kept Holland away from what roused his curiosity.

If the past two days were any indication, Grim and Dec would soon join them, and the little cabin would become unbearably crowded.

Charis hung on to the railing as she climbed the stairs leading toward the deck. The sun was a shade brighter than it had been two days ago when Charis was last on deck, but the air instantly nipped at her cheeks and stiffened her fingers. Raising one arm to block the sun from her eyes, she moved to the edge of the boat, ignoring the scattered Rakuuna on deck.

If she acted like she belonged, she was more likely to eventually blend in. One could make valuable observations when one was overlooked.

A Rakuuna much farther down the port side called to another, and then two of them reached over the edge and hauled another Rakuuna out of the water. Charis tried not to stare at the way the water glittered against the creature's scales or the way her limbs moved as though they had an extra joint.

Maybe they did. That could explain why their legs and arms were so disproportionately long compared to their bodies or how they could swivel their heads like owls.

She filed away that bit of information in case it was useful and rubbed her hands together to bring some warmth back into them.

The Rakuuna who'd come from the sea was carrying a large net on her back. She dumped it, and a load of fish squirmed and flopped onto the deck. Immediately, one of the other creatures squatted and began tearing the heads off each fish and stuffing them into his mouth.

Charis turned toward the sea and tried not to gag.

"It likes fish?" A voice spoke directly behind her. Instinctively, Charis grabbed a dagger from her wrist sheath as she spun on her heel to face a female Rakuuna with broad shoulders, what looked like a tattoo of a constellation on her bony chest, and a length of brown seaweed woven into her tangled braid. The female held a headless fish in her hands, skewered on the end of one claw, but the offering she'd been extending toward Charis was snatched back when she saw the knife.

"Make me bleed?" The Rakuuna hunched her shoulders, hissing as she threw the headless fish to the side and snatched Charis's wrist instead. Her grip was painfully tight, but Charis kept her expression neutral. A predator only respected another predator. Mother had taught her that.

"I only pulled the dagger because you startled me." Charis held the creature's gaze, though looking into black eyes with no white rim felt like falling into an abyss.

"It should be down below."

"I was told I could come onto the deck."

"Wrong. Not if it makes us bleed." The Rakuuna shook Charis's wrist sharply, and the dagger fell to the deck as Charis's wrist went briefly numb.

"Why do you care? We can't harm you. You've proven that." Charis watched her carefully. If she was afraid of physical harm, then they were vulnerable to weapons. Charis just had to learn how.

"Dishonorable."

Charis's laugh was an icicle, shattering on impact. "Do not speak to me of honor. We did you no harm. And yet you sank entire ships full of innocent people. Invaded my kingdom and killed anyone you met. Families out celebrating. Children dancing in the street. The queen herself. The Rakuuna are many things, but honorable isn't one of them."

"It does not speak against my queen." The Rakuuna hauled Charis closer.

So they were deeply loyal, then. Charis appreciated that, even as it meant finding a Rakuuna to exploit for information might be difficult. So be it. She was adept at tricking others into giving her far more than they'd planned to.

"Your queen ordered the slaughter of innocents, both here and in Rullenvor. What kind of monster does that?" Charis threw the words at her.

"A good queen saves her people." Spittle flew from the Rakuuna's mouth, spraying Charis's cheek. "It knows nothing of this. It runs away from its people."

Interesting. What did the Rakuuna queen think she was saving her people from by invading peaceful kingdoms? Or was that simply the excuse she'd given the foot soldiers, who might balk at the idea of colonizing for wealth?

She softened her voice, infusing it with pity. "Your loyalty is admirable, but it is not honorable to kill innocents, even to save your own."

The female bared her fangs and hissed, her claws breaking the skin on Charis's wrist. With a jerk, she yanked Charis toward the stairs, sending her tumbling to the deck, where she was dragged by one arm. The Rakuuna took the stairs in three bounds, slamming Charis against the steps as she went, and then threw her against the wall outside her cabin. Charis's head rapped sharply against the wood. Bending low, the Rakuuna whispered, "It stays quiet until it gets to

Calera and our queen kills it."

Charis tried to respond, but her head was fuzzy, and everything hurt as though she'd been trampled by a horse. The door to the cabin opened as the Rakuuna stalked away, and someone gasped.

Charis tried to rise, only to crumple to the floor.

"Charis!" Tal ran forward and dropped to his knees beside her. "Where are you hurt?"

Her vision wavered as she turned her face toward his.

"I'm fine," she rasped.

"Liar," he said softly.

She gave him a look of murderous fury. Or at least she tried to. Her body didn't want to obey messages from her brain.

"I'm going to lift you and get you into bed," he said firmly, as though expecting an argument. Which was fair, given that in the past two days, she'd either snapped at him or ignored him entirely.

This time, she simply closed her eyes and said nothing.

The Rakuuna had said her queen was going to kill Charis when she arrived in Calera. Was that the truth? Or just an assumption?

Tal slid his arms beneath her back and scooped her up. Cradling her against his chest, he made his way into the cabin. Holland was gone. Probably checking on the other Calerans. As Tal carefully settled her on the bed, he parted her mass of curly hair and examined what he found.

"You've got a pretty good knot here," he said as he ran his fingers along the rest of her scalp, likely hunting for more injuries.

Charis batted his hand away none too gently.

The Rakuuna had been telling the truth as she knew it. Maybe it came from the understanding that to fully control a kingdom, its former ruling family had to be eradicated, the way it seemed the Rakuuna had done in Rullenvor. Or maybe the female who'd dragged

Charis down the stairs knew that her queen had to make an example of Charis to break the rebellion brewing in Calera.

Charis had believed the bounty had been placed on her head as a way to use her to gain King Alaric's jewels, but any heir to the Caleran throne would satisfy the treaty. He could marry one of his children to Holland, Nalani, or, seers forbid, Ferris, and it wouldn't change a thing about what he stood to gain. If the Rakuuna queen killed Charis, however, she could destroy the spirit of rebellion in Calera by snuffing out their symbol of hope.

"What happened?" Tal asked as he dipped a cloth in the basin of icy water and then carefully positioned it against the bump on her head.

"Nothing." She ought to feel scared. Defeated. Angry. *Something.* Instead, she felt numb.

"I've been with them for weeks, and they've never attacked me like this. Was there something . . ." He gave her a long look. "You didn't goad her into doing this to you, did you?"

She looked away.

"Charis, that's incredibly dangerous." He looked worried, and she had the sudden urge to laugh. It bubbled up, raw and bitter, and once she started, she found she couldn't stop.

"What's so funny?"

"Warning me . . . that something is . . . dangerous." The laughter burned now, scraping against the chasm within her as though it was a thing born from darkness. "I'm going to die, Tal." Her voice rose as the laughter faded away. "They're going to kill me, so what does it matter if it happens on this ship or after I disembark? The least I can do is get useful information for my people in the time I have left."

The room was really spinning now, and Charis felt sick to her stomach. Her eyelids fluttered closed on a final glimpse of Tal's face, stricken and pale, and then something heavier than sleep took her.

Charis woke with a dull headache and the unwelcome sight of Tal slumped in a chair, his head resting on the side of the bed as he slept. The cabin was pitch dark except for a lantern burning on low beside the vanity basin. Holland snored comfortably from his bunk above Charis.

Tal must have spent the entire day and most of the night at her side.

It was ridiculous to feel warm at the thought of him still pretending to care.

Irritated with herself, she sat up, wincing at the pain in her head, and took satisfaction in the way Tal jerked awake, wild-eyed and confused.

"Go away," she said, her voice still husky with sleep.

He scrubbed a hand over his face, ran it through his hair, and then sat back in the chair. "No."

She froze, her chin lifting as she stared him down. "What did you just say to me?"

"I said no." He sounded calm—a bold choice given that she was absolutely certain the look on her face screamed murder.

Her hands curled into fists, and he gave her a rueful little smile.

"Hit me if it will help you feel better. I won't try to block it."

She sat up straighter. "I don't need your permission."

"That's true, but you do need my help."

"I'd rather die." She threw the truth at him, the words vibrating with fury and pain, and his eyes darkened.

"I'm sorry, Charis." He tried to hold her gaze, but she looked past him at the faint sheen of starlight drifting in through the porthole. The apology of a traitor was worth nothing.

"Leave me alone," she said again. She wasn't going to untangle the sheets from her legs and subdue her hair with him as an audience.

"I will, but first we need to talk."

"I have nothing to say to you." A lie, but one she'd defend with her last breath. Better to shut him out completely than to risk showing him just how badly broken she felt inside.

"Fine. Then you can listen." He shot a glance at Holland as though checking to make sure he couldn't overhear them, but his snores remained undisturbed.

She opened her mouth to protest, sure he was about to dive into a discussion about their relationship, but instead he said quietly, "We are going to discuss your assumption that you're close to death once I've earned enough of your trust for you to listen to me."

Her lip curled, and he hurried on. "In the meantime, I have information that you need. I've been gathering it for weeks."

"By cozying up to your enemy, no doubt. One of your greatest talents." Her words were dagger-sharp and bleeding fury.

"It worked." His voice was flat. "I gained their trust, and they no longer pay attention to me as I wander the ship."

"How foolish of them."

"Maybe." He leaned his forearms on his knees, and Charis ignored the treacherous flutter of her heart when this motion brought him closer to her. "There are several Rakuuna aboard this ship who are terribly sick. Skin flaking off, unable to eat, feverish, lungs filling with fluid. Maybe other problems, too, I'm not sure. Sometimes I volunteer to help. Two weeks ago, I overheard one of the Rakuuna who runs the medical bay say that the serpanicite from Rullenvor's mines was nearly gone."

"Serpanicite?" Charis frowned. Lady Ollen from the royal council had worn a huge serpanicite ring, proud to own such a rare piece. "What are they buying with it and from whom?"

Why would the Rakuuna focus on such a rare gem when others were more easily accessible? What was so expensive that they needed serpanicite to afford it? And which of the sea kingdoms was bartering with the Rakuuna?

"I don't know." Tal stretched, his back popping as he arched it. "I've also learned that the captain is the queen's nephew or uncle . . . his Caleran is rudimentary, so I'm not certain. Anyway, they're related."

She looked away. That meant the captain was privy to accurate information about the queen and her plans, which meant the assumption that Charis was being taken to her execution was likely true.

How could she keep her promise to free her people if she was going to die once she reached Calera's shore? The answer that came to her made her clench her jaw until it ached.

She'd rather use Reuben. Holland. Any member of her crew.

Anyone but Tal.

But of every captive on board this ship, he had the best chance of survival. His father was the one who had the jewels the Rakuuna needed, which meant Tal had leverage. The Rakuuna queen wouldn't risk angering King Alaric enough that he'd refuse to make a deal with her.

Fine. She'd use him. Her people mattered more than her pride.

But there was a fine line between using him and allowing him into her inner circle, and she wasn't going to forget on which side of the line he belonged.

"King Alaric agreed to help me retake my kingdom. Perhaps you and Holland can use some of his serpanicite as leverage to bargain with the Rakuuna queen. Obviously, he doesn't have enough to satisfy them or he'd have already paid the ransom for you, but you just need to distract the queen long enough to stage an attack she doesn't see coming."

Tal's mouth twisted into a bitter smile. "I wouldn't put too much faith in my father."

"I don't put much faith in any royal from Montevallo," she said crisply, ignoring the flash of hurt in his eyes.

If he hurt, it was only a small fraction of the pain he'd given her. She expected him to argue the point, to try to get her to see his actions in a better light, but all he said was, "I don't either. However, I'm not sure an attack against the Rakuuna will be successful. I've observed them for weeks, and other than the illness in the sick bay, I haven't seen signs of any physical weakness we could take advantage of."

An idea formed as she looked out the window to avoid his gaze. An idea daring enough that even Holland would approve. Maybe she could still make a few moves in her deadly game against the Rakuuna queen. Maybe she didn't have to spend her days willing the despair away as her fate closed in on her.

And maybe she could still keep the promises she'd made to her people by using the traitor who'd broken her heart.

As the sound of footsteps in the corridor drifted past the closed door, she said softly, "I learned something, too." Pulling the small satchel of moriarthy dust from her belt, she dangled it in front of him. "And I've got a plan."

SIXTEEN

"I LIKE THIS plan," Holland announced as he hefted his sword and moved into the third rathma position. "It involves food, courage, and the deaths of my enemies—three of my favorite things."

Tal grinned as he nodded his approval of Holland's form and signaled him to move to the fourth rathma.

Holland matched the grin with one of his own and then scowled. "Stop trying to make me like you. You still have a disemboweling in your future."

"Elbow raised even with your shoulder. Chin down. Not sideways, *down*." Tal moved around Holland, scrutinizing him carefully. "If you can't even do four of the rathmas, how are you going to successfully disembowel anyone?"

"Care for a demonstration?" Holland straightened, his sword pointed at Tal's midsection.

"Can we get back to the plan?" Charis asked from her perch at the edge of her bed. She'd spent three days recovering from her injuries, and while she still hadn't slept much and had swallowed only a few bites before pushing the disgusting slop the Rakuuna called food around on her plate to make it look like she'd eaten more than she had, at least the room had stopped spinning, and her head ached less and less.

"Of course," Tal said promptly, while Holland once again tried to master the flow from the third to the fourth position. "Chin *down*. Like you're trying to touch your chest, except stop before you get there. And swivel your hips. Not like that, are you trying to break a bone? Like you're dancing."

"I hate dancing."

"It shows." Tal raised a brow in Charis's direction as though inviting her to see what a struggle it was to teach Holland, but she looked away.

Tal wouldn't get banter or playfulness from her. She was using him to save her kingdom. When his usefulness ended, so would her interaction with him.

A tiny voice in the back of her mind wondered if Alaric felt the same way about his son and that was why Tal was still a prisoner of the Rakuuna, two months after they'd demanded his ransom.

Once upon a time, that thought would've softened her with compassion, but everything soft within her had been whittled down to the bone.

Holland tripped over his feet and sprawled onto the cabin floor, nearly sending his sword into Tal's shin.

"Charis, do you want to run through the plan again while I show him what it's supposed to look like?" Tal asked, reaching down to help Holland to his feet.

"As long as you both pay attention to what I'm saying. These lengthy sparring sessions are getting ridiculous."

Especially because it meant listening to Tal's voice, and the way he accommodated the needs of the person he was speaking to. And it also meant watching him flex his muscles and demonstrate the lithe, graceful strength of his body . . . which meant remembering how it felt to be held by him, cared for by him.

Kissed by him.

Tal hefted his sword and flowed smoothly into the seven rathmas, his body moving as if there was music playing in his head. His broad shoulders strained against his tunic as the sword cut a graceful arc through the air, and then he dipped low, his leg sweeping out.

Had he been practicing like this his entire time aboard the ship? No wonder he'd been able to pick her up as if she weighed nothing. No wonder the calluses on his fingertips still felt rough against her skin as he checked her for injuries.

"Are you feverish?" Holland demanded.

Blinking, Charis tore her gaze away from Tal to find Holland looming over her, staring intently at her face. Instantly, Tal dropped his sword and rushed toward her.

She threw her hands into the air. "I'm fine. Stop hovering."

Tal's eyes were filled with concern. "You look flushed. Holland, feel her cheek."

"I'm not a nurse." Holland put his palm against her face.

"No, use the back of your hand. Didn't your mother ever check your skin for a fever?" Tal asked.

"I had the good sense to never get sick." Holland reversed his hand and smacked it gently against her forehead. "Seems warm."

"I'm fine. You two are going to be the death of me if this keeps up." She paused as her words struck something within her, echoing into the abyss where she'd pushed her grief. The echoes felt like fresh wounds, and she frantically reached for the willpower to focus on her duty instead. "Actually, the Rakuuna are going to be the death of me, but not before we have a plan in place to take them down."

"Stop saying things like that." Holland glared at her. "It isn't set in stone just because some stupid Rakuuna said it was."

She shrugged, because arguing with him was pointless. "Fine. Now, Holland if you can try to pay attention to what I'm saying instead of just watching Tal, we can continue."

"You were the one watching Tal and forgetting to speak, not me." He sounded offended.

The concern in Tal's eyes softened into something warm and knowing. Something that used to send butterflies through her stomach. She glared at him. If anything, her stomach was still nauseous from the few bites she'd eaten of the cold fish stew they'd been served for breakfast. Not a butterfly in sight.

A tiny, crooked smile played at the edge of Tal's mouth as he returned to the center of the room and scooped up his sword.

"We have very little moriarthy dust, and we need to figure out how it's most effective," Charis said sternly, as though Tal's movements weren't distracting in the least. "That means we need to find a way to make a Rakuuna ingest it, we need to wipe some on a Rakuuna's skin, and we need to put some into an open wound."

"Several of our crew members are helping in the kitchen since the food these monsters serve is about as edible as licking the bottom of my boots." Holland brushed his hair out of his eyes and mimicked Tal's motions, watching closely. "We can have them put the poison in that fish stew they like so much."

"We don't have enough to poison the entire thing unless they're really sensitive to it, so let's sneak it into two individual bowls. Then we can see how effective it is." Charis turned to the porthole to admire the way the clouds scudding across the sky created gray, green, and muted violet-blue shadows in the water below. It was certainly preferable to admiring anything or anyone inside the cabin.

"I can wipe some on a Rakuuna when I'm on deck stretching my legs," Holland said.

"If you do that, and they react, they'll know it was you," Tal said as he held the final position, sword guarding his chest, feet ready to lash out at an opponent.

"What if we just wipe it on something we know the Rakuuna often touch?" Charis turned back to the porthole when she found herself staring too long at Tal. Her traitorous body might respond to the sight of his, but her heart had learned its lesson well.

"The stairwell railing?" Holland raised his arm, checking to see that his elbow was even with his shoulder.

"The one who dragged me down the stairs took them three at a time. No railing needed." Charis tapped a finger on her chin as she thought. What did the Rakuuna often touch that the humans could easily access without raising questions? "The helm is impossible for us to get to. The rigging? The door leading into the mess hall?"

"The portrait of their queen." Tal nudged Holland's back until he was satisfied with the position. "It hangs down the opposite corridor where the Rakuuna sleep."

Charis met Tal's gaze. "They touch it?"

"They bow and then press the back of their first two fingers to her collarbone every time they walk past."

"You really are a good spy." Her words were needle-sharp and tipped with venom.

"I've learned to be." His shoulders dropped as he turned away from her to examine Holland's next attempt.

"Have you seduced any of the female Rakuuna yet?" She hadn't meant to say it. The words rushed out, an arrow shot from the wound he'd given her.

He stiffened and turned to face her, devastation on his face.

Instantly, she realized she didn't want the answer. Didn't want to open the door to a discussion she didn't think she'd ever be ready to have. Better to spend her final days focused on what she could accomplish, rather than on the pain that had stitched itself to her as though it had always been there.

Quickly, she said, "Never mind. It doesn't matter. What's important is finding a way to test the poison on an open wound. That's going to be more difficult because we can't actually wound them."

"I bet their skin slices open if you get close enough with a sword." Holland tried the complicated footwork between five and six and nearly fell on top of Tal.

"And then they know you're the one who did it, and they learn about the poison. Plus, they'll kill you for it." Charis blew out a breath and searched for other options. "Everything we try has to seem like a fluke. A strange accident that can't be traced back to us. And since we can't even get very close to them—"

"I can do it." Tal's voice was quiet, but there was a note of resignation in it.

"How?" She forced herself to meet his gaze.

"The sick Rakuuna." He swallowed and looked away. "They have open sores."

Charis's stomach sank. It was one thing to go up against a soldier in battle. It was another to ambush one who lay helpless and dying. No wonder Tal looked upset. She supposed even he had a code of honor.

"Why are the two of you looking like someone kicked your favorite puppy?" Holland asked. "They might be sick now, but they were only on this ship in the first place because they joined their queen's mission to kill our people and take over our kingdom. If you can't stomach putting the poison on their sores, I will."

"They won't trust you anywhere near the medical bay." Tal squared his shoulders. "It has to be me."

"Well, it shouldn't be too hard. If you can trick Charis into falling in love with you, surely you can manage poisoning some monsters, right?" Holland sounded genuinely curious.

Charis tried to breathe past the sudden ache in her chest. Her face burned, and she was exquisitely aware of Tal's silence.

After a long moment, Tal said flatly, "I said I'd do it, and I will. Now, Charis, it might be a good idea for you to brush up on your sword skills, too."

Fine. If he could speak as though it didn't matter that he'd tricked her into falling in love with him, so could she.

"It's not like we can get past the Rakuuna's long reach," she said because she did *not* want to be on display in front of him.

"No, the impostor is right. The poison might not kill them." Holland walked to Charis and handed her his sword. "It might just weaken them. We have to be ready for anything."

The sword dipped toward the floor as Charis struggled to hold its weight.

When had she become so weak?

Setting it aside as though she'd always intended to and not because she was about to drop it, she reached for her dagger instead, begrudgingly grateful that Tal had retrieved it for her from where she'd dropped it on the deck during her confrontation with the Rakuuna. "I prefer weapons that they can't see coming until it's already too late."

"The fact that they think you're safely imprisoned on their ship and therefore aren't a threat to them any longer is proof they'll never see you coming." Holland sounded confident, but a whisper of doubt snaked through her.

She hadn't seen the Rakuuna coming until it was too late. Hadn't seen Tal's betrayal coming either. If she couldn't trust her instincts, what could she trust?

Abruptly sick of being near Tal, she said, "I'm not going to practice with my dagger in front of the two of you. I'm going to check on Reuben after this latest bout of seasickness and then make sure the rest of our people understand the plan."

"Are you sure you should tell everyone what we're going to do?" Holland frowned.

"Figuring out how the poison works is only the first step." Charis sheathed her dagger and headed for the door. "Once we reach Calera, one of us has to survive long enough to get that information to Nalani. While I think Tal has the best odds, the three of us are the Rakuuna's prime targets, and I don't feel comfortable assuming any of us are going to live long enough to even send a palloren."

"You flatter us with your optimism." Holland swept his hair out of his eyes and picked up his sword again.

"You can figure out a way through this," Tal said quietly. "You always do."

Something dark and heavy blossomed in her chest until she thought she might come apart at the seams.

The old Charis could scheme and strategize, confident that she could outwit any foe. This new, hollowed-out version of herself couldn't see the chessboard clearly, couldn't understand her enemies, and clearly, given Tal's true identity, didn't even know how many enemies she faced.

All she had left was the ability to learn how the poison worked and the desperate determination to get that information to Nalani before the Rakuuna executed the queen who stood between them and crushing the Caleran rebellion.

SEVENTEEN

CHARIS INSISTED ON going with Tal to the medical bay the next morning. She needed information, and while Tal had proven to be an excellent spy, seers curse him, he didn't read his opponents as quickly as she did. A sick Rakuuna, already defenseless, might be more prone to accidentally giving information away.

The medical bay was on the bottom of the ship, in the opposite corridor to the brig. It was damp and cold, the smell of rotting fish and mold heavy in the air. The main corridor was filled with buckets, piles of soiled rags, and trays with bowls of half-congealed fish soup gone cold. The bay itself was filled wall to wall with thin pallets of woven grass, most of which were occupied by Rakuuna who looked horrifyingly close to death.

Charis choked on the overpowering stench of rot as she followed Tal into the bay. Seven Rakuuna lay on pallets, their scales flaking into the air as they struggled to breathe, their bones jutting against their skin as though they might split the surface at any moment.

In the back corner, a male Rakuuna crouched beside the bed of a female. He rocked back and forth as one trembling hand smoothed the female's hair. Bubbles of brackish-looking blood rose from her mouth.

"What kind of sickness is this?" Charis whispered, her skin crawling at the thought of catching what was killing these creatures.

"I don't know." Tal handed her a damp cloth and then took one as well. "But I've helped in here often and haven't become ill. We should be all right." He glanced at the satchel of moriarthy dust tied to her belt and looked away.

She swallowed as bile rose to scorch the back of her throat. The smell in the room was overwhelming, but if she was honest, her stomach's distress had more to do with trying the poison on a creature who was already in so much pain than it did with the stench.

Charis stood rooted to the floor, breathing through her mouth, as Tal busied himself wiping the nearest patient clean. Another Rakuuna, this one looking young enough that Charis wondered if he was even fully grown, sat between two pallets, spooning swallows of fish soup into the patients' mouths on either side of him. The patient in the corner gurgled, and the Rakuuna who was attending her let out a long, haunting cry that rose in pitch until Charis had to cover her ears to stop the pain.

What illness was this? Had they caught something from the raw fish they ate? From a sickness in Rullenvor that affected Rakuuna, but not humans?

And how fast did they become sick once they were exposed to it?

Maybe she didn't need to figure out how to use the poison. Maybe all she needed was to find a way to expose the Rakuuna queen and her loyal soldiers to whatever was wrong with the creatures on this ship.

The patient shuddered violently once more and then went slack.

The male Rakuuna curled over her body, his cries undulating through the air.

His pain struck the darkness within Charis, and her own grief echoed back. Her throat suddenly aching, her eyes burning with unshed tears, she forced herself to look away from the corner.

They weren't her people. In fact, they were part of the reason her people were in pain. She couldn't confuse the Rakuuna's grief with her own. Not if she wanted to gain the information she needed.

Clutching her damp cloth with shaking fingers, she tried to block out the sound of his mourning as she followed Tal's lead and crouched beside another Rakuuna, who appeared to be quite a bit younger than Charis.

A child soldier.

What kind of queen sent children into war?

She dabbed at the child's forehead, wincing at the film of scales that clung to her cloth. The pouch at her side felt heavy as she contemplated the task in front of her.

Yes, this child soldier was part of the army that had hurt and enslaved Charis's people, but how much choice did a child truly have? His queen was to blame, not him. The idea of experimenting on him with poison filled her with revulsion. Surely an adult Rakuuna would be easier to bear.

"What are you doing here?" A high, raspy voice came from behind Charis, and she turned from the child, grateful to have something else to focus on.

A Rakuuna with some kind of patch on his tunic stood in the doorway, a slim jar of green powder in one hand and a pitcher of water with a long wooden spoon resting inside in the other. His Caleran accent was much clearer than any of the other Rakuuna she'd met on board the ship.

"We're helping," Tal said quietly as he switched his dirty rag for a clean one and moved on to the next patient. As he passed Charis, he whispered, "He's their physician."

"Not her." The physician set the pitcher and jar down on a small table and glared at Charis.

"Why?" Charis kept her voice calm. "It looks like you need the assistance."

"No assistance from the one keeping us from getting medicine." He bared his fangs at her, and she rose to her feet, her thoughts spinning.

"I'm not keeping you from getting medicine."

"You are." He whipped the wooden spoon out of the water pitcher and aimed it at her as though he was contemplating striking her with it.

She frowned. "Is that what you're buying with the serpanicite you got from Rullenvor? Expensive medicine?"

He snatched up his supplies and stalked past her to the child on the pallet, bumping her hard enough that she would have hit the floor if Tal hadn't leaped forward to steady her. Shaking off Tal's supportive hand, she watched the physician closely.

"You could pay for it with other jewels. I'm sure King Alaric would—"

"Serpanicite!" The physician raised the bottle of green dust at her and then carefully measured out two pinches and dropped it into the water pitcher. As he stirred, the water became a murky green.

Charis was missing something. It seemed like he was saying the green dust was serpanicite, which would mean the rare jewel the Rakuuna were after was medicine to them, not currency for trade.

But why would they need so much medicine that they'd had to drain Rullenvor of its supplies and then turn their sights on

Montevallo, with Calera as the gateway? Unless . . .

"How many are sick?" she asked.

The physician knelt at the side of a thin sailor whose scales were flaking off, leaving gaping sores behind. He murmured in their language, and she obediently opened her mouth to receive a swallow of the murky green liquid.

"How many?" Charis asked again.

The physician glared at her again as he moved to the next pallet. "Many. Old, young." He gestured at those in the room. "Every ship is like this. Home is like this."

"And serpanicite is your medicine?" She stepped back as he crouched beside the child's pallet.

"You know that it is." He gave the small Rakuuna a swallow of liquid.

"I didn't know that until just now." She glanced at Tal, and he shook his head. He hadn't known, either.

"Many die." The physician rose to his feet, towering over Charis. Anger filled his voice as he shoved the water pitcher in her face, shaking it slightly for good measure. "Almost out of serpanicite. Nothing stops the sickness without it. This makes you happy?"

"Of course not." Why was he angry at her and not at his monster of a queen who was busy invading and crushing kingdoms instead of bartering for the medicine she needed to save her species?

Choosing her words with care, she said, "I can see that your people are dying. What I don't understand is why, instead of helping them, your queen is off killing my people instead."

"You had the chance to help us, and you refused!" The physician's voice rose, scraping against Charis's ears.

When had she had the chance to help Te'ash with this horrifying disease? The only time the Rakuuna had ever approached her was through Ambassador Shyrn of Rullenvor with their offer to help defeat Montevallo in exchange for an indefinite pass to set up camp in Calera with access to Tal's kingdom.

Access to the serpanicite they needed.

She frowned. Why not just tell her the situation and ask for safe passage to Montevallo where they could bargain with King Alaric for what they needed?

Unless they didn't have a way to pay for the gems.

Or unless there was still something Charis was missing—some crucial piece of information that would help her make sense of everything that had happened.

Facing the physician as he stooped to give medicine to another sick Rakuuna, she said softly, "If your queen had simply told me the situation, things would be different. I would have helped, had I known. She made the wrong decision, and it cost many Rakuuna their lives."

Behind her, Tal sucked in a little breath and then stepped forward as if to angle himself between the physician and Charis. Whatever he intended, it was too late. The Rakuuna sank his claws into Charis's shoulder and shook her until stars flickered at the edge of her vision.

"You will never come to this room again," he snarled. "You're lucky my queen wants to kill you herself. The blood of my family is on your hands."

He shoved her, sending her stumbling into Tal, who quickly steadied her and then guided the two of them out of the sick bay.

Charis's shoulder stung, and dizziness came in waves, but even though she hadn't learned what the poison would do to open wounds, she had something just as valuable. She knew why the Rakuuna wanted serpanicite from Montevallo, and she knew that someone— clearly Lady Channing—must have told the queen not to be honest with Charis about their true situation—a lie by omission that had set in motion the chain of events leading to Calera's ruin.

This would end either with Alaric paying the Rakuuna enough jewels to get them to leave or with Nalani's armada destroying the monsters. Charis just needed to stay alive long enough to see this through.

EIGHTEEN

THE FOLLOWING AFTERNOON, Charis was at the bow of the ship, clinging to the railing as the vessel climbed a massive swell before plunging down and sending a spray of icy water onto the deck. The sky pressed close, an ominous bruised indigo full of thick, metal-gray clouds. Just ahead, the skyline blurred, as if the ship was hurtling toward a curtain of rainfall.

"Your Majesty." Reuben's voice beside her was unsteady. "We're sailing into a storm. We should go below."

"Soon." She didn't want to go below. Everything inside her was stretched too thin, scraped too raw, and if she had to spend the hours between now and nightfall trapped in a cabin with Tal and Holland, she was going to break.

Staying in a different cabin wasn't even worth considering. She'd tried staying with others on her crew, but they all looked at her with such deference and hope in their eyes.

It was the hope that gutted her.

They saw their fierce, indomitable queen, who was only imprisoned because she chose to become bait and outsmart their enemy.

Imprisoned, but not conquered. Temporarily inconvenienced, but still viciously capable of winning.

Charis knew the truth.

If she was the conquering Rakuuna leader, she would never allow Calera's queen to survive. Especially when that queen had become a symbol of resistance to the people whose subservience she needed.

Charis had been dead the instant the Rakuuna ship found them on the open seas.

The ship shuddered as it plunged down another long swell and slammed into the valley below it. Charis gripped the railing harder as Reuben bent over and vomited.

"It's done." Tal's voice spoke directly behind her, nearly startling her into losing her grip.

She spun toward him and found misery in his eyes. Thunder rumbled through the air, and rain began pelting the deck.

"I put some on the queen's portrait." He swallowed. "And I put some on one of the clothes a sick Rakuuna is using to dab his sores. It—he used the cloth before I left the sick bay."

Lightning split the sky, snaking in four directions and raising the hair on her arms.

"Your Majesty," Reuben croaked. "The storm—"

"What happened?" Charis asked, her fists clenched so hard, her fingernails pressed deep half-moons into her palms.

The poison had to work. She had nothing else to use against her enemy.

A muscle along Tal's jaw worked, and then he said, "He screamed as if someone had poured boiling oil onto his wound. The sore was bubbling and hissing, and it—there was a lot of blood."

She nodded as another fork of lightning blazed overhead. All around, Rakuuna were hurrying to secure rigging and safeguard their ship from the storm. Reuben vomited again.

"It works," she said, feeling more weary than triumphant. "At least we know if we find a way to wound them first, the poison works."

"Your Majesty—" Reuben paused to dry heave.

"We should go below," Tal said, glancing at the sky and reaching for her.

Reaching for her. As if she was just going to take his hand and follow him.

"I'm capable." She turned away from Tal's outstretched hand. There was no point staying where it wasn't safe, even if she couldn't stand the thought of being cooped up in the cabin. Besides, Reuben would refuse to leave her side, and as sick as he was, he was likely to get washed overboard.

There was a time when she would have welcomed that. Now she needed his loyalty and unwavering commitment to the Caleran crown if she was going to see this through.

The understanding that she'd come to rely on the man who'd killed Milla sat uneasily, pricking at her heart.

It could join the rest of the thoughts that kept her up at night and clawed at her composure during the day.

They slipped and skidded their way to the stairs and climbed below. Tal hesitated when he reached the cabin door, and Charis glared at him. "I'm going to get Reuben settled and check on the rest of the crew."

"But then you'll return so Holland and I can make sure you're safe?" He was watching her far too closely, and she was reminded of all the times he'd seen past her words to read her thoughts instead.

"Of course," she said as if he was a fool for thinking otherwise.

His eyes narrowed, but when he saw her guiding Reuben into the next cabin, he finally went inside and shut the door.

"Go lie down," Charis said as she maneuvered Reuben into his cabin. The ship pitched forward, and Charis caught herself against the wall.

"What if we sink?" Reuben's voice wavered and sweat dotted his brow as he swallowed hard.

"The Rakuuna wouldn't dare let that happen." She straightened with the ship and drew in a shaky breath. The tattered remnants of her outward calm were fraying rapidly.

"You don't know that, Your Majesty." Reuben slid forward, banging into a chair, as the ship crested on another swell and then plunged forward.

"I'm of no value to them if I'm lost at sea." She used the same voice on him that had worked on Tal. "And they're capable of steering the ship from both the helm and those handholds they have below the surface. If they can steer it, they can stabilize it. Now go to bed."

He reached his bed and gripped the edges. "You'll be in your cabin with the traitor and Lord Farragin?"

"Yes. Now lie down before you fall down."

She closed his door behind her and then braced her hands against the wall to consider her options.

She'd intended to check on the rest of her crew, but they would need reassurances she didn't feel capable of giving. And she'd intended to resign herself to hours in the cabin with Holland and Tal, both of whom had become increasingly persistent in asking her how she was doing. The thought sent a restless, agitated sort of energy humming just beneath her skin.

She was fine. She was always fine. What other choice did she have?

Abandoning the idea of heading for her cabin, she wandered into the empty mess hall, gripping one of the tables that was bolted to the floor as the ship rolled to its left before righting itself.

Despite what she'd said to Reuben, she knew the ship might go under. The thought of the unforgiving sea rushing through corridors, filling rooms, and stealing the breath from her lungs should have been horrifying. Instead there was a weary sort of longing within her to just let the water in. Let it wash away the pain and the wreckage of the life she had and bring her to where her parents waited.

No more grief. No more fury. No more wishing things were different.

The dark chasm within her would seal shut, and she'd be free.

She'd be free, but her people would still be trapped. Her allies still at risk. Her promises unkept.

Something unfurled within her, raw and tender to the touch, and she dug her nails into the table as it spread, pressing against her bones, tearing through her veins, spilling across her tongue until she threw back her head and screamed.

Panting, she closed her eyes and listened, trying to come up with a story to explain away the noise if anyone came to check on her, though surely the sounds of the storm had drowned her out.

The ship's timbers groaned as the wind battered the vessel, and a sharp crack rumbled through the air, though she couldn't tell if it was lightning or a break in one of their masts. The rain drummed steadily against the deck above her, but no voices called out in worry.

It was better this way.

No one here to see her falter and break. No one to offer help when there was nothing anyone could do to change what was.

Her throat closed, as if a fist was wrapped around her neck, and she sank to her knees while her next breath shuddered and clawed its way into her frozen lungs.

There was no changing the truth. No matter what she did, what risks she took, how far she pushed, nothing she did would bring back what she'd lost. Mother's fierce spirit would forever be silenced. She'd never visit Father's sunny chambers again and curl up against him while he soothed her.

Her head spun, and a tingling sensation spread through her limbs as the air in her lungs thinned.

How could she be strong when everyone she'd looked to for strength was gone?

She could no longer feel her hands as she pressed them against the floor, bracing her elbows as the ship shuddered and heaved. Lights danced at the edge of her vision, and the sound of the storm became muffled and faint.

"Charis!" A firm voice intruded on the gathering darkness within her mind and then something cold was shoved against the back of her neck.

Water dripped from the rag at her neck and slid down her spine. Her eyes flew open, and she gasped in a breath as she found Tal on his knees beside her, hovering anxiously as he pushed her head between her knees and pressed his cloth against her skin.

"I'm fine." She meant to sound commanding, but her voice was weaker than Hildy's tiny meow.

"Obviously." He pulled the rag away from her neck, and she eyed him suspiciously.

He sat back on his heels and studied her.

She looked away.

The ship pitched to the right, and she slid into him. Instantly, he wrapped one arm around her and grabbed a table leg with the other, steadying them both.

"Don't touch me."

"If I let go of you, you'll slide across the room until you hit the wall." His voice rumbled in his chest, a sound so achingly familiar and so altogether infuriating.

"I'd rather hit the wall than lean on you." She swallowed against the fist that was still closed around her throat.

"I know." He held on as another wave slammed into the boat.

She tilted her head back so she could see his face and instantly regretted it. He was entirely focused on her, his brown eyes worried as he held her close, trying hard to shield her with his body. The ship slid sideways, and they hit the table, Tal's shoulder taking the brunt of the impact.

He grimaced in pain but kept his grip on her.

Once upon a time, this would have been comforting. She could have leaned against him, safe and secure in the knowledge that no matter what came for her, he was at her back.

Now he was another piece of the world she'd lost, and nothing could change that either.

Her jaw went numb. It felt as if a horse was sitting on her chest, and it was impossible to move. Impossible to breathe.

The ship spun in the opposite direction, and Charis spun with it, limp as a rag doll. Tal strained to hold on to the table as he pulled her back to his side.

"Hey." His voice was low against her ear. "Stay with me, Charis. I'm right here."

But he wasn't. Not really. His heart was in Montevallo, and it always had been.

She was utterly, impossibly alone.

"Take a breath, please."

She couldn't, even if she wanted to. Lights danced along her vision once more, and she welcomed them.

Let her fade into oblivion while the storm raged and keep her there until the wound inside her stitched itself back together.

Vaguely, she was aware that she was sliding across the mess hall and into the kitchen, only there was a pressure under her arms, as if she was being dragged. And then, without warning, a sharp, acidic odor was thrust beneath her nose.

The darkness parted, the lights at the edge of her vision vanished, and she was left sprawled across the kitchen floor, blinking up at Tal, who knelt beside her holding a rag soaked in vinegar to her nose.

"What are you—did you *drag* me?" She tried to sit up, but her head spun, and the room seemed unaccountably crooked.

"I pulled you. Vigorously."

She pushed the rag away with trembling fingers and glared at him as if she was seated on her throne, not lying on the floor. "That's the same thing."

"We can argue semantics later." He placed the rag at his feet. "First, let's discuss why you were in the mess hall, alone, in the middle of a raging storm, when you're obviously unwell."

Her eyes narrowed. "I'm not unwell."

"Right. Because healthy people pass out twice in the space of five minutes."

"I'm fine." The lie fell from her lips with practiced ease, leaving bitterness in its wake. "Just got a little sick from the ship rolling around."

He crossed his arms over his chest and gave her the look that used to send little sparks of warmth racing through her blood. It was an invitation to match wits with him. To spar outside the practice arena, using nothing but her mind as her weapon.

Leaning forward, he said softly, "Liar."

She bared her teeth. "You would know all about that."

"Indeed I would." He sounded pleased, as if she'd conceded a point.

She frowned.

"I know you're lying, Charis, the same way I know you aren't eating or sleeping. The same way I know you're putting too much pressure on yourself and are in danger of collapsing." His voice softened. "I know you're lying, because I know *you*."

"You don't know me anymore."

"No?" The ship rocked violently, and he grabbed her arm to keep her from hitting the cabinets. "Then tell me what's changed."

"I'm not telling you anything."

"Why not?" he asked as if this was a perfectly reasonable question. As if he hadn't betrayed her and broken her heart only two months ago.

She opened her mouth, snapped it shut, and glared at him as she struggled into a sitting position, her back against the cabinets.

"Do you think you have to be strong for me?" He tilted his head as if trying to figure her out.

"Don't be ridiculous."

"I'm not the one who passed out on the mess hall floor and then claimed I was fine, Your Majesty."

"I didn't—that's not even—why are you still here?" Her voice rose. "Go back to Holland." And seers curse him for making her wish she could ask him to stay so she wouldn't be alone with the darkness inside her.

"And leave you to pass out again all by yourself? I think not." He settled against the cabinet beside her, his shoulder touching hers.

They sat in silence for a long moment while the ship rocked and the winds howled, and then he said quietly, "You don't have to be strong in front of me, Charis."

She bit down hard, clenching her teeth as she swallowed the truth that rose to the surface.

Of all people, she had to be strongest in front of him because he alone had seen her at her weakest, and he'd buried a knife in her back.

"Breathe." He reached for the vinegar rag as though worried she might lose consciousness again. She pushed his hand away, and as she drew in a jagged breath, the dam within her burst.

"You have a lot of nerve sitting next to me and pretending to care." The words were sharp as a blade, and she hoped they sliced him to the bone. "I know you're watching me. I can feel it. The first chance you get, you'll run and tell your father everything you know about Calera's situation, and if Alaric thinks we're not strong enough to do what needs to be done, he'll refuse to honor the treaty. Refuse to help us with his army. And then . . ."

"Then?" he asked gently, as if she hadn't just wounded him, though she could see the pain in his eyes.

"Then it's all gone. All of it!" Her voice rose, wild and fierce, and she turned on him with her fists ready, though he wasn't putting up a fight. "Mother is gone. Father is . . . I didn't even get to say goodbye."

A sob caught in her chest, and she hurled the last of it at him, the darkness spilling out of her with every word. "I have a kingdom of people depending on me to be strong enough and smart enough to make everything right, but nothing will ever be right again, will it? Because nothing I do will bring back who we've lost. And the worst of it is that Mother was telling the truth all along."

"About what?" He brushed a hand against her skin as he gently tucked a curl behind her ear, but she barely noticed.

"There's no one I can truly trust anymore. To rule is to be alone. And I am utterly, completely alone."

Her voice broke, and she turned away as tears slid down her cheeks.

"Charis, I'm sorry." He placed one warm hand against her back and waited. When she didn't order him to stop, he kept it there. "I wish we'd both had a chance to say goodbye to your father. He was the best man I've ever known."

Sobs shook Charis until it seemed she'd never stop. Dimly, she was aware of him anchoring her body next to his so that she wouldn't slide with the movements of the ship. He whispered against her ear, but she couldn't hold on to anything he said. There was nothing but the agony of missing Father and wishing she could turn back time and undo what was final.

When at last, her sobs quieted, she felt weary to the core. She leaned away from Tal, resting her head against the cabinets just to put distance between herself and the boy she'd just shown weakness to. She needed to do something about that, but right now it would take far too much energy, and her eyelids fluttered.

"You aren't alone, Charis," Tal said quietly, his voice aching with the same pain that lived within her. "I know it's hard to see it, now, but I swear it's true. I'll prove it to you, if you'll let me."

She wanted to tell him he'd already proven everything she needed to know the night he was revealed as a spy, but she was no longer sure that was the truth, and she was too tired to figure it out.

Instead, she rested her head against the cabinet and let her eyes close while the storm raged on, knowing he wouldn't let anything happen to her while she slept.

NINETEEN

THE STORM LASTED for most of the night. About an hour in, Tal had escorted her back to the cabin and watched her fall into bed, where she'd slept, deep and dreamless, for the first time in weeks. She woke feeling focused and clearheaded with no one else in the cabin. It was time to pull herself together, check on her crew, and then figure out how to sneak some poison into a soup bowl or two.

With that plan in mind, she splashed her face with freezing water, subdued her hair into a thick braid, and opened the door to leave the cabin. Holland, however, was standing on the other side, Tal right behind him.

"I'm going to check on the crew," she said, waiting for them to move.

"You have some explaining to do." Holland bit off his words as if he was struggling to keep his voice down.

From farther along the corridor, the brittle bones sound of Raku-una talking to each other drifted down, and the smell of rotting fish stew lay heavy on the air. Charis stepped back to let the two of them into the dubious safety of the cabin. Tal was carrying a rough wooden platter holding what looked like a fish—a proper, baked fish, rather than a bowl of the disgusting stew Charis was usually served for breakfast. Tal settled the tray on the room's small desk and then pulled out a chair in a clear invitation for her to sit down.

She ignored him and turned to Holland. "What do you mean I have explaining to do?"

"I won't sugarcoat it." Holland placed a mug of water onto the desk with a *thunk*. "You're too thin, you look terrible, and now the impostor tells me you passed out. Twice."

She turned on Tal. "You *told* him?"

"Don't get mad at him," Holland snapped, and then paused. "I mean, stay mad at him for all the things he did wrong, of course. No one here is forgetting we owe him a disembowelment. But he was right to bring this to me."

"I'm *fine*."

"You need food." Tal's tone didn't ask for an argument, but she'd never required an invitation.

"I need to check on the crew and then solidify our strategy for the rest of the poison."

"You can talk while eating." Tal gestured at the tray. "And the poison has already been handled."

"Handled by whom?" She patted the satchel she always kept tied to her waist. Did it feel a little lighter than it had yesterday?

"Ayve was in the kitchen, so it just made sense to put a pinch of poison in a few soup bowls." Tal gestured toward the chair again.

"Did the Rakuuna know Ayve was in the kitchen? Because if something goes wrong, and they can tie it back to us . . ." She stopped at the stricken expression on Tal's face.

"Risks are part of war," Holland said firmly.

The room spun, and she reached out to hold on to something for balance. It was unfortunate that the closest object to her was Holland's arm. He swore, and the next thing she knew, she was in the chair, and Holland was spearing a bite of fish onto a fork.

"Eat it by choice or force me to have the impostor feed you." Holland shoved the fork into her hand.

She lifted her chin, but then Tal said softly. "Grim, Lohan, and I started fishing at dawn so we could have something other than fish stew to serve our people. Ayve and Dec risked a lot to convince the Rakuuna who runs the mess hall to let them cook for us this morning. Even Reuben dragged himself out of bed to stand guard outside your door so you could enjoy this breakfast without interruption. When was the last time you ate a meal?"

Charis tried to lie. To tell them this was ridiculous, and she was fine. To order them to leave her alone.

The words wouldn't come. Instead she drew in a breath and said quietly, "It's been a little difficult to feel hungry." It had been impossible to swallow more than a bite or two when everything tasted like dust and the idea of chewing seemed like an insurmountable task.

"I'm never too upset to eat," Holland said. "Unless it's Lady Shawling's cookies. Those are an insult to the mouth."

"They were pretty awful."

"And yet you ate them, just to be polite." Holland waved at the fish. "Tell yourself it's impolite to refuse something your people worked so hard to give to you and get it done."

"Besides, if the poison works, we may have a volatile situation on our hands. You'll want to be clearheaded." Tal locked eyes with her, and she glared.

It didn't seem fair that he still understood exactly what to say to motivate her.

The first bite tasted like nothing, but she chewed anyway. There was a knock at the door and Ayve entered, followed by Dec, Grim, and Lohan. Reuben, looking positively ghastly, stood guard outside.

Ayve's long red hair was roughly subdued into a loose braid, and her cheeks looked a bit too pale, but her eyes glowed with enthusiasm. She held a small piece of baked dough in her sturdy fingers. It smelled like the cookies Charis loved to eat at winter solstice parties.

"Your Majesty, we found some flour and spices the Rakuuna took from a merchant ship. It isn't much, but if we stretch it out, we can have little pastries every day between now and when we reach Calera."

Charis took the pastry with the same care and ceremony with which she'd once received gifts from ambassadors and kings. "This looks delicious, Ayve. Thank you."

As the others began whispering to each other about the poison and how likely it was to work when mixed with stew, Tal leaned down and said softly, "I told you I'd prove that you weren't alone."

She swallowed hard, took a sip of water, and made herself meet his gaze, though it felt like she was prey exposing her belly to a predator.

"About that whole scene in the mess hall . . ."

"Yes?"

"I don't suppose you'd be willing to forget about it?"

His eyes softened, and his lips quirked in a small smile as behind them Holland ordered Grim to have more sense and Grim, in turn, offered to throw him to the sea monsters. "I'm not going to forget about it because it was important to you."

Her eyes narrowed. "Then promise me you won't use it against me."

His smile disappeared. "I would never do that."

"Never?" She speared another bite of fish with so much force, it disintegrated onto the plate.

He leaned close again, his eyes finding hers. "The only informa-tion my father ever received from me had to do with understanding what kind of person you are and the best way to approach you and your mother to bring an end to the war. Every personal thing you ever shared with me is still with me and me alone. I swear."

"And I'm supposed to take your word for it?"

"Are you ready to let me explain myself?"

Before she could respond, an unearthly wail tore through the corridor, rising to such a feverish pitch that Charis dropped her fork to cover her ears. Ayve collapsed to her knees, Grim stumbled into a wall, and Dec clapped one hand on his friend's arm to steady him and the other over one of his own ears.

Tal and Holland each drew their swords as the Rakuuna cry grew louder. Someone shouted outside the cabin, and then the door was flung open.

A Rakuuna lurched into the cabin, oily black blood leaking from a hole in her throat, and headed straight for Charis.

TWENTY

IN THREE STRIDES, the Rakuuna reached the center of the cabin, her black eyes glittering with fury as she lunged with outstretched claws.

Tal and Holland thrust themselves in front of Charis, their swords pointed at the creature.

Charis scrambled to her feet, her dagger already in her hands. If this Rakuuna was already wounded, surely they had a chance of finishing her off. She flexed her muscles, feet sliding into the first rathma position as though she'd never stopped practicing.

Too late, she realized she wasn't the creature's target.

The Rakuuna buried her fingers into Ayve's hair, grabbed a fistful, and yanked the woman to her feet. The creature hissed, sending a spray of black blood out of her neck, and bared her double row of fangs. Her claws dug into Ayve's head, and she shook the woman like a child's rag doll.

"Hurts us." A terrible choking sound issued from the Rakuuna's throat, and more blood sprayed, hitting the side of Ayve's face.

Holland, Dec, Lohan, and Grim rushed for the Rakuuna. She used her free arm to send them sprawling across the floor. Tal planted himself in front of Charis, sword held steady.

From behind the Rakuuna, Reuben staggered in, a cut in his head bleeding profusely. His sword shook as though he'd been injured too badly to hold it steady, but still he aimed it at the monster's back.

Lohan was closest to the Rakuuna. He belly-crawled toward her, his dagger in his hand. The creature kicked him in the chest. He crashed into the wall, twitched once, and lay still.

Holland roared and sprang to his feet, sword ready.

He was going to die. They were all going to die if Charis couldn't find a way to control this.

"Stop!" She used Mother's most commanding tone.

Her people froze. The Rakuuna did not. Instead, the creature shook Ayve and howled as the hole in her neck slowly widened, as though the skin was continuously burning away, like thin paper held to a flame.

From the corridor came more wails, followed by the dry rattle of the Rakuuna's language. The bearded Rakuuna who captained the ship burst into the room, followed by three others, including the female with bluish skin and a crown of braids. A long, charred opening from the base of her neck to the tip of her chin poured black blood, and she was supported by another Rakuuna.

"You did this." The captain pointed at Charis.

She let her eyes widen and shook her head. "Please tell us what's happening."

He hissed, and the Rakuuna who held Ayve spat a few words to him. Her voice sounded weak, and her black eyes were glassy.

Good to know the poison was this effective. A larger dose might have killed her outright. If Charis could talk their way out of this, she'd have all the information she needed for Nalani.

She glanced once at Lohan's body and looked away.

holding him moved swiftly toward Charis, Tal, and Reuben while the captain turned his attention to Holland.

"Watch it," Holland snapped. "I like this coat."

"Careful," Charis breathed as Reuben squared his shoulders.

The Rakuuna captain's hands were damp and chilly. Charis held herself as still as possible while he searched her, trying not to focus on the scaly translucence of his skin or the smell of rot and brine wafting from his mouth.

When he found nothing, he turned to Reuben while one of the others searched Tal. In seconds, the captain yanked the satchel from Reuben's pocket and pried open the knot. He peered inside, frowned, and then shook a small amount of moriarthy dust onto the floor. The red-brown poison glittered dully in the light of the porthole. Charis schooled her expression into calm disinterest and tried to breathe normally, though everything inside her felt sharp as glass.

The herbologist in Solvang hadn't known exactly how moriarthy dust affected the Rakuuna because it had been so long since it had been used. Maybe the Rakuuna wouldn't recognize it. Maybe she could think of a convincing lie. Maybe—

"What?" The captain pointed at the satchel before baring his fangs at Reuben.

"Medicine," Reuben said, looking queasy enough that the idea of him carrying medicine might make sense.

"For what?" The Rakuuna looked dubiously at the powder.

"My stomach." Reuben burped and patted his stomach gingerly, looking even sicker than he had a moment before. Blood from his head wound congealed on the side of his face, a stark contrast to his pasty complexion.

The captain's black eyes stared unblinkingly at Reuben, and then he said, "Eat."

Charis bit her tongue and shot Holland a look as the captain raised the satchel to Reuben's mouth. She had no idea if moriarthy dust was safe for humans to eat. If it wasn't, Reuben was about to die a horrible death, and her plan to poison the Rakuuna invaders would be revealed.

The satchel met Reuben's lips. He clenched his fists but slowly opened his mouth. The powder spilled across his tongue, and he grimaced, though Charis couldn't tell if it was from pain or from the taste.

The entire room seemed to hold its breath as Reuben struggled to swallow the gritty dust. Finally he opened his mouth for the captain to see that the powder had gone down harmlessly. Charis slowly unclenched her hands, relieved. It didn't affect humans the way it affected the Rakuuna. That gave Nalani more options for the barrels of poison Orayn was bringing her.

Slowly the captain swung his face from Reuben to Charis. His head swiveled to the side as he studied her for a long moment. She kept her hands open and her expression neutral, though her mind was racing.

He wasn't convinced.

"Search other rooms," he said to his crew.

Behind him, Ayve made an awful gurgling noise in the back of her throat and slumped against the floor.

"May we tend our wounded?" Tal asked in the soft, nonthreatening voice he'd used to lure Hildy from her hiding place in the orchard where he and Charis had found her.

The captain shifted his focus to Tal. "That one touch stew." He pointed to Ayve.

"She was helping in the kitchen this morning," Tal said. "But you've seen for yourself that we have no way to hurt you—"

"Hurt!" The Rakuuna grabbed Tal's chin and wrenched his face toward the sight of the two now-dead Rakuuna with their throats still oozing black blood. "Never before."

"Can we help?" Dec asked. His voice was as quiet and controlled as always, but there was a tension in his body Charis had never seen before.

He was scared the captain was going to kill the prince he was supposed to protect.

"Two dead Rakuuna," the captain said in a voice as vicious as Charis at her best. "Two dead human. Same."

"Same," Tal agreed.

The other Rakuuna returned to the room and spoke in their own language to the captain. Abruptly, the captain released Tal and turned back to Charis.

"No more up here. Live below."

Before she could respond, the Rakuuna grabbed them and hauled them into the corridor where her other crew members were already lined up waiting. In moments, they'd all been dragged into the belly of the ship and locked in the brig.

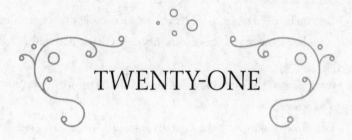

TWENTY-ONE

Days turned into weeks as the ship sailed south with the Calerans trapped in its belly. It was hard to keep track of time in the brig. There were no windows in the long, rectangular cage that spanned half the length of the ship. Moldy mattresses and thin, rough blankets were scattered about, and there was a privy pail and a small table with two chairs bolted to the floor.

Charis estimated they'd been down there for nearly three weeks. They had to be getting close to making port in Calera, and the chasm that had opened within her the night of the invasion felt large enough to swallow her whole. Every hour that passed seemed to tighten the pressure in her chest, until her heartbeat was frantic, feverish.

She would see her kingdom again.

And then she would die.

At least she'd be with her parents again soon. But before that happened, she had to be sure Nalani had the information about what the Rakuuna were after and why, and about how to use the poison. And, seers curse him, the only person in the brig she was sure the Rakuuna queen didn't plan to kill was Tal.

King Alaric might not have rescued his youngest son, but even the Rakuuna must understand that murdering the son of the man you hope to extort jewels from was a poor strategic decision.

That meant that Charis and Tal needed to have a conversation, something she'd been avoiding at all costs. However, ignoring him because she didn't want to appear vulnerable was one thing. Refusing to talk to him when he could help her keep her promises to her people would be foolish.

As most of the crew settled onto their mattresses for yet another period of rest—they had no idea if it was dark outside—Charis forced herself to approach Tal and say quietly, "Would you join me at the table?"

Instantly he was on his feet and moving toward the small table, where an assortment of discarded objects were strewn. Bits of fishing net, wire hooks, torn burlap sacks, and a few rusted tools—nothing helpful. The satchel Reuben had returned to her with its small amount of moriarthy dust was the only useful weapon in the entire brig.

She settled into a chair, expecting Tal to sit opposite her. Instead he leaned against the table itself, just to her left.

"We should reach Calera soon," she said, her tone as impersonal as she could manage.

"I owe you an explanation."

She stiffened. "That's not what I asked you here to talk about. Nothing you can say will change what you did."

"I know."

"So what's the point of discussing it?" She pressed her hands against the table as if to stand and walk away, her mouth suddenly dry.

"Afraid you might not be able to stay mad at me?" He threw the challenge at her and waited.

"No."

She'd yet to walk away. He didn't waste any time.

"I was ordered by my father to become a spy in the Caleran palace because I have an ear for languages and could speak with a flawless northern Caleran accent and because having spent my life around royalty, I knew how to behave." He swallowed as though it was difficult to force himself to speak the entire truth. "I suspect that my father expected me to get myself killed, which would save him the trouble of dealing with the son he's always hated."

She sniffed and looked away.

"I was supposed to get as close to the royal family—your family—as possible. Father wanted information that would help him bring the war to an end."

Her eyes narrowed. "And the information you gave him inspired him to destroy an entire farming village despite the fact that there were no soldiers present?" She turned on him. "You remember Irridusk, don't you? You visited the refugee camp there. You met the survivors—old women, a few children—and heard how the rest of their families were slaughtered like animals."

His voice shook. "I didn't have anything to do with that. I'd only been your bodyguard for a few weeks at that point, and I hadn't passed on any information other than that you were driven to be everything your mother expected you to be and that removing the queen wouldn't give my father an easier road to victory as he'd assumed."

"And I'm just supposed to take your word for that?" Her chin rose, and she pointed a finger at him. "You're a liar."

"I *became* a liar." He sounded like he was in agony. "I had to be if I wanted to survive. I was simply following orders."

"If that's supposed to make me feel better—"

"You would have done the same thing if you were in my place. Why can't you see that?"

She glared at him. "Because it isn't true."

He threw his hands in the air. "If your mother had ordered you to go undercover as a spy in my father's keep, you would have done it. No hesitation."

"That's not the same thing."

"It's not—I was following orders! Just like you would have done."

"Did you really follow orders?" She stood, a strange energy vibrating through her, and Tal rolled to the balls of his feet as if anticipating an attack. "Or did you improvise? Because I've met Alaric, and I don't think he has the imagination to design the kind of betrayal you—"

"What would you have had me do differently?" Now he was the one taking a step forward, frustration practically humming off him. "Disobey my father—my *king*? Become a traitor to my kingdom and my family and end up with my head on a pole? Or maybe you think your mother was the only parent in this equation who demanded absolute obedience. Charis, trust me, if you'd been sent to spy on me in Montevallo, you'd have done whatever it took to fulfill your mother's expectations."

"I wouldn't have taken your heart." Her words sliced through the air, tipped in agony, bleeding regret. He looked as though she'd struck him.

"I *tried*." Pain filled his voice. "I expected to see you as nothing more than Calera's formidable, warmongering princess. And you lived up to those expectations beautifully for a week or two. But then . . . then you weren't eating or sleeping well. You were having nightmares when you did sleep. You were taking care of everyone else at the expense of yourself, and it became increasingly clear that you cared deeply about your kingdom and about stopping the war."

She opened her mouth to argue, then snapped it closed and watched him warily. He ran a hand through his hair and leaned against the table as if suddenly exhausted.

"I thought it would be all right to be your friend. Someone needed to watch out for you the way a friend does, and I told myself it was my job. That, somehow, I could be what Father expected of me and also be what you needed." He scrubbed his hand over his face and looked at the floor. "I didn't realize how far gone I was until I learned about your betrothal to Vahn." His lips twisted. "I stood there in the war room near you, my heart bleeding in my chest like the fool I am as you announced what you'd done to secure a treaty."

She was quiet for a moment as she sorted through his words, hunting for lies. Finally she said, "You stopped talking to me for nearly two weeks after that."

"I was terrified." He met her gaze without flinching, though she could see that baring his heart like this was costing him. "I should have been excited and happy about the treaty. My people would finally have port access. No more starvation or being forced into the army to risk their lives fighting Calera. I would be able to go home and resume my normal life again."

Slowly she sank back into the chair, still watching him as though at any moment he might make a sudden move.

He hesitated, and a faint pink flushed his cheeks. Then he said, "I didn't feel happy. I felt like you'd just reached into my chest and cut out my heart."

The silence that followed his words was punctuated by the mast creaking and the dull slap of water against the boat.

"You should have either told me the truth or walked away," she said quietly.

"I know." He looked into her eyes, and she couldn't find any deception. "I was selfish. I wanted to stay at your side, and I kept convincing myself I had more time before I told you the truth. If I'd just trusted you with it instead—"

"You'd probably be dead."

"It's a good possibility."

"If Mother had learned of it, it's the only possibility."

"I never intended to hurt you. I might have hidden my true identity from you, but I never hid *myself*." He let his hands fall to his sides. "You know me better than anyone else, and so someday I hope you look beyond my name and my job and see my heart, because in there, I'm exactly who I've always been—just a boy in love with a girl he knew he could never have."

His words settled between them, and she waited for him to ask her for more. For forgiveness, for understanding, or at the very least for an explanation of her own feelings, but he didn't. Instead he gave her a sad, crooked smile and sat across from her.

"You called me over here for a reason. What do you need?"

For the next hour they strategized, and it was infuriating how easy it was to fall back into old patterns. She could still finish his thoughts. He could still anticipate hers. They could fill in the gaps between words with a single look.

By the time she was ready to rest, she was certain that if she was unable to get a message to Nalani herself, Tal knew exactly what to say. The armada would know how to use the poison, and Tal's time spent helping in the sick bay had given him insight into exactly the kind of desperate situation the Rakuuna queen was facing, which Nalani could use to pressure the queen into taking whatever deal Alaric offered once Nalani agreed to marry Vahn.

Maybe Charis couldn't trust Tal with her heart again, but she could trust him with this. He'd traded his own life for the safety of her people. This asked far less of him.

Three days later, the boat slowed noticeably. A flurry of hushed conversation erupted throughout the brig.

"We must be entering Arborlay's harbor," Tal said as he and Holland approached Charis.

Her knees threatened to give out.

All this time, she'd been running toward vengeance because saving her kingdom was all she had left. Now, faced with the real possibility that she'd done everything she could to keep her promises yet wouldn't be alive to see it through, pain spread through her, tender and raw.

She'd never see the streets of her city lit for the Sister Moons Festival again.

She wouldn't have children she could nurture like Father had nurtured her.

She'd never dance again, kiss again, sink her teeth into a ripe summer peach and let its juices run down her chin.

But maybe, if her last act was to make sure her people and their allies could drive the invaders from her land, she would be remembered as the young queen who gave everything she had to Calera.

She rolled her shoulders and craned her neck, trying to loosen knots of tension.

"What's the plan for meeting the Rakuuna queen?" Tal was watching her carefully, and she stopped trying to release the knots in her shoulders.

"I'll do what I can to appeal to her desire to have power in Calera and to save the Rakuuna who are sick." She couldn't resist stretching her stiff neck once more. "If I can manage it, she'll honor you for being Alaric's son, and you can do what we discussed."

"Would you like me to help with that?" Tal gestured toward her neck.

She lifted her chin, ignoring the angry pull of her muscles. "Absolutely not."

"I mean no disrespect. I just thought perhaps you'd want to look more . . . royal when you arrive." He glanced once more at her. Heat flushed her skin as she realized he'd been talking about her wild mess of tangled hair.

"He's right." Holland gave her a long look. "You've been without a handmaiden for quite some time, and it shows. Let him help you at least look like the queen you are. I'm going to go make sure the others know that if they reveal the truth about the poison, I'll gut them where they stand."

Charis met Tal's gaze, and the heat beneath her skin spiraled into her belly.

Somehow the thought of him doing her hair was even more daunting than the idea of him rubbing her neck, but he and Holland had a point. She didn't want to meet the invader queen looking like a vagabond who'd never seen a hairbrush.

"I'm ready to be of service. Unless you'd rather Holland try his luck." He quirked one eyebrow, and she sighed.

"Fine. It's not like you can do much anyway. There are no supplies in the brig."

"Hmm." He was already hunting through the small stash of fishing gear on the table, muttering under his breath.

Moments later, Charis was seated, with Tal standing behind her, an assortment of objects strewn at his feet. As he began gently tugging his fingers through her snarled curls, untangling them bit by bit, she checked and double-checked her nails as if it was the most important thing in the world, despite the fact that she'd already cleaned them as much as was possible in her current situation.

If she closed her eyes, she could almost be back in her chambers in the palace, seated at her vanity, while Tal undid whatever monstrosity of a hairdo her older handmaiden Mrs. Sykes had given her. Laughing at his jokes. Leaning against the solid warmth of his chest. Feeling something deliciously fizzy spread through her veins as he whispered against her ear.

She wanted to tell herself those moments were lies. The callous game of an expert spy.

But if she believed Tal's story of accidentally falling in love with her, then those moments were real and precious and gone forever.

She wasn't sure which was worse.

Her eyes stung with unshed tears, and the table blurred as she tried to blink them away. Behind her, Tal stilled, his hands wrapped in her hair, and then he said quietly, "Do you remember when Mrs. Sykes put your hair up in that awful bun? You looked like someone's grand-mother. The kind that smacks your hand if you reach for a cookie."

She drew in a shaky breath and said nothing. He began scooping her curls toward the top of her head.

"Or that time when I still hadn't admitted to myself how much I wanted to be with you, and you wore that dress, and I walked into the bath chamber, took one look at you, and forgot how to talk in complete sentences?"

"I don't want to do this." She'd meant to sound firm and com-manding, but her voice wavered with grief.

"I'm almost done." He bent to grab some things from the floor and then resumed work on her hair.

"I meant . . . I don't want to remember." The table blurred again, and she blinked furiously before any tears could fall.

He was silent for a long moment as he worked on her hair. Then, letting his hands rest on her shoulders, he said softly against her ear, "And I don't want to forget."

His breath warmed her neck, and his fingers traced a gentle pattern against her skin. Something warm unfurled in her belly and spread, leaving a trail of heat in her veins. A slight tip of her head, and she could lean against him. A small turn of her chin, and her mouth would be next to his.

"Charis." He whispered her name, his lips grazing her earlobe, and she tilted her face toward him.

For a long moment, his lips hovered a breath away from hers. Nothing existed but the heat of his skin and the delicate ache of longing within her.

Then Holland barked an instruction to Grim, and Charis was suddenly, exquisitely aware that she had an audience and that she'd nearly made the foolish choice to give in to her attraction to Tal.

She leaned away from him. Before she could figure out what to say, he stepped around to face her, looked her over with a critical eye, and said, "It isn't the fanciest updo I've ever managed, but it will do." His cheeks were pink, and he sounded out of breath. The warmth in his eyes as he looked at her sent another spiral of heat through her veins.

Quickly, she reached up to pat her hair and found her curls arranged beneath a small length of fish net and secured with hooks bent into coiled hairpins. Casting about for something, *anything*, that would steer the conversation into safer territory, she said, "If being a spy doesn't work out, you could always be a hairdresser."

He leaned toward her and said with sudden ferocity, "You aren't going to die today, Charis Willowthorn. You're a force of nature. You're faster, smarter, and stronger than anyone who comes against you. Don't you dare walk into that palace thinking you don't have options."

He wrapped his hand around hers and squeezed. "There are always options. Always one more strategy that you can see, even if no one else can. When you meet their queen, remember who you are. The only person who should be terrified today is the invader sitting on your throne."

The ship bumped up against the pier with a jolt. Above them, the door opened, and the slap of a Rakuuna's steps echoed from the stairs.

The chaos within her steadied as she held Tal's gaze. He believed in her, and despite how much pain it brought her to admit it, he knew her best. "Thank you," she said before she lost the courage to allow him to see that his words had helped.

As a Rakuuna opened the brig and ordered the humans to leave the ship in a single file line, Charis raised her chin and strode toward her destiny.

TWENTY-TWO

Rain swept the streets of Arborlay in silvery sheets as Charis, Holland, Tal, and Grim rode in the carriage provided by the Rakuuna guards who'd greeted the ship at the dock. Burk, the other surviving Caleran crew member, followed in a separate carriage with Reuben, who was clearly worried that he was needed beside his queen.

Charis recognized the boy who drove her carriage. Before the invasion he'd been a groom in training at the palace. She'd tried to make eye contact with him, but he'd stared at his boots, his shoulders hunched against the rain.

Was he still willing to be loyal to the true heirs of Calera's throne, even if it meant risking his life? Or was the fact that he worked for the Rakuuna proof that he'd refused to join the rebellion?

"Good to know those monsters are still afraid of horses," Grim said from his place beside Tal. His freckled forehead seemed permanently wrinkled in a frown as he peered out the carriage window. "Can't even drive the carriages."

Charis glanced out the window and shuddered at the sight of a trio of tall Rakuuna guards walking a short distance away from the vehicle, clearly keeping pace with the cargo inside while still remaining safely away from the horses. Their too-long limbs moved in graceful tandem. Every few steps, their black eyes would flick toward the carriage, as though making sure the humans inside hadn't tried to escape.

Beyond the creatures, the hazy outline of Arborlay's buildings was a dark smudge through the curtain of rain. Charis leaned closer and drank in the sight, somehow feeling more homesick now that she was back in her kingdom than she had at sea.

There, just past the line of warehouses that hugged the dock, were the elegant lines of the merchant sector, their shops closed now due to the weather. Thesserin trees bent before the wind, their slender branches stripped of their golden leaves. And in the distance, just visible in the shifting light of the storm, the narrow steeple of the seers' temple pierced the iron-gray sky.

"Maybe we can make a run for the palace stables." Holland leaned forward as if he planned to leap into action. "I'll tell the coachman to keep going—"

"If the simple act of riding horses was enough to overthrow our enemies, don't you think the people here would've already done it?" Tal's voice was sharp. Charis tore her gaze from the window. His hands were clenched into fists.

He was scared.

"I don't see you coming up with any brilliant ideas, impostor." Holland swept his hair out of his face, a quick, impatient movement that usually meant his mood was balanced precariously on a knife's edge.

He was scared, too.

She couldn't blame them. The thought of facing the Rakuuna queen made her feel as though snakes were squirming in the pit of her stomach. There was nothing Charis could do about her own situation beyond hoping she could somehow convince the queen she was more useful to her alive than publicly executed to put an end to the rebellion. However, Tal should have nothing to worry about, and if Charis could convince Holland to lie for once in his life, he could be safe, too.

Abandoning the temptation to stare at her rain-soaked city, she reached for the icy control that usually had people rushing to do what she asked. "All of you need to take a deep breath and stop looking like you're about to face your own beheading. We can't go into the palace like whipped dogs afraid of our fates. I'm the one the queen needs to kill. If you each do exactly as I say, you'll be safe." She hoped.

Three pairs of eyes swiveled to meet hers. Grim seemed confused. Holland was clearly offended. And Tal looked furious.

Charis ignored their expressions. "Grim, once you leave the carriage, speak nothing but Montevallian and stick close to Tal. Have Dec do the same. It will be clear that you're his guards, and that you aren't Caleran."

Before he could reply, she turned to Holland. "You can either use your Solvanish family's last name and pretend to be an envoy from Solvang sent to supervise my trip to the northern kingdoms—"

"You want me to act like a diplomat?" His lips curled into a sneer.

"Or you can speak your best Montevallian and pretend to be one of Tal's guards. Either way, as long as the Rakuuna queen doesn't realize you're my heir, you'll be safe. If the captain who took us tells her I said my entire crew was related to me, I'll tell her he didn't understand enough Caleran to translate my words properly."

He opened his mouth as if to argue, but she was already turning toward Tal. "And you have nothing to worry about."

"Really?" His tone matched his furious expression.

"If the Rakuuna wanted you dead, you'd be dead already. It doesn't serve the queen to kill you when doing so would jeopardize her ability to get your father to give her the serpanicite she wants. You'll be safe."

"Safe." He threw the word at her.

"Yes. Safe." She turned back to the window. If this was her last trip through Arborlay, she didn't want to miss a single chimney, window box, or cobblestone.

"Do you want to explain reality to her, or should I?" Tal asked.

"You can have that pleasure." Holland sounded like he had the night his mother had insisted he dance with at least seven girls before slinking off to the palace armory to admire the Willowthorns' cache of weapons. "But I want it noted that being aligned with you is highly uncomfortable for me, and I'd appreciate it if we could go back to being sworn enemies at our earliest convenience."

"Of course," Tal said.

Charis ignored them. The road curved gently before beginning its steady ascent to the distant palace. She didn't have much time left. Either she was going to talk her way out of this, or she was going to die. She'd thought there would be a small measure of peace at the thought of silencing the ruin within her and leaving this mess for others to clean up. But there was nothing but the frantic thudding of her heart and a desperate desire to stay alive, even though it hurt.

The carriage creaked as someone opposite her adjusted themselves—she didn't look to see if it was Grim or Tal. As the carriage rounded another bend in the road, the white stone palace with its narrow turrets and tall windows came into view.

Charis's hands began to shake.

Something creaked again, and then Tal was on his knees in front of her, his brown eyes finding hers and holding.

She frowned and drew back, but he didn't reach for her. Instead he said with quiet intensity, "We aren't worried about our own safety, Charis. We're scared of losing *you*."

Her throat tightened, and she glanced sideways to find Holland glaring at her. He made another impatient gesture and said, "Obviously."

"You don't have to—that's very . . . It's not good strategy to prioritize me." She looked back at Tal and found him leaning close in a way that used to make something warm and tender bloom within her. Now it made her heart beat a little faster.

"Not good strategy?" Holland's voice rose. "Well then, that takes care of it. How foolish of us to care about you when, strategically, we ought to turn our loyalty to someone else."

"You should!" She turned to him, grateful to avoid Tal's gaze, which had gone from furious to wounded. "I will either survive my encounter with the Rakuuna queen, or I won't. Nothing you do now will change that. The fate of Calera is what truly matters, and that deserves all your focus."

"No." Holland sounded mutinous.

"We can care about both." Tal's voice was gentle as he took her cold, shaking hands in his and squeezed gently. When she whipped around to face him, he held her gaze, waiting, clearly ready to let go of her if that's what she wanted.

It *should* be what she wanted. He'd broken her heart and betrayed her trust. Leaning on him for comfort before facing her enemy was exactly the sort of weakness Mother had tried so hard to stamp out of her daughter. She stiffened and reached for the cold rage that she'd always associated with Mother.

This time there was nothing but the growing ache within and the memory of Father's blue eyes lighting up when he talked to Tal.

Father had trusted Tal. More than that, he'd loved him. And while Father hadn't been half the political strategist Mother was, he'd been an excellent judge of what mattered most to him: people's hearts.

He'd thought Tal had a good heart.

And if Charis was honest, so did she. Despite the pain, the betrayal, and the loss of trust, she believed Tal when he said he hadn't shared personal details with his father. She believed him when he said he'd shown her who he truly was, even if he'd lied about his name.

It didn't heal the wound he'd dealt her, but it did stem the bleeding. And right now, about to face the enemy queen with nothing but her wits to keep herself alive, Charis couldn't force herself to refuse the comfort of those who cared about her fate.

When she didn't pull away, Tal's grip firmed. As the carriage drove into the palace's inner courtyard and turned onto the semicircle drive that would take them to the entrance, he said with quiet intensity, "I've watched you manipulate a room full of contentious nobles into doing exactly what you want while believing it's their own idea. I've seen you turn grown men into quivering fools. And I witnessed you terrify an assassin into telling you the truth with nothing but the threat of what you *might* do when you left her cell. The Rakuuna have a physical advantage here, but no one can outthink you."

"He's right." Holland bumped his shoulder against hers as the carriage slowed. "You're as smart as your mother, and you can be just as scary when you want to be."

Charis swallowed against the sudden dryness in her mouth. "They're monsters."

"They're political opponents who want something. Figure out

how to use that against them, and you'll have the leverage you need." Tal leaned closer, until his breath fanned the chilled skin of her hands. "Nobody uses leverage better than you, Charis."

Her thoughts felt as slippery as vapor as the carriage creaked to a stop. She didn't know how to convince the Rakuuna queen of anything. Nothing about their invasion made sense. Destroying Calera just to put pressure on Alaric in Montevallo wasn't a viable strategy, no matter how often Charis examined it.

The air in her lungs thinned, and lights danced at the edge of her vision.

She had no leverage. No trick up her sleeve she could pull when the timing was right. She had nothing but the hope that she could deflect attention away from Holland and the rest of her crew and somehow talk her way out of an execution.

"You're going to be all right." Tal's voice was fierce as he let go of her hands and hauled her against his chest instead. He pressed his cheek to the crown of her head. "Remember who you are. Be everything your mother trained you to be."

A loud, haunting cry rose from the courtyard as one of the Rakuuna who'd escorted the carriage announced their arrival. Charis dragged in a thin, shaky breath and leaned against the solid warmth of Tal's chest.

She could despise herself for this weakness later—if she was still alive.

"You know how to make yourself invaluable to the Rakuuna." Tal pulled back slowly as their coachman dismounted from his perch. "If nothing else, they should keep you alive just so that my father will pay the ransom to ensure there's still a marriage treaty that allows Vahn to sit on Calera's throne."

"Calera only has one throne." The words were a reflex. Muscle memory from years of Mother's rigid expectations. Yet as soon as they left her lips, a flicker of rage kindled to life in the corner of her heart again.

"And whose throne is it?" Tal's eyes burned into hers, his expression fierce.

Her spine straightened. Her chin lifted. The rage within burned brighter, and somehow that made it easier to breathe.

"Whose throne is it?" Tal repeated.

She imagined a crown on her head as she stood over the bodies of her enemies. *"Mine."*

The door was wrenched open, and a long, scaly arm reached into the carriage, wrapped around Charis's hand, and yanked her forward. Tal yelled, and Holland lunged for the doorway as though planning to fight the creature, but the Rakuuna was faster and stronger. She pulled Charis into the courtyard and began dragging her up the steps to the palace.

"I can walk." Charis drew herself upright with the dignity befitting Calera's queen.

The Rakuuna chattered at her in their language, and Charis laughed with every ounce of viciousness she possessed. When the creature paused at the top of the steps to stare at Charis, black eyes unblinking, Charis reached out and deliberately peeled the monster's fingers away from her hand, one talon at a time.

"A queen does not enter her palace like a criminal." Her tone was polished marble.

Let them kill her. Let them sear her name into the mind and heart of her people so that she would forever be the battle cry that roused every Caleran from their slumber and sent them racing toward their enemies with fire in their bellies. Let them believe her death would end the rebellion instead of igniting it into a firestorm they had no hope of containing.

Charis would face every second of her fate like the queen she was born to be.

"It comes with us," the creature hissed, reaching for her hand again.

Charis slapped the Rakuuna's face.

The creature recoiled, chattering rapidly, but Charis ignored her as she swept into the palace, the hairs on the back of her neck standing on edge as she braced for the retaliation sure to come.

"I've come to see your queen," she announced to a Rakuuna who stood just inside the door, his pale skin dotted with silvery gray scales. "Where is she?"

Behind her, the Rakuuna she'd struck was still chattering, and others were joining in. Perhaps urging her to retaliate? Perhaps warning her that only the queen got the pleasure of killing Charis?

Either way, their focus was wholly on her and not on the rest of her people.

Silently willing Holland, Tal, and Grim to instruct the others on what to say to put distance between themselves and the idea that they were part of her bloodline, Charis glared at the Rakuuna who stood before her.

"Where is she? Or should I simply search the palace myself?"

His pale lips curved into a snarl, revealing his double row of fangs. "No queen," he said in heavily accented Caleran.

Charis blinked, her thoughts racing. No queen? Was she gone from Calera? Or simply not at the palace right now?

"Too late."

"Is she dead? My condolences." Her words were spun sugar dipped in venom.

The Rakuuna made a sound that reminded Charis of the howling wind in a snowstorm. It took a moment to realize he was laughing. The sound sent a chill down her spine.

"She is not the queen who dies," he said. He turned to gesture for someone behind him to come forward. "The day is too late. You see our queen tomorrow."

Charis glanced at the wall of windows that graced the entrance hall. Rain still fell in thick sheets, reducing visibility to almost nothing. Still, it looked darker than it had before. She'd lost track of time completely in the ship's brig. If it was twilight, the Rakuuna queen would want to wait until the storm passed and there was enough light that the audience she would surely compel to attend Charis's execution got a good look at the symbol of their rebellion before she died.

"Tomorrow." The Rakuuna smiled at her as though she was a delicacy offered on a buffet table to a slew of ravenous beasts. "Take her." He stepped aside to reveal a woman with dark red hair, a disheveled apron across her palace maid uniform, and a bruise blooming along her left cheekbone.

The maid scurried forward, chin tucked toward her collarbone as though anticipating a blow, and whispered, "Please come with me."

Charis went. There would be no getting information from the Rakuuna in the entrance hall, and he might punish the maid for any defiance on Charis's part.

The maid remained silent, moving so quickly that Charis had to lengthen her stride to keep up. They moved down the main corridor, past the ballroom, up one set of stairs, and then followed a curved corridor until they reached the southern wing, the one Mother had always reserved for guests.

Rakuuna were everywhere. Lingering in hallways. Standing on

the stairs. Posted outside the door leading to the southern wing's suite of rooms.

There would be no escape through the palace.

The maid escorted her past the Rakuuna guards and down the hallway, to the fifth door on the left. Behind her, the rest of her people were being herded into the hallway as well. Tal and Reuben immediately rushed to Charis's side. Holland took one look at the room a different maid offered to him, Dec, Grim, and Burk and joined Charis as well.

"Thank you," Charis said to the maid beside her, keeping her voice low so the guards standing just outside the wing's entrance couldn't hear her. "How many humans are working in the palace? And do you know how to get in contact with any of my mother's royal council members?"

If she could find a way to send Lord Thorsby a message, she could make sure the rebellion connected with Nalani and saw this fight through to the bitter end.

A whisper of sound came from the guards, and the maid quickly shook her head. Flinging the door open, she ushered them inside, lit a lamp resting on a table just inside the entrance, and then rushed from the room, closing the door behind them without saying another word.

Charis stood for a long moment, shoulders stiff, body braced, while Tal and Holland hurried to light sconces along the walls of what turned out to be a suite of three rooms with a small sitting area and bath chamber. Reuben assigned himself the couch in the sitting area where he could watch the door in case anyone came for Charis. Holland and Tal each took a small bedroom, leaving Charis with the larger room at the back of the suite.

She told them she was too tired to have a lengthy discussion about their situation and ordered them all to get some sleep. And then she shut the door to her room with shaking hands, moved to her bedside, and collapsed to her knees, burying her face in the soft coverlet atop her bed.

She was back home in familiar territory.

She had a group of loyal Calerans rebelling against the enemy.

She had a supply of moriarthy dust somewhere out at sea.

And she had no idea how to use any of it to convince the Rakuuna queen to keep her alive.

TWENTY-THREE

DAWN WAS A faint splinter of gold outside her window as Charis awakened from a fitful slumber. She'd dreamed of monsters and blood and the unforgiving depths of the sea dragging her to her fate.

Shivering as the remains of her nightmares crept back into the shadows of her mind, she stretched and climbed out of bed, moving as silently as possible.

Where were the Rakuuna guards? Outside the wing? Outside her door? It had been nearly impossible to fall asleep knowing they could come for her at any moment. The idea of washing and then getting herself dressed with that threat hanging over her head sent her stomach churning.

Reuben was snoring on the sitting room couch, his sword hand clenched as though he imagined he still held a blade. The Rakuuna had confiscated all weapons upon their arrival in the palace. Perhaps the queen, unlike the ship captain, now had enough experience with humans to realize that even when the odds were against them, people were courageous and foolish enough to fight for their freedom.

The doors to Holland's and Tal's rooms were still closed. Charis slipped into the bath chamber, quietly closing the door behind her. Her fingers shook as she lifted the lid on the chamber pot, straining to hear any hint of sound.

When would the Rakuuna queen send for her? And would Charis be summoned alone, or would Holland and the other Calerans who'd been with her be punished as well?

When she'd finished with the chamber pot, she crept to the sink and turned the water on low. She was nearly finished washing her hands when she finally found the courage to look in the mirror.

It was like looking at a stranger.

She was pale and gaunt with hollow cheeks and smudges of exhaustion beneath her eyes. Her brown curls tumbled wildly, and her body appeared to be carved from paper-thin stone, all sharp lines and blunt edges.

Slowly she straightened her shoulders. Appearances no longer mattered. Only strategy remained.

The Rakuuna queen might believe she was summoning a defeated rival to her execution, but Charis had to prove her wrong. Charis knew how to read situations, detect lies, and exploit the tiniest of openings. She could negotiate with a vengeance and gain more for her people than her opponent even realized she'd given up.

And even if Charis couldn't convince her enemy to let her live, all she needed was to get a message to the leaders of the rebellion. If they exchanged pallorens with Nalani in code, they could set up an invasion of their own, using the moriarthy dust to obliterate the Rakuuna. Holland and Tal would see that the message was sent, even if Charis wasn't able to do so herself, so long as one of them survived.

Quickly she bathed herself, scrubbing at the dirt beneath her fingernails and attacking her snarled curls with a wide-tooth comb. The closet in her room had a sparse selection of clothing for both men and women. Charis chose a blue velvet dress with a belt made of tiny silver interlocking links. She'd just tucked her curls behind her ears and straightened the belt when someone opened the suite's door.

For an instant, time seemed to hold its breath.

Then, as Charis stepped from her bedroom, doing her best to wear an expression fit for a queen, Tal and Holland flung their doors open and rushed into the sitting room, each brandishing a makeshift weapon. Tal had an iron fire poker. Holland had what looked like a bedpost he'd snapped in half. Neither of them was wearing a shirt.

Reuben lunged off the sofa and snatched something from the floor. Charis frowned as her guard whipped his weapon into the air. Was that a *curtain rod*? Her lips lifted slightly.

The Rakuuna queen may have taken her people's blades, but their courage was out of her reach.

A pair of Rakuuna guards entered the suite, ducking to avoid hitting their heads on the doorjambs. Their lips were peeled away from their fangs in a snarl, and their black eyes swept the room before landing on Charis.

"It comes with us." The female guard stepped forward, only to draw up short as Reuben slapped the curtain rod against her stomach. "Stupid human." She batted the rod away, sending Reuben stumbling into the side of the sofa.

Tal and Holland lunged forward, throwing themselves between Charis and the advancing guards. "Not today!" Holland whipped his broken bedpost into the air.

The male guard sniffed scornfully. "Can't stop us or it dies."

Charis's hands began to shake as Tal swept into the first rathma position while Holland looked one second away from charging the Rakuuna. They were committed to defending her, but it was going to cost them their lives.

"I'll go." Her voice cracked, and she cleared her throat as every gaze in the room found hers.

"Absolutely not." Holland glared at her.

"I agree with Holland." Tal rolled to the balls of his feet.

The female Rakuuna strode forward, clawed hands extended, fury on her face. Hastily, Charis said, "I'll go peacefully. Stand down."

"Charis—"

"I mean it, Holland." She skewered him with a look designed to shut him up, for all the good that ever did. "Stay alive."

"You stay alive," he muttered, his bedpost still raised threateningly.

"No more time." The male Rakuuna leaped forward, slammed into Holland, and sent him spinning into Tal. Both of them hit the wall beside Charis's bedroom door. "It comes with us."

"I am coming." Charis's voice shook. "Leave them alone."

There was a commotion at the suite doorway, and then Dec and Grim raced into the room, headed for Tal. The male Rakuuna turned to face them as Tal yelled at them to stop before they got themselves killed.

Look who was dishing out the same order he'd failed to obey when it came from Charis.

"Bring them all." Another Rakuuna entered the suite, her gray-white hair flowing down her back, her skin so translucent, the threads of blood beneath its surface resembled thin, black snakes.

"Go peacefully," Charis said before Holland could finish climbing to his feet. He gave her a mutinous look, but then Tal clapped a hand on his shoulder and steered him toward the corridor, speaking quietly in his ear.

Moments later, Charis, flanked by Reuben and Holland, left the southern wing and headed toward the center of the palace, following the first guard who'd entered the room. Tal, with Dec and Grim on either side, was on her heels, and the male guard took up the rear.

They passed guards at every turn. Charis's skin crawled at the way their black eyes watched her while they spoke to each other in their language. Desperately, she reached for strategy.

What could she say to convince the queen to keep her alive?

What could she say to bargain for the lives of her people?

And what leverage could she use if all of that failed?

It didn't matter that she'd spent most of the night wrestling with those questions—she still didn't have answers that felt like a solid plan. Her chest pinched, making it harder to breathe.

Before she was ready for the confrontation, they were at the door that led to Mother's sitting room. There was no more time to strategize. There was only the painful thud of her heart, the smell of Mother's favorite dried herbs sitting in a dish on the table, and the sight of a tall, lithe Rakuuna with silver-blue scales in delicate patterns on her white skin, long white braids woven with blue beads, and a dull green crown of what looked like moss-covered metal on her head.

She was sitting in Mother's favorite chair.

The queen glared at Charis, and her thin lips peeled back into a snarl. A pair of guards stood on either side of her. The pinching in Charis's chest exploded into fury.

This was Mother's room.

Mother's chair.

Mother's kingdom.

And if not for the creature in the mossy crown, Mother would still be alive to rule it.

The female guard said, "I present Charis Willowthorn, Queen Bai'elsha."

"Renegade princess." Bai'elsha's words trailed off into a snakelike hiss. Her Caleran was accented but much clearer than her guards' or that of those on the ship.

Charis moved fully into the room, chin held high, thoughts sharp as knives as the guards herded her people against a side wall.

"Renegade *queen*." Charis strode forward, ignoring the way the Rakuuna's guards tensed in response. "And you are sitting in my chair."

There was a collective gasp from the side of the room, but Charis ignored it. There was nothing but Bai'elsha and the verbal duel Charis couldn't afford to lose.

"I earned this." The Rakuuna queen swept her taloned hands out to encompass the room.

"You stole it." Charis's voice shook with the heat of her anger.

"In my kingdom, if you kill the owners of a house, you get the house." The queen smiled, revealing both rows of fangs. "But of course, I haven't killed all the owners of Calera. Yet."

Charis took two steps forward and gracefully perched on the edge of the cream-colored chair opposite Queen Bai'elsha. Running her hand over the smooth marble surface of the coffee table between them, she tapped a fingernail against the base of the heavy crystal candlesticks Lady Channing gave Mother for her last birthday. Had she already decided to betray Mother then?

Meeting Bai'elsha's gaze, Charis said, "You won't get what you want from King Alaric if you kill me."

Bai'elsha's smile widened. "You know nothing of my business with King Alaric. He'd prefer you to be alive when he arrives, but he'll make do with the other heirs if necessary." Her eyes sparked with malice. "Let's see if it's necessary."

Charis's stomach plunged. This was it. The moment where she

either found a way out of this or died trying.

Cocking her head to the side, Bai'elsha studied Charis for a long moment. Charis crossed her legs as if nothing worried her and folded her hands in her lap. There was a faint ringing in her ears, and she had to remind herself to breathe.

"You are not scared?" Bai'elsha asked.

Charis was terrified. Heart pounding, mouth dry, palms damp. But showing her fear would gain her nothing.

"I do not cower before my enemies." Charis waited a beat and then said with confidence, "Neither do you."

The faster she could establish a connection between them, the faster she could shift the queen's intentions.

"No, I do not." Bai'elsha slid one taloned finger down the arm of Mother's chair. "Your people are loyal to you."

"As are yours to you." Charis cocked her head as though studying Bai'elsha the way the Rakuuna queen watched her.

"I recently put to death two people who tried to sabotage my ships. Members of this silly, doomed rebellion. They pleaded not for their own lives, but for yours." Bai'elsha's mouth curved into a sneer.

Was the scorn in her voice because she didn't respect a queen whose people spoke up on her behalf? Or was the sneer aimed at all Calerans?

"They understand that I'm of far more use to you alive." And please, *please* let that be true.

"An enemy without usefulness is best killed quickly." The queen rose to her feet, moving with startling quickness.

"I agree." Charis stood as well, praying that her shaking knees would hold her. There was a scuffle from the people lined up against the wall, and Tal said something in a voice Charis barely recognized, but Charis didn't look away from the Rakuuna queen.

Would Bai'elsha tear out her throat? Stab her in the heart? Or would she order one of her guards to do it?

Quickly she said, "I was never your enemy, Queen Bai'elsha. Why were you mine?"

Bai'elsha drew back as though startled, her watchful eyes flicking a glance toward the others against the wall before returning to Charis. "My people are dying. Without serpanicite, we will be gone in five years. Maybe less. What kind of queen would I be if I didn't do what was necessary to save them?"

"Then why not schedule an audience with my mother and present your case? You could have asked for help—"

"We did!" The queen's voice rose. "Your Lady Channing presented our request. It was denied." She swept out a hand to encompass the room again. "And now this is mine."

"Lady Channing did not tell me your people were dying, or that you needed a specific jewel from Montevallo to make medicine for them." Charis kept her voice even, though everything inside her wanted to scream. "And you had already begun sinking our ships before she ever came to us with your offer. You set yourself up as our enemy, but if you'd simply told us the truth, we would have welcomed you as a friend."

Bai'elsha leaped over the table to close the distance between them faster than Charis could blink. "You know *nothing*."

The Rakuuna queen whipped her hand into the air and wrapped long, taloned fingers around Charis's throat. Tal, Holland, and Reuben shouted in protest, and there was a brief skirmish as several Rakuuna guards rushed forward to keep them from getting to Charis.

Pain, sharp and biting, as the queen's talons sank beneath Charis's skin. She squeezed, and it was suddenly impossible to breathe. Charis's hands flailed, searching for a weapon. Her fingers brushed against the glass candlestick, and she grabbed it.

"I trusted your Lady Channing," the queen whispered against Charis's ear. "And this is the result."

Gray spots danced at the edge of Charis's vision. Lifting the candlestick, she smashed it against the table's edge and then thrust the broken shard she held into the queen.

Instantly, the Rakuuna let her go, her dry bones language spilling out of her as black blood poured from the wound on the back of her hand. Strong arms grabbed Charis from behind and the glass was yanked from her grasp.

Charis coughed as air flooded her lungs again, and then said quickly, "I could have stabbed you in the heart. I didn't."

"Weak." The Rakuuna queen glared at Charis, blood falling from her fingertips to stain Mother's rug.

"Strategic." Charis held the queen's gaze. "I don't wish to be your enemy. Your people can be saved, and so can mine."

For a long moment, Queen Bai'elsha glared, and the only sound was the steady *drip, drip, drip* of the Rakuuna's blood hitting the floor.

Finally, the Rakuuna queen said, "My kingdom will be saved. Stay in the palace. Do not cause problems. Otherwise, I will kill you."

Charis held herself still while hope, fragile and aching, bloomed within. She was still alive, and so were her people. Maybe everything would be all right. Once Alaric arrived and traded serpanicite for Charis, the Rakuuna would leave, and she could rebuild her kingdom.

"Take her to her chambers and lock her in." The queen turned away. "If she tries to escape, kill her."

Before Charis could utter another word, she was dragged from the room.

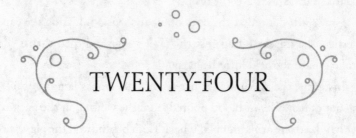

TWENTY-FOUR

FIFTEEN MINUTES LATER, Charis, Reuben, Holland, and Tal were back in their suite. Dec and Grim had attempted to stay with Tal, but the Rakuuna refused to allow it. Apparently, both boys had landed blows on the Rakuuna guard who'd subdued Tal, and their punishment was exile to their room.

"You survived," Holland announced as the door closed behind the guards, leaving the four of them alone. "Now what?"

"Now we keep our heads down until King Alaric arrives and makes the trade," Reuben said.

Before Charis could respond, someone knocked on the suite's door. Charis's stomach pinched.

Had Bai'elsha changed her mind? Or was Charis to be separated from her people the way Tal had been separated from Dec and Grim?

The knock sounded again, and Charis frowned as she met Tal's eyes. Why would the Rakuuna guards bother knocking? He nodded as if to say he'd been wondering the same thing. Quickly, he and Holland grabbed their makeshift weapons from where they'd been abandoned on the sitting room floor.

"Enter," Charis said as she rose to her feet, braced for disaster. Reuben instantly pivoted to put his body between hers and the door.

She still half expected one of the Rakuuna to enter, but instead her fourth cousin, Ferris Everly, walked in, his cheek bruised, and his blue eyes anxious.

"Charis!" He rushed toward her, his pale face looking drawn and weary. "Father said you'd returned, but I had to see it for myself."

Revulsion fought with relief at the sight of him. Relief won. Maybe Ferris had always been a thorn in her side, but his father was a respected member of the royal council, and despite his grasping, greedy nature, Ferris had taken the news of her betrothal treaty in stride, even though it meant his dreams of marrying her and becoming king consort were dashed.

In fact, his ability to quickly pivot to the most practical path forward reminded her a bit of herself. Maybe Ferris couldn't help his sense of entitlement when it came to holding a position of power in her kingdom. He was a product of his father's ambitions as much as Charis was a product of her mother's. It was possible she'd been too hard on him.

"You're looking . . ." His eyes wandered down to her bosom. "Underfed."

Then again, perhaps she'd been exactly as hard on him as he deserved.

"You'll watch how you speak to your queen, or I'll be happy to remove your tongue." Holland hefted his bedpost and glared at Ferris.

"Oh, wonderful, you returned with her." Sarcasm dripped from Ferris's words. "I suppose Nalani is going to have a few nasty things to say to me next. I swear by all the seers, if you Farragins had half an idea what those of us trapped here have been through, you'd shut your mouths."

"I don't have time for petty arguments today," Charis said.

Ferris took one look at her face and sketched a quick bow. "Forgive me, Your Highness—"

"Your Majesty."

He blinked and then said quickly, "Of course, Your Majesty. I apologize. I'm out of practice with court protocols. The Rakuuna queen has her own way of running things." He stared past Charis for a moment as though looking at something only he could see. A muscle along his jaw tightened.

Maybe he was odious on his best day, but he was right. Charis and her crew had no real idea what those who'd remained in Calera had been through.

Speaking in a gentler voice, she said, "Why are you in the palace, Ferris?"

"Father, Mother, and I live here now." His voice was bitter. "We're prisoners in this wing, along with all the Calerans Queen Bai'elsha is using as palace staff."

"Why would they want *you* around?" Holland looked baffled.

"Because we're useful," Ferris snapped. "You might try it sometime."

Holland waved the bedpost menacingly. "I volunteer to be of use right now. Your Majesty, permission to remove the pestilence from this room."

"Permission denied." Charis faced Ferris, whose cheeks had turned an unbecoming shade of pink. Tal moved around Holland to stand at Charis's side, his fire poker held like a sword.

Ferris's eyes widened. "Are you really going to let them treat me like a threat?" His voice rose. "My family came to the palace the morning after the invasion to find Queen Letha, King Edias, and *you*. Instead, we were greeted by monsters who assumed we were there to fight them for the throne. If Father and I hadn't managed to convince them we had the connections to act as a go-between for their negotiations with Montevallo, we'd be dead."

"I'm grateful you're still alive," Charis said calmly.

"But why did you come back?" Ferris sounded agitated. "You should've just kept running as far and as fast as you could."

Charis frowned. "We didn't return of our own accord. The Rakuuna hunted us down and captured us."

His shoulders slumped. "I was afraid of that."

"And I wasn't running, Ferris. I was getting help for our kingdom."

His eyes widened. "You have help for us?"

Perhaps the incredulity in his voice could be attributed to the horrors he'd witnessed in her absence. Or perhaps he'd never had enough faith in her from the start.

"I do." She just had to get a message to the rebellion so Nalani and the retired admiral who'd agreed to help Calera could coordinate with the admirals of Solvang, Thallis, and Verace in planning an attack on the Rakuuna.

"Father is going to want to hear all the details." Ferris glanced over his shoulder as the door opened to admit the redheaded maid from the night before carrying a tray with bowls of pumpkin porridge and a plate of spiced brandyberry muffins. "He's busy getting Mother's medicine, but he'll return soon. You can't imagine the lengths we have to go to now just to get medical supplies that used to be readily available."

"The Rakuuna allow your father to leave the palace?" Tal asked.

Ferris barely spared him a glance. "Don't be daft. We have a contact who knows how to get in and out of the palace without getting caught. Father is meeting him in the servants' quarters. Father and I would be missed if Queen Bai'elsha decides she needs us for something, but she doesn't even know he exists."

The maid carried the food past Charis, and her stomach pitched uneasily at the smell.

Holland snatched a muffin from the tray, and Ferris said something derogatory, prompting another argument.

Leaning close, Tal said softly, "Why did the Rakuuna need to negotiate anything with Father? Vahn already offered to pay whatever jewels the Rakuuna required. Father wanted port access and dignity for our people, which you gave him through the betrothal treaty. He should have willingly paid whatever price was needed to get the Rakuuna to leave."

"If he'd been willing to pay, then why would the Rakuuna have felt they needed you as a prisoner in the first place?" Charis whispered back.

"I don't know," Tal admitted as Holland offered to stuff Ferris's mouth full of porridge just to shut him up while Ferris swore that his father was going to hear about this.

"Maybe they asked for more than he has?" Charis caught the maid's eye and motioned her close while the boys continued to bicker over their breakfast.

"We've been without port access for nearly two decades, which means we've been without robust trade with other kingdoms." Tal caught the muffin Holland tossed his way. "Trust me, Father has more stockpiles of jewels mined from our mountains than he knows what to do with."

"What's your name?" Charis asked the maid as she curtsied. Tal handed Reuben the muffin and raised his hand to catch the next one Holland tossed.

"Lannibelle, Your Majesty, but most just call me Lanni." She shot a look over her shoulder at the door leading to the corridor beyond. "I can't stay. The guards expect me to keep delivering trays."

"Then I'll make this quick." Charis met the woman's eyes. "Where do your loyalties lie?"

A direct question, coming at an unexpected moment, always revealed the truth. Those with nothing to hide answered freely. Those with secrets fumbled or paused, even for an instant, as they chose their words with care.

"With you, Your Majesty." Lanni's eyes sparked with fervor, and she curtsied again. "As do those of many Calerans."

"Many?"

The maid's cheeks grew flushed, and her voice lowered until Charis had to lean forward to hear her. "There are . . . rumors that we would be better off without you because the Willowthorns caused the invasion."

"Where do those rumors come from?"

Lanni shrugged and glanced at the door again. "Your Majesty—"

"One last question, Lanni." Charis lowered her voice. If the Everlys had a contact who could sneak into and out of the palace, then there was hope that Tal or Holland could too. They could deliver the message to the rebellion and put Charis's plan in motion, but only if they knew where to go. Praying Lanni could help, Charis said, "If I needed to find Lord Thorsby, where would I go?"

Lanni's eyes widened. Quickly she whispered, "He is rumored to be with Lady Ollen, Your Majesty."

"At her house?"

Lanni frowned. "I think her house was destroyed. All I know is that she enjoys a good afternoon tea."

Tal choked on his bite of muffin. "How is that helpful?"

Lanni shrugged again, looking miserable. "That's what Cook said to the milkman when he delivered supplies the other morning. I thought maybe it meant something because it was a strange thing to say, but I could be wrong. Your Majesty, please, I must go, or I'll be punished."

"Thank you, Lanni." Charis turned to Tal as the woman hastily left the room, closing the door behind her.

Tal shook his head. "We'll need to ask other people about Lord Thorsby. Maybe Ferris can—"

"I know where Lady Ollen is." Charis gripped Tal's arm. "Her favorite tea shop is the two-story bakery on the northwest side of the merchant district. I can't remember the name of it, but there's an alchemist shop across the street and a bookbinder next door."

Tal gave her his crooked smile. "I do love your brain."

"And I love yours." The words left her lips before she'd truly realized what she meant to say. His eyes darkened, and he leaned close enough that she was suddenly, exquisitely aware of the rise and fall of his chest and the way his collarbone caught the early morning light.

"So where is Nalani? I wanted to—what is happening here?" Ferris demanded, staring at Tal and Charis, who were standing far too close to one another.

"Nothing that concerns you," Tal said at the same time that Charis said, "Strategy."

Ferris stilled, his eyes narrowing. "Why is Charis blushing?"

"It's nauseating, but you get used to it." Holland grabbed the last muffin and moved toward Charis.

She pivoted toward Holland, reaching out for the muffin as an excuse to put a little bit of distance between herself and Tal.

"Eat that." Holland shoved the food into her hand.

"Fine." Charis held the muffin without taking a bite.

Ferris craned his neck to look at the bedrooms. "Where is Nalani? We need her so we can start planning how to manage things. I know what Queen Bai'elsha is really up to."

Charis glanced at Tal, Holland, and Reuben. Each of them looked as wary as she felt. "Nalani isn't with us. And how do you know what the queen is planning?"

"What do you mean Nalani isn't with us?" Ferris set down the remains of his muffin. "Where is she?"

"She's still in Solvang." Holland crossed his arms over his chest. "She's safe. Now, I think you'd better explain yourself."

"Safe." Ferris took a deep breath and blew it out slowly, then nodded. "Good. That's good. It buys us more time."

"How does that buy us time?" Charis asked.

Ferris met her gaze. "Because the terms of King Alaric's agreement with Queen Bai'elsha state that all four heirs to the Caleran throne must be present before he will deliver the jewels. He's camped just far enough inland that the Rakuuna can't reach him. They have to spend time in the sea each day, or they grow very weak."

"All four heirs—that doesn't make sense." Tal turned to Charis. "Father only needs one heir to fulfill the betrothal treaty. Why would he care about anyone but you?"

"Father?" Ferris's voice was sharp. "Who exactly are you?"

"He's Prince Percival Talin Penbyrn, King Alaric's younger son." Charis waved that announcement aside as Ferris left the food tray and moved toward them. They had bigger problems than Tal's identity. "Would your father be trying to force the Rakuuna to keep the line of succession safe?"

"Again, how does that benefit him—hey!" Tal stumbled back as Ferris planted his hands on Tal's shoulders and shoved.

"You treacherous, lying dog." Ferris spat the words. "The only reason I can think of that your father wants the four of us gathered together is to go through with the wedding and then kill us all, leaving your brother as the sole ruler of Calera. And he has his monstrous allies here to help him make sure it happens. No doubt you were in on it the entire time. You're nothing but a filthy traitor, and I should kill you where you stand."

Holland dropped the bedpost, curled his hand into a fist, and plowed it straight into Ferris's face.

Ferris hit the floor and lay gasping, blood leaking from his nose. "How dare you—"

"Tal is much more than a filthy traitor, and nobody gets to kill him except for me." Holland glared down at Ferris.

"You hit me to stake a claim on the honor of killing him?" Ferris sounded incredulous.

"No, I hit you because nobody talks about my friends like that."

Tal looked at Holland as though he'd just been given something priceless.

Ferris wiped blood from his nose and sat up. "You just said you wanted to kill him."

"No, I said I get to kill him. Keep up."

From outside the suite's door, the unmistakable rattle of the Rakuuna talking to each other drifted in. Holland leaned down and snatched both the bedpost and Ferris off the floor.

"I can stand on my own." Ferris glared at Holland.

"Enough," Charis said as Reuben moved to position himself between her body and the door. "Ferris is right. The only explanation that makes sense is that Alaric plans some kind of treachery. We'll deal with your feelings about that later, Tal. Right now, we need to move fast to get a message to Lord Thorsby and Lady Ollen so we can warn Nalani to hide before the Rakuuna queen realizes she's still in Solvang."

Ferris took a big step back, putting a healthy distance between himself and Holland. "What message? I can give it to our contact."

Under no circumstances was Charis trusting something this delicate, this important, to a person she'd never met. "It's a message that must be delivered in person."

Ferris sighed. "Well then, you're out of luck, because no one seems to know where Lady Ollen and Lord Thorsby are staying."

Trust Ferris and his parents to not even consider checking in with the servants as a source of information.

"I know where they're staying," Charis said. "I just need you to show us how your contact gets out of the palace."

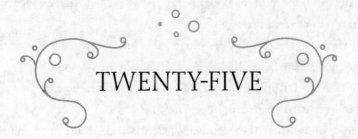

TWENTY-FIVE

Night seemed to take forever to arrive.

All day long, Rakuuna guards patrolled the halls of the southern wing twice an hour, often stepping inside rooms to stare at the occupants for long, uncomfortable moments before moving on. It was unnerving feeling their large, black eyes on her, and she couldn't afford for the guards to get used to seeing her in her suite's sitting room when she planned to sneak out that evening, so she, Holland, and Tal had made a habit of going into their respective rooms and closing their doors, leaving Reuben alone on the sofa.

Besides Charis and her people, there were at least thirty people staying in the wing. The Everlys, eleven people Charis recognized as palace staff from her mother's tenure, and quite a few others who were working as servants under Queen Bai'elsha, but whose faces Charis didn't recognize.

Lady Everly appeared a bit frail—Charis supposed it was because she no longer had regular access to her medicine. Lord Everly, however, looked as dour and somber as ever, his words slow and careful as he assured her that he and Ferris had done their best to negotiate a favorable deal between Alaric and the Rakuuna, but that he, like his son, was deeply concerned over the requirement that all four Caleran heirs be present for the wedding and subsequent jewel payment.

Lord Everly had also echoed Charis's concern that Nalani be apprised of her tenuous situation immediately so she could hide. Based on what Charis now knew about the Rakuuna, it would be enough for Nalani to move inland and stay with her father's family. As long as she was more than a day's journey from the coast, the Rakuuna would have difficulty hunting her.

However, there was nothing to stop the Rakuuna from destroying the people in the capital city of Ooverstaad, including Gareth and Vyllanthra, in their efforts to find Nalani. Which meant Charis needed her allies to assemble an armada and use the moriarthy dust to wipe out the Rakuuna in Calera as soon as possible.

Lord Everly also wanted a full accounting of Charis's time away from Calera, but she'd kept the details to a minimum. The last thing she needed was for one of the other Calerans to learn about the moriarthy dust or the gathering armada and curry favor with the Rakuuna by reporting it to Queen Bai'elsha. Instead, Charis had assured the Everlys that Solvang had given asylum to their refugees, that Nalani was working on shoring up alliances with the other sea kingdoms, and that spreading news of Alaric's potential treachery would at least give Charis some leverage she could use to negotiate with him when he arrived.

None of Calera's allies would look kindly on a ruler who had gained not just a throne, but an entire kingdom through bloodshed and bad-faith agreements.

The Everlys had also agreed that making contact with Lord Thorsby and Lady Ollen was urgent, and so they'd hung one of Lady Everly's pink handkerchiefs on the railing of her sitting room balcony as a signal to their contact that he needed to return that evening. Unfortunately, they'd insisted that Ferris should go along with them since he was more accustomed to navigating around Rakuuna patrols.

Charis considered pointing out that dodging scheduled, predictable guards within the palace was much different than navigating the dark streets of Arborlay after Queen Bai'elsha's curfew, but what was the point? She had no energy for arguing. Everything in her was solely focused on escaping the palace, finding the rebellion's headquarters, warning Nalani while also getting her Caleran allies ready to help her, and then returning to the palace before her absence was noticed the following morning.

She'd briefly considered not returning at all, but the Rakuuna had no respect for human lives. Queen Bai'elsha would torture and kill the other Calerans left behind as she hunted for clues to Charis's whereabouts, and their blood wasn't something Charis could stomach having on her hands.

When night finally arrived, Charis, Holland, Tal, and Ferris waited in her suite of rooms for the guards to complete their walk-through. All were dressed in dark pants, sweaters, and boots. Reuben stood off to the side, looking furious at Charis's decision to exclude him from the outing. As soon as the Rakuuna left the wing, Ferris beckoned them into the hall.

"Remember the plan?" he asked, as if they might have forgotten the details they'd been discussing all day.

"Go to the parlor at the end of the wing, ride the dumbwaiter down to the servants' hallway, take the back stairs up to the third floor and climb out the balcony of the seventh room." Holland moved through the door before he was finished speaking. "Let's go before the guards do another sweep of the palace. We know the schedule for this wing.

We don't know the schedule for anywhere else."

"Your Majesty." Reuben placed a hand on her arm before she could follow Holland. "For the last time, I must protest. I should go in your stead. Or if you won't allow that, I should go with you."

Charis pulled her arm free of his grasp. What if Lord Thorsby or Lady Ollen were lying like Lady Channing had been? What if they were working with King Alaric? Charis had to see their faces when she spoke to them. It was the only way she could be reasonably sure. "You can protect me by staying here. If you're gone, and the Rakuuna check on me, they'll immediately know that I'm gone, too. We'll be back as soon as we can."

Before he could say another word, she moved into the hall, followed immediately by Tal.

The dumbwaiter was tucked into the wall behind a cupboard door decorated with a trio of painted birds resting on a thesserin branch. It was a square the size of a carriage door, just large enough for a full-grown human to crouch on their hands and knees, which meant they spent nearly ten minutes slowly sending their party of four down the servants' hallway, one person at a time. From there, they raced to the narrow staircase at the end of the hall and climbed two sets of stairs as quietly as possible.

For once, neither Holland nor Ferris said a word.

Once they reached the third floor, they found themselves in an abandoned wing of guest suites. Quickly they made their way into the seventh room, crossed the tiny sitting area, and opened the door that led out to a balcony overlooking the palace courtyard. Charis was about to order Ferris to make the small leap into the cradle of the closest thesserin tree, when a shadow unpeeled itself from the wall beside the balcony's door, sending her heart crashing in her chest.

"My lords, my lady," the shadow whispered, stepping closer so that in the faint moonlight, Charis could see the shape of a man with a narrow face, a long nose, and a mustache the size of a large mouse spread across his upper lip. "My name is Mason. I got the message that you needed an escort through the city. Where are we going?"

"The merchant district," Charis said. "Northwest side."

He nodded. "Stay quiet. The courtyard patrol is about to pass. Give them five minutes to turn the corner and move away from us, and then we'll head out."

Charis pressed her body against the wall and watched the tall, lithe shadows of two Rakuuna guards move across the courtyard. Her pulse beat wildly, and her hands trembled as she double-checked that the small satchel of moriarthy dust was tied securely to her waist.

This was madness.

If they got caught, they might be killed. At the very least, they'd be thrown into the palace dungeons. But Nalani's life was at stake, and Charis needed to put her plan into action if Calera was to be saved.

Five minutes crept by with agonizing slowness, punctuated by the occasional cry from a night hawk and the soft shush of fabric brushing against stone when one of their party readjusted themselves against the balcony wall.

When the Rakuuna had long since rounded the far corner of the palace, Tal turned to her, his hand outstretched. "It's time. Ready?"

Charis hesitated for a moment, waiting to feel rage or pain at the sight. Instead, the small, warm light Tal had once lit in her heart burned steadily—the beginning of a new, fragile friendship between them.

She took his hand.

"Ready."

"You were right, Holland." Ferris moved past Charis and climbed the railing. "It is nauseating."

"I'm always right. Do make sure your foot doesn't slip," Holland said cheerfully. "We wouldn't want anything to happen to you."

"Keep your voices down," Mason whispered. "And move quickly."

The chilly air smelled of the woodsmoke that drifted lazily into the night sky from chimneys across the city. It had rained that afternoon, and the stone balcony was still damp. Once Ferris and Mason had climbed down the tree, Tal, Holland, and Charis approached the railing.

"You first," Holland said, gesturing at Charis.

"Be careful," Tal said, giving her hand a quick squeeze before letting go. "The bark is wet."

"I can manage." She climbed over the railing and reached for the closest branch, dimly aware that Tal was holding on to the back of her sweater. Once she was securely in the tree's cradle, she shimmied down the trunk and strained to hear any sound from the Rakuuna patrol while she waited for Tal and Holland to descend.

The instant everyone reached the courtyard, Mason started moving, trusting them to follow. The sister moons were directly overhead, partially shrouded by clouds, their ghostly blue light lending a faint glow to the stones beneath their feet.

The oil lanterns that used to be lit around the palace at night no longer burned. Maybe the Rakuuna could see well at night without them. The thought sent a chill down Charis's spine.

All the more reason to get off the palace grounds and into the city proper as fast as possible.

Moving quickly, they skirted the edge of the courtyard, heading west, keeping to the line of thesserin trees and the dubious coverage their bare branches allowed. When they reached the edge of the courtyard, Mason brought their group to a halt. Charis waited, every muscle coiled with tension.

What if there was a patrol on the rooftop?

The instant they left the protection of the thesserin trees, they'd be exposed.

"Move quickly but silently." Mason's voice was grim. "The patrol will be close, and we can't afford to give ourselves away."

Charis's stomach twisted as she took one step into the courtyard, then another, feeling utterly exposed. The dim blue light of the sister moons, which moments ago had seemed nothing but a faint shine in the darkness, now felt like a torchlight illuminating her every move.

Another three steps. Five.

On the sixth step, Ferris's boot slid against the gritty, damp stone, a loud screech of leather against rock. He froze.

Mason, however, didn't. "If anyone is close, they'll have heard that. *Run*."

They took off, sprinting across the exposed space. Charis tried to run lightly, her focus entirely on the overgrown garden that flanked the far edge of the courtyard. If they could make it inside the arched, vine-covered entrance before the patrol came, they'd be out of sight.

From somewhere over her left shoulder, the high, undulating cry of a Rakuuna rose, piercing the night and sending a rush of cold fear through Charis's veins.

She pushed herself to run faster.

An answering cry came from the right.

Were they coordinating their attack? Alerting other guards to chase them down?

The courtyard had never felt so vast.

She raced under the archway just behind Mason, ripping at the vines that tangled in her hair, and whirled to face the courtyard. Tal skidded to a stop beside her, his breath coming quickly. Holland and

Ferris lunged beneath the archway and stopped beside Mason. All five of them stared at the courtyard, bodies tensed to run again.

For a long, agonizing moment, they waited, sure they'd been discovered. The wind whispered through the vines and rattled twigs along the garden path. The palace sat, still and silent, bathed in moonlight.

Charis turned to Tal and whispered, "I think we're—"

A scream tore through the night, raw and brutal.

Tal stepped in front of Charis, though he had no weapon.

"That was human," she said softly.

"Someone got caught breaking curfew." Mason's voice was nothing more than a breath. "Stay quiet."

Another undulating cry rose, this time from farther away, followed by the unmistakable dry rattle of Rakuuna talking to each other. Charis's breath clogged her throat as the patrol rounded the corner and entered the courtyard.

Tal remained in front of her, body positioned to take the brunt of an attack, but the pair of Rakuuna never looked at the tangled, overgrown garden at the far edge of the courtyard. Charis swallowed against the dryness in her mouth as the pair seemed to take forever to walk that side of the palace and eventually turn the corner.

The instant they were out of sight, Holland said, "Someone got hurt."

"Or killed." Mason turned toward the garden path. "We need to get off these grounds before we're next. There's a gap between bushes two minutes east of here. We can use the orchard for cover as we move toward the road. Let's go."

Nearly an hour later, after silently creeping through the gardens—which, by the state of things, had been untended since the invasion—and carefully moving through the orchard, hugging one tree after another to blend in with the shadows, they reached the road that led into the city.

"Stick to the shadows," Mason whispered, though they were already doing so.

The streets of Arborlay were eerily still. No torchlights were lit, giving more credence to the idea that the Rakuuna could see well in the dark. Starshine glittered against windowpanes, and porch timbers creaked as the breeze kicked up, tearing at Charis's clothing and slapping damp air against her cheeks.

The bakery was deep into the merchant district. They'd been walking for nearly thirty minutes, trying hard to stay pressed against buildings, listening intently for any signs of Rakuuna. Tal consistently put his body between hers and the street beyond, while Holland walked two steps behind them, ready to face any opponent that came at their backs. Mason and Ferris walked in front, sometimes talking in low voices that never reached Charis's ears, sometimes moving in silence.

She found herself falling into rhythm with Tal, at once new and achingly familiar. Him protecting her with no thought to himself. Her matching her movements to his, syncing up with his steps, his speed, and the cadence of his breathing.

They were two blocks from the bakery when a haunting cry rose from somewhere on their left.

As the cry was still rising in pitch, Tal pivoted. "We need to hide."

"Go low or go high, but get off the street," Mason whispered as he and Ferris raced to climb one of the thick, sturdy oak trees lining the street.

Charis had no interest in being that exposed. Quickly, she scanned their surroundings and then pointed to a raised wooden porch on a cobbler's shop two stores ahead of them. "There."

Without another word, Charis, Tal, and Holland ran, sprinting from one building to the next, while behind them, the Rakuuna's alert hit fever pitch and began to fall. Another cry sounded, this one from somewhere ahead. It sounded as if it had come from the street they were on.

It was too late to choose another location to hide.

If they'd been seen already, their lives could be measured in seconds. All that was left was to pray as they hurtled toward the porch. Gaps between the boards surrounding it were barely wide enough for Charis to shimmy through. She reached it, grabbed the edges of the boards, and launched herself into the darkness beneath, landing on her hands and knees. Tal tried to follow but got stuck partway through.

Whirling, Charis grabbed his hands, planted her feet, and pulled with everything she had. For a moment, nothing happened, and she tugged even harder.

He slid forward with such force, he slammed into her and sent her flat on her back, his body landing heavily on top of her. Holland launched himself through the opening, his momentum sending him crashing onto the two of them.

The air left Charis's lungs, and she gasped. Immediately she covered her mouth with her hands, while Holland rolled to one side and Tal rolled to the other, his hair brushing against her face as he went.

Rakuuna voices drifted down the street, and Charis froze as the sound crept closer.

Tal pressed his body next to hers, anchoring himself between her and the outside world. As the slap of footsteps reached their ears, she fumbled through the dark until she found his hand. Lacing her fingers through his, she squeezed her eyes closed and prayed that this wasn't the end.

She wanted to restore her kingdom.

She wanted to bury her parents and say a proper goodbye.

She wanted to explore this new flame within her battered heart.

The steps paused just shy of the porch.

Every breath felt too loud. Every heartbeat a drumroll announcing her presence to the predator outside.

The dirt beneath her was cold and unforgiving, and the darkness played tricks with her, tempting her to believe something else was entering the gap between porch boards.

She forced herself to think of nothing but the feel of Tal's hand in hers. The roughness of his fingertips and the steady cadence of his breath as he pressed himself to her side. The way she fit against him as though he'd never left.

On her other side, Holland was so quiet, he seemed to be holding his breath.

The footsteps started up again, and a shrill cry rent the air.

Had they found Ferris and Mason?

Tal's hand tightened on hers, but the Rakuuna were receding. Searching other streets for anyone foolish enough to violate curfew.

As the noise faded into silence, Charis became exquisitely aware of the warmth of Tal's body and the heat of his breath fanning the side of her neck.

Softly, he said, "Are you all right?"

"I've been better." Holland stretched, and a popping sound came from his back. "What did I land on?"

"Me." Charis and Tal spoke simultaneously.

"Ugh." Holland began scooting toward the gap between boards. "Let's never speak of this again."

Tal shifted his weight, and his mouth brushed against her ear. She shivered.

"Are *you* all right?" He breathed the words against her skin.

She nodded, not trusting her voice, and scooted toward the hole between porch boards. "We should get going."

He squeezed her hand once and then let go so he could follow her back onto the street.

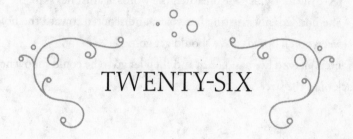

TWENTY-SIX

THE TWO-STORY TEAROOM and bakery was nestled between a book-binder's shop and a store selling sewing notions. Ferris and Mason were waiting at the mouth of the alley, pressed against a tree. They joined Charis, Tal, and Holland in silence. The scent of sugared icing and yeast bread hung in the air as Charis's group approached the back door. Clouds drifted across the sister moons, making it difficult to see in the narrow alleyway that cut between shops.

Charis wasn't convinced the lack of moonlight would affect the Rakuuna's vision the way it did hers. Every second she spent outside felt like exposing her neck to a sharpened blade.

They'd nearly reached the bakery's door when a shadow detached itself from the stairwell, and a quiet male voice said, "Who goes there?"

Holland stepped in front of the group and answered softly. "Her Majesty, Queen Charis Willowthorn, requests an audience with those inside."

The shadowy figure froze, then said, "Right. The queen is just wandering the streets after curfew. Listen, go on back to wherever you came from. Nothing special going on here anyway. Just me and my workers baking bread for the morrow."

Holland glanced back at Charis, and she moved to his side. The tension in the man's body belied the forced casual tone of his voice. He was lying, which meant he had something to hide. Relief turned her knees weak. She'd found the resistance. Her kingdom could still be saved.

"We've taken great risk to come here tonight," Charis said softly. "Perhaps we could simply step inside for a cup of tea before our journey back to the palace?"

"Wasn't expecting company." The man shifted his feet, blocking the door at his back.

Charis clenched her jaw. Was there a secret phrase she was supposed to know to gain entrance? It was too dark for the man to see her clearly, and he obviously hadn't recognized her voice. What else could she do to convince him that she was truly Calera's queen and meant them no harm?

"Now, you listen here, you flour-dusted fool." Ferris managed to sound both imperious and desperate. "How dare you leave us standing on the street where we could get killed by the Rakuuna—"

"Enough, Ferris." Charis kept her voice low. "He's right to be cautious."

"I might have a solution," Tal said, sounding calm and agreeable. "Perhaps you could ask one of your more senior workers to come to the door for a moment? He's a fussy man, always wears a handkerchief in his breast pocket, though usually he's busy using it to wipe his forehead. He's known the queen since she was a child. He'll recognize her."

Charis looked from Tal to the man in the shadows. If Lord Thorsby was indeed here, this was a risk worth taking. If he wasn't, there was no chance the sentry would allow them in now.

The man considered Tal for a long moment, and then said, "No one here matches that description."

Again, he was lying.

Charis stepped forward. "I appreciate the difficult position we've put you in. Would you be willing to deliver a message from me to your most senior worker?"

He stared at her in silence.

"Ten years ago, when I was seven, I once borrowed my mother's wax and royal seal and stamped it all over the finalized draft of a trade agreement with Morg because I thought it looked pretty." Charis lowered her voice as a sound from a nearby street echoed into the night. "Your worker found it before my mother did and spent hours redoing the document without ever telling her what I'd done. Only the two of us know about that incident. Tell him that story, and he'll know for certain that I am who I say I am."

For a moment, the man did nothing but stare at her. Finally, he said, "Wait here. Times being what they are, my sword hand gets real twitchy if anyone tries to enter my property without permission."

"We won't move from this spot," Tal said.

They remained silent as the man ducked inside the bakery, locking the door behind him. Something skittered along the rooftop across the alley. Tal and Holland both pivoted to put themselves between her and the noise. From the mouth of the alley, four buildings down, the rattling sound of Rakuuna speaking to each other drifted through the air.

The hair on the back of Charis's neck rose. She couldn't see the patrol, but that didn't mean they couldn't see her.

And while she had a small chance of the Rakuuna at the palace recognizing who she was and deeming her too valuable to kill yet, the city patrol had never set eyes on her. She'd be treated to the same body-breaking consequences as the rest of her people who were caught out after curfew.

Moving slowly, hardly daring to breathe, Charis stepped back to press herself against the cold brick wall of the bakery beside Ferris and Mason.

The sound of the Rakuuna patrol came closer.

They'd turned down the alley.

There was nowhere to run. No time to hide. She was going to have to either fight or somehow convince the patrol that she was valuable to their queen.

Holland and Tal spun to face the threat.

The chattering between the Rakuuna guards stopped abruptly, and Charis's mouth turned to dust as one of them raised the alert, a high-pitched, undulating cry that sent a shaft of pain through her head and nearly brought her to her knees.

"Run," Tal said firmly. "I'll give you time to find a place to hide."

Ferris and Mason were already sliding along the wall as if they meant to dive between buildings and flee.

"No." Her voice shook, but a fire burned in her heart. These monsters had taken enough from her. She couldn't outrun them. They weren't going to take her life while she fled like a coward and left Tal to die.

She wouldn't pound on the bakery's door and ask them to let her in, either. The Rakuuna couldn't discover where Lady Ollen and Lord Thorsby were organizing the rebellion.

"This is not the time to argue, Charis, *run*." Tal's voice was desperate.

Holland rolled to the balls of his feet.

Behind them, the bakery door swung open, releasing a gush of warm, sugarcoated air, and a man's voice, sounding utterly annoyed, said, "Oy! Break time's over. Get back in here and help us finish. These tea cakes don't bake themselves."

The Rakuuna alert abruptly dropped into silence, and then, from the darkness, a cold, lilting voice said, "It works here?"

"Yes, geniuses, they work here. Your queen ordered a tremendous number of pastries for the upcoming wedding feast. An order like that takes a large crew working nights." The man stepped onto the back stoop, snatched Charis's arm in his, and dragged her into the bakery. Glancing back at the others, he snapped, "I swear, if you don't hurry up and get your aprons back on, I will turn you into a pie."

Tal quickly entered the bakery, followed by Holland, Ferris, and finally Mason. The baker slammed and locked the door. Charis drew in a shuddering breath and stared at the lock, expecting the Rakuuna patrol to tear the door from its hinges at any moment. The door remained closed.

"The person you wanted to see is down in the basement. Stairs are at the end of the kitchen to your left." The baker picked up a bowl and a whisk. Delicious scents wafted from the nearby ovens. "I'll keep watch up here while I work."

Mason and Ferris exchanged glances and began moving toward the stairs.

There was a big difference between trusting someone to guide her through the dangerous city streets and giving him a front row seat to her secrets. Quickly, Charis said, "Ferris, I'd like you and Mason to keep watch with—what's your name?" She looked at the baker.

"Rames, Your Majesty."

"Keep watch with Rames. Use the time to locate multiple escape routes out of this building if necessary."

Ferris looked as if she'd ordered him to scrub the floor of a bath chamber. "Keeping watch is for underlings."

"Nobody with any class uses the word *underlings*." Holland brushed past Ferris on his way to the stairs.

Charis moved to Ferris's side. There was no time for Ferris's sense of entitlement, but shaming him in front of others wouldn't accomplish her goal half as quickly as simply making him feel important.

"I need someone I can trust to watch our backs. I've only just met Rames. I'll fill you in on anything important once we return to the palace."

Ferris glanced once more at Mason and then dipped his head respectfully. "Yes, Your Majesty."

"Don't stay up here all night gawking at the pastries." Lady Ollen's brisk voice cut through the air from the far side of the kitchen.

"Lady Ollen!" Charis walked across the tile floor toward the noblewoman, skirting a long trestle table laden with bowls of rising bread dough resting beneath tea towels.

Lady Ollen swept into a deep curtsy, her dress billowing out around her plump figure, her gray hair shining in the muted lamplight. "Your Majesty, we are at your service."

"Thank you, Lady Ollen." Charis took the woman's hands in hers and smiled. "Your loyalty is without question."

"Which is more than I can say for some. Shall we talk?" She nodded toward the stairwell behind her. It was tucked into a corner, beside a large shelf full of flour bags and jars of sugar. Charis, Tal, and Holland followed her down the narrow wooden staircase.

The basement was easily the size of Charis's bedroom and sitting room combined. There were barrels lining one wall and a stack of old tables and chairs near the far corner. Additional tables, chairs, and sleeping pallets were scattered across the scarred wooden floor. The wall beside the stairway was entirely devoted to storing stacks of plates and saucers, along with several rows of spare teacups. Three dusty lanterns burned bright, lending a soft, golden glow to the space.

Two people were asleep. Three others sat at a table, huddled over a small stack of papers. At the closest table, Lord Jamison Thorsby, Mother's chief advisor and head of the royal council, sat nursing a cup of tea. Even in these conditions, his dress coat and cravat looked immaculate.

"Lord Thorsby!" Charis rushed forward.

He leaped from his chair, nearly spilling his tea. "Your Majesty!" He bowed.

"I'm so glad to see you safe and sound." Charis grasped his arm as he fished a silk handkerchief from his coat pocket and dabbed his eyes.

"And I, you, Your Majesty. We'd hoped for your return, and we spoke about it as a certainty to keep people's spirits high, but to actually see you here . . . I'm overcome. Forgive me." He waved a hand at his face as he tried to stop the tears.

"A Rakuuna patrol saw us." Holland moved into the room and plopped himself down in the chair beside Thorsby's. "Rames pretended we were workers on a break, but we should make this quick."

"We'll need to find a safe place for Her Majesty to stay." Lady Ollen looked around the room. "She certainly can't sleep on the floor. Besides, if the patrol saw such a large group entering the bakery, this won't be a safe hiding place much longer."

"No need to find places for us to stay. We're going back to the palace." She patted Lord Thorsby's arm and then sank into the closest chair. Tal immediately stationed himself beside her, silent and watchful.

"Are you certain that's wise?" Lord Thorsby sounded faint as he settled into his chair.

"If we don't, the Rakuuna will tear through the city hunting for us, and I'm not willing to be responsible for those deaths."

"Is that Ferris Everly I saw upstairs in the kitchen?" Lady Ollen asked.

"Yes, more's the pity," Holland said.

"Does Lord Everly send any news?" Lady Ollen perched on the edge of a chair and leaned toward Charis. "They've been living in the palace since the morning after the invasion. Made to work for the Rakuuna, is my understanding."

Lord Thorsby looked to Charis. "The Rakuuna knew they needed to obliterate the leadership in Arborlay immediately if they were going to take the country in a single night. They burned down the homes of many who were close to your mother. Or they turned the properties into barracks for their soldiers. The Everly home was the first to burn."

"And what did they do when it happened? Did they turn to friends or find hiding places like we did? No. They moved into the palace itself and started speaking on behalf of the queen." Lady Ollen spat over her left shoulder as though warding off a curse.

"Did they move there of their own accord? Or were they taken prisoner?" Charis asked, remembering the rumors that the High Emperor of Rullenvor had become a mouthpiece for the Rakuuna before ultimately dying when his usefulness to them ended.

"Well . . ." Lady Ollen's dark green serpanicite ring flashed in the light. "They were searching for your family, and then they stayed on to be negotiators for that monster on the throne. But really, there's no excuse. I would rather have died than be useful to those who killed our queen." Lady Ollen jabbed a finger at Lord Thorsby. "And so would you, Jamison."

He nodded, desperately dabbing at his shiny forehead. "Just so, Lady Ollen. Just so. Still, one does what one must to survive, and as they were the only members of the royal family left, it stands to reason that the Rakuuna wanted to use them to convince King Alaric to return to Arborlay." He met Charis's gaze. "Our best information indicates that the Rakuuna have demanded a rather large shipment of jewels from Montevallo."

Charis nodded. "That's correct. And I can confirm that the Everlys are living in captivity, along with the rest of the palace staff. We're being kept in the same wing."

"Clearly they know a way out, so why not just leave?" Lady Ollen frowned.

"Where would they go?" Charis asked softly. "King Alaric has demanded that all four heirs to the Caleran throne be present when he arrives. If the Everlys flee, the Rakuuna will hunt them down, the same as they did me."

Lord Thorsby took a sip of tea and folded his handkerchief. "If the Rakuuna need all four heirs for King Alaric, why wasn't a bounty placed on the Farragin twins?"

Charis blinked. Why indeed?

Holland looked offended. "I hadn't thought of that. That could've been my one opportunity to have someone put out the call to bring me in dead or alive."

"Knowing you, I'm sure there will be more," Tal said.

"Thank you." Holland appeared somewhat mollified.

"It still doesn't answer Lord Thorsby's question, however." Charis tapped her fingers on the table. "Something doesn't add up."

"If they'd placed a bounty on all three of you, they'd have alerted you that there was a plan in place to get rid of every rightful heir to Calera's throne." Tal sounded miserable. "And knowing how your mind works, that would've been all the warning you needed to hide Holland and Nalani far from the Rakuuna's reach."

"The Rakuuna don't know how Charis's mind works or they'd

never have allowed her the opportunity to leave Calera alive in the first place," Lady Ollen said.

"The Rakuuna don't, but King Alaric does," Tal said flatly.

Charis glanced at him and found him staring at the floor, jaw clenched. Turning back to those at the table, she said, "What Alaric doesn't know is that the heirs aren't without resources. I have a plan. Tell me everything I've missed in my absence, and then I'll tell you what we're going to do."

Two hours later, Charis sat back, mind racing as Holland, who'd managed to eat his way through an entire loaf of bread while they'd talked, brushed crumbs from his duster and said, "We'd better head back to the palace unless we want to be skewered by a Rakuuna. We should get across the city while it's still dark outside."

Charis nodded, her attention still on the papers Lord Thorsby had placed in front of her at the start of their discussion. The first was a list of nobles who'd declared loyalty to the Rakuuna, rather than to Charis. She could forgive them their desire to survive at any cost, but still, she committed every name on the list to memory. Once she had her kingdom back, not one of them would be welcome to advise her, serve her, or even hold the privilege of living in Calera's capital.

There was also a list of those who'd died. It was horrifyingly long and included many respected nobles, merchants, and peasants who'd been unfailingly loyal to Queen Letha. A list of properties destroyed or currently being used by the Rakuuna. A list of safe buildings throughout the city and the surrounding area with basements or inner rooms in case someone needed a place to hide. A list of the actions the rebels had taken against the invaders, which included burning two of the homes they'd turned into barracks—something Holland bemoaned he'd missed out on—sinking four of their ships, and poisoning the fish supply that was delivered to their quarters, among other things.

All done in her name by those who'd refused to give up hope of her return.

The weight of that courage and loyalty was heavier than any crown she'd ever worn, but she bore it with gratitude. Her people were worth fighting for. Worth dying for.

Worth saving.

She'd explained the urgency of contacting Nalani to Lady Ollen and Lord Thorsby and had been assured there was a farm outside the city limits with pallorens that were never intercepted by the Rakuuna. She'd also told them about the moriarthy dust, the promise of ships from Solvang, Thallis, and Verace, and the retired admiral who'd agreed to create the battle plans that would end in the Rakuuna's destruction. And because they'd questioned why she was relying heavily on Tal's understanding of Alaric to inform her decisions, she revealed his true identity as well. In the end, they had steps in place to put Charis's strategy into action.

If Alaric truly wouldn't honor the deal with the Rakuuna until all four heirs were present, Charis had hopefully bought her allies enough time to bring war to Arborlay's doorstep and ruin the Rakuuna. She'd deal with Alaric's potential treachery once she had her kingdom firmly under her own control again.

Still, something about the situation with Alaric felt off. If he'd wanted to destroy Calera's ruling family and install his son as the king, why not wait to have the Rakuuna attack after she'd already married Vahn?

"We're missing something." Charis tapped on the papers and looked to Tal.

"I agree."

"I hardly think we need an impostor's opinion on the matter." Lord Thorsby spoke brusquely, his handkerchief once again summoned to deal with his forehead.

"Lord Thorsby, while I sympathize with the sentiment, I must insist that all talk of Tal as an impostor ends now." Charis swept the table with a look, finding indignation on Lord Thorsby's face, speculation on Lady Ollen's, and a single raised brow on Holland's. "He was following his father's orders, and he made a tremendous personal sacrifice to ensure the safety of Calerans. Plus, should we discover there was no treachery on Alaric's part, Tal will be my king consort's brother. We cannot allow a whiff of controversy to taint my reign."

It was impossible to think of Vahn as her king consort without wanting to flinch, and so Charis hurried on. "I don't trust that we understand all the details of this situation. There are too many things that don't make sense. And because of that, we need to be prepared for treachery from unexpected places." She tapped the second pile of papers in front of her—her notes about their allies and potential battle plans.

Yes, the armada's soldiers would be well equipped to kill the monsters. But Charis had seen how quickly the Rakuuna could sink a ship from below the water. Soldiers who were let off at a northern port and made their way down to Arborlay could do plenty of damage, but the ships at sea would be sunk as soon as they were close enough to the capital to catch Queen Bai'elsha's attention.

However, the Rakuuna in Calera weren't the only ones who could die by moriarthy dust.

"We need leverage," Tal said softly, as though he'd read her mind.

"Yes, we do." She looked to Lady Ollen. "In your message to Lady Nalani, I want you to include orders to send three ships, each supplied with some moriarthy dust, to Te'ash."

"Te'ash?" Lady Ollen shifted in her chair. "You're sending them to the Rakuuna's homeland?"

Charis bared her teeth. "I am. Queen Bai'elsha brought her best warriors with her, leaving the old, the young, and the sick behind. If the only way I can ensure her cooperation is to order the deaths of every single Rakuuna left defenseless on Te'ash, I want to have that option."

Holland grinned. "Now we're having some fun."

When the others looked askance at him, he sighed. "Fine. I'm having fun. The rest of you may continue being serious."

"The Rakuuna aren't the only threat. We have to be prepared for treachery from every quarter." Charis glanced over the lists in front of her again, running her fingers over the papers as a plan came together. "If the worst happens and Nalani is captured, Alaric will come to Arborlay and demand the wedding be held immediately. Can your network find a way to provide my people with weapons at the feast? I don't want to face an execution with nothing but my wits and the little bit of moriarthy dust I carry with me."

Lady Ollen shared a long look with Lord Thorsby, who cleared his throat and set his handkerchief down.

"We'll do our best to get weapons to you if the feast takes place. But we can provide you with some extra protection now." He fished a hand into his breast pocket and came out with a small envelope, no bigger than the width of two fingers held side by side. Reaching across the table, he handed it to Charis.

There was something inside. She shook it gently and raised an eyebrow at what sounded like a teaspoon's worth of sand granules sliding against each other.

"Dried mursilla herb," Lady Ollen said. "Those of us who are privy to the names and locations of everyone involved in the rebellion keep some with us at all times, just in case we're captured. That way, they can't get the information from us by torturing us to death."

"Skip the torture and go straight to death." Holland slapped his hand against the table. "That's smart."

"If things don't work out the way we hope . . ." Lord Thorsby cleared his throat, his eyes suddenly glistening. "I'm sorry it's such a slow-acting poison. Supplies are quite low, and we don't have anything stronger available to us at the moment. I don't want you to use it, but I know you'd rather die than give up Nalani's location, if it comes to that."

"As would I," Holland said solemnly and then waved his hand as Lady Ollen pulled out her tiny envelope of poison. "You need it, too, and I have no compunctions about simply impaling myself on the nearest sword before betraying my sister."

"Thank you." Charis closed her hand over the envelope, its contents feeling suddenly fraught with risk. "We'll take our leave now. I deeply appreciate how hard you're fighting to save our kingdom."

Lady Ollen's eyes glistened, too. "Hurry back to the palace. The street patrols don't check in with the queen before sentencing people to death if they're caught breaking curfew without an excellent explanation."

TWENTY-SEVEN

CLOUDS OBSCURED THE sister moons as Charis and Tal followed Holland up the stairs and through the kitchen. Trays of steaming hot tea cakes and loaves of bread were set out on the counters to cool. Ferris and Mason were standing by the back door, their heads together as though having a discussion. Rames was busy whisking a large bowl of sugar icing. He set down the bowl and bowed as they approached.

"My apologies for not immediately recognizing you, Your Majesty."

"No apology necessary." Charis smiled at the man. "I appreciate your caution, along with the use of your bakery."

"Can't be too careful." He returned to whisking. "There's them that have decided showing loyalty to the monsters is the best way to stay alive. Especially when your own loyalty to your kingdom is in doubt. Glad to see you're still on our side."

Charis stopped abruptly. "You doubted my loyalty to my people?"

Holland snatched up a kitchen knife. "I regret having to do this, as you make an excellent tea cake, Rames, but no one insults the queen's integrity in my presence without paying the price in blood."

Rames dropped his whisk and held his hands up, palms out. "I meant no harm, sir. Just listening to the conversation in my tearoom each day. I'm grateful to know that the whispers about Her Majesty got it wrong."

Charis shook her head at Holland, who scowled but reluctantly set down the knife. Lanni, the maid who served Charis her meals, had said something about rumors as well. "What exactly are people saying?"

Rames looked from her to Holland and back again before picking up his whisk. "Oh, things like you made a deal with the Rakuuna and brought them to our shore, but then you didn't pay them, so you had to run away."

Charis stared at him while Tal muttered a curse under his breath, and Holland once again looked ready to pick up the knife.

"What kind of deal do people think I made?" Years of training kept her voice calm, but it took effort.

Rames tugged at his collar as if it was too tight and didn't meet her eyes. "Seems like folks think it was to get the queen out of the way, quick-like, so you could have the throne to yourself."

The room tilted, and Charis slapped a hand on the table to keep her balance as the memory of her mother's body falling at the hands of the attacking Rakuuna collided with that of her father lying on his bedroom floor, his throat torn to shreds. Bile rose, and she swallowed desperately as she fought to push the memories back into the shadows where they belonged.

How could anyone believe she would kill her own parents— people she'd loved with everything she had—just to gain power that was already within her grasp?

"Charis," Tal murmured, his hand a spot of warmth against her back as he leaned close.

"Tell me who's been spreading this rumor so I can cut out their tongues." Holland sounded furious.

"I don't know." Rames shrugged as he set the bowl of light green frosting beside a tray of tea cakes. "I mean, I can give a few names, but I don't know which of them actually believed it and which were just gossiping."

"It doesn't matter." Charis forced the words out, though her lips felt numb, and her mouth seemed to have forgotten how to work properly.

"Of course it matters!" Holland glared at her and then turned the full force of his anger on Tal. "Tell her it matters. Explain it."

"I don't need anyone explaining anything to me." Charis straightened, though it still felt as though she'd been punched in the stomach. "It doesn't matter who's spreading the rumor. It matters who started it."

"Who benefits?" Tal murmured, a frown digging into his forehead.

"Whoever needs me to look like the villain." Charis met his gaze. "If I'm the cause of Calera's woes, no one will want me for their queen."

"But how does that benefit either the Rakuuna or my father?" Tal asked.

"If you're removed as queen, that leaves me as next in line, and I am not interested in wearing a crown." Holland smacked his hand beside a row of green frosted tea cakes, earning him a glare from Rames.

"Well, not to put too fine a point on it, but the rumors include Lord and Lady Farragin as well, though of course your parents are still alive." Rames moved the tray of completed tea cakes away from Holland. "If you want my honest opinion, I don't think there's a single source. I think this is a result of hundreds of conversations from thousands of people who all wanted to understand how the three of you could leave us behind and not come back and fight for your throne."

Silence fell, broken only by the ticking of a clock above the fireplace, the soft patter of rain against the cobblestones outside the window, and the hushed argument happening between Ferris and Mason.

"That's reasonable," Charis said slowly. "Rames, can you start a new rumor for me?"

Rames paused in the act of smoothing a coat of pale green frosting across the etched surface of the tea cake. "I can try."

"Tell people that I've returned, and that I'm committed to fighting for my people. In fact, tell them I spent my time away gathering alliances to help us do just that."

"Are you sure that's wise?" Holland reached for one of the frosted tea cakes, and Rames snatched the tray into the air and slid it onto a nearby shelf. "What if that gets back to the Rakuuna, and they try to question you about it? Or worse, what if they send word to Alaric that you're gathering support against him?"

"No, actually, this could work." Tal began pacing. "Father never does anything that won't benefit him politically. If he believes future alliances with other kingdoms would be at risk if something happens to Charis, he might reconsider her value to him."

"Or he might order the Rakuuna just to kill her now, and I really think that ought to be a higher priority for you," Holland said.

"Nothing is a higher priority for me than Charis." Tal stopped in his tracks and glared at Holland.

"Then maybe we shouldn't encourage her to goad her enemies with a rumor about alliances," Holland shot back.

"Or maybe we should trust that she knows what she's doing." Tal's voice rose.

Charis moved away from them and said quietly to Rames, "Do as I asked, please."

"Yes, Your Majesty."

Was it risky potentially letting the Rakuuna know she had allies willing to help her? Yes. But if she didn't turn the tide of public opinion back in her favor, she'd risk driving out her enemies only to be faced with civil war.

She was banking on the Rakuuna feeling so secure in their physical prowess that they'd never suspect she had a weapon capable of hurting them until it was too late.

Ferris and Mason were still in a heated discussion as Charis began moving toward the door, leaving Holland and Tal arguing beside the trestle table.

She didn't have the patience or the energy to face the long, dangerous journey back to the palace, think through the strategies she needed to employ to win back her people's favor without jeopardizing the safety of her allies at sea, *and* silence two separate arguments. Her jaw clenched as she neared the door, where Ferris and Mason were staring intently out from behind the curtained window while whispering back and forth.

She wasn't the only one scared to make her way back to the palace. Her future wasn't the only one balanced on a sword's edge. Arguments were bound to happen, and getting upset with her allies wouldn't help anyone.

Drawing in a deep breath, she reached for something compassionate to say as she neared the door.

"I don't have orders from your father," Mason's fierce whisper reached Charis's ear, and she froze.

"Orders from me are the same as orders from Father, and you'd do well to remember your place, Bartho." Ferris strained to look out the window. "This rain is going to make the journey that much slower. We can't afford a delay."

He turned from the window, but Charis was already back beside Rames, her skin prickling, her limbs screaming at her to *run*.

He'd said Bartho. Not Mason.

Bartho.

Why hide Mason's identity? And why did that name strike a chord of dread deep within her?

She pretended to study a frosted teacake as her thoughts raced. Bartho . . . She'd heard that name before the invasion, but what was the connection? Rullenvor? That didn't feel right. Was he involved in the war with Montevallo? No, she remembered every emissary Mother had ever received. Had he been on Lady Channing's staff? Charis shook her head, though the chill on her skin refused to leave.

Could he be Montevallian? She froze as a memory surfaced. She was standing in a dungeon cell, her dagger to an assassin's throat, promising to destroy the woman and everyone she'd ever loved unless the assassin gave up the name of the person who'd hired her to kill Charis.

The name she gave was Bartho.

They'd never found a trace of him, but maybe that was because he'd been sheltered all along by a respected member of Mother's royal council. By a member of her *family*.

Charis's thoughts tumbled wildly, snatching at details, connections, and puzzle pieces, slotting them into place. She couldn't let Ferris see that she'd overheard him. If his family was connected to the man who'd orchestrated assassination attempts against Charis, then everything Ferris had told her from the moment she'd set foot in Calera was a lie.

And if everything she thought she knew about Alaric, the

Rakuuna, and her situation in Calera was a lie, then she, her crew, and the people using the bakery as a safe house were in danger the instant the Everlys realized their deception had been exposed.

"We need to leave now, Your Majesty," Ferris called. "It's a long walk back."

She nodded, thankful that Holland was still delivering a parting shot in his argument with Tal. Using the volume of Holland's voice as cover, she leaned close to Rames and said quietly, "Do not react to anything I'm about to say. I'm going to take a teacake as if that's my only reason for being close to you—but the instant we leave this building, get everyone out. We've been betrayed."

She grabbed a teacake and turned away. Rames picked up his bowl of frosting and stirred briskly. Tal took one look at her face and turned abruptly from Holland. She gave Tal a look that clearly said to keep quiet and smoothed her expression before saying, "Holland, that's enough. We have to get back to the palace. Look, I convinced Rames to give you a teacake."

Holland snatched the pastry from her hand, took a bite, and headed to the door, Charis and Tal on his heels.

Moments later, the group was moving swiftly and silently through the rain-drenched night. Ferris and Bartho took the lead, Tal and Charis followed several paces behind them, and Holland brought up the rear. Tendrils of fog rose from the sea, belly-crawled over the shore, and wound their way sinuously through the city streets. It was impossible to see more than a carriage length ahead, much less watch out for the Rakuuna patrol.

Charis dearly hoped the lack of visibility affected the creatures the same way it affected her, but she wasn't going to bet her life on it. Instead, she and the others clung to the sides of buildings and moved through swirls of fog when they had to cross a road.

The entire time, Charis had one ear straining for any hint of pursuit, and the rest of her mind was fully engaged on the problem at hand.

Ferris knew Nalani was in Solvang. Was it possible Lady Ollen could get a palloren to Solvang before the Everlys sent a Rakuuna to hunt Nalani down? Charis knew firsthand just how fast the Rakuuna ships cut through the water.

Ferris also now knew the location of Lady Ollen and Lord Thorsby, leaders of the rebellion. Charis prayed Rames got everyone far away from the bakery before Ferris returned to the palace and reported it to Queen Bai'elsha.

Fortunately, Charis hadn't told Ferris about the moriarthy dust or the allies committing ships to her cause. She still had the ability to wage war against her enemies, but she was just now realizing she hadn't truly realized who was on the other side of the dangerous chess match she'd been playing.

Tal grabbed her arm and anchored her to his side, pressing them both against the gnarled bark of a sugar maple tree. She froze. From somewhere to the east, the rattling of the Rakuuna's voices whispered through the air. She had no idea where Ferris and Bartho were and could only hope Holland was hiding nearby.

It was impossible to judge how close the Rakuuna were. The gentle patter of the rain and the heavy, muffled quiet of the fog made the entire world feel shrouded in wool, obscuring all sound.

Her damp sweater snagged on the tree's trunk as she silently adjusted her stance, ready to fight. Not that she'd do much damage.

For long moments, they stayed still, huddled against the tree at the very edge of the palace grounds. And then, from the road behind them, the slap of webbed feet on cobblestones. The rattle of quiet words exchanged. The whisper of danger sent a chill over Charis as she prayed desperately for the fog to protect their meager hiding place.

Then the sound of the patrol faded, swallowed by the fog. The rain was nothing but mist now, gently encasing Charis and Tal as they climbed through the orchard, slipped into the overgrown palace garden, and then tiptoed across the courtyard until they reached the thesserin tree outside the balcony.

"I need you to come to my room," she whispered as she grasped the damp trunk with cold fingers. "Alone."

He paused for a beat and then said, "Of course."

Her cheeks grew warm. "And not because . . . Not for anything . . . We need to talk."

"Yes, we do." He created a cradle with his hands and waited. She placed her foot into the cradle and leaped for the branches as he hoisted her up. The instant she started climbing, he shimmied up the trunk behind her.

The night sky was slowly fading into a murky violet as she reached the balcony. Dawn was less than an hour away. She hoped the message she'd ordered sent to Nalani was already safely outside the city's border, along with those who'd been at the bakery.

Tal climbed onto the balcony and together they crept in through the door, closing it quietly behind them just as the palace patrol rounded the corner and entered the courtyard below.

Holland was already in the room.

"There you are." He glanced behind them. "Where are Ferris and Mason?"

"They were ahead of us, so they must have arrived first," Charis said, keeping her voice even, though it took effort.

If—no, *when* Holland learned that the Everlys were connected to Bartho and that his sister had just been put in even more danger than

before, Charis was going to have a hard time stopping him from going after the entire Everly family with his bedpost.

Maybe that was the best strategy. Maybe it wasn't. Charis needed time to think it through. She needed to look at all the angles. She needed confirmation that she was right before she effectively sentenced the Everlys to death.

She glanced over to find Tal watching her closely, a crease in his brow as he studied her.

"Nice of them to wait here to make sure we all arrived safely," Holland said, shaking water from his hair.

"It's Ferris." Charis moved toward the hallway. "What do you expect?"

Quietly they left the room, hurried down the stairs to the dumbwaiter, and hauled themselves one at a time back up to the southern guest wing. Charis was first inside the dumbwaiter. It was dry.

If Ferris were back inside the palace, he hadn't used the same path as before.

The guest wing was quiet, the hallway dimly lit by a few flickering sconces along the walls. Ferris stood beside their bedroom door, looking worried.

"Hurry!" he mouthed, pointing at the end of the corridor where the Rakuuna patrol would soon be making their rounds.

Charis looked at the floor as though being careful not to slip in her wet boots as she walked past Ferris. It was that or spit her fury in his face.

"You're back." Reuben shot off the couch, his face pale and weary.

"We're fine," Tal said softly. "Get some sleep."

"Shouldn't we talk about what you learned from Ollen and Thorsby tonight?" Ferris asked.

Charis nodded. "Of course. But the patrol might hear us speaking, and we're all exhausted. Get some sleep. We'll speak about it tomorrow."

She managed to make eye contact with him and smile, though it turned her stomach to do so.

Ferris left, Reuben settled onto the couch and began dozing, and Holland wandered into his room and shut the door. Charis walked to her room, Tal behind her, and turned as he quietly closed the door behind him.

"We have a problem," she said the instant the door clicked shut.

"What's wrong?" He moved closer. "Something's been off with you since we left the bakery."

"I overheard Ferris call Mason by the name Bartho." Her voice shook, and she sank slowly onto the chair that rested in front of the vanity.

Tal stared at her in silence for a long moment, his eyes dark, his jaw tight. Finally, in a voice she barely recognized, he said, "Stay right here. I'm going to go beat the truth out of Ferris."

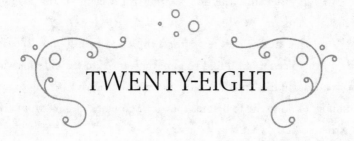

TWENTY-EIGHT

"You can't go pick a fight with Ferris," Charis said firmly.

"Watch me," Tal snarled, turning toward the door.

"Wait!" She scrambled to her feet. "What if I'm wrong?"

"Are you?" He held her gaze, fury in his eyes.

Slowly she shook her head. "No."

"Then I'll be back here momentarily with a bloodied and beaten Ferris. In fact, I think I'll invite Holland and Reuben to the party, and we'll make sure Lord Everly gets his due as well." He grabbed the doorknob.

She threw herself between him and the door. "No."

"Charis." He looked at the ceiling as if searching for patience and then tipped his head down to meet her eyes. "That man hired the assassin who shot an arrow at your heart. And you were poisoned, remember? At the Everlys' house! It must have been his voice I heard saying to put poison in your dinner in case you hadn't already ingested enough from your drink."

"I know."

"That means the Everlys must have been working with Lady Channing all along."

She sagged against the door as the true weight of the Everlys' treachery sank in.

"And that means they're traitors who tried to kill you. Repeatedly." His voice shook. "I told you I never wanted to see you slip away from me again like you did on the floor of the Everlys' dining room, and now I know who to blame. You aren't going to stop me from giving them exactly what they deserve."

"I have to." The words scraped over her tongue, bitter and raw. She was so furious she wanted to tear the Everlys apart piece by piece until there was nothing left, but a chess match wasn't won with emotion.

"Why?" He placed his hands against the door on either side of her and leaned close. "If they were working with Lady Channing, then they were working with the Rakuuna from the start. Which means Father isn't the one who wants all four heirs here for the wedding. The Everlys do. Those rumors about you?" His breath fanned her face, and she caught a whiff of black tea and peppermint. "I'd bet every drop of blood in my body the Everlys started them. They can't just kill you, Holland, and Nalani. They have to discredit you first so that Calerans accept Ferris as their king."

"I know," she whispered.

"Then why protect them?" He went still, his eyes boring into hers. "Is this about us? It is, isn't it? You don't trust my motives, or my will to do what's necessary, or—"

"It's not that." She waited for a twinge of pain from the wound he'd given her, but somewhere along the way, it had knit itself back together, and the scar tissue held.

His eyes locked onto hers. "It isn't?"

She shook her head, and the fragile hope that bloomed in his eyes made the small torch he'd once lit within her glow a little brighter.

"Then help me understand, because right now, all I want to do is hurt the ones who've hurt you, and I don't see a single reason why I should hold back."

"Because taking the Everlys out of the equation creates additional problems right now." Her eyes drifted down to his lips, and she ordered herself to stop it immediately.

They were surrounded by enemies. Her life hung by a thread, and her power-hungry cousin held the blade. Everyone she loved was in danger. Now was the time for strategic thinking and careful planning, not for wishing she could have one last, wild kiss with Tal just to see if the scar tissue held and the ache inside softened into something tender.

"Please stop looking at me like that," Tal said quietly, his voice full of the same longing that lived within her.

She dragged her gaze back up to his eyes. "I'm not looking at you like anything."

"Liar." He breathed the word, tipping his head and bringing his face closer to hers. "You're distracting me from vengeance, and you're doing an excellent job, but I'm still going to walk out of this room and do what needs to be done."

"I'll do what needs to be done." Charis lifted her chin. "But it has to be public. I need to unmask the Everlys in front of both the Raku-una and those with influence in Calera. If I do that, I can silence the rumors about me with the truth about them, and I can force Queen Bai'elsha to switch her allegiance to me or risk losing the serpanicite she needs from your father."

He was silent for a long moment, his face still close to hers, his scent wrapping around her like a memory she'd almost forgotten. Finally, he said, "You're right."

"I know."

He smiled a little, but it disappeared quickly. "There's only one event that will bring the Rakuuna, the Everlys, and those with influence in Calera into the same room."

She couldn't meet his eyes. "The wedding."

He stepped back. Silence fell between them, broken only by the patter of rain against her window and the faint crackle from the wick of the lamp lit beside her bed. Then he put a hand into his coat pocket and said, "I once thought seeing you marry my brother would be more than I could endure, but I was wrong."

She frowned.

"I can endure the wedding ceremony, and the thought of you with him, and the years of marriage afterward. I'll hate every second of it, but I can survive it." He pulled something from his pocket and stepped closer. "What I can't endure is not being the one to protect you. To stand between you and the rest of the world that always seems to want something from you but very rarely gives you anything in return."

"Tal—"

"I can't endure hurting you. I can't survive losing your trust. Losing *you*."

It was impossible to look away. She could see his heart written on his face, and the tender, aching warmth within her flared a little brighter.

His eyes darkened as he watched her expression, and then he said, "I brought you a present."

She blinked as he opened his hand to reveal a teacup painted in delicate swirls of blue and silver, just like the ones in Rames's basement. "What's this?"

"My favorite teacup."

"Your . . . what?"

"I don't have a holster, but I could get one. I'm a prince, so it would probably be pretty easy. Just commission it or—"

She held up a hand to stop the flow of words. "What are you talking about?"

His voice softened. "Remember when we went horseback riding and discussed which odious son of King Alaric you might have to marry? We joked that fussy Prince Percival wore his favorite teacup in a holster."

She eyed him warily. "I remember."

"I don't believe we've been properly introduced." He bowed, low and extravagant. "Prince Percival Talin Penbyrn, at your service."

She let out a tiny, incredulous snort of laughter. "I know who you are."

He gave her his crooked smile. "You know almost everything important there is to know about me, except this."

"A teacup?" She stared at the delicate thing. Had Tal lost his mind? Months of captivity at the hands of the Rakuuna after being tossed to the wolves in Calera by one's own father would be enough to break anyone.

"Remember? We were discussing your upcoming marriage, and you were worried about managing a man you'd never met."

She nodded, watching his face closely.

He held up the cup, his eyes fixed on hers. "I told you. Every man has a favorite teacup. Once you know what that is, you have the leverage you need to break him if you want to."

She stared at the cup for a long moment while the tender thing inside her became almost painful to the touch and then finally said, "You've never even seen this thing before today."

"I drink from it all the time."

"You stole it from the basement of Rames's bakery."

"I would never."

"Liar." Her voice was nothing but a breath.

He knelt in front of her, holding the cup out to her as if he was offering her a crown. "You're my teacup, Charis. All you need to do to break me is to tell me to leave you. Please, *please* don't tell me to leave."

He was right. She did know all the important things about him. She knew the depth of his loyalty, and how, even as the world crumbled around them, his only thought was to sacrifice himself in return for the Rakuuna's promise to let the Calerans live. She knew that he'd lied about his name, but not about his heart. And she knew that his weakness was that he'd wanted more time with her before his truth drove them apart forever.

He'd wounded her, but doing so had wounded him, too.

And she didn't want to face her fate without him by her side.

With trembling hands, she reached out and wrapped her hands around the teacup, her fingers resting against his. Quietly she said, "I don't want you to leave."

His voice trembled as he asked, "Does that mean that you can forgive me?"

Once upon a time, she'd sworn that forgiveness was impossible. That the wound he'd dealt had been a killing blow. But now she found the pain had become a dull bruise, fading a little more every time Tal proved who he truly was in his heart. She pulled him to his feet.

"I forgive you." She placed the teacup on the vanity with care and turned to find him standing there, longing on his face as he watched her.

"You need to know that I'm still in love with you. I don't expect you to love me back. I just wanted—I can't stand keeping secrets from you."

She couldn't look away from him.

"I want to kiss you," he said. "Would that be all—"

She closed the distance between them and pressed her lips to his, and for a few glorious moments, nothing existed but the heat of his skin, the way her body fit against his, and the brilliant light burning in her heart.

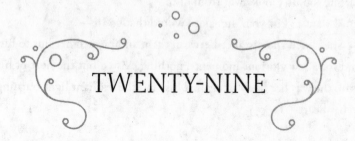

TWENTY-NINE

THE NEXT MORNING, Charis waited until Lanni had served breakfast before beckoning Holland, Tal, and Reuben into her room.

Tal stationed himself beside the door, leaving it open a crack so he could see if anyone entered their suite. Charis had considered simply locking the suite door, but if the Everlys came to discuss her meeting with Lady Ollen and Lord Thorsby, they couldn't find anything out of the ordinary.

Besides, the Rakuuna patrol would come back through in less than twenty minutes, and a locked door earned the occupants a very unpleasant search of both their belongings and their bodies.

"What are we doing in here?" Holland asked.

"We're having a discussion where we won't be overheard, and where we'll have a bit of warning if someone walks in." Charis stood with her hands folded at her waist, calm and certain of what she needed to do. Fury had hardened into the icy rage she'd used to survive Mother's expectations. Charis was the immovable cliff her enemies would crash against, not realizing the danger until they were already in pieces at her feet.

She met Tal's gaze and found the same immovable certainty in him. "You'll keep him contained?"

"I will." Tal glanced at Holland and then moved his feet into the first rathma position. Reuben took one look at Tal and hefted his curtain rod, though he wasn't yet sure what was going on.

"Keep who contained?" Holland demanded, looking from Charis to Tal.

"You." Charis drew in a deep breath. "You aren't going to like what I'm about to say."

Holland's eyebrow rose. "If you think the impostor is enough to stop me if I . . . Wait. Why would the impostor need to stop me from doing anything? Aren't we on the same side?" He glared at Tal. "Don't make me regret being your friend."

"This isn't about Tal." Charis kept her tone gentle, though the ice within her wanted to cut something to ribbons. "It's about Ferris."

"That little weasel?" Holland snorted. "What's he done now?"

"I overheard him call Mason by the name Bartho when they were arguing in the bakery last night."

Holland frowned. "Bartho? Who's that? It sounds familiar, but I can't—"

"It's the man who hired the assassins that came after Charis." Reuben's voice shimmered with violence. "Tal is going to have to stop me as well, Your Majesty, because if Bartho is working for the Everlys, that makes them—"

"Dead," Holland said flatly. "They're on borrowed time; they just don't know it. Reuben, let's go."

Tal pivoted, using his body to block the door as Reuben and Holland advanced.

"Out of the way," Holland said. "I'd hate to have to hurt you."

"I, on the other hand, wouldn't mind at all. Stand aside." Reuben lifted his curtain rod like it was a sword.

"I felt the same when I first heard about it, but you need to listen to Charis before doing anything." Tal sounded calm, but his cheeks were flushed. "Trust me, when it comes time to destroy the Everlys, I'm going to be first in line."

Charis unclasped her hands. "We have to be strategic. The Everlys have protection. Lady Channing confessed to setting the assassination attempts in motion—"

"Which means the Everlys were working with her. Yes, I've got the gist of things, Charis." Holland's voice rose. "What I don't understand is why we're hesitating to drop them where they stand." He turned on Tal. "You of all people ought to be ready to kill them for what they did to Charis. I'm usually happily oblivious to how other people feel, but even I can tell that you love her."

"I'm more than ready," Tal said, anger sparking in his eyes. "But Charis has good reasons to wait."

Reuben looked to Charis, his already-pale face losing any trace of color. "Your Majesty, Lady Channing also confessed to working with the Rakuuna. That means the Everlys are working with them, too."

"Yes, which complicates things." Charis stepped closer to Holland as his eyes widened and his hands curled into fists.

"Nalani." Holland's voice shook. "They know where she is. They know where the rebellion is headquartered, and they know about the message, and—I have to leave. I need to get to Solvang."

He turned to find Tal still blocking the door. "Get out of my way, or I'll go right through you."

Charis moved to Holland's side. "I warned Rames to get everyone out the instant we left, so we can hope they're all safe—"

"*Nalani* isn't safe." Holland met Charis's gaze. "She's not a fighter. Not with weapons, at least. She doesn't stand a chance if they find her, and now we've told them exactly where to look. If we contain the Everlys before they deliver the message—"

"It's too late," Charis said gently. "Holland, it's too late, and you know it. We gave her location to Ferris yesterday morning. I'm sure some Rakuuna were sent to Solvang before lunch was served. The palloren won't reach her in time. There's nothing we can do to save her from being taken."

It was an awful truth, and it had kept her up most of the night, sick with fear.

"No." Holland whirled and plowed straight into Tal. Tal deflected the first punch, absorbed the second, and then spun Holland into the wall.

"Stop," Tal said quietly. "You can't get to your sister before the monsters do. Charis has a plan that ends in the deaths of those who deserve it, but she needs your help."

"Let me go!" Holland shoved at Tal, but then Reuben was there, wrestling Holland's free arm while Tal pivoted, flowed into the third rathma, and drove Holland to his knees.

Charis crouched in front of him and gripped his shoulders. "I'm scared, too. I want her safe. I want them dead. But if we aren't careful, the Everlys will decide it's too risky to keep you, Nalani, and me alive long enough to frame us for the invasion. They want the throne. If they think for one minute that we know the truth, we're all dead. Do you see that? I need you with me, Holland, or we are all *dead*."

He held her gaze, his dark eyes desperate. "I'm supposed to keep her safe. She's my *sister*."

"You can keep her safe by helping me." Charis prayed she was speaking the truth. She had very little leverage now that Nalani would no longer be in Solvang to coordinate. Surely someone else there would take up the job in her absence. Unless Charis's allies decided

Calera was a lost cause and instead divided the moriarthy dust among themselves in case the Rakuuna came for their kingdom next.

Holland closed his eyes, his jaw clenched tight, and then drew in a breath. "Fine." His eyes opened. "What's your plan?"

"First, and most important, we have to pretend that nothing's wrong around both the Everlys and the staff. We don't know who we can trust."

Holland made a noise in the back of his throat. "If you expect me to be nice to the Everlys, you're in for some disappointment."

"Just behave like you usually do. You're never nice to them," Tal said.

"Because clearly I'm an excellent judge of character." Holland shook off the hands that held him and climbed to his feet.

Charis rose to hers as well and said softly, "We're going to act like we trust them, but we aren't going to tell them anything they don't already know. I'm sure they've already sent a message to King Alaric telling him he can bring the jewels in exchange for marrying his heir to ours. At the wedding feast, I'm going to get the Everlys to expose their treachery, thus silencing the rumors about us, and I'm going to make Queen Bai'elsha swear allegiance to me instead of the Everlys so that she doesn't kill us on their orders."

"How?" Reuben asked as the door to their suite clicked open.

Charis smiled, cold and regal, as Ferris and Lord Everly walked into the sitting room. "By being the queen my mother raised me to be."

Charis moved past Tal and swept into the sitting room, icy composure firmly in place. "Oh good, you're both here. We were just discussing how to handle King Alaric's alliance with the Rakuuna. I'd love to hear your thoughts."

Behind her, Reuben and Tal filed into the room, taking up their posts on either side of her chair as if she was seated on a throne.

Holland stalked past the Everlys, not even sparing them a glance, entered his room, and shut the door.

"What's wrong with him?" Ferris asked.

Charis sighed. "You know Holland. He can't stand being cooped up like this, and it's made him grumpy."

"Never mind Holland." Lord Everly leaned forward, avarice in his eyes. "My son says you found Lady Ollen and Lord Thorsby. What plans have they made? How can we assist them from inside the palace?"

Charis matched his body language and lowered her voice as if sharing a secret. "To be honest, I expected better than what I found. The rebellion is nothing more than a handful of people, poorly organized, with no solutions to the current problems our people face, and no ideas worth implementing. One would think Lord Thorsby, at least, would have put some administrative infrastructure in place, given his years of experience running the royal council, but perhaps I'm being too hard on them. These are difficult times."

"Surely they knew something of value that could help us." Lord Everly exchanged a glance with Ferris. She had to give them something if she wanted her lie to appear credible.

"Indeed." She sat back, spine straight, every inch a queen. "They've compiled a list of nobility who've apparently sworn loyalty to the Rakuuna instead of to the Willowthorns. Once we've managed to save our throne from King Alaric's treachery, that list will come in quite handy as we fill our dungeons."

"That's it?" Ferris's lip curled. "Months of sneak attacks and spreading rumors about how strong the spirit of resistance is within the Caleran people, and they're just tattling on others for saving their own skin?"

Charis inclined her head as though to credit Ferris with this piece of wisdom. "I'd hoped for more organized support for our most pressing issues, but unfortunately, it looks like we can't rely on them for help until we've already figured out how to save ourselves. Thankfully, I have one of Mother's most trusted advisors at my side. Now, Lord Everly, you've had two months of experience dealing with both Alaric and the Rakuuna. What wisdom can you offer?"

As Lord Everly began speaking, filling the room with vague assertions and half-truths that continued to point the blame at King Alaric, Charis held herself perfectly still, her expression carved from glass, and hunted through his words for a weapon she could turn against him when the time was right.

THIRTY

A WEEK PASSED, and then another. Charis had settled into a routine. Wake early and check to make sure Holland hadn't changed his mind and snuck out of the palace at night. Force herself to eat a few bites of breakfast because, if she didn't, Tal threatened to feed her himself. Remain stoic as the Rakuuna patrol searched her quarters and her person as they'd taken to doing the day after she'd returned from her clandestine visit to the bakery. Endure a visit from the Everlys and yet another interminable discussion about the upcoming wedding feast. Pick through their words and carefully guard her own. Watch Holland spar with Tal until he wore himself out and feel grateful that Tal was willing to give Holland an outlet for his fury. Feel grateful for the few afternoons that Dec and Grim were able to sneak out of their room to spar with Holland so that Tal could have a break. Pretend to enjoy dinner though she could barely stomach swallowing a bite. And then sit with Tal in the quiet of the night, trying to find and hold on to her equilibrium so she could do it all over again.

Tension coiled within her like a spring, tightening every time the door opened, every time she heard Ferris's voice, and every time she had to stop Holland from exploding.

Her plan to expose the Everlys and force Queen Bai'elsha to swear allegiance to Charis instead was paper-thin. She couldn't count on Lady Ollen and Lord Thorsby to somehow smuggle weapons into the feast when they'd had to flee the city. She couldn't depend on Nalani to coordinate an attack with the retired admiral from Solvang. She couldn't trust that any of her allies would honor her request to send three ships to Te'ash to threaten Queen Bai'elsha's people. She had no leverage and no power.

Everything depended on being three steps ahead of her enemies, saying the right words at the right time, and bluffing a species of monsters capable of tearing her limb from limb in seconds.

If she failed at any point, all was lost.

The oatmeal she'd been trying to swallow tasted like dust in her suddenly dry mouth. Her heart pounded, a jarring rhythm that made her feel slightly sick. She reached for water to wash down her breakfast, but her hands shook, and she knocked the cup to the floor instead.

It shattered on impact, water spreading across the wooden floor, shards of glass gleaming in the morning light.

"I'll get it," Reuben said brusquely as she moved to pick up the pieces.

She forced the oatmeal down her throat and said, "I can clean up my own messes."

"A queen doesn't need to do that," he replied as Tal and Holland came out of their respective rooms at the same time.

"What happened?" Tal asked, glancing from the shattered glass to Charis.

"I knocked it over." She drew in a breath, cursing the tension in her chest that made it feel like she couldn't properly fill her lungs no matter how hard she tried. "Just clumsy this morning, I guess."

Holland snorted. "You're never clumsy." He stalked over to the breakfast tray, grabbed a slice of pumpkin bread, and looked at Charis. "Are you sick? Tal, she looks sick."

If she looked sick, Holland wasn't much better. His eyes were shadowed with worry, his body bruised from the merciless sparring sessions he and Tal participated in every afternoon. He looked utterly exhausted even as he kept himself in perpetual motion.

"I'm not sick. No, I'm—That's not necessary." She flinched as Holland smacked the back of his hand against her forehead. "See? No fever."

"Then what's wrong with you?" he asked as he took another bite and began prowling around the sitting room.

Tal crouched next to her as Reuben swept the mess into a towel. "Holland is right. You don't look well."

It was on the tip of her tongue to say that she was fine—a lie no one in the room would believe, but one she'd stand behind because the fate of her kingdom depended on her strength—when the suite door opened and a pair of Rakuuna guards walked in.

"On its feet," he said, his high voice scraping over Charis's nerves like a razor.

"Hey, genius, I'm already on my feet," Holland snapped. "It's like you have two brain cells and both of them are competing for third place."

The guard snarled, swiveling his head in Holland's direction.

Charis stood quickly, sending her bowl of oatmeal tumbling. Tal caught it before it hit the floor, but Charis was already rushing to put herself between the guard and Holland.

"We're ready for your search," she said, trying hard to sound calm even as her heart slammed against her chest as though it meant to tear itself free.

"We're sick of your searches," Holland said. "We aren't allowed to leave this wing, and we barely leave this room. What do you think you're going to find that you haven't found already?"

"Holland, just get it over with," Tal said.

"Fine." Holland raised his fists and assumed a fighting stance as he faced the guard. "Come search me if you can."

The guard lunged forward, his pale, webbed hands shoving Charis out of the way as he went for Holland. Charis slammed into the sofa and tumbled to the floor. Reuben snatched his curtain rod and leaped to her side while Tal vaulted over the back of the sofa to crouch beside her.

Holland roared in fury and grabbed a heavy brass candelabra from the side table. "Come and get what you deserve."

The guard crashed into Holland, and they both collided with the table. Holland swung the candelabra at the Rakuuna's face, but the guard wrapped his too-long fingers around Holland's hand and wrenched the weapon free. He grabbed Holland's throat with his other hand and squeezed. Holland bucked and twisted, clawing at the monster to no avail.

"Stop him," Charis said as she struggled to her knees. "*Please*, Tal."

Holland was going to goad the Rakuuna into killing him, and there was nothing Charis could do.

Tal ran toward the pair as from the doorway behind Charis, the other Rakuuna guard said something in her own language. Instantly, the guard who was choking Holland let go, though he kept Holland pinned beneath him.

Holland coughed roughly and then said, "Get off me if you

know what's good for you."

"Holland?" A familiar voice filled the room, and Charis twisted toward the door to see Nalani standing just inside the sitting room. Her dark eyes were fearful, and a bruise shadowed the side of her neck. The air left Charis's lungs as if she'd been struck.

Holland froze.

Tal used the opportunity to reach his side and press a calming hand on the other boy's shoulder. Quietly, Tal said to the guard, "We apologize for the disturbance. He was worried about his sister. Please understand."

The Rakuuna hissed at Holland, but the female guard said something, and he got to his feet in a lithe, graceful movement that was far more fluid than anything a human could manage.

Tal grabbed Holland's hand and pulled him to his feet. The instant he was upright, Holland rushed to Nalani and threw his arms around her. Nalani hugged Holland, her forehead pressed to his chest, her shoulders heaving as she sobbed.

Tears stung Charis's eyes as she waited her turn to hug her cousin. She barely noticed the guards searching each room, hardly felt their hands as they swept over her. They ignored the satchel, believing their ship captain's report that it was medicine. She'd stuffed the little envelope of mursilla herb given to her by Lord Thorsby into the satchel, too.

The guards muttered to each other as they left, closing the suite door behind them. Holland patted Nalani's back and said fiercely, "Don't you ever scare me like that again."

Nalani pulled back, her breath shuddering. "You've got a sack of hay for a brain if you think *you* were the one who was scared. I got dragged out a *window* in the middle of the night, thrown into a ship's brig with the nastiest-tempered Rakuuna you can imagine, and spent a week on the water wondering if I was ever going to see anyone I loved again."

Holland patted her one more time before slowly letting go. "Only a week?" His voice was thick with emotion, and he cleared his throat. "Charis, Tal, Reuben, and I spent a lot longer than that in a Rakuuna brig."

"And that's another thing!" Nalani raised a finger and pointed it in his face. "You were supposed to watch over Charis and stay alive, and what do you do? You let her act as *bait* for the monsters and then you join her."

Holland raised an eyebrow. "Well, I certainly wasn't going to be left out."

Nalani threw her hands into the air and turned to Charis. "I expect it's been difficult spending so much time with my brother." One final tear slid down her cheek, and she swiped at it with her palm.

"You have no idea," Tal muttered as Charis rushed forward and hugged Nalani.

"I heard that." Holland folded his arms over his chest.

"You were meant to." Tal moved closer to Nalani and said, "I'm really glad you're safe."

Holland laughed. "No one in this room is safe."

"You know what I meant." There was a warning in Tal's voice, but Holland paid no attention.

"I know that all four heirs are now in the palace, which means the filthy traitors in our midst will be trying to kill us soon." For the first time in weeks, Holland sounded like his normal self. He settled into a chair, draped one leg over the edge, and snatched another slice of pumpkin bread.

Tal grabbed breakfast for himself and sat on the sofa while Reuben stood by the door, ready to cause a distraction if the Everlys entered during a discussion of their treachery.

Charis ignored them all and simply held her cousin. Nalani had lost weight. Her bones pressed sharply against her skin, and she trembled as she leaned against Charis.

"I can't imagine how awful that trip was when you were all alone," Charis said. "And Holland's right. We aren't safe here. But I am so glad to see you alive and well."

Nalani clung to her and whispered, "I thought you all must be dead. Why else would they send for me? They needed an heir to exchange with Alaric, and I thought I must be the only one left."

"If Ferris gets his way, none of us will be left," Holland said, an edge of fury to his voice.

"Ferris?" Nalani stepped back, wiping more tears from her face.

"It's an explanation that can keep for a few more minutes." Charis shot a look at Holland, and he closed his mouth. "Let's get you cleaned up and fed."

An hour later, Nalani was bathed, dressed in a plain gown of green wool, and had eaten a bowl of oatmeal and two slices of bread. Charis had eaten more as well—not because she was hungry, but because Holland was right. Now that Nalani was here, the Everlys would soon make their move, and Charis had to be clearheaded if she was going to have any chance at defeating them.

As if her thoughts had summoned him, the suite door opened, and Ferris entered. Holland choked in the act of swallowing the rest of his sister's bread and coughed so hard, he gagged.

Ferris's lip curled. "That's disgusting. Go be sick in the bath chamber."

Holland coughed once more and then said, "I can't be the only one you have that effect on, Ferris."

"One of these days someone is going to have to teach you some manners." Ferris brushed his hands against his shirt as if wiping off the taint of being near Holland.

Holland raised his head and pinned Ferris with his dark eyes. "Want to try?"

"I see nothing has changed," Nalani said, dusting crumbs from her dress.

"If by that you mean that your brother is still an embarrassment to Caleran nobility, then you are correct." Ferris moved closer to Nalani, and Holland made a warning sound in the back of his throat.

Nalani raised one eyebrow in a look that was a copy of the expression her twin usually wore. "I meant that you're still as insufferable as you ever were."

Something flashed across Ferris's face, and a chill spread over Charis's skin. Holland opened his mouth, but Charis said, "Enough arguing. Ferris, would you like some bread? We have one slice left."

"Thank you, Charis, but I've been sent by Queen Bai'elsha to deliver a message, and I can't stay long."

"We're heartbroken." Holland took the final slice of bread and stuffed half of it in his mouth.

"What message?" Charis asked, folding her hands in her lap to hide their trembling. She knew what he was going to say before he said it. All four heirs were here. It was time.

"She welcomed King Alaric and his traveling companions to the palace several days ago. Now that Nalani is here, she and Alaric have agreed to hold the wedding feast this evening so that Alaric will send for the jewels the Rakuuna need." Ferris stepped back. "We're to dress appropriately, of course, so a maid will bring clothing fit for the occasion."

Charis met his gaze and inclined her head. "Thank you. Do you want to join me in discussing how to convince Alaric not to go through with his plan to kill us all once the wedding is finalized?"

Nalani sucked in a breath but said nothing.

Ferris waited a beat and then said, "I wish I could, but Father needs me."

"Of course." Charis kept her expression open and somewhat friendly as Ferris left the room.

Seconds after the door closed behind him, Nalani said, "Somebody start explaining what in the seers' name is going on."

THIRTY-ONE

THREE HOURS LATER, they had explained the situation to Nalani, and she, in turn, had filled them in on what had happened with their allies after Charis's ship had sailed from Solvang.

It was as bad as Charis feared.

The retired admiral had made a battle plan, coordinating with admirals from Solvang, Thallis, and Verace, and enough ships had been committed to the cause to truly qualify as an armada. However, once Orayn and his crew returned with the moriarthy dust without knowing how to use it and word spread that Charis had offered herself as bait to the pursuing Rakuuna ship and hadn't been heard from since, the rulers of Calera's allies had kept their ships in port.

The pallorens Charis had tasked Lord Thorsby with sending would have arrived in Solvang by now, provided he'd been able to get out of the city before Ferris and Bartho alerted the Rakuuna to his whereabouts. But even if Charis's messages had been received, it didn't change her situation or her plans. Yes, her allies would know how to use the moriarthy dust, but they wouldn't have had enough time to reach Calera yet.

And that's if they were even coming. It was smarter for them to consider Calera a loss, divide the poison among them, and shore up their own defenses while praying the Rakuuna never decided to pay them a visit.

Either way, the result was the same. Charis and her people were facing their enemies alone.

Lanni served lunch, and when they were finished eating, Charis insisted that everyone get some rest. Whatever happened at the feast that night, they all needed to be alert and ready.

Nalani joined her in her bedroom, the two of them curling up on the wide four-poster bed. As soon as they were settled, Nalani spoke.

"So Tal is back."

Charis blinked. "Um, yes. I guess we skipped that part of the story."

"The fact that Ferris and his family are going to try to frame us for their own treachery and then kill us was important information." Nalani flipped over to face Charis and snuggled into her pillow. "But now I'm desperately curious to know how Tal is part of the picture again, why Holland hasn't killed him, and how you feel about all this."

Charis's cheeks grew warm as she told the story of reuniting with Tal on the Rakuuna ship and how it had made sense to work with him since he understood his father.

"I think you're leaving out all the good parts." Nalani poked Charis's shoulder. "Tal must have had a very good explanation for his actions, because I know for a fact Holland was ready to gut him the instant he saw him, and I was pretty certain you were never going to speak to him again."

"I didn't speak to him—or at least, I didn't say much, for a long time. And Holland was prepared to slice him open as soon as we entered the cabin, but Tal stopped him."

"How?"

Charis smiled a little. "By telling Holland that we needed Tal's help getting our kingdom back and that once all of this was over, he wouldn't fight back because nothing Holland did to him would be worse than how it felt to know he'd hurt me."

"All right, I know you don't want to hear this, but I think that proves Tal is who we thought he was all along. Only his name is different." Nalani stretched and then caught sight of Charis's face. "Or maybe you *do* want to hear nice things about Tal."

"It took a long time, but I was able to forgive him." Charis pulled the blanket up to her chin. She didn't expect to sleep. Not when every move she made and every word she said tonight had to be choreographed as precisely as a ballet. But Nalani looked like she needed days of sleep, not just the few hours they had before they had to dress up in wedding finery and fight for their lives.

Nalani smiled a little. "I forgive him, too."

"Try to get some rest." Charis closed her eyes to encourage Nalani to do the same. It was hard to lie still. She wanted to pace. To hold a sword in her hand and swing it at a target. To throw her head back and scream at the unfairness of it all.

How could she rest when, in a matter of hours, she would either manipulate and bluff her enemies into a corner or she would die, along with those she loved?

Nalani gave a wet sniff, and Charis's eyes flew open. Her cousin was huddled against the pillow, tears streaming down her face.

"Nalani?"

"I'm sorry." She hiccupped and then cried harder.

"It's all right." Charis scooted closer and wrapped her hand around Nalani's. "You can cry if you need to."

"I'm not ready to die," she whispered.

Charis's throat closed, and she had to swallow twice before she could speak. "I'm not, either."

"I haven't seen Mother and Father in months. They won't know that we're innocent. What if they aren't even there tonight to say goodbye?" She sucked in a sharp breath. "Or what if they are there, and they have to watch us die?"

"We can't think like that." Charis tried to sound firm, but her voice shook.

"I've never even been kissed." Nalani sniffed again. "I know that's a stupid thing to think about right now, but I want so much out of my life. I loved being ambassador to Solvang. I was good at it."

"You're good at a lot of things." Charis blinked as tears stung her own eyes.

"So are you. I had dreams for the two of us. I wanted to live a long, useful life and be remembered as a strong, smart woman who changed our kingdom for the better." Nalani squeezed Charis's hand. "I wanted you to be remembered as the best queen Calera has ever known. And together, we would be unstoppable."

Charis used her free hand to gently wipe tears from Nalani's cheeks. "Who says we aren't?"

Nalani choked on a laugh that sounded suspiciously close to a sob. "We're surrounded by traitors and monsters, but you don't waver. You don't break."

"I can't."

"Even if you need to?" Nalani lifted tearstained eyes to hold Charis's gaze.

"Even then." Charis blinked before her own tears could fall.

"I want you to know that I have faith in you." Nalani's voice was earnest. "I know I'm a mess right now, but I won't be tonight. I'll be proudly standing next to my queen, ready to help you take back our kingdom. I won't break when it counts."

"I know you won't." Charis soothed, feeling raw and unsettled. She wanted to crawl into Father's arms and believe everything would be all right just because he said it would be. She wanted to follow Mother into the dining hall, taking her cues from the fiercest queen Calera had ever known.

She didn't want to find the strength to carry the weight of her kingdom's fate on her shoulders.

She didn't want to, but she would.

It was her job to tell others it would be all right and make them believe it. Her time to become the fiercest queen in Calera's history.

Nalani's eyes fluttered shut, and she slid into sleep. Charis lay still, eyes wide open, thoughts racing as she considered every possible scenario that might happen at the wedding feast and chose the best countermove. Tonight was the final chess match between her and her enemies. She couldn't afford to lose.

Hours later, as the sun was disintegrating into fiery ribbons across the horizon, Lanni brought clothes for each of them and set them out. Nalani had chosen to get ready with Holland, who'd taken to pacing again while strongly advocating for simply breaking the Everlys' necks before they ever had a chance to leave their rooms.

Someone knocked softly on her bedroom door as Charis surveyed the clothing laid out on the bed. "Come in," she called.

Tal entered wearing a formal dress coat, trousers, shirt, and cravat. He stared at her bed, where a frothy, pale blue confection of a ball gown lay. It had long sleeves that still left most of her shoulders bare, and delicate swoops of lace and ribbon decorated the skirt, which glittered with tiny bits of sea sapphires woven into its threads.

Tal pointed at the dress. "Isn't that—"

"The wedding gown my seamstress was creating for me before the invasion? Yes." She moved to the bed and brushed her hand over the skirt. A pair of silver dancing heels rested on the floor. "Getting fitted for this seems like a lifetime ago."

"That was the first time Bartho tried to have you killed," Tal said, coming to stand beside her. "Seems appropriate to punish his bosses tonight while wearing this."

"I'm going to need help getting into it."

His eyes widened. "Do you want me to—"

"Get Nalani for me? Yes."

He cleared his throat. "That's exactly what I was going to say."

An hour later, Charis was in her gown, and Nalani was in the sitting room talking quietly with Holland.

"Look at you, dressed up for a ball but without a hairstyle to match." Tal came up behind her as she sat in front of her vanity, his brown eyes warm when they met hers in the mirror, though there were shadows of worry within.

"I seem to make a habit of that," she said, reaching for one of the small bottles of perfume that were clustered in the corner of the vanity. It was the same scent Father had given to her on her seventeenth birthday.

If she was going into battle, it was only fitting that the man who'd loved her unconditionally should be part of her armor.

"Why the pageantry?" Tal gestured at his outfit and then hers. "If Ferris is going to accuse us of treachery, why clean us up as if we still have power?"

Charis dabbed the fragrance behind her ears, a pang in her heart at the delicate scent of plum and thesserin flower. Father was the only person in the world who had ever seen Charis as delicate.

"For the benefit of the audience." Charis set the perfume bottle down with care and reached for a stack of hairpins. "The Everlys will present your father and the Caleran nobility with what they expect to see. Ferris and his father can't afford to look like they have more power than I do."

"It would make people nervous."

Charis nodded and selected a hairpin that looked like a sapphire dagger. "If Ferris seems like he's reluctantly revealing the truth, building a case against me and the Farragins, then it will look like he's worthy of the power the crowd will confer on him, rather than appearing to have stolen it when no one was looking."

"Do you want to talk through the plan again?" he asked.

She drew in a cleansing breath and pushed it out again. "I have to goad the Everlys into revealing that they were working with Lady Channing. The simplest way to do that is to get under Ferris's skin until he gives Queen Bai'elsha an order."

"Even if they're working together, what makes you so sure the Everlys would dare order Queen Bai'elsha to do anything?" He frowned as he took the hairpin from her hands.

"Lord Everly wouldn't." She shook out her curls. "But Ferris thinks everyone's beneath him. He's the one I have to focus on. If he slips up, the nobility in the room will see the truth. That will silence the rumors about me, and then I can tell Queen Bai'elsha that I will honor the deal she made with your father. I marry Vahn—" Her voice shook, and she cleared her throat. "I marry him, and Alaric pays the serpanicite ransom. If she accepts that, the Everlys have no support, no power, and no way to avoid being punished for treason."

His eyes met hers. "And if Bai'elsha won't listen to you?"

She clenched her fists and then forced her hands to open. "Then

I use the moriarthy dust on the closest Rakuuna and convince her I sent ships to kill every living thing on Te'ash unless she works with me instead of against me."

They were silent for a moment, their expressions grim. Anything could go wrong tonight. *Everything* could go wrong. And those she loved would pay the price.

"It's going to be all right." Tal's hands came to rest on her bare shoulders, warm and steady. "Just breathe."

"I am."

"Liar." He said it tenderly.

He was right. The air felt too thick, her lungs too thin, and the boulder on her chest grew heavier. If Mother had been here, she'd have told Charis that she was raised to be faster, smarter, and stronger than anyone who dared come against her. If Father had been at her side, he'd have hugged her and said he loved her and not to forget to rely on others who loved her, too. She'd rarely taken Father's advice—mostly because Mother's expectations were the standard Charis was striving to reach—but this time he was right. She needed to be faster, smarter, and stronger, but to do that, she needed support.

"Charis?" Tal squeezed her shoulders gently.

"What if I fail?" She forced the words out before she lost her courage.

He closed his eyes for a moment, and when he opened them, all she could see was his faith in her.

"You won't. You'll read the people around you and gain information no one realizes they've given up. You'll find a gap in Ferris's plans, and you'll exploit it. He ought to know this about you, so he's a fool for even letting you in that door."

She drew in a shaky breath. "But I could still fail."

"Yes." He leaned down so that his face was beside hers and they were looking at each other through her mirror. "But you won't fail alone. We're all in this together."

She swallowed, her heart beating a little faster as the scent of his soap enveloped her.

He knelt beside her, turning her chair slightly so that she was looking down into his upturned face. "I believe in you. I know we're up against tremendous odds, and there's no one else I'd rather trust to get us through it."

She stared at him, her whole world narrowing down to the way his eyes lingered on her face and the tremble in his hands when he reached for hers.

"You are the best person I know." He swallowed hard. "You still take all the air out of a room for me when you enter. I think about you far more often than I should. I even dream about you sometimes—"

"You do?"

"I— Yes, but I'm not going to tell you about those, so don't even ask."

She raised an eyebrow. "You're the one who brought it up."

"A decision I regret." His eyes softened. "I have a lot of regrets, Charis, but you aren't one of them. I love you, and I'm with you every step of the way."

She bent swiftly and pressed her lips to his, swallowing his words as she kissed him. He froze for an instant, and then his arms came around her, and he crushed her against him.

Everything else faded away until all that was left was his lips, his hair in her fists, and her desperate need for him. She kissed him as if she meant to conquer him, and maybe she did. She wanted his surrender. His loyalty. The way he made her laugh and the way he understood her before she even said a word. She wanted every part of him to belong to her, and the sword at their backs left no time for hesitation.

When she finally pulled back, her heart racing, her breath catching in her throat, she felt as if the torch he'd lit in her heart had spilled into her veins, wild and delicate.

"I don't want to go into tonight without telling you that I still love you, too," she said, and he gave her his crooked smile before kissing her again.

Then he let go of her and stood. "I could kiss you all night, but we don't have that luxury. We need to do something about your hair."

She turned to face the mirror and found her curls in a wild halo around her face. "Have any ideas?"

His smile widened. "As a matter of fact, I do."

When the Rakuuna guard opened the door to summon the Calerans, Charis was standing in her silver heels, her gorgeous gown glittering in the lamplight, pieces of her hair twisted into small rosettes above her ears and secured with hairpins that looked like snakes. The rest of her hair fell free down her back. Nalani was glowing in a sea-blue gown, Holland looked dashing even if he'd refused to give up his battered duster for a dress coat. Even Reuben looked more like he used to in his freshly pressed palace uniform.

Tal turned and offered his hand to Charis. "Ready?"

She lifted her chin and called on the fury in her heart to be her shield. "Ready."

Together, they followed the Rakuuna from the room.

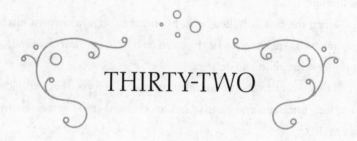

THIRTY-TWO

CHARIS'S STOMACH CHURNED as she entered the palace's formal dining room, Tal and Reuben at her side with Holland and Nalani following behind.

Jeweled chandeliers glittered above rows of tables draped with dark blue linens. Vases of bold red winter roses were flanked by ivory candles dripping wax, and the palace's best gold dishes graced the place settings.

Charis and Tal were surrounded by Rakuuna guards, the scales covering their nearly translucent skin shimmering in the golden light. More Rakuuna were stationed around the room, sealing off every exit. They carried no weapons, but the talons on their long fingers could cut like a blade, and the double rows of fangs in their mouths appeared needle-sharp.

Was the extensive Rakuuna presence due to the Everlys making sure Charis's allies didn't try to rescue her? Or was it Queen Bai'elsha ensuring that the Everlys didn't double cross her? Maybe both were worried that Charis, Holland, and Nalani would try to run.

Charis had no intention of running. She'd promised herself the night she'd sailed away from Calera that she'd return with a vengeance and either secure freedom for her people or die trying. Tonight, one way or the other, her quest would come to an end.

Queen Bai'elsha sat at the end of the table to the far right—a place of honor without being given the same ranking as the Calerans who would be seated at the head table with the Montevallians. Charis studied the Rakuuna queen in her sheer green sleeveless gown, its flowing swaths of fabric reminding her of the ocean's current. Bai'elsha's dark eyes were watchful, her pale lips parted to reveal her fangs.

Did the Rakuuna know she'd been slighted? Did she care? Or was she so singularly focused on making sure her deal with the Everlys came through that nothing else mattered?

She hoped it was the latter, because Bai'elsha's desperation and the small pouch of moriarthy dust were the only leverage Charis possessed.

"Your Highness, how lovely you look." Ferris approached, his voice carrying to the surrounding nobility, who immediately fell silent. "Of course, I realize you'd prefer we address you as Your Majesty, but since we haven't held a legal coronation yet, the council feels obligated to proceed according to Caleran law."

Charis tore her gaze from Bai'elsha and faced him. So he'd already begun to make his case against her. Accusing her of flaunting Caleran law in a clear grab for power would only play well with nobility who already suspected the Willowthorns of caring about power above people. She took the measure of the room again, slowly this time, and her heart sank.

Every person in attendance was a name on Lord Thorsby's list of those who'd chosen loyalty to the Rakuuna above their own people. There wasn't a single ally to the Willowthorns in the room. Would they even care if they learned of the Everlys' complicity? Or would they believe the Everlys, like themselves, bore no responsibility for the invasion and had simply been pragmatic in their choices?

Of course, people whose loyalty was only to themselves were also no true ally to the Everlys. Maybe if Charis could somehow convince them she was the better choice to help them save their own wealth and position, they might turn on Ferris and his father like starving wolves.

She faced Ferris and spoke with icy precision. "I'm curious which members of the council decided to meet in secret and declare that the coronation held on a Caleran ship by a Caleran captain before the required number of noble witnesses was illegal. Since Lord Thorsby and Lady Ollen have already accepted the coronation's outcome, that would leave your father, Lady Whitecross, and Lady Channing. Lady Whitecross has not been seen since the night of the invasion. Lady Channing was revealed to be a traitor and is dead. So that leaves . . ." She pretended to tick council members off with her fingers until she had just one finger raised in the air. "Your father, acting without the rest of the council, deciding that he alone could dictate whether the true heir to the throne received her crown. Am I missing anything?"

Holland made a scornful noise behind Charis, but thankfully kept his thoughts to himself. There might be a moment that evening when Charis would need Holland's forceful insistence on speaking only the unvarnished truth, but that time hadn't come yet.

Thunderclouds gathered in Ferris's eyes, though his expression remained excruciatingly polite. "Perhaps we can sort out the misunderstanding once we've finalized the treaty with King Alaric. He awaits us at the head table."

Charis sensed Tal stiffen at her side, and she glanced past Ferris to see King Alaric at the opposite end of the room, the purple jewels knotted into his long, graying blond hair glittering beneath the chandeliers. He looked at Tal and smoothed his maroon and black dress coat as though his hands needed something to do.

Prince Vahn stood to Alaric's right, his gaze finding Charis's and holding. His mouth still held the hint of cruelty she'd seen months before, but there was a shadow in his brown eyes that she couldn't identify.

On Alaric's left stood a tall young woman with blue eyes and Tal's jawline. Her maroon gown was accented by a silver sword sheathed at her waist. She barely glanced at Charis. Her full attention was on Tal, and the relief on her face made Charis decide that she liked Tal's sister, Zale, a great deal more than she did the rest of his family.

"How are we going to sort out a misunderstanding about Charis's title after finalizing the treaty?" Tal asked. "You told us King Alaric planned to kill us all once the ceremony was complete."

Ferris glanced around as though worried about others overhearing and said softly, "Yes, that seems to be his plan. But Father and I have been working to get a different bargain into place, so just go along with whatever happens, and you'll be safe."

"Tal is already safe," Nalani said. "We're the ones in danger."

"That's what I meant." Ferris sounded impatient. "All of you will be safe."

Interesting. Charis swept past Ferris and headed toward the Montevallians. Ferris wanted her to believe he was still on her side. Either he was worried she posed a threat—unlikely, or he wouldn't have even allowed her into the room—or there were at least a few people in the crowd who the Everlys were unsure of. They needed her to be compliant so they could incriminate her before she even had a chance to put up a defense.

Charis planned to be anything but compliant.

The nobles in attendance murmured as Charis, Tal, and Reuben began heading toward the Montevallians. Ferris kept pace beside them. Holland and Nalani had paused to take an appetizer from a serving girl's tray.

As they passed the middle of the room Charis looked to her left. Servants were taking wraps to the coatroom or delivering goblets of fizzy winterberry wine to each guest. One coat bearer met her gaze boldly and held it for a long moment before looking away.

Charis tracked his progress across the room until he entered the coatroom. Was he simply curious about the princess who'd gone missing after the invasion and had returned as a captive queen? Had he been ordered by the Everlys to keep an eye on her?

When he didn't reappear immediately, Charis kept walking. She couldn't afford distractions. Her plan to goad Ferris into exposing the Everlys, shift the Calerans' loyalty, and convince Queen Bai'elsha to align with her was a stack of cards. A single misstep would send the entire thing crashing down.

Tal cleared his throat as they approached his family. Charis turned her attention to King Alaric. She couldn't warn him of the Everlys' planned treachery without letting Ferris know that she knew what he'd been hiding. And even if she did warn Alaric, what could he do? He had four guards with him, plus Vahn and Zale. Not nearly enough to fight off both the Rakuuna and any Calerans who'd decided to swear fealty to Ferris instead of Charis. "Princess Charis, how nice to see you again." Vahn inclined his head respectfully, but his gaze quickly skipped past her to rest on Tal, a speculative gleam in his eyes. "I see you still have your bodyguard in tow."

"Someone had to care enough to rescue him." Charis aimed the words at Vahn but looked to Alaric, whose eyes narrowed as he turned from her to examine Tal. Never mind that Charis hadn't actually followed through on her plan to rescue Tal. Between Vahn, Alaric, and

Charis, she was the only one who'd even entertained the idea.

"Ah, so you know his identity now." Vahn sounded amused. "And his head is still attached to his shoulders. I guess you aren't really the formidable opponent he said you'd be."

"I'm no longer an opponent of anyone from *Montevallo*."

She looked hard at Vahn, willing him to be even half as intuitive as Tal. Would he understand that Charis had other enemies circling?

"We should take our seats," Ferris said, stepping between Charis and Vahn as if to direct the Montevallians to their designated chairs. "The ceremonial feast is about to begin."

Charis scanned the room once more, heart pounding as her gaze skipped from one person to the next. Not a friend in the bunch. Not even the servants would look at her. Only Bai'elsha met her eyes, but Charis couldn't read the expression in the Rakuuna queen's black eyes.

Charis was seated between Tal and Ferris, with Holland and Nalani just down from Tal. Alaric sat across from her, flanked by Vahn and Zale. Lord and Lady Everly sat beside the Montevallians. The head chair was empty. She supposed the Everlys wanted it to symbolize that Calera was without an official ruler until the wedding ceremony and coronation took place after the feast.

"I'd like a real explanation for why you're suddenly calling me Your Highness when you've spent two weeks calling me Your Majesty," she said to Ferris as the first course was placed in front of them. Let him think she was anxious and wanted him on her side. The closer you kept your enemy, the easier it was to cut them off at the knees.

Ferris's gaze shot toward his father and then at those seated at the surrounding tables.

"Laws and traditions must be upheld," he said primly, dabbing his mouth with his napkin. "We can't afford for Alaric to think we aren't marrying his heir to the proper ruler of Calera. He could back out of the treaty."

Except Alaric wasn't the one worried about keeping up the appearance of following Caleran law. Lord Everly was. And he would only worry about that if he wasn't sure he had enough support for the coup he had staged.

Maybe no one in the room would meet Charis's eyes, but that didn't mean they were all convinced they should support the Everlys. They simply didn't want to be killed by the Rakuuna as punishment for going against what was planned. This pageantry was for their benefit. To assure their continued loyalty once the monsters had gone back to Te'ash.

If Charis could take the Rakuuna out of the equation, maybe she—as well as the Montevallians, Holland, and Nalani—had a chance of surviving what was to come.

"I'd like to hear more about the bargain you've made." Charis lifted her spoon.

Ferris paused, his next bite of spiced pumpkin soup hovering over his bowl. "What bargain?" His gaze shot to his father and then back to her as a frown pinched his brow.

She leaned close and said softly, "The one you said you and your father made. The one you said keeps all of us safe."

Ferris set his spoon down. "I can't—I'm not at liberty to share all the details just now."

"Why wouldn't you be at liberty to share the details with your queen?" Charis arched an eyebrow and managed to swallow a bite of soup, though her stomach pitched.

"Father doesn't think it wise," Ferris said. Charis longed to wipe the smug condescension off his face.

Nalani leaned past Tal and said, "It isn't just his decision to make, Ferris."

"Father is a trusted council member." Ferris's tone was sharp.

"And I am your *queen*." Charis watched with satisfaction as Ferris's cheeks reddened. He might be a much better liar than she'd ever given him credit for, but he was far too emotional to keep the truth under wraps for long.

"Just trust us, Charis. This will be over soon," Ferris muttered, turning away as the soup was cleared and a plate of roasted winter vegetables with cream sauce was set down in its place.

Alaric leaned forward and raised his voice to be heard clearly. "I'm pleased to see you alive and well." His gaze moved from Charis to Tal and back again. "This business with your kingdom has been most concerning."

"It has been concerning to all of us as well," Lord Everly said from his place two seats down. "We're simply grateful that you've brought payment for the Rakuuna so that we may honor our treaty with you and move forward as allies."

"It does seem strange, though, that the Rakuuna are only now accepting King Alaric's payment when they could have had what they needed much earlier." Charis raised her voice as though to make sure Lord Everly could hear her. The nobility nearby grew quiet as they listened.

Lord Everly's cheeks flushed pink. "Who can understand the mind of a monster?"

Charis shrugged and pushed her plate aside, no longer interested in pretending to be hungry. "I don't find the Rakuuna difficult to understand. Or perhaps you were speaking of a different kind of monster?"

"The Rakuuna are the only monsters here." Lord Everly sat back as the servants cleared his dish, and then he leaned past Zale to speak to Alaric. "The strain of this situation has been difficult on all of us, but Charis and the Farragin twins seem less worried over the outcome."

Holland tossed his fork down. "Perhaps you'd like to see just how worried I am?"

Lord Everly drew himself up straight. "You lack any sort of manners."

Nalani elbowed Holland before he could reply.

"I'm sure Charis's mother trained her well," Zale said, her voice firm but kind. "She was simply managing a crisis, and her two closest heirs followed her lead."

"A leader cannot risk showing too much emotion when those who depend on her need to see strength." Alaric lifted his fork to his lips, but then paused and looked at Charis. "However, I do have a few questions I'd like answered before we proceed with the wedding that will bind our kingdoms together."

"Yes, of course." Ferris pushed his food around on his plate. Apparently committing treason was sapping him of his appetite. "What questions do you have?"

Alaric didn't look away from Charis. "Why did I receive contradictory messages from Calera?"

She frowned. It was time to put on a show and hope those around her bought what she was selling. "What do you mean? I sent you two pallorens, and neither of those messages contradicted each other."

Vahn pushed his plate away untouched, watching Charis closely.

Ferris cleared his throat and opened his mouth, but Alaric got there first.

"Your emissary in Arborlay offered plans different from yours." He took a bite and continued speaking around the mouthful. "I get worried when it seems that a queen doesn't know what her underlings are doing behind her back."

"Underling?" Ferris clenched his fork hard enough to turn his knuckles white. "I am in line for the throne, and with Charis and the Farragins gone, it was up to me to open negotiations with you."

Charis met Alaric's gaze. "I hope you'll forgive the confusion Ferris caused. He apparently didn't realize I was not only alive, but actively negotiating with our allies to get help taking back our kingdom. Once he learned his true queen already had things well in hand, of course he was delighted to step down from a role he no longer needed to play."

Ferris opened his mouth, but before he could say anything, Lady Everly knocked her plate off the table. It struck the marble floor with a tremendous crash and shattered.

There was a brief moment of silence as though the room itself was holding its breath, and then from the wall closest to Charis's table, the coat bearer who'd met her eyes whipped a dagger from beneath his sleeve and yelled, "Death to traitors!"

From all around the room, others wearing service uniforms dropped what they were holding, pulled weapons from hidden sheaths, and attacked.

THIRTY-THREE

Chaos erupted as those with weapons screamed "*Death to traitors!*" and lunged at the guests closest to them. Rakuuna backed away, watching warily. Tal stood so quickly, he sent his chair flying onto the floor behind him. He and Reuben took fighting positions on either side of Charis as she jumped to her feet, though they had no weapons.

Charis's hands shook as screams rose.

Who were these people?

Had Lady Ollen and Lord Thorsby sent help?

If so, surely they knew better than to order the murder of Calerans in Charis's name. Especially Calerans she needed to convince of her innocence.

The attackers closest to Charis's table struck a woman in a purple feathered dress four seats down from the Everlys and then ran around the table to get to those seated on the other side.

The Montevallian guards converged on Alaric, Vahn, and Zale, surrounding them, swords out, feet sliding into the first rathma position.

The Everlys stood and backed away from the table until they reached the wall.

Holland grabbed his fork and knife as though they were weapons and leaped to his feet. Nalani grabbed hers as well and followed suit.

Ferris ducked under the table.

More screams. More blood. People panicked and ran for the door, but Queen Bai'elsha called out in her language and the Rakuuna blocked anyone from leaving.

Charis's head spun, and there was a ringing in her ears as her throat closed. Her vision wavered, and she was back in the Farragin ballroom watching her friends and fellow Calerans frantically fight their way across a blood-slicked floor, hoping for escape. A woman's thin, high wail became the cry Charis imagined Mother had made as the Rakuuna converged on her.

"Tal, weapon!" a man's voice yelled.

Charis blinked, and she was back in the royal dining hall. Tal spun toward the other side of the table in time to catch the holstered dagger Vahn tossed his way.

The coat bearer and three others stabbed Lord Vickery at the opposite end of Charis's table and then he locked eyes with her. For a breath, they stared at each other, and then, his eyes flickering with something she couldn't identify, he screamed, "Death to traitors in the name of Queen Charis!"

"No." The word was nothing but a horrified whisper. She swallowed and yelled, "No!"

The boy and his fellow attackers ignored her and kept coming.

Holland leaped between the boy and Reuben, brandishing his knife. His fork was already embedded in the face of a girl who'd tried to slash at Tal when his back was turned to catch Vahn's weapon.

"Stop." Charis raised her voice. No one listened.

They weren't here to obey her.

She stumbled back as Tal fought two attackers at the same time. Her legs struck the edge of her chair, and she nearly fell.

There were at least seven fighters surrounding Charis now. Reuben was fending them off with a chair. Tal used his dagger, but he was losing ground as four attackers took him on at once. Holland had snatched a plate from the table and was using it as a shield while he kicked and punched his way to Tal's side, both fighting to keep the assailants from the person who was clearly their real target: Charis.

Panic blazed through her as the truth hit home. They weren't here to kill in her name. They were here to make it look like she'd ordered the deaths of defenseless Calerans and then silence her forever before she could defend herself.

One of the attackers slipped under Tal's outstretched arm while he was fending off two others and buried his dagger in Tal's side.

"No!" Charis screamed, lunging for him as he stumbled back.

King Alaric barked an order and suddenly four of the five Montevallian guards were standing in front of Tal, swords flashing, flowing through the seven rathmas like graceful dancers delivering death with beautiful precision.

Tal shook as he crumpled to the floor at her feet.

She fell to her knees beside him. "You're going to be all right." She took his face in her hands, and his eyes found hers.

He hissed in a breath as he reached for the wound and found blood pouring down his side and dripping onto the floor.

Reuben crouched down next to her.

"Take Tal's dagger and get them away from us," Charis said.

Reuben slumped against her side and slowly slid onto the marble beside Tal, his glassy eyes staring at nothing. Charis made a noise as though she'd been the one with a blade in her chest.

She'd hated Reuben. Fought with him. Resented him. And then learned to rely on his unquestioning loyalty to whomever wore Calera's crown. He'd taken Milla, Luther, and Fada from her on Mother's orders. And then he'd given his life for hers. It was impossible to identify the swell of emotion within her.

Tal rolled his head to the side to look at Reuben. "Is he—"

"Yes." She pressed her skirt to Tal's wound, trying to stanch the bleeding as behind her the sounds of fighting ceased.

"Tal?" Zale pushed her way past her guards and took in the bloody scene in a swift glance. "Here." She snatched a napkin and bent to press it against her brother's wound. It worked better than Charis's skirt, so Charis eased back.

"Hi, sis," Tal said weakly.

"Hi yourself." Zale looked at Reuben's body and then lifted her gaze to something a few paces away. "Oh, Charis. Your Majesty. I'm so sorry."

Charis turned to see where Zale was looking, and the breath left her body. A hoarse wail tore its way past Holland's lips as he dropped to his knees beside Nalani, still holding a fork in her left hand, a dagger thrust into her chest.

THIRTY-FOUR

"No, no, no." Charis crawled past Reuben, her dress catching on splinters of the chair Tal broke when he leaped to her defense. When she reached Holland's side, she reached for Nalani's neck, her fingers shaking so badly, she couldn't tell if she could feel a heartbeat.

"Somebody help," Holland yelled. "Somebody help my sister."

Charis curled over Nalani's face and pressed her ear to her cousin's mouth.

Nalani lay so still. The roaring of Charis's frantic pulse made it difficult to focus.

Nalani had to be all right. She wasn't gone. She couldn't be.

Pain was a living thing, tipped in fire, unfurling within Charis and spreading through her veins until everything hurt.

"Charis?" Holland whispered. "Will she be— Can we fix this?"

A faint tickle brushed the side of Charis's face. She jerked back, staring at Nalani. Seconds later, Nalani's eyelashes fluttered.

"She's alive." Charis's voice shook as much as her hands. Frantically, she snatched at a fallen napkin. "Don't pull the dagger out. It's helping slow the bleeding. Press this around the wound."

Holland snatched the napkin from her and tenderly placed it around the exposed blade, pressing to help keep the wound from losing too much blood.

Tal and Nalani needed immediate help, but Charis was in no position to get it for them.

They were trapped in a room with no allies. People had just been murdered *in her name*. At any moment, the Everlys would blame her for the ships that had been sunk, for the invasion, and for the bloodbath that surrounded them. Reuben was dead. Charis, Nalani, and Holland would be accused of treachery and put to death, and no one would be punished for tearing her kingdom to pieces.

"Charis, she needs a physician. Quickly." Holland's voice was a ghost of its normal strength.

"I'm sorry," she whispered. "I don't know how to make that happen."

The pain within Charis coalesced into a single, burning flame as he collapsed, laying his face against Nalani's cheek, his dark eyes full of misery.

"What do I do now?" he asked, though he wasn't looking at Charis.

There was nothing he could do.

There was only Charis, with her little satchel of moriarthy dust and her willingness to be the most ruthless person in the room.

As Lord Everly called the room to order, instructing the servants who hadn't taken part in the fight to haul the bodies off to the side of the room, Charis climbed slowly to her feet.

Loosening the mouth of the satchel, she plunged her hand inside, brushing against the little envelope of mursilla herb to let the last of the moriarthy dust trickle over her fingertips.

She was smarter. She struck harder. She never wavered. Never faltered. Never broke.

The Everlys should have killed her when they'd had the chance.

Her body moved stiffly, as though she was a stranger in her own skin, as she walked past the wreckage of Tal's chair, past Reuben, and past Tal, who was speaking softly to Zale.

She held his gaze and saw the moment he understood what she was doing. He struggled to get up, but Zale refused to let him.

Ferris was still under the table, his eyes wide as he watched bloodied bodies being dragged across the marble.

Charis's lip curled.

Coward.

And this is who Lord Everly wanted to crown king of Calera?

A true king didn't hide from danger. Didn't flinch at the result of his own choices.

But then Ferris never had been worthy of being king.

She had seconds before the Everlys noticed that she was no longer distracted. Quickly, she withdrew her hand from the satchel, watching Lord Everly closely while she set her trap.

The instant he noticed her, she spoke in a cold, clear voice that rivaled Mother's on her best day. "People of Calera, we will deal with the horrifying violence we were just subjected to—"

"Too right, we will," Lord Everly blustered. "We all heard them say—"

"We have a treaty to fulfill." Charis raised her voice. "And it cannot be put off. I know Lord Everly will join me in advocating that we keep our word to King Alaric tonight."

She locked eyes with King Alaric.

Zale said quietly, "I agree, Father. Let's get this done."

"Indeed." King Alaric watched Charis closely. "I've waited long enough."

"I'm sure you have no argument against us honoring King Alaric's wishes, do you, Ferris?" Charis turned as Ferris hastily climbed to his feet.

"I— That is, I'm not certain if we . . . Father?" Ferris glanced between Charis and Lord Everly.

"Do you speak only your father's thoughts, or do you have your own?" she asked, reaching for her glass of fizzy pink wine.

Ferris's jaw tightened. "You know I have my own."

"Then stop checking with your father and answer me. King Alaric wants us to complete the treaty. I think we ought to honor our agreement with him, don't you?" Her fingers closed around the glass stem, and she prayed they wouldn't shake.

"Of course, but—"

"Thank you, Ferris. I quite agree." She lifted the glass, her mouth dry, her heart thunder in her chest. The goblet trembled in her hand, and she tightened her grip.

It was time.

"I'd like to propose the first ceremonial toast."

THIRTY-FIVE

CHARIS'S WORDS ECHOED throughout the dining room, and for an instant everyone blinked in surprise. An instant was all Charis needed.

Standing in her bloodstained skirt, Reuben's loss and Nalani's fate carving a hole into her, she raised her wineglass and said, "To King Alaric and his family for their continued interest in peace between our kingdoms."

The crowd of nobles, though still in a state of shock, were well trained in royal etiquette. Most of them grabbed their glasses, raised them, and mumbled, "To King Alaric and his family!" before taking a sip. Charis sipped as well and watched Ferris, whose face was a rather unbecoming shade of pink, take a hurried swallow so that he wouldn't stand out.

Lord Everly rose from his seat. "I really think—"

Charis raised her glass again, fury a brilliant fire coursing through her. "And to the *loyal* Calerans who embraced me as their queen and never lost faith that I would free our kingdom from tyranny."

Queen Bai'elsha stirred in her chair, her goblet untouched—did

Rakuuna even drink wine? It didn't matter. Charis had something entirely different planned for her.

The nobles once again raised their glasses, but the murmur of "To loyal Calerans" was far less enthusiastic than their response to the first toast.

Fine by Charis. Every person who'd given the Everlys any shred of confidence in their coup had Nalani's blood on their hands. Her words weren't meant to make them comfortable.

Barely waiting for those around her to finish swallowing, she lifted her goblet again and said in a voice that shook with rage, "And to the Everlys, who took it upon themselves to speak for me to King Alaric and work with Queen Bai'elsha of Te'ash without my knowledge."

This time, her words caused a ripple of consternation, starting with Lady Everly, who choked on the sip of wine she'd just tried to swallow. People glanced nervously at each other and then hesitantly said, "To the Everlys."

It wasn't lost on any of them that Charis had separated the Everlys from her mention of loyal Calerans. Or that she'd said they had spoken for her without her permission. The line was drawn, and those who decided to support the Everlys now did so in obvious defiance of their true queen.

"I am an heir. I spoke for you because you left us." Ferris held his glass in a crushing grip.

"And finally." Charis lifted her goblet once more. The pale pink liquid was almost half-gone. "Finally, a toast to the Rakuuna, who could have simply asked us to help them negotiate a shipment of jewels from Montevallo but instead decided to sink our ships, invade our lands, kill our royal family, and hold us captive until tonight. Strange how a queen so desperate for the jewel she needs to make medicine for her people would turn down multiple offers of that help months ago, but who am I to criticize how little another queen values her people?"

The consternation in the room slid toward pandemonium. Nobles took hasty sips from their goblets, though most of them couldn't force their mouths to form the words that would bring honor to the Raku-una. Queen Bai'elsha had risen to her feet in a lithe, fluid motion that reminded Charis just how fast the creatures could move.

She was playing a cat and mouse game with death, winner take all.

"That's enough." Ferris slapped his half-full goblet onto the table and grabbed her arm.

"I agree." Charis set her own glass down and turned on him. "You've gone far enough. No more charades, Ferris. Show us who you really are."

Ferris pushed on her arm, trying to get her to sit down, but Charis was fueled by rage and desperation, and she wasn't going down until she no longer had the strength to stand.

Apparently realizing the futility of his actions, Ferris changed course. Turning to the room, he shook his head and said in a tone bleeding with regret, "I'm afraid Father and I cannot let this wedding go forward without revealing some rather distressing information we've come across."

King Alaric leaned forward, dark eyes boring into Charis. She lifted her chin, and the corner of his mouth curved upward in a knowing smirk she'd seen on his son a hundred times.

He knew she was up to something, and he was watching it play out because the outcome didn't matter to him as long as a Caleran heir was ready to marry one of his children and assume the throne.

Lord Everly cleared his throat, tugged his dress coat into place, and spoke with the same gravity with which he'd used to open Moth-er's royal council meetings. "I regret that we must speak out in such a public setting, but Charis's actions leave us little choice."

Charis bared her teeth in a vicious smile. "Let's discuss *your* actions, shall we? Let's tell everyone here the truth."

Ferris leaned close and whispered, "Stop this, or I will order the Rakuuna to kill your precious Tal."

Charis met his eyes and said in a voice dripping with contempt, "You don't give orders, Ferris. Your father does. You have no power here, and we both know it. Now, be quiet; the adults are talking."

Ferris would break. He had to. Otherwise, the only weapons she had to fight against the Everlys' accusations were words, and that wouldn't be enough to overcome the fact that unarmed Calerans had just been killed in her name.

Lord Everly's voice shook with fervor. "It is my solemn duty to inform both King Alaric and the esteemed nobles of this court that evidence has come to light that Charis Willowthorn allied herself with Lady Channing and the Rakuuna months ago in a treasonous plot to kill her own parents and take over this kingdom by force."

It was one thing to know what the Everlys would say about her to make their case. It was another to hear herself accused of coldly arranging the deaths of the people she'd loved most in the world. The air in her lungs seemed made of fire, and her throat closed.

Tal fought off Zale's restraining hands, climbed to his feet, and spoke in a voice that barely contained his fury. "Show your proof."

"Excuse me?" Lord Everly faltered, staring from Tal to King Alaric, who was watching the confrontation with avid interest.

"Did I whisper?" Tal bit his words into sharp little pieces. "You accused Charis of murdering her parents. Show us your proof."

Lady Everly reached into her rather substantial handbag and produced a sheaf of papers bearing Lady Channing's green seal. "All the proof is here in her correspondence with Lady Channing." She stood, waving the papers toward the crowd so they could see for themselves.

Tal laughed derisively. "Really? That's the best you've got?" He turned to face the room, one hand pressing the bloody napkin against his wound. "Every person in here knows better than to believe that someone as smart as Charis would put a plan like that in writing." He turned back to the Everlys. "You are *pathetic*. Charis worked night and day to discover who was sinking Calera's ships, and then she unveiled Lady Channing's treachery at the Sister Moons Festival."

"She had her co-conspirator killed." Ferris cleared his throat and then continued. "And then she ran away while her people suffered under the Rakuuna occupation."

"Why?" Charis asked, noting Ferris's flushed face with interest. "Why would I run if I'd just achieved what I wanted?"

He tugged on his collar as every eye in the room fell on him. "Let's ask Queen Bai'elsha. She's the one who made the deal with you. Isn't that correct?" He aimed the question at the Rakuuna queen.

"Yes." The queen's high, cold voice captured the room, and more than a few shivered as she swept her gaze over those assembled. "We are here because we were told that killing the royal family and occupying Calera was the only way to get King Alaric to agree to supply the serpanicite we need."

"And who told you that?" Charis asked, raising her voice to make sure the entire room heard her. "You had to send a ship of warriors to capture me and return me to Calera. If I'd made a deal with you that benefitted me, why wouldn't I have stayed here to reap the rewards?"

"Because you needed it to look as if the Everlys were behind it." Bai'elsha met Charis's eyes without hesitation. Charis had to admit, the queen lied as if she was being paid to do it.

Which, of course, she was.

"You see?" Lord Everly sounded solemn. "The Rakuuna queen admits Charis's involvement and bolsters our testimony that she is behind Calera's pain and suffering. And you all saw what happened tonight. Her assassins attacked us—"

"You shut your mouth right now, you haggard old fool, or I will shut it for you." Holland rose from the floor, his tearstained eyes wild.

Lord Everly hurried to stand behind his chair as if it would protect him.

Ferris cleared his throat. "Queen Bai'elsha has stated that Charis arranged for the Rakuuna to invade our kingdom."

"Look around you!" Tal gestured at the entire room. "We're surrounded by Rakuuna ready to rip us to pieces if we step out of line. Now, who, I wonder, do they obey? Charis?"

"That's a good question." Charis looked to Bai'elsha. "Do you obey me?"

Bai'elsha hesitated, looking from Ferris to Lord Everly as if hoping for a lifeline.

"You should have admitted your guilt," Ferris said. Really, his face was the most unbecoming shade of red. "I warned you what would happen to Tal if you didn't."

Charis's entire body trembled as though she were a plucked string, and her voice rose, filled with the icy rage that burned so brightly within her. "I don't give in to threats, Ferris. I issue them. And I've grown tired of this farce. You and your family colluded with Lady Channing and the Rakuuna to bring death and disaster upon this kingdom. You arranged for assassins to be present tonight in an attempt to make me look guilty, but you made a grave mistake when you ordered them to kill people I love."

She locked eyes with Bai'elsha. "I sentence Ferris Everly to death for the crime of treason. Have one of your guards kill him immediately."

"You can't sentence my son to death!" Lord Everly thundered.

"Wrong answer." Holland leaped across the table, collided with Lord Everly, and threw the man into the wall behind him. Before Ferris's father could finish staggering to his feet, Holland shoved him against the wall and pressed his forearm against the man's throat. "Not. Another. Word."

Charis faced Lord Everly and his sniveling wife. "I am the rightful queen of Calera. By law, I can sentence any traitor to death. I believe what you mean to say is that I can't use the Rakuuna to do my bidding. Isn't that right?"

She looked at Bai'elsha, who stood three paces away from her seat, fangs bared as she glanced from Charis to the Everlys. When the Rakuuna queen remained silent, Charis pivoted to face the rest of the room.

"The Everlys and Lady Channing saw an opportunity to get the Willowthorns out of power in Calera, and they took it. They were unhappy with the way the war was being run, and the Everlys especially were furious over the treaty we signed with King Alaric because it meant Ferris couldn't marry me and become king."

She glanced at Ferris and found him wiping sweat from his brow, anger in his eyes. Turning back to the room, she continued, "They made a deal that ensured that the royal family would be killed, but Tal negotiated for my safety and the safety of the rest of Calera. He bargained with his own life."

Vahn stirred in his seat, his eyes seeking his brother's face.

"These are lies. Queen Bai'elsha herself said so." Ferris gripped the back of his chair with both hands.

"Then why hasn't she obeyed my order to kill you?" Charis asked.

"Enough of this!" Lady Everly's shrill voice cracked. She waved the sheaf of papers above her head. "We have proof. Charis is the traitor and should be put to death, as should Holland Farragin for colluding with her and for hurting my husband."

Bai'elsha rattled off a command, and a Rakuuna with silver hair and scales the color of pale moss peeled away from the closest wall and stalked toward the head table, moving impossibly fast.

Charis's shaking hands reached for the pouch at her waist and yanked it free.

A swell of panicked cries swept the crowd as the Rakuuna lunged for Charis. Tal leaped forward, putting his body between Charis and the monster.

The Rakuuna slammed into Tal, raking his body with her talons before tossing him aside like a child's discarded rag doll. Zale and Vahn rushed toward their brother's crumpled body.

Charis didn't have time to see if Tal was all right. She plunged her hand into the pouch, scooped up the final pinch of moriarthy dust, and held it in her fist as the Rakuuna readied herself to stab her talons into Charis's throat.

The Rakuuna lunged.

Charis ducked low and launched herself forward. Colliding with the Rakuuna's chest, she slapped her hand across the creature's mouth, releasing the moriarthy dust as the fangs closed on her palm.

Pain exploded down Charis's arm. The Rakuuna grabbed her shoulders, talons digging in. Charis struggled to free herself from the creature's crushing grip while behind her, people gasped or cried out, as if afraid they might be next.

Blood poured down Charis's arm as the Rakuuna's teeth sank deeper into her palm. She kicked and fought, but the monster's hold on her shoulders only grew tighter.

Fear blazed through her, and she struggled harder.

What if the poison didn't work before she was torn to pieces?

What if there hadn't been enough moriarthy dust to kill her attacker?

The Rakuuna hissed, releasing Charis's hand. Her black eyes found hers, rage simmering in their depths, and then her claws burrowed in, sending rivers of agony through Charis as the creature began pulling her shoulders as though she meant to tear her in half.

Someone shouted, and then a sword flashed, whistling past her face to embed itself in the Rakuuna's chest. Its hilt was Montevallian. The creature stumbled back, and Holland stood there, breath heaving, black hair disheveled, clothing slightly askew as though he'd already fought a battle just to reach her side. Charis craned her neck to look at Nalani and found Lord and Lady Malinson, who'd been seated near Nalani, on their knees beside her, keeping both the dagger and the napkin stable.

"Kill him, too," Ferris shouted, his voice rough.

"You can try. Who wants to go first?" Holland yanked the sword free and turned to see who was coming for him.

Bai'elsha spoke and three more Rakuuna rushed toward the head table, but then an ear-piercing scream split the air. For an instant, everyone froze as the Rakuuna who'd attacked Charis wailed, rising in pitch until Charis's ears ached. The scream tapered off as the Rakuuna began coughing, black, brackish blood spraying from the hole that was rapidly eating its way through the creature's jaw. Another hole, this one the size of Charis's fist, tore open in the monster's throat as if her skin was nothing but wet paper.

The Rakuuna began shaking violently. She reached for her throat, but the damage was done. Blood poured from her wounds, soaking her chest where Holland's sword had done little damage. Bai'elsha chattered in her dry bones language, and more Rakuuna began moving toward Charis as her attacker slid to her knees, her breath gurgling in her throat.

Holland swung his sword in a wide arc as he placed his body

between Charis and the incoming Rakuuna. "There's more where that came from!"

Charis didn't dare glance at Tal's prostrate form as she lifted her chin and found the strength to speak in clear, ringing tones. "Queen Bai'elsha, you see that I can kill your kind. Have your guards stand down, or every Rakuuna left behind on Te'ash will suffer the same fate."

Bai'elsha said something, and every Rakuuna in the room paused, watching their queen carefully for her next order. She turned to Charis. "You cannot get to Te'ash if you cannot leave this room."

"I don't need to get to Te'ash." Charis spoke with absolute certainty. No hint of hesitation or doubt that would weaken the lie she needed Bai'elsha to believe. "I spent my time away from Calera assembling an armada of ships from every sea kingdom. Each ship is equipped with a supply of moriarthy dust, and I sent them to Te'ash. If my admirals don't hear the correct coded message from my representative in time, they will proceed with the plan to destroy every single Rakuuna you left behind when you decided to invade my kingdom and kill my people."

At Charis's feet, the Rakuuna coughed wetly, shuddered, and lay still.

"This one is dead." Holland twirled his sword. "Who wants to be next?"

Bai'elsha bared her teeth and then said, "You could be lying."

"I'm the one person you've dealt with in Calera who has never lied to you." Charis held the other queen's gaze. "You could have sent emissaries directly to King Alaric to arrange a trade for the jewels you needed if you'd simply asked. You could have received the palloren Vahn Penbyrn sent offering you payment in full if you'd leave our shores except the Everlys intercepted it and made sure you didn't. You could have had the medicine your people needed *months* ago, saving hundreds of lives. The reason you didn't is because your allies—the Everlys—lied to you so they could keep using you in their treasonous plot to overthrow the legal rulers of Calera."

"Enough of this!" Lord Everly shouted. "Charis and Holland must die for their part in the plot to— Ferris? Son?"

Lady Everly dropped the sheaf of papers she was holding and raced toward the head of the table where Ferris stood swaying in place, his face pasty white, his eyes bloodshot and bulging. Foam bubbled at the edges of his mouth.

"What's happened? Ferris!" Lady Everly launched herself toward her son but stopped short as the broadside of Holland's sword slapped against her stomach, stopping her in her tracks.

Charis faced the room, acutely aware of Tal lying on the floor, his siblings pressing Vahn's dress coat to his wounds to stop the bleeding. He was all right. He had to be. She had no more space within her for that kind of all-consuming grief.

Ferris coughed, a wet, gagging sound that produced more foam.

"What have you done?" Lady Everly screamed at Charis.

"I sentenced him to death by slipping some mursilla herb into his drink." Charis scanned the room slowly, noting with grim satisfaction that every eye, Rakuuna and human, was locked on her. "Surely you didn't think I made four toasts in a row because I was feeling festive."

"But you—how—he's my *son*." Lord Everly rushed to join his wife as Ferris tugged his collar open, revealing the sweat pooling along his collarbone.

"And they were my parents. My friends. My people. You dare say that to me when my loyal guard is dead and one of my closest friends could be dying just a short distance away?" Charis's voice was a whip-lash. "You killed thousands of innocent people. Ships from our allies. Ships from our merchants. Our navy. People celebrating our most sacred night of the year. And all because you thought you were enti-tled to power that was never yours." She met the Everlys' anguished gazes as Ferris crumpled to the floor, his body convulsing. "Power that will *never* be yours."

Lady Everly keened, a cry of bone-deep grief, as Ferris became still.

"Why are you crying?" Holland snarled. "You'll be joining him in a moment."

Charis turned to Bai'elsha. "I am offering you a choice, one queen to another. You can take the serpanicite your people need and leave for Te'ash immediately with the promise that if you need more, you will simply send a palloren informing me of the situation so that I can arrange shipment to you. Or you can try to kill me."

"Come any closer to my queen, and I get to fill you full of holes." Holland hefted his sword.

"You keep your word?" Bai'elsha asked, voice heavy with suspicion.

"Always." Charis held the Rakuuna's gaze for a long moment. "You can have me as an ally or an enemy. The choice is yours."

A chair scraped and then King Alaric spoke. "As our two king-doms unite today, I will add my promise to Her Majesty's. I will honor the agreement I made with Calera, which includes a generous shipment of serpanicite for you, but only if you leave today and never come back. If a single Rakuuna is ever spotted in southern waters again, you will never receive another jewel. I don't care how many people you kill."

The ensuing silence was broken only by Lady Everly sobbing and Zale murmuring to Tal. Charis stood tall, blood trickling from the gouges in her shoulders and palm, grief hollowing out her body until it felt impossible to bear, and waited to see if Bai'elsha would capitulate.

Finally, the Rakuuna queen gave a single nod. "We have an accord." Her voice rose in the undulating wail that Charis had first heard so many months ago on the open sea. Instantly, every Rakuuna in attendance moved to her side and then left the room.

THIRTY-SIX

WITH THE THREAT of the Rakuuna lifted, Charis called for a physician and rushed to Tal's side, trusting Holland to hold the Everlys captive until she could deal with them and seeing that the Malinsons were still caring for Nalani.

Vahn saw her approach and leaned back to make room for her at Tal's head. She dropped to her knees, her entire body shaking as if she was caught in a windstorm.

It was over. She'd won, but the cost was impossibly high. She couldn't bear to add Tal to the list of those she'd lost.

Zale kept Vahn's dress coat pressed against the bloody gashes in Tal's chest but whispered softly, "He's going to be all right."

Charis raised a trembling hand to Tal's face and said, "I forbid you to die, Tal Penbyrn."

"As do I," Holland spoke from above them. "You promised me a disembowelment, and a true gentleman keeps his word."

"My guards have detained the Everlys, Your Majesty," Alaric spoke from somewhere behind Holland. "And now, young man, I'd like my sword back." Holland handed back the sword and hurried to Nalani's side as the palace physician rushed into the room.

Charis leaned down until her mouth was beside Tal's ear. "If you don't wake up right now, I will never forgive you."

His lips parted. "Liar."

His voice was a shadow of its usual strength, but she didn't care. Taking his face in both her hands, she kissed him. "It's over."

"I never doubted you." His eyes fluttered open and found hers before slowly closing again.

"Get another physician in here." Charis looked at the palace staff as she climbed to her feet. "I want this hero's injuries treated immediately. Go!"

Two uniformed servants rushed from the room.

Charis faced the assembled nobles, many of whom were looking at the exits as if they were hoping to leave now that there were no monstrous guards blocking the doorways. Before they could move, Charis spoke with the icy calm Mother had used to bring order out of chaos.

"You have one opportunity to prove your loyalty to me. I will not threaten you to gain your compliance. I will offer you a choice, just as I offered to the Rakuuna." It hurt to see Reuben's body lying on the floor. Charis swallowed against the lump forming in her throat. "We need healing, not division. We are entering a time of rebuilding. I need people in Arborlay who are willing to work hand in hand with each other to restore our beautiful kingdom to its former glory."

Every eye in the room was on her. She paused as a second physician entered the room and was directed to Tal, and then she continued, "You came here tonight because you believed the Everlys were the best choice to rule our kingdom. You've now seen that the Rakuuna answered to them, not to me. You've heard that all this could have been avoided had they brought the Rakuuna's needs to my mother and me immediately. You know the tremendous cost that Calera has paid for their treachery. You also know that I have the confidence of King Alaric and every allied kingdom on the sea."

She scanned the room slowly, fire burning in her belly. "If you still believe someone else would be a better leader, you are welcome to leave. Take your families and move to the countryside. Or to Solvang or Thallis. I don't care where you go, but you can't stay here. If, however, you believe that you put your faith in the wrong people, and you're ready to submit to my sovereignty, I will accept your fealty and expect to see you working harder than most to restore our city."

She paused to let her words settle and then said, "If you've chosen to live elsewhere, get up and leave now, and nothing will happen to you. However, if you stay, and I learn that you are causing discord, you will find yourself in my dungeon faster than you can draw your next breath. Make your choice now."

A few people got up, shamefaced and looking at the floor as they crept out of the room. Two more hurried after them. The rest stayed where they were.

"Show your queen the deference she deserves." Holland's tone brooked no arguments.

As one, the Caleran nobles dropped into curtsies and bows. Charis stood, tall and proud, eyes burning, heart pounding, imagining she could hear in the distance her parents whispering that they were proud of their daughter.

When the crowd had once again found their seats, she turned to the Everlys. "You have been found guilty of treason. The punishment is death."

"I volunteer to do the job." Holland's lip curled as he aimed his sword at Lord Everly.

"In my kingdom, traitors have their heads removed and stuck on the fence posts that line the palace gates." King Alaric moved to

Charis's side, his gaze barely landing on Tal before moving away. "It's remarkably effective in discouraging others from moving against me."

Charis thought the rage within her was spent, but the sight of Alaric's callous disregard for his son sparked it anew.

She waved a hand at a page. "Lead the guards to the dungeons and make sure the Everlys are in separate cells. They will be publicly executed in the square tomorrow at noon. And get Ferris's body out of here."

As her orders were obeyed, she turned to Alaric. "I know we need to have a wedding ceremony, but it will have to wait a few hours to allow everyone to change into clean clothing and to let the physician stitch Tal's wounds."

Vahn's head lifted, surprise written across his face. "You're still going through with the wedding tonight?"

King Alaric laughed. "Barely waiting for the blood to dry. You're every bit the queen your mother was, I'll give you that."

Yes, she was. And she'd done what she'd sworn to do when she'd fled her kingdom. There was just one more task awaiting her.

Two hours later, grateful that Nalani, though seriously injured, would live and that Tal would also recover from his wounds, Charis dressed in the blue gown that had once caused Tal to stumble over his words when he saw her, and had the nobility moved to the throne room.

With no member of the royal council present to perform the ceremony, she'd sent for the magistrate of Arborlay. It was time to solidify her treaty with Montevallo, pay the Rakuuna to leave and never come back, and begin the process of rebuilding her kingdom. And it was time King Alaric realized that, while he might not see the kind of treasure he had in his youngest son, others did.

Vahn was waiting for her in the corridor outside the throne room. "Tal is all right."

She nodded. "I received word that his wounds were dressed, and he'd been given clean clothing."

"He'll be along shortly. I just . . . I wanted to talk to you. Before we go in." He looked uncomfortable.

"What is it?"

"I'm a bit surprised that you're going through with this."

She faced him, softening at the sight of his brother's blood on his snowy white shirt. "I keep my promises. And our kingdoms cannot continue to be at war."

"I agree." He swallowed, looked over his shoulder as his father's voice called his name from inside the room, and then said in a rush, "I'm just surprised that you're marrying me without protest. Of course, Tal can remain your bodyguard, and I'll do my best to look the other way if the two of you— It's awkward, but— Perhaps we—"

"Tal won't continue on as my bodyguard."

Vahn's brows rose. "It's clear that you two love each other."

"We do."

"Then why . . . Oh." He drew in a breath and blew it out slowly.

"I will honor the treaty, down to the letter." She raised her voice so that Alaric, who was approaching, could hear her, too.

"I should hope so," Alaric said, glancing down the hall where Tal was walking toward them, supported by Holland, who looked weary.

"I already know you plan to honor our treaty as well," Charis said. "After all, you made it clear that you'd support me if I won my recent power struggle but wouldn't be too bothered if I lost because there were still heirs to choose from to fulfill the treaty."

"Don't sell yourself short, Your Majesty." Alaric clapped Vahn on the back. "I much preferred you as Calera's ruler than that pompous Ferris Everly."

"Excellent." Charis turned to her friends. "Holland, if Tal needs help staying on his feet, don't let him fall."

"Tal doesn't need to be on his feet for this," Alaric said as Zale left the throne room to fuss over her brother.

Charis ignored Alaric.

"Please help him onto the dais," she said to Zale, who was hovering anxiously at Tal's side.

"The dais?" Alaric looked from Charis to Tal. "Why?"

Charis leveled him with the look that used to send the nobility scrambling to get back in her good graces. "Because he risked his life to save my kingdom and then risked it again tonight to save me." She moved past Alaric and said, "Because I honor those whose courage deserves it."

Moving through the room, past clusters of nobility having hushed conversations, she mounted the steps to the dais. Alaric followed her to the base of the steps. She turned to him. "And because I plan to finalize our treaty by obeying it to the letter."

Beside Alaric, Vahn snorted. When his father turned to look at him, Vahn immediately assumed an expression of grave dignity.

"Well, then Vahn should be up there, too." Alaric motioned for Vahn to step to the dais.

Charis cleared her throat and said loudly, "Thank you to all who've remained to witness this momentous occasion. Please take your seats."

As the crowd settled into their chairs, Holland and Zale approached the dais with Tal. The magistrate climbed the steps behind them, his wide girth making for slow progress.

Charis looked at the magistrate. "The treaty between Montevallo and Calera states that one of their heirs must marry one of ours." She turned as Alaric followed Vahn on to the dais.

Vahn gave her a rueful look and shrugged.

"Prince Vahn Penbyrn of Montevallo will make a fine ruler one day, and I'm sure his kingdom will be grateful for his leadership." Charis's voice rang out, and she hastened on as Alaric's cheeks reddened and his mouth dropped open. Beside her, Tal turned to see her face, his eyes wide with wonder.

"Prince Percival Talin Penbyrn has demonstrated constant, unwavering loyalty to me and to the well-being of Calera and has proven adept at balancing that loyalty with his concern and love for the people of Montevallo. I can think of no better king consort to have at my side as I begin my queenship."

Turning to Tal, she whispered, "Is this all right with you?"

He gave her his crooked smile. "Are you asking me to marry you?"

"I am."

"I might have to think about that for a while."

Her lips lifted slightly. "Liar."

He leaned close and whispered, "You own my heart. I'd be honored to marry you."

She reached for Tal's hand, and he intertwined his fingers through hers, his gaze warm. The torch he'd lit in her heart, once nearly extinguished, blazed with brilliant light.

"We had an agreement," Alaric snapped.

"Yes." Charis smiled at Tal. "One of our heirs would marry one of yours. Tal is one of your heirs, is he not?"

"He is, but that wasn't the plan."

"Father, she said Tal will be nothing more than a king consort." Vahn sounded nearly as arrogant as he had the first day Charis had met him. "I decline to be a consort. With me as your heir in

Montevallo, and Tal as king consort here, we can enjoy the benefits of a long, profitable partnership that strengthens both our kingdoms."

Charis raised an eyebrow at Vahn, and he raised one right back. She hadn't expected him to give up the idea of marrying her so easily, but she also hadn't expected him to show such concern over Tal's wounds. It seemed that, like her, Vahn had shown the side of him that his father expected him to show when they'd first met.

"Are you absolutely sure, after everything we've been through, that I'm the one you want?" Tal whispered as the magistrate began a short wedding ceremony.

"Are you trying to get out of this?" She narrowed her eyes, and he smiled.

"I wouldn't dare."

"You dare a great many things."

His smile widened, and the rest of the room faded away until he was just a boy standing in front of a girl telling her he loved her enough to marry her—not because of her position, but despite it.

As the magistrate read the vows, she leaned close to Tal and said softly, "I can't promise I'm going to be easy to live with."

"I'll take my chances."

"I might start a few arguments."

"I'll argue right back."

She moved closer. "We've got a lot of work ahead of us, and it isn't going to be easy."

He closed the distance between them and whispered, "I never did care for things that were easy."

The magistrate finished speaking and said, "The royal couple will now share their first kiss."

The pain within her over those who'd been lost was still raw and tender, but somehow joy existed beside it, threaded through the ache so that both felt as much a part of her as breathing. She was the bereft daughter. The vengeful queen. The grieving friend, and the blushing bride. She looked at Tal. "Ready?"

Tal's smile matched hers, full of happiness and grief in equal measure. "Ready."

She kissed him, slow and sweet, her heart pounding in rhythm with his, drowning out the applause around them, and for the first time since the night everything went wrong, she felt like she was truly home.

EPILOGUE

FOUR MONTHS LATER, when the ground had thawed and the meadows were once again filled with cheerful wildflowers and the hum of bumblebees, Charis stood beside a tree on Father's property in northern Calera late one afternoon and looked at the freshly carved stone at her feet.

Edias Stephren Lorrinton Willowthorn
Beloved father, mentor, friend

"It's perfect," Tal said, his hand finding hers and squeezing gently.

"It doesn't say that he was a king consort." She'd gone back and forth on that, agonizing over how to encapsulate everything Father had meant to her and his loved ones, worrying that decades from now, those who saw this stone wouldn't realize the man it honored had been an integral part of who Queen Charis Willowthorn had become.

"He wouldn't want it to." Tal leaned down to brush a stray piece of grass from the headstone.

They'd had an official burial for Mother soon after the wedding, along with a burial ceremony for Reuben, who'd been awarded the kingdom's prestigious Sapphire Star for courageous service to the crown. Immediately after, Charis had ordered the kingdom into the traditional one month mourning period for a queen, while simultaneously working to restore everything the Rakuuna had destroyed.

Ships had been rebuilt. Buildings had been repaired. Royal medals had been awarded to Orayn, Finn, and the rest of Charis's crew, along with Lady Ollen and those who'd helped her. Lord Thorsby hadn't survived the Rakuuna and had been awarded a medal posthumously. Every crew member who'd died during the journey and every Caleran resistance fighter who'd fallen had been awarded one too. The Everlys and their lackey, Bartho, had each been put to death for treason.

There was still much to do. New fields had to be plowed and planted to combat the food shortage the Rakuuna had caused by burning warehouses. Infrastructure had to be repaired. Trade had to resume to deal with shortages in medicine, cloth, and metal, but that also required negotiating with Montevallo for the jewels to pay for things since Calera wouldn't be able to trade crops again until the fall.

Holland, now a royal council member, had joined the navy as an officer with plans to work his way up to admiral over the years. Sailing the open seas had the benefit of taking him far from his mother's matchmaking schemes while also reviving his hopes of seeing a kraken.

Nalani was serving as ambassador to Solvang and, despite her busy schedule, still found time to consistently send pallorens with suggestions for reforms to Caleran law. Delaire had stayed in Solvang to assist Nalani while also enrolling in the prestigious Ooverstaad University, where she was studying international law in preparation for becoming an ambassador herself.

And now, this long after winning control of her kingdom from the Everlys and banishing the Rakuuna, Charis had finally made time to take her father's body home to be buried in his beloved north.

It had taken this long because somehow the idea of giving him a final resting spot made his death real. Final.

"He'd love it here," Tal said, as if reading her mind. "You brought him exactly where he'd want to be, and we will visit him often."

She leaned against Tal, tears gathering in her eyes. Grim and Dec, now serving as guards, stood a short distance away, respectfully watching their surroundings while ignoring Charis and Tal.

"I miss him." She could barely speak the words without her throat closing.

"I miss him, too." Tal sounded close to tears, but then laughed a little as Hildy, now fully grown, wound her way through his legs, sat on the headstone, and began licking her back. "Apparently, so does Hildy."

Charis's laugh wobbled a bit, but still, it felt right to sit in the sun, pet Father's cat, and remember the man who'd loved her unconditionally and had anchored her to the better part of her nature.

She leaned her head against Tal's chest as he told a story about Father tricking Ilsa into giving them sweetcakes for breakfast. The land rolled away from the tree in gentle dips and curves, dressed in long grass and delicate flowers. Small coils of smoke drifted up from the distant village houses, and somewhere nearby a bird sang cheerfully.

It was simple, unpretentious, and peaceful, just like Father had been.

"I'm grateful he sent me to be your bodyguard," Tal said as the sun dipped toward the horizon. "He trusted me with what was most precious to him, and I'll spend the rest of my life making sure I don't let him down."

"Better make sure you don't let me down, either."

"I wouldn't dream of it." He gave her a sly grin. "Unless, of course, we're discussing your desire to cheat during sparring."

"I never cheat during sparring."

"Liar."

She snuggled close, a smile on her face and peace in her heart as the sun slowly disintegrated into crimson fire along the horizon.

ACKNOWLEDGMENTS

First, as always, thank you to Jesus for loving me and being a constant friend, no matter what life throws my way.

Huge thanks to my husband, Clint, who is my biggest fan and who is always willing to listen to me talk through plot issues for hours until he helps me find the missing piece. I love you!

Thank you to my kids, Tyler, Jordan, Zach, Johanna, and Isabella, who don't all read my books (I get it, it's weird to read a kissing scene written by your mom!) but who are proud of me and always cheer me on. Extra thanks to my fabulous daughter-in-law, Hannah, who DOES read all my books and who was the very first reader of Charis's story. Your texts at two a.m. were exactly the encouragement I needed! I also appreciate my sister, Heather, who is fabulous at many things, including brainstorming plots, cooking excellent meals, being a safe place for my kids, and coming in clutch with all the forensic knowledge one could ever need in case one wanted to hide a fictional (I swear!) body. Thanks also to my brother-in-law, Dave, who fixes my tech issues (It's me. Hi. I'm the problem, it's me.) and who always makes me laugh. I'm also grateful to my parents for raising me in a library and letting me read to my heart's content.

Every book comes together differently, and this one took several iterations before I finally found the right way to finish Charis's story. I deeply appreciate my editor, Kristin Rens, and my agent, Holly Root, for their patience with the process and their continued belief in me as a writer. I'm also grateful to the team at Balzer+Bray, who are consistently a delight, and the team at Root Literary, who are some of the best humans on Earth.

Writing is often a solitary endeavor, but I'm never in it alone. Thanks go out to Jodi Meadows, who always drops everything to help me fix a synopsis or unsnarl a plot point and who is, in fact, one of the most loyal friends anyone could ask for. I'm also grateful to the Writer's Sanctuary—in particular, the Red Herrings Society. Getting to hang out with you daily in our virtual group and having the honor of mentoring you, teaching you, and seeing you accomplish your incredible dreams is absolutely amazing. (If you're a writer who needs a positive, supportive community, you should check them out!)

And finally, I dedicated the book to you, but I'm going to mention you here as well. To Mary Weber, my soul sister and partner in (alleged) crimes, I'm so grateful for your friendship. For daily phone calls and big ideas and Airbnbs and international travel and Taylor Swift and fierce encouragement and dreams that align every single time. It may have taken us forty years to find each other, but we were always meant to be besties. Now, I'm pretty sure you owe me some cake.